JUST
for
NOW

RICHARD WALL

authorHOUSE®

AuthorHouse™ UK
1663 Liberty Drive
Bloomington, IN 47403 USA
www.authorhouse.co.uk
Phone: UK TFN: 0800 0148641 (Toll Free inside the UK)
*   UK Local: (02) 0369 56322 (+44 20 3695 6322 from outside the UK)*

Published by AuthorHouse 12/08/2022

ISBN: 978-1-7283-7530-4 (sc)
ISBN: 978-1-7283-7531-1 (e)

Print information available on the last page.

This book is printed on acid-free paper.

CONTENTS

CHAPTER ONE

Just for Now

Walter was dozing off when a red-faced manager flung the door open and yelled, "Train on one!" Walter was scrambling to his feet when the man sitting in the corner, who hadn't stirred for half an hour, stopped him.

"Sit down, you prat. You're not on the fucker," he said.

He seemed to know what he was talking about, so Walter did as he was told. No sooner had he taken his seat before another red-faced manager stuck his head in and bawled, "Train on one!"

"I'm not on the fucker," Walter told him.

"Someone must be on the fucker," muttered the red-faced manager and left.

"Close the shaggin' door," shouted the nearly comatose man in the corner after him. "He can get those pissed up pricks out of the pub," he added and closed his eyes. Suddenly he sat bolt upright and stared intently at Walter.

"Tell me this," he said, then paused.

Walter waited.

"What the fuck made you come on this shower of shite?" the man demanded.

"Desperation," Walter told him.

The man looked delighted.

"I knew it. Blokes come on here—they're either thick or desperate. Welcome to The Post Office, the legion of the undead," he said, and closed his eyes again.

"It may not be the legion of the undead, but it's bloody weird," Walter muttered. "How did I end up here?" he added.

He was beginning to think the fatalists were right and it was all preordained. He didn't choose The Post Office. Perhaps it had been lying in wait for him from the moment he was born.

He decided it was no use kicking against the pricks. He just had to work under them.

CHAPTER
Two

Another Fresh Start

Walter had to get a job. His past was lamentable and his future dire. It looked rather as though The Post Office was his last chance. He might even fit in there. Everyone knew about The Post Office. That was where you went when it had all got too much for you. It was a place of refuge. The entire country was full of people rambling on when drunk about how when it all got too much they would either become the landlord of a village pub or go on the post. On balance, he preferred the post.

For a start, the series of advertisements they were running made it obvious they were desperate to find people prepared to do the job. This suggested the job didn't amount to much, but it probably also meant they might take him on. His employment record would not recommend him to those looking for thrusting, dynamic young executives.

Apart from anything else, he was no longer young. It had to be the post. He would fill in the bloody form. In truth, he no longer cared about a career; he just wanted a job. He resolved that if any of his friends told him that being a postal worker was better than walking the streets, he would thump them.

His heart sank when in what seemed like a suspiciously short time he was called for an interview. Was the job that bad? They weren't being very selective. It looked rather as though they were taking anybody. They were in no position to be choosy—but then neither was he. It could prove to be an ideal match. The job centre's dream—a hopeless man slotted into a crap job. He decided to attend. What had he got to lose?

The answer to that question quickly became apparent at the interview. He stood to lose his health and very possibly his sanity. He sat gazing at The Chief Inspector and wondered if he should make a bolt for it. Clearly, The Chief was right off his rocker. He seemed a very amiable man, but he shouldn't have been out on his own, let alone holding down a responsible position.

He'd begun by admitting that the basic pay was deplorable, but then went on to point out the marvellous opportunities that were available to supplement these starvation wages by working overtime. What was appalling was the monumental scale of the overtime he said was on offer. The Chief had been living in an enclosed world for so long he simply couldn't grasp what a horrifying prospect he was holding forth to the poor benighted souls before him.

"When you've been here for a bit, you'll be able to work regular nights," he said.

None of the interviewees looked thrilled.

"And that's another ten pounds a week in your pocket," he went on.

One or two men began to look vaguely interested. The Chief beamed round.

"But that's just the start," he told them. He sat there like an angler who knew he was about to hook a few fat juicy fish. "Once you're on regular nights, you might get lucky." He paused and gazed at his audience—some were now visibly tempted and intrigued. "What do you think you might get?" he asked.

"Back on days?" said someone who was not showing the right spirit.

The Chief looked at him with pity. "You might get five hours overtime a night before your job starts six days a week," he said. He seemed gratified by the gasps this announcement provoked, although whether they sprang from terror or delight, no one could possibly know.

The Chief sat beaming at them all. Then he produced the clincher. "And if you're really in luck, you could do your five hours before your job, six nights, a week and if someone goes sick and he's on delivery, you can do his walk after your job, and that could be another thirty hours a week."

A man who had to be madder than The Chief, if that was possible, looked thrilled. He had found what he had been looking for, an organization where lunacy was the norm.

Walter was in shock. He was numb. Looking back, he often asked himself why he had not walked out there and then. It was, he decided, because the sheer enormity of it all paralysed his will to the extent that he no longer had the power to resist. He had to give it a go, but only until something better turned up.

CHAPTER
THREE

Bringing Harmony

It was not a good time to be a postal worker. A dreary harpy had become Prime Minister, and after piously promising to bring harmony, had started to kick the crap out of what she obviously thought of as the truculent lower orders. Despite his good intentions, Walter did not take naturally to the work. Having to get up at the hour when the secret police called because you were at your lowest ebb caused him great difficulty. He was permanently tired.

He soon realized that the general perception of The post Office as a haven of tranquillity for those looking for an easy way out was completely fallacious. The delivery room floor at half five in the morning was frantic. Row upon row of men were desperately preparing their deliveries so they would be ready to catch the van. The uproar was deafening. Since it was the depths of winter, a bewildered Walter would climb down from the back of the van and stare bemusedly into the murky gloom. Wandering round in the dark, trying to deliver mail, seemed to him distinctly barmy. No wonder the old Chief had gone peculiar. He wasn't born to be mental, the institutionalized lunacy had tipped him over the edge. Walter wondered how long it would be before he found himself slipping into the void. Most of the delivery staff struck him as being distinctly odd. He put it down to years of sleep deprivation. It was bound to have an effect sooner or later. What alarmed him most was the thought that if he started going peculiar, he would in all probability be blissfully unaware of it. For all he knew the process could have started already.

Blundering about in the dark, trying to establish whether he was in fact in Acacia Avenue, he asked himself the question out loud, "Am I going weird?" An answering voice came out of the gloom, "Don't worry, Postie. The whole bloody country is going weird," it said. The clink of bottles told him it was that other creature that roamed the streets during the unearthly hours. He watched with something akin to envy and admiration as the milkman scurried about with an enthusiasm that suggested he was determined one day to own his own dairy.

After a dog had attempted repeatedly to bite his arse and its owner had repeatedly assured him it was allright he began to think that perhaps the Old Chief wasn't as daft as he had at first thought him. Suddenly the idea of working nights was enticing. Surely sleeping in daylight would be sheer bliss. The thought of the five hours overtime before the job officially started to be followed by hours of delivery work when it ended caused him to quail, but he resolved to face that problem when it arose. What he had to do now was get off delivery work. He'd have to find something a bit more congenial until something better turned up.

To his intense relief he found himself on nights quite quickly. There were vacant slots because so many men said adamantly that 'they wanted some sort of fookin' social life' and insisted on working the early turn. Walter could not understand how it was possible to achieve a social life when you were in a state of catatonic exhaustion and assumed they were all members of a club for zombies where they sat slumped in corners maintaining a social life against all the odds. You had to admire the resilience of the human spirit. His own social life was in any case negligible and he was quite prepared to sacrifice it. Anything to get off delivery.

After a few unhappy weeks during which a variety of dogs of all shapes and sizes attempted to bite his arse while their owners assured him they were all right, and a number of unpleasant people had accosted him in the street and demanded that he hand over their fookin' giro, he looked at the duty sheets and saw that he was detailed to work at the railway station, on nights with three hours standard overtime before the job. This effectively removed any possibility that he might have some sort of social life during the day. However the money would be useful and sooner or later a dog would manage to sink its fangs into his buttocks so he decided this was a gift horse and he would not look it in mouth.

He signed on at the Mail Porters' room on the station and went into the back where a strange sight awaited him. There was an enormous wooden table in the middle of the room that looked as though it might at one time have been in a seedy baronial hall. A huge kettle, seemingly designed for giants, was boiling on the gas stove, pouring out so much steam the place looked like a Turkish Bath. No-one seemed to be making tea and no-one seemed inclined to turn the gas off. A number of the men had the high colour of habitual drinkers and looked pissed. Some fierce looking men were playing cards at one end of the table, another man was asleep at the other end with his head resting on a newspaper. Walter couldn't tell if he'd fallen asleep or passed out.

At that point the door was flung open and a furious looking man stormed in. 'Is any fucker going to help me unload this fucking train or not?' he demanded. The response was immediate: 'Fuckoff' roared every member of the card school as they continued the hand. The sleeping man raised his head briefly, bellowed 'cunt' and went back to sleep. The kettle continued to boil, the cards were shuffled, the sleeping man opened one eye and gazed blearily round. No-one seemed in the slightest way interested in the train. It all struck Walter as being very strange, indeed downright surreal. He edged towards the door. One of the redfaced men glared at him.

'Where you going?' he demanded. 'To do the train' said Walter.

'Are you on the fucker?' asked another red faced man.

'Let them fuckers come out of the pub and do it' bellowed one of the card school.

'They wouldn't recognize a train if you showed 'em one' said one of the card players as he threw his hand down in obvious disgust.

A man in a suit appeared in the doorway. 'Train on one' he said. 'We're not on the fucker' the dealer told him.

Get those idle coonts out of the pub' said the man who had given up on the card game in none too good a temper.

'The fookin' train won't stay here forever. They'll blow it out soon' said the man in a suit. 'The sooner they blow the bastard out the better' said one of the red faced men. The man in the suit was looking desperate. His eye fell on the man with his head resting on the paper. 'Is he on it?' he asked hopefully. 'He can't stand up' he was told. 'He's bloody useless' fumed the man in a suit. "He might be but at least he's here. Not like those pissed up prats in the pub' said the dealer.

A railwayman with flag and whistle came in. 'I can't hold the bugger much longer' he said. The man at the end of the table slowly raised his head. 'If you can't hold the bugger you'll have to let it go' he said. No-one could counter that. The man in the suit gave up. 'I'll have to fill in a report' he said. No-one seemed bothered. The kettle continued to boil, the steam wreathed its way round the room. The dealer fixed his eyes on the man in the suit: "Don't stand there like a twat. Get your fags out' he instructed. The man in a suit who seemed to be in charge did as he was told.

Walter soon realized that the scene he had witnessed on his first night at the station was typical. The arrival of every train provoked a passionate argument as to who was and who was not 'on the fucker'. The Gaffer was forever being urged to get 'those pissed up prats' out of the pub. For reasons unknown to Walter, The Gaffer was very unwilling to follow this advice. He seemed anxious to leave the pissed up prats where they were. The railway foreman regularly appeared in the doorway saying he couldn't hold the fucker much longer, and the card school showed absolutely no interest beyond telling him to let the fucker go. The Gaffer said he'd have to fill in a report, and one of the card school invariably told him not to stand there like a twat and to get his fags out. Walter wondered what happened to all the reports.

He also wondered if this station was unique, or if all over the country trains were arriving loaded with mail, postmen were swearing blind they were not on the fucker, and the trains were carrying on with their cargo untouched by the men of the Royal Mail. He knew from his time on delivery that letters were arriving in the sorting office in abundance, but just how this happened was completely beyond him. Perhaps those pissed up prats in the pub were sneaking over and slinging the bags off while the blazing rows went on in the room.

After a few days of being told 'sit down you wanker you're not on it' Walter decided the best course was to sit quietly and read his book. He scarcely dared open his mouth because he found the old hands terrifying. A few trains came and apparently left as they arrived since no-one was 'on the fucker', he sat there immersed in his book until one of the fierce red faced men glared at him and demanded: 'are you doing the fucker or not?' Walter went out and was immediately told to fetch a barrow. He found a barrow, grasped the handle and was then told to 'leave that fucking barrow alone'. They were difficult men to work with. It was hard as well to get to know their names since at least half of them were apparently called twat. Others were perpetually absent and thus referred to as that twat. It was all very confusing. The huge kettle on the gas stove seemed to be boiling twenty fours a day.

Gradually Walter got to know who was who. There were four or five men who he tended to think of collectively as The Card School. Their trousers were apparently nailed to the chairs and they only left the room in the face of severe provocation, such as when the Gaffer in a last despairing attempt to get them onto the platform called them a bunch of useless idle twats, and ran out onto the station where they couldn't thump him without witnesses. There was Paddy who worked down at the loading bay and arrived in the room several times a night, purple faced and effing and blinding furiously Walter could never grasp what the subject of Paddy's tirades were, and since no-one took any notice he decided it need not concern him. After ranting and raving for a while Paddy took himself off looking as though he felt better for getting it off his chest.

All the men smoked, some of them gambled, most of them drank and some did all three. 'A man called George usually arrived on platform one around midnight, red faced, grinning from ear to ear and saying he had had 'a great fucking night'. As yet Walter couldn't attach names to the 'two pissed up prats' but as it looked as though they never left the pub it seemed unlikely he was going to meet them. Apart from the 'two pissed up prats there were another pair known as The Ghost Squad. One of the fierce looking men, called Joe, was supposed to be working with them and claimed he hadn't seen them since just after the war. There were vague rumours that they were actually supernatural.

Walter felt that this tight self-contained little unit could not continue indefinitely without interference from the outside world. Some bugger must be reading all those reports he mused.

What actually happened was they came for George.

CHAPTER
FOUR

The Arrest

They came for George just as the clock struck twelve and he'd as usual beamed round and told everyone he had had a 'great fucking night'. There were two of them, a grizzled Sergeant and a taut faced young Constable keen to get on. The parcel train was being unloaded. The Gaffer thought he had done his prospects of promotion a power of good, Stung beyond endurance when he was asked if he had any bollocks or not he had gone over to the pub and returned in triumph with the two pissed up prats one of whom was now puking miserably down onto the track. When The Gaffer had flung open the door of the room and shoved the two pissed up prats in the effect was instantaneous. The dealer dropped the pack. 'Have they been barred?' he asked.

'They're doing the train' said The Gaffer.

'We're not on the fucker' protested one of the pissed up prats.

'We've never been on the fucker' said the other.

'You're on the fucker now' The Gaffer told him.

As one man The Card School rose to their feet and headed for the door.

'Where are you going?' asked The Gaffer.

'We're going to do the train' said The Dealer. 'You're not on the fucker' The Gaffer told him. 'We're not missing this' he was told. Everyone piled out onto the platform. Thus it was that George's arrest took place before an unprecedented full house, which was why he didn't go quietly. At first he didn't realize fate had caught up with him. He thought it was just another routine patrol. It wasn't until they closed in on him and The Sergeant spoke to him in an official sort of tone he realized that he was about to be detained.

The Sergeant looked him up and down: 'Mr. Sampson?' he asked. George was annoyed. He had a great fucking night, it was near the end of the shift and he didn't need this. 'You know bloody well who I am' he retorted. 'I have reason to believe you have been drinking on duty' The Sergeant said. George breathed beer all over him. 'Who shopped me? he demanded.

'Say fuckall George' said the Pissed Up Prat who seemed to have finished puking. I'm saying fuckall' said George. The Constable made a note. 'What are you writing down there?' asked George, breathing all over him. The Constable recoiled. 'Fuckall' he answered. "That won't stand up in Court' said one of the card school. I'm not going to court' said George. Wanna bet? retorted The Constable. George didn't care for his tone and decided he needed representation. 'Where's the bloody union man?' he asked. No-one knew.

During all this Ronnie, who claimed he had last seen the Ghost Squad shortly after the end of World War Two, had been unloading one of the brakes. He was on his own and obviously disgruntled. He looked accusingly at The Sergeant. There was no other figure of authority in sight since The Gaffer, overwhelmed by his success in getting the Two Pissed Up Prats out of the pub, had gone over for a celebratory pint. 'There's supposed to be three men on this door' Ronnie told The Sergeant. 'Oh yes' said The Sergeant trying hard to look interested. 'Can you see three men mate?' Ronnie persisted. Can't say I can mate The Sergeant conceded. 'We've got the time and motion twats here this week'. 'Are the time and motion twats at your place?' Ronnie asked politely enough.

The Sergeant was plainly puzzled by this line of enquiry and was by no means certain he should be answering questions, but he'd been told to cultivate as benign an image as possible among the general public, and on balance postmen just about came into that category, even though they were on strike once a week and showed every sign of enjoying their pariah status. He decided to stall.

'Why do you ask?' he countered. He then stepped back as George angrily thrust his face into his; 'Why answer a fookin' question with another fookin' question? he asked. 'Answer the shaggin' question said one of the card school. There was a low rumble of assent. The Sergeant felt the situation was getting a little out of hand. It was not supposed to be like this. Miscreants were supposed to come quietly, snivelling about stress and their responsibilities to their wives and hordes of children. That was the trouble with waiting until George was positively awash with ale. It made him even more argumentative than usual and he refused to take this charade seriously. The Sergeant was finding it difficult too. George had been pissed on duty for at least twenty five years and no-one had minded. Now all of a sudden he was a menace to society and had to be apprehended.

Joe on the tractor wasn't much help either. 'Say you've gone senile George' he advised. 'We'll back you up' he added as a somewhat malicious afterthought. George wasn't impressed with this piece of gratuitous advice. 'Are you saying plead guilty?' he demanded angrily. Joe nodded emphatically. 'Say you've gone suddenly senile, do two months in an open prison, have a rest, come out and sue the bastards for wrongful arrest. 'That's what they all do now' he said. He then drove off, parked his tractor and went round to the back door of The Lion and The Lamb for a quick pint.

George decided the best thing to do was follow the line taken by other more prominent transgressors, including some of those responsible for the legislation he was being done under. 'I've done nothing wrong' he announced. 'He's not a fucking criminal' said a man George had bought a pint just before he came over. 'No he shaggin' ain't' chimed in Ronnie as he peered up the station steps which he hoped against hope his two absent mates might come wobbling down. The Sergeant shook his head wearily and thought vaguely about early retirement.

The taut faced Constable who had hopes of a glittering career, rapid promotion to Sergeant followed by a meteoric rise through the ranks, and in due course a knighthood, decided it was time to remind The Sergeant he was there. He thrust what he hoped was an unsmiling menacing face into George's, and was about to ask him with as much intimidatory force as he could whether he wanted to do it the easy way or the hard way when he caught a whiff of George's beery breath, winced, muttered 'kin'ell' and withdrew from the proceedings.

At that moment Paddy arrived from the shed and the whole situation descended into pure farce.

There's some dodgy looking characters hanging about down the shed' he bellowed. There was no response from the law.

'Do you hear what I'm saying? Paddy demanded. He'd been drinking and his temper was a bit short. 'Not now Paddy we're busy' The Sergeant said. Paddy was outraged. 'Busy' he bellowed. 'Busy doing what? Sure you're standing here either side of George like a pair of bookends. You're propping him up as though he's War and Shaggin' Peace'

George is under arrest' Ronnie said. 'Under arrest. That's a load of bollocks' said Paddy unable to believe what he was hearing.

'What's he under arrest for? He's not a fucking criminal' roared Paddy. Ronnie nodded his agreement. 'He's not a fucking criminal' he confirmed. 'That's for the court to decide' said The Constable, keeping a wary eye on Paddy. 'What bloody court?' asked George. There was no reply.

Ronnie sat down on a pile of bags determined to stick it out until The Ghost Squad turned up. He reckoned they could still be alive. Paddy glared at The Sergeant. 'Has he committed murder? he asked. The Sergeant shook his head. 'Has he stolen something?' Paddy persisted. The Sergeant again shook his head. 'Has he thumped somebody?' asked Paddy. Again The Sergeant had to shake his head. Paddy thought for a moment.

'Has he ...? At this point The Constable felt he wasn't prepared to stand there while Paddy went through a list of all the possible felonies known to an irate Irishman with a skinful and said with all solemnity: 'He has been drinking on duty' Paddy had to sit down. He shook his head as though the sheer overwhelming evidence of man's inanity was more than he could bear. He rounded furiously on The Sergeant.

'There's mass murder going on all over the world, there's rape, there's pillage, there's starvation, embezzlement, drug running, massive corruption, perversion of justice and you're here to arrest a man who's had a drink. What the fuck have you got to say for yourself? Challenged to defend his role in that context The Sergeant was at a loss for words. He sat down and got out a cigarette. Ronnie stuck his head out of the brake.

'That twat of a Gaffer should be here when one of his blokes is in the shit' he said. 'Everyone knows the fucking Gaffer is useless' said Paddy. Everyone nodded, including The Sergeant. 'That's why they made the eejet a Gaffer in the first place' Paddy explained for The Sergeant's benefit. The Sergeant drew on his cigarette. He looked round the group. 'I've got two years to do. I'd like to tell 'em to shove it right now. Everyone including George nodded in sympathy. 'It's a bastard' said The Sergeant. 'It's all bollocks' said Paddy. 'I've done nothing wrong' said George.

'Is this supposed to be an impartial inquiry? It looks like a jockin' frameup to me' said Paddy.

'What about Habeas Corpus?' said Ronnie, having decided that as no-one was going to come to his rescue he might as well join in wholeheartedly in the only activity that was now taking place on the entire station.

'Yes' said Paddy. 'Get that useless idle drunken fucker out of the pub.'

The Constable put his book away and moved purposefully towards Paddy.

'Now look here mate' he started but got no further. Paddy planted himself in front of him.

'I suppose you're a Freemason?' he asked in sufficiently aggressive a tone as to make it perfectly clear he intended it as a rhetorical question. The Constable was taken aback.

'It's nothing to do with you' he said defensively.

'You'll get nowhere if you're not' Paddy informed him.

The Constable struck a pose. 'I have no conflict of interest. My allegiance is to The Great British Public' he declared, having spotted two somewhat bemused members of the said Great British Public who were wandering around trying to find someone who might be able to tell them if there was any possibility of getting a train somewhere.

'Excuse me Officer' the First Hopeful Traveller ventured.

'Not now mate The Constable responded.

'What about these bandits down the bloody shed? Paddy asked.

'Why don't you go and find out if they've been drinking? said George.

'We can't be in two places at once' The Sergeant said somewhat testily.

'It's a question of priorities' said Mike The Union Man.

'Exactly' The Sergeant said, glad of a little help.

'And arresting George, and kicking the crap out of him is more important than stopping a gang of shaggin' hooligans stealing our fucking vans' said Paddy.

'Fucking brilliant' said Ronnie.

'No-one's going to kick the crap out of George' said The Sergeant.

'Too bloody true they're not' said George, preparing to face an imminent assault.

The Second Hopeful Traveller thought he saw a glimmer of hope and there might after all be a chance of getting off the station in the foreseeable future.

'Do you suppose there might be a chance these shaggin' hooligans pinching your crappy old fucking vans might give me and my twat of a mate a lift back to poxy Sheffield?' he asked. Paddy thought about it for a moment.

'They seemed a nicely spoken bunch of criminals' he said.

'We'll try 'em said The Hopeful Traveller and set off towards The Shed.

'But I think they're planning to go to shaggin' London' Paddy called after them.

Ronnie looked gloomily at the daunting pile of mailbags in his brake.

'Any chance these friggin' hooligans might come and rob me of a few of these bastards?' he asked.

The Constable spoke to The Sergeant in a pained undertone.

'This is all a load of old bollocks Sarge' he opined.

The Sergeant looked at him with the withering scorn reserved for those who persist in stating the blindingly obvious under the impression they are making a great revelation.

'Of course it's a load of old bollocks. What do you expect? What else could it possibly be? The whole country's a load of old bollocks. That's the way things are now. I give it two years and the Universities will be offering bleedin' degree courses in loads of old bollocks' he said.

The Constable looked horrified.

'It's not that bad surely' he said without a great deal of conviction. Then he perked up.

'Let's forget this crap and go down to The Shed and deal with these hoodlums. They'll probably make a run for it in one of the Post Office's shagged out vans, and if they haven't stolen our car we can have a high speed chase' he said looking eager and suddenly years younger.

The Sergeant sighed wearily.

'It's not like television' he explained. 'If there are any villains there, which is highly unlikely, Paddy has probably seen a courting couple or some blokes having a slash, but if there are any villains they could be tooled up. Fancy being shot?' he asked.

But they could be doing a mail robbery The Constable objected. The Sergeant sighed and shook his head.

'Did our superior officers say anything to us about mail robbers? He asked. The Constable shook his head. The Sergeant warmed to his theme.

'They're not even remotely interested in mail robbers' he continued' "They're not bothered about terrorists.

What they care about is George having a couple of pints when he is specifically forbidden to do so under the railway by laws. George is a naughty boy. He thinks it's all a load of old bollocks. He does not keep this opinion to himself. According to him we are being run by a collection of idiots. George has to be made an example of. You can't have people ignoring stupid regulations. We have somehow to get George off this platform away from this shower and get him to blow into the little bag. If we can do that we will have done our little bit to restore Britain's former greatness.

'You have to face the fact that the patients are running the asylum.' he concluded.

At that point The Gaffer arrived somewhat the worse for drink. He glared at George.

'It's your round' he said. George bridled.

'I know it's my round' he retorted.

Ronnie spotted The Gaffer. 'There's supposed to be three men at this door' he started.

'Oh fuck off' said The Gaffer.

Ronnie pointed at The Constable. 'Write that fucker down. That'll sound really great when they read it out in court. The Great British Public'll really love that fucker' he said.

It slowly dawned on The Gaffer that all was not well.

'What's going on?' he asked, trying to sound as though he were something more than nominally in charge of the situation.

'George is under arrest' said Ronnie gloomily. 'He's helping the Police with their enquiries' he added.

The Gaffer turned pale. 'What's he done?' he asked.

'I have done nothing wrong' said George.

'We have reason to believe he has been drinking on duty' said The Constable.

'Why do you say that?' asked The Gaffer.

'For Chrissake will you look at him' answered The Constable.

The Gaffer looked at George, noted his bright red face and decided he didn't wish to be associated with him any further. He moved discreetly a few steps further away. Paddy glared at him.

'Are you going to stand by your man?' he demanded.

'That's a song ain't it? said Ronnie.

The Gaffer edged a few more tiny steps away.

'We all know drinking is against the law' he said self righteously.

Paddy was disgusted. 'Call yourself a fucking Gaffer. A decent Gaffer stands by his blokes when they're in the shit' he roared.

'I am not in the shit. I have done nothing wrong' said George.

Paddy turned to The Constable.

'Write that fucker down' he instructed. 'He says he's done nothing wrong. That's evidence.'

The Constable shook his head.'

'That is not evidence' he told Paddy firmly, at last wholly sure of his ground. 'Evidence is when he blows in the bag and pisses in the bottle' he declared.

George shook his head. 'I'm pissing in no bottle' he told him and folded his arms with the air of a man who considers the subject closed.

Paddy turned to George in triumph …

'You're right George. No fumes in the bag, no piss in the bottle, no fucking evidence' he said.

Mike nodded enthusiastically. 'Paddy's right. Say fuckall. Don't blow in the bag. Don't piss in the bottle. No fucking evidence. No fucking evidence, no fucking case, it's sheer fucking harassment' he declared.

Joe arrived back from the pub with an alcoholic flush and a truculent air. He got off the tractor with some difficulty.

'Write to your bloody MP George. Slip the fucker a few quid and he'll ask a question in Parliament' he said. 'You'll be in Hansard as well as the Police Gazette' he added.

Mike snorted derisively. 'The only question our MP will ask will be where's the nearest bar still serving' he said.

Paddy returned to the attack.

'Where's the so called Gaffer?' he demanded. No-one replied. The so called Gaffer had disappeared.

Ronnie shook his head wearily. 'Bloody fine set up down here. Even the bastard Gaffer's on the shaggin' Ghost Squad.' You'll not see him again tonight' he said.

'Too bloody true you won't' Paddy bellowed. 'He'll have gone sick. That's what he always does when there's trouble and one of his men is in the shit' he added, his face turning purple with indignation.

'I am not in the shit. I have done nothing wrong. There is no evidence. It's one law for us, another law for them, I am being victimised' George complained, obviously believing every word he said.

Ronnie piped up. 'You can call me as a witness. Harassment, victimisation and discrimination. It's postman prejudice he said.

The Constable was taken aback. His mouth fell open and his jaw sagged.

'Postman prejudice? What the fuck is that?' he asked The Sergeant. The Sergeant shrugged. 'I don't know, but I don't like the sound of it' he said. The Constable looked worried.

'Prejudice is tricky. If we're not careful George'll be out of the shit and we'll be in it. It's all right for you, you've only got a few years to do. I can't afford to drop in the shit' he said, edging uneasily away from The Sergeant. The Sergeant pointed a finger at him.

'If you're thinking of going sick, forget it. You're in this with me, shit or no shit' he said firmly. The Constable sighed. The prospect of early promotion that had so recently seemed to be looming was all at once a mere illusion, about as likely as a big win on the pools.

The West Country Boys working in the sorting section of the train had finished their tea. It struck them that it was high time one of the Station Men started handing in the bags for sorting. The Man On The Tick Sheet stuck his head out. He called politely down the platform.

'Excuse me'. The Station Men ignored him. He decided the time had come to assert himself.

'Is anyone going to hand in these fuckers or not?' he asked. Paddy rounded on him.

'Do you care about fucking justice or don't they have that down in Bristol?' he shouted.

The Man On The Tick Sheet rose to the challenge. He stepped down onto the platform and strode purposefully towards Paddy.

'What's up with you Paddy?' he asked. Before Paddy could tell him The Man On The Tick Sheet spotted George.

'Come on George. What are you playing at? We can't stop here all bloody night, even though Derby Station is a lovely spot' he said.

'I have done nothing wrong' George told him. The Man On The Tick Sheet agreed.

'You've done fuckall wrong. You've done fuckall right either. In fact you've done fuckall. What about these fucking bags?'

George had reached the stage where he couldn't switch his channel of thought.

'I am not pissing in the bottle' he said. The Man On The Tick Sheet was understandably mystified.

'I'm not asking you to piss in the bottle George' he said. He got no response so decided to make his requirements abundantly plain. He pointed at the pile of mail bags on the barrow outside his door.

'See those bags?' he asked, speaking very slowly and clearly as if to a child. George nodded. The Man On The Tick Sheet felt he was making some progress.

'I don't want you to piss on them. I want you to hand them in to me'; he explained.

George shook his head gloomily. 'You'll have to make other arrangements' he said.

The Man On The Tick Sheet was visibly shaken.

'What now?' he asked. George nodded.

'But the fucker's due out in five minutes' protested The Man On The Tick Sheet. He headed back to his door absolutely furious.

'It's no fucking skin off my fucking nose. If we haven't got the fuckers on board we can't sort the fuckers. We'll have to play fucking cards' he shouted.

Paddy bellowed after him. 'They've arrested George.'

The Man On The Tick Sheet stared hard at The Sergeant and The Constable. 'What Batman and Robin here?' he asked. The Constable felt he ought to protest but somehow found he simply hadn't the heart. All he wanted to do was get off the Station, put as much distance between himself and George as he could manage, and never set eyes on him again.

Paddy nodded and glared at the Constable and The Sergeant. The Man On The Tick Sheet was astounded. A thought struck him.

'Here is this a fucking wind-up? he asked. Paddy shook his head. The Man On The Tick Sheet raised his eyes to heaven.

'What for?' he asked.

'Ask them' Mike chimed in.

The Man On The Tick Sheet was about to do so when Ronnie stuck his oar in again. 'It's postman prejudice' he said.

The Constable winced and began to think with something akin to horror of having to take up a career in security.'

'He's not a fucking criminal' said Ronnie, wondering if he should perhaps chuck off a few bags so he could claim he'd been a zealous worker, abandoned by his superior, his mates, and finally overwhelmed by the sheer enormity of the task.

'They say he's had a drink' said Paddy.

'So fucking what?' said The Man On The Tick Sheet.

The Constable muttered something.

'You what? Said The Man On The Tick Sheet.

'He's broken the law' said The Constable miserably, wondering why he felt so unutterably stupid.

'Fucking arseholes!' said The Man On The Tick Sheet.

The Constable sat down defeated. He put his notebook away. Ronnie objected.

'Get that shagger back out and write the bugger down' he said. The Constable ignored him.

Suddenly there was an almighty commotion of frantic shouting and whistling at the end of the platform. The sorters stuck their heads out of the brake.

'Come on Reggie. Fuck the mail. We're off' they shouted.

'Hang on. They've arrested George' yelled The Man On The Tick Sheet.

The sorters came piling off the train and charged down the platform.

'What's he done? Who's he thumped?'

'He's had a drink' said The Man On The Tick Sheet.

'Yes but what's he done?' they clamoured.

At the end of the platform the railwayman in charge was jumping up and down.

'What's he saying?' asked Paddy.

'Fucking something' said Ronnie.

'It's time that thick twat learned to express himself properly. He's been over here twenty five years and he's continually incoherent' said Paddy censoriously.

The Man On The Tick Sheet looked dismissively at The Railwayman.

'He never could string two sentences together' he said. He turned to The Sergeant.

'Now then what's all this bollocks about George?' He's not a fucking criminal' he said.

The Sergeant decided it was time to play a straight bat.

'I don't make the rules. Don't blame me. I'm only following orders' he said.

The sorters set up an indignant protest to the effect that drunk or sober George was the best postman on the station, one of the select few that knew what he was doing. The Constable began to hear warning bells ringing all round. He saw himself disappearing forever into the loathsome maws of Group Four Security, working all the hours God sent, for a pittance, no longer a member of a respected, long established force. He drew The Sergeant aside.

For Christ's sake Sarge let's get our arses off this fucking station. We've got no chance. We're getting no co-operation. He's saying fuckall. He won't blow in the bag, he won't piss in the bottle. That old prat in the brake is going to accuse us of postman prejudice. We'll be crucified in the media. None of our Gaffers will stand by us. They'll drop us right in the shit to save their own necks. And to top it all, if that's not enough, this bunch of fucking West Country Worzel Gummidges are going to make that red nosed wanker postman of the fucking year. Let's pissoff' he said and nipped round a corner.

A moment later The Sergeant's radio crackled. He responded: 'Sergeant Green' The Constable walked rapidly to the steps leading off the platform speaking authoritively into his handset.

'Proceed at once to Chesterfield Station, suspected break in' he said and mounted the steps two at a time. From the bridge he glanced down and saw The Sergeant making his way most enthusiastically towards the stairs. The postmen gave him a round of what was obviously derisive applause.

At the end of the platform The Railwayman had thrown away his flag and jumped on his whistle. He stormed up the platform and when he reached the postmen was beside himself with rage.

'Close them fucking doors or it'll go without you' he snarled.

'Get bollocksed' said The Man On The Tick Sheet. 'We wait for you fuckers often enough while you try and get your act together. You can give us five minutes while we get the stuff on board.

'Come on George' yelled The West Country Lads.

Suddenly there was a frenzy of activity. It was this scene that greeted the Members of the Ghost Squad as they descended the stairs in the confident expectation that the work would have been done in their absence as usual. They halted in their tracks and stared at the train in horror. They checked their watches. Surely there was some mistake. Ronnie spotted them.

'Come on you two idle twats. Get your fat arses over here' he yelled triumphantly. The Ghost Squad moved towards the train like a pair of zombies. Ron stared at one of them.

'You've gone bald since I saw you last' he observed.

The Ghost Squad gazed in horror at the heap of bags requiring attention.

'I've saved a few for you' Ronnie told them gleefully.

'Idle old sod' they muttered resentfully and addressed themselves to the pile of bags with evident distaste. The train was loaded in no time at all. The Platform Supervisor looked ruefully at the remnants of his whistle, and from that time on The Constable always made it perfectly plain that if any assignment involved contact with George he wanted fuckall to do with it.

CHAPTER
FIVE

The Platform One Players

After the forces of law and order had been sent off with their tails between their legs morale was for a while at an unprecedentedly high level. The men began to believe they might be able to win. They were soon to find out they had no chance. Whilst they had won a skirmish, perhaps even a small battle, the tide of the war was running inexorably against them. The generals had declared war on their own troops, whilst maintaining that their welfare was a top priority. As Great Britain had its former eminence restored, virtually rammed up its arse, life grew steadily more intolerable for people who were unfortunate enough to be doing useful work. The mental homes were closed down, the inmates turned out into the streets to cope as best they could. Some adapted to the new environment so well they rose to the highest levels of government and management. Life became increasingly unpleasant for those foolish enough to cling to their sanity. There was no escape. Anyone wishing to progress had to become barking mad, or at least pretend they were certifiably insane. The better it was all declared to be the more horrifying the actuality became.

As the physical conditions on The Station grew daily worse, and rail travel became ever more hazardous because of the grossly irresponsible cost cutting, so the regulations governing the wretched lives of the defenceless workers became more oppressive and hypocritical. The ghastly truth was that nothing mattered but money. It wouldn't do for the authorities to be seen to be obsessed with saving money to the point where even the lives of the self important mobile phone carrying executives who travelled on The Master Cutler were deemed to be of little consequence when weighed in the balance against the promise of more economies, more cuts in the subsidy and ultimately yet more cash handed over to the already obscenely rich. Management had to demonstrate that despite all the evidence to the contrary they really did care for the people who placed their lives in their hands.

Naturally the budget didn't provide for much in the way of elementary precautions so a pretence had to be maintained that passenger safety was the first consideration. Announcements were made to this effect, a stringent regime would be imposed, anyone willfully endangering the lives of fare paying customers would be severely dealt with. These provisions only applied to those at the bottom of the heap who were doing their utmost to keep their beloved service going. It was now generally understood, if not actually stated, that offences were something that could not in any circumstances be committed by those who had mounted the managerial ladder, Even the Ten Commandments no longer applied to them.

As the workers were declared to be no longer required managers sprang up like dragons' teeth. They were everywhere. Indeed they were now so numerous there was very little for them to do. Most simply had no function. They were total parasites. For the most part those who could advance some sort of justification for their existence were incapable of performing what meagre function they had, so they applied themselves with great zeal to doing what they were best at. This was pointlessly oppressing those who fate and a series of Tory administrations had placed entirely in their power. They set about persecuting the workers. They carried out this campaign with maliciousness and remarkable stupidity. As The Mad Witch proclaimed she had set the people free thousands of revolting Little Hitlers sprang up across the land.

The persecution was pursued with some ingenuity. Had the same zeal been directed to improving or even preserving the service it would have been laudable. A favourite technique was to introduce a regulation declared to be necessary to deal with particular offences being committed by a clearly specified group of employees, and then also apply the rule with the same severity to those not remotely connected with the original group of potential malefactors. A prime example of this was the drive against drink and drugs. Rules were introduced that were supposed to ensure that no-one under the influence of either should drive a train. The Unions wholeheartedly gave their support. No one was going to argue against the desirability of having drivers in full possession of their faculties.

Unfortunately that was just the beginning. Very soon a reign of terror was imposed. Minor clerks with forty years service found themselves being threatened with dismissal because they had drunk half a pint of beer at lunchtime. Safety had nothing to do with it. Intimidation was rife. The workers had to fear. They had to obey without question. What had been introduced as a necessary measure very quickly turned into a mess of spite, bullying and pettiness. Stupidity was rampant and amply rewarded. It paid to be an arsehole. At management levels it was virtually a condition of employment. Decent people were not required.

Not surprisingly staff morale was very low. As the workers were systematically ground under the heel they were assured that management valued and cared for them. They were unable to accept these assurances that were shown to be insincere several times during each working day. The more nervous of them developed a haunted, hunted air as they skulked about hoping no one would notice them. The bolder spirits were openly derisory. It was of course the nervous ones who bore the brunt of the vileness.

Rod Williams was a Station Manager and the new dimwitted regulations suited his mean spirit and microscopic brain. The fact that there was now far more likelihood that trains would collide at high speeds did not greatly concern him. He came to work by car. He now had the power to virtually destroy someone's life; not for endangering those poor benighted souls who were naïve enough to entrust themselves to the bedraggled remnants of British Rail, but for what was considered to be a far greater crime, failing to acknowledge the total power vested in whatever idiot was deemed to have the right to manage, which all too often meant the power to act like a malignant village idiot suddenly placed in charge.

Like most of those now in charge Rod was a pathetically inadequate personality. The able people with decency and integrity had been got rid of. They were regarded as an obstacle, a hindrance. They threatened the Great Plan. Suddenly finding power thrust upon him Rod became more and more objectionable. The widespread oppression, the increasingly inane official absurdities boosted his hitherto feeble ego. He found self belief because someone passed a regulation. He was able to ruin people far superior to himself unless they unquestioningly deferred to him. What he said went.

The Adenoidal One who had begun her regime standing outside Ten Downing Street quoting Saint Francis of Assisi imposed upon the people who actually made the country run the constraints of totalitarianism, and ghastly legions of Rod Williams stood beneath her banner and drooled at the prospects she held before them. Suddenly hordes of nonentities found they had been accorded the privileges of dictatorship within their work place, constrained only by a framework of regulations that could be safely ignored. The roles of Prosecutor, Judge and Jury were now carried out by the same person. The sheer enormity of it all was breathtaking. Resistance was sporadic and disjointed. One by one the bulwarks painfully raised over decades to protect workers from the worst excesses of capital were removed and organized labour, despite some valiant rearguard actions, was soundly defeated.

Amid great enthusiasm from those who were doing very nicely out of all this misery Great Britain was declared to have been restored to its former glory. Some people actually believed this to be the case. The Unions were made totally impotent and were supposed to have been given back to their members. Hundreds of thousands lost their jobs and the unemployment figures continued to mysteriously fall. The virtues of honest money were proclaimed, and embezzlers thrived.

Their virtues were trumpeted and when their chicanery was exposed their escape from The Sceptered Isle was expedited.

This was the background against which the Platform One Repertory Players came into existence and began to plague the hitherto triumphant Rod Williams. The first intimation that something alarming was afoot came when a group of postmen, apparently waiting for the parcel train outside his office, sat themselves down on barrows seemingly waiting for some sort of show to start.

Rod ignored them. Just a bunch of peasants, well under the thumb. One of them began tapping on a steel barrow. Tap tap tap. Rod peered out. He wondered if there was a regulation that forbad tapping on steel barrows. Suddenly he heard a startling noise. A high pitched voice rang round the Station.

'Can anyone tell a poor old seaman who's lost the precious sight of his eyes in the service of his blessed majesty King George wheresoever he may be asked.

Rod was outraged. 'It's a Goddam beggar outside my office' he hissed and headed towards the door, determined to sort this wretched mendicant out, and make sure that wherever he pursued his chosen profession in future it was not outside the Station Manager's office. He felt he knew what would ensue if this was not nipped in the bud. It would only be a matter of time before the passengers disembarking from The Master Cutler were accosted and asked for alms. That simply would not do.

As he went to open the door he heard a second voice that stopped him in his tracks.

'You are at The Admiral Benbow Inn sir' it said.

Rod went and sat behind his desk. He had to think. This was puzzling. Certain things did not add up. He was pretty sure for instance that King George was not on the throne. He took out his wallet and had a look at a postage stamp to make sure. He had to be sure of his facts. He was quite certain that despite the deplorable antics of certain postmen this was not The Admiral Benbow Inn. It was Derby Station, and it was officially an alcohol free zone. He considered the facts, the conclusion was obvious. All the postmen out on the platform were ratarsed. They had to be. He knew for a fact that you couldn't get on

The Post Office unless you were practically an alcoholic. He put on his hat and purposefully straightened his tie. He'd show these bastards what was what. They seemed to think work was an occasion for hilarity. He'd soon disabuse them. As he again reached for the door handle the high voice caused him to freeze. The hair at the back of his neck rose.

'I hear a voice, a young voice, a kind voice' it said. It was eerie.

'Give me your hand young sir' it went on with an appalling insinuating tone.

Rod tiptoed across to the window and peered out. What he saw horrified him. A postman was standing in front of the group, his arm stretched out in a balletic pose towards another postman. The second postman gave his hand to the first one, whereon it was seized fiercely and dragged towards the first man.

'Now boy take me to The Captain' he shrieked.

Rod winced. The tone was penetrating enough to disturb important people sleeping in The Midland Hotel opposite The Station. There could be complaints. He must stop this.

'And when we get there you say' the terrible voice continued.

Despite himself Rod wanted to know what would come next. What would the boy, who he couldn't help noticing was at least fifty years old, have to say?

'You say here's a friend to see you Bill' shrieked. The Man With The Terrible Voice.

Suddenly The Man With The Terrible Voice who had supposedly lost the sight of his eyes serving The King underwent an alarming change. He flung away the hand of the fifty year old boy, stalked away from the group, and became somehow a mass of conflicting angles. To Rod's eyes he comprised entirely of writhing arms and legs which appeared to be going simultaneously in all directions in a way that struck Rod as most peculiar. Rod was horrified and yet fascinated. It was all compellingly hypnotic, this strange scene being enacted outside his office. He watched roundeyed.

The Apparition, strangely garbed in Royal Mail gear, but unlike any postman Rod had ever clapped eyes on, moved towards the group sitting on the barrows, but did so in a weird manner, with sudden changes of direction, slow cautious advances and hasty retreats. It gazed about it in a manner full of apprehension. It seemed to see everywhere the most terrifying sights. Rod sympathized. He was undergoing a similar experience. Suddenly the ghastly figure shot out a scrawny arm and seized the forearm of the nearest postman. It turned a glittering eye towards him and froze. It stood absolutely motionless. The group waited, all attention. Rod waited too. The still figure moved. It raised its other arm and pointed in the direction of the signal box.

'Are you off that boat out there in the bay Matey?' he asked.

There was no reply. The strange figure suddenly moved forward and grabbed a postman by his lapels. The man was dragged off the barrow towards the center of the platform where the strange figure released him. The strange figure moved away and then turned and again grabbed the postman.

'Is there a one legged sea cook on board?' he asked. Without waiting for an answer he continued after gazing fearfully round in all directions, apparently expecting to see something unbearably horrifying.

'I fear that man as I fear no other. He once had an entire crew fetching up their entrails for five days after they'd scoffed his Irish stew. What's your name Matey?' he asked.

It sounded to Rod as though the other man said his name was Knobhead, which struck him as strange, but the strange figure continued.

'I'm poor Ben Gunn I am Jim lad and I haven't spoken to a Christian these three years. But Jim lad' and here he drew Jim lad away from the group on the barrows, looked round in a conspirital way, and clutching his arm, said:

'I'm rich.'

The concrete that filled Rod's skull began to stir a little. He was never happy when this happened. It was disturbing. However what he was witnessing and hearing began to seem somewhat familiar. Somewhere he'd seen and heard it before. It was the same and yet not quite the same. Reluctantly he tried to think. His brow creased with the unaccustomed effort.

Ivor, The West Indian Platform Manager, came in, cheery as ever.

'Great show on platform one' he said with proprietal pride.

Rod sat with his brow knitted trying to remember.

Ivor continued. 'That guy shouldn't be here' he said.

Rod agreed wholeheartedly, but how could he get rid of him?

It then became apparent that he and Ivor were not on the same wavelength.

'I hate to see talent wasted. He's wasting his time here. He should be at The Playhouse' Ivor said, and left leaving Rod even more confused. This was quite extraordinary and entirely beyond his limited powers of comprehension. There were people who actually approved of what was being done outside his office. He was not capable of articulating what he found deeply disturbing, but what it was was the sense that something subversive was gathering momentum and he had the misfortune to be directly in its path.

Suddenly he remembered what had seemed vaguely familiar. He'd seen it on television recently, or at least something like it.

'It's Treasure Island' he said out loud.

Sean, The Irish Porter, came in. 'Not now it isn't' he told Rob. 'They're doing Saint Joan.'

Rod's first thought was that a devout lady was being subjected to uncouth attentions, but he no longer trusted his first instincts. Doubt had been instilled in his mind.

He peered at Sean. 'They're doing what?' he asked.

The terrible voice, now much lower, and if anything louder, thundered outside the window.

'No eggs. No eggs. A thousand thunders what do you mean by telling me there are no eggs?' it roared. It was a most intimidating sound and Rod had no wish to confront the man making it. He took off his cap. Suddenly he thought it unlikely he would be leaving his office for a while. A second voice said something he couldn't catch, although it might have been something to the effect that there were no chickens, and the terrible voice resounded in his ears.

'Blasphemy! First you tell me there are no eggs and then you blame your Maker for it' it roared.

Sean's eyes were shining. He sat down uninvited. Rod again sensed he was in the track of something alarming.

'That's wonderful' said Sean. He eyed Rod; 'I take it you're familiar with the work?' he asked.

Rod shifted uncomfortably in his seat, his attention rather divided between his interrogator sitting in his office and his tormentor resonating unashamedly on his platform. He didn't have a clue what it was. The complaint about the lack of eggs made him wonder if it was a commercial for the Egg Marketing Board.

Fortunately Sean couldn't resist the temptation to air his knowledge and so spared him further embarrassment.

'The undisputed masterpiece of Ireland's greatest man of letters, George Bernard Shaw' said Sean, looking to Rod's mind as smug as if he'd written it himself.

'Didn't he write My Fair Lady? Rod asked, anxious to show that he wasn't entirely lacking in culture. The words had no sooner left his mouth before he regretted uttering them. Sean assumed the infuriating air of superiority he now displayed all too often since he enrolled for an O level course in English Literature.

Ireland's greatest wrote a play called Pygmalion on which the musical My Fair Lady is based' he said.

Rod felt like hitting him. He decided to put the upstart little Irish git, who hadn't written a masterpiece and was the merest menial on the station, firmly in his place. Before he could do so his ears were assailed by a vocal eruption outside. It contained such savage fury he shrank back in his seat.

'Forty thousand thunders, fifty thousand Devils. Do you mean to tell me that that girl who had the audacity to come here asking to see me three days ago, and whom I told you to send home to her Father with my orders that he was to give her a sound thrashing is here still?' it blasted.

'That's training for you, that's breath control' said Sean appreciatively.

This sort of behaviour was way beyond Rod's comprehension. He sought an explanation and could find none. Clutching at straws he asked:

'Is he drunk?' Sean shook his head. 'He's not had a drop.'

Rod persisted. 'Is he on something?' he asked hopefully. Sean shook his head.

The huge voice roared out, different again. Now it had a distinct West Country sound.

'You can't stop here' it said. Rod was just able to hear someone ask: 'Why not?' The voice resumed. 'This Station's haunted.'

Sean stood up. Rod hadn't told him to. Things were falling apart.

'They're going onto The Ghost Train. I'm not missing this' he said and went out faster than Rod had ever seen him move. He sat with his head in his hands trying to gather what in his case had to pass for thoughts.

The dreaded voice went remorselessly on: 'Last Summer it were. On this very spot poor old Walter Holmes lost his reason. It were a wild night and the wind were howling. You could hear poor old Walter out on the platform singing. Rock of Ages. Up and down he went singing his heart out' it continued. Now several voices broke out in a somewhat disjointed rendering of Rock of Ages. And then again The Voice of Thunder.

'And then the clock struck twelve' it declaimed, every word articulated and drawn out. The Chorus took over. 'Boing. Boing. Boing. Rod realized he was going to hear this sound twelve times. At the same time Rock of Ages continued in a low murmur, and the voice was raised just as Rod was attempting to console himself with the thought that it couldn't possibly get any louder. It could and it was awesome.

'The door suddenly juddered open. And there stood Walter Holmes, framed against the night sky, his lamp still burning in his hand, as large as life, and he were ... ... as Rod looked anxiously at the door, the mighty voice and chorus outside joined in unison on STONE DEAD.

Rod was appalled. Sean stuck his head in:

'Did you enjoy that? It's my favourite. The Ghost Train written by Arnold Ridley, nowadays best known for his role as the ancient private with a chronically weak bladder in the tv series Dad's Army' Sean informed him. He left as suddenly as he had arrived.

Rod glared after him. 'That bloody leprechaun wants sorting out' he muttered. His gloom deepened. 'They all want sorting out' he added.

Suddenly there was an almighty commotion outside. A train had been seen nearing the station. Rod felt a sensation of sheer relief. Normality had been resumed. He reached for his hat. At the very moment when he felt his redemption had occurred he heard possibly the most horrifying sound so far. Right outside his window.

'Hee haw hee haw.'

The voice had now changed into a thunderously braying donkey. Its cries met with a response from donkeys all over the station. From every corner came the vile sound: hee haw hee haw" Rod took off his hat with an air of finality. He hung it on a hook. He opened the drawer of his desk and took out a sheaf of paper. There was nothing else for it. He would have to make out a report. He took up his pen. The donkeys continued to bray. They all sounded damnably cheerful. He reviewed the events he sought to relate. He put his pen back. He knew if he committed all this to paper enquiries would be made as to his mental state. He decided to bide his time. He put his hat on and took himself off to the Executive Toilet. After locking himself in he took out his pen and wrote on the wall: POSTMEN ARE A BUNCH OF FUCKING ASS'OLES.'

He felt better.

CHAPTER
Six

Dr. Llewellyn

As the process of setting the people free continued apace so the suffering spread and intensified. It spread to the extent that it was difficult to grasp why the tories kept getting returned to power. The Scots and the Welsh voted overwhelmingly against the prevailing bestiality, but for some strange reason The English opted with enthusiasm for things that anywhere else could only be imposed with the aid of tanks on the streets and machine gun nests on every corner.

Doctor Llewellyn couldn't understand it. Neither could he understand why the Scots and the Welsh, who everyone knew perfectly well had made it abundantly clear they were against all this nonsense, should have nonetheless to put up with it because the English seemingly have a marked streak of masochism, or as he thought in his blacker moods which were become increasingly frequent, were simply bloody stupid.

Surgery was by now the sheerest purgatory. He found himself wondering if there was a doctor anywhere in the British Isles who didn't fervently wish he was a vet. He was beginning to feel he couldn't cope much longer with the hordes of workers complaining of exhaustion, and The Managers who sat opposite him twitching, chewing their fingernails and wittering on about stress. Ulcers were out. Stress was the in thing. He got so fed up listening to the tales of the challenges these tosspots continually faced at work and the resultant carnage caused amid their lives that he told one bloke to pull himself together and stop sniveling. He then with some relish quoted Richard Nixon, whom he heartily loathed, 'if you can't stand the heat, get out of the kitchen.' He hadn't seen this particular patient since and didn't know if he had taken his advice and joined the millions who regularly waited for the arrival of the giro, if the prescription had worked and he was now happily kicking ass and subjecting others to stress, or if he'd got the hump and taken his card to another practice. He had to admit that he didn't really care.

He was in a particularly foul mood because he'd had a look at the appointments list and had seen the name Rod Williams at the top.

'I can't stand any more consultations with that moron' he'd complained.

'We all have our crosses to bear' said The Receptionist.

Doctor Llewellyn suspected her of being a secret Tory voter. The entire state of Britain appalled him. Probably what appalled him most was the astoundingly low quality of the people who were now running things. He found the fact that Rod Williams was actually in charge of a sizeable railway station entirely inexplicable. Surely the English had wankers enough and to spare without having to import them from Canada. Were there perhaps adverts in the Toronto Times and the Ottawa Post:

'Are you a wanker? You are. Splendid. Come to Britain and be a Manager.'

Doctors were reputed to be clueless about their own health, but he knew that having to continually listen to the whinges of a bunch of elevated halfwits was having a dire effect on his. His professional manner he realized had become distinctly confrontational. It had to. Each consultation was now in the nature of a contest, or so it appeared to him. There was a clear conflict.' His aim was to cure the useless bastards, theirs to make him as deranged as they were. He raised his fist and pounded the bell.

'Round one' he bellowed.

In the waiting room the exhausted workers, the twitching managers, the women who couldn't conceive and those who couldn't stop having babies and had difficulty in remembering who the Fathers were quailed. The door of the consulting room opened and Rod Williams walked in. Before he could open his mouth or even reach the chair Doctor Llewellyn got in first.

'I don't want to hear any more about shaggin' George' he said.

'Don't talk to me about shaggin' George' Rod replied.

Doctor Llewellyn picked up his pen.

'Is it a repeat prescription?' he asked.

He knew damn well it wasn't but he couldn't help trying.

'I want a consultation' Rod told him.

Doctor Llewellyn regarded Rod, trying hard to hide his acute distaste. What the British Medical Association would undoubtedly condemn as an unworthy thought struck him.

'I wish he had piles. I'd sooner stare up his arse than have to try and peer into the murky recesses of his subterranean mind' he told himself.

'You don't have piles?' he asked.

Rod looked puzzled.

'No I don't have piles' he affirmed.

Doctor Llewellyn looked cheerful.

'Well at least your arse is allright' he said and made a note.

Rod looked even more puzzled. His bafflement made his stupid face look dimmer than ever. Doctor Llewellyn gave him a smile of encouragement.

'So what's the problem?' he asked.

He wrote down the answer before Rod gave it. 'Stress.'

Rod sat twitching opposite him, a most nauseating spectacle. Doctor Llewellyn wrote down the answer to the next question. Worse.

'Is the stress better or worse?' he asked.

He thought it would save time if he answered his own question and did so.

'So what's making it worse?' he asked, hoping against hope that he hadn't guessed the answer correctly and Rod would have the decency to liven things up by providing him with a much needed laugh.

'I'm worried about the Area Manager' said Rod, chewing savagely at what remained of his fingernails. The extent to which Dim Managers were terrified of the people above them never ceased to amaze Doctor Llewellyn, since so far as he could make out they were if anything even more stupid than the unprepossessing specimens who haunted his surgery.

It really was extraordinary. He kept reading in the press, which was admittedly voluntarily in the government's pocket, how wonderful things were and what an example Britain was to the rest of the world, which stood aghast and wondered at our breathtaking achievements, consumed with envy, and anxious to the point of desperation to follow our inspiring example. Then he saw them, the people who were supposed to be responsible for this miracle. Those who weren't completely knackered were idiots terrified of the idiots above them.

He had to cling to the hope that somewhere in the country there were some rational intelligent people. He realized he was unlikely to come across them, but he did need to believe they were there somewhere, waiting patiently for the tide of the all prevailing lunacy to recede.

Meanwhile here he was with the demented Rod Williams.

'Why are you worried about The Area Manager?' asked Doctor Llewellyn.

'That guy knows everything' said Rod.

Doctor Llewellyn thought it highly unlikely that omniscience was a quality possessed by an Area Manager of British Rail but he held his peace.

'What really worries me' said Rod twitching alarmingly 'is that there's a spy on the station.'

Doctor Llewellyn cheered up immediately. This was better. Instead of a snivelling half witted bundle of neuroses he had a genuine lunatic on his hands. He forgave Rod Williams for the hours of tedium he had inflicted on him.

'What makes you think there's a spy on Derby Station?' he asked.

The answer delighted him. It was so splendidly bizarre he could have shaken Rod Williams by his wet trembling hand.

'There's a spy on every station' said the quaking creature.

'Do you mean to tell me British Rail is riddled with informers?' said Doctor Llewellyn.

'Oh sure. It's part of the new enterprise culture. Keeps everybody on their toes' said Rod.

'Then if it's routine, why are you bothered?' asked the doctor.

'Because I don't know who the bastard is' said Rod.

'Do people usually know who the bastard is?' asked the doctor.

'Oh sure' said Rod.

'How can you tell?' asked Doctor Llewellyn.

'It's always the guy who takes an interest in what's going on' said Rod.

'So what's the mystery? Why can't you tell who it is?' asked Doctor Llewellyn.

Because now none of British Rail staff take an interest. They all want out' said Rod.

'Then you're in the clear. If there's no interest there's no seething discontent. Everyone's given up. The dissidents are crushed. The Area Manager must trust you. There is no spy' said Doctor Llewellyn.

'Oh yes there is' said Rod.

He leaned towards The Doctor.

'It could be that Longhaired Bastard of a Postman' he said.

Doctor Llewellyn was delighted. This was wonderful. The years of study might not have been a complete waste of time after all.

'Why would a Longhaired Bastard of a Postman be spying for British Rail? Surely if he's going to spy he'll spy for The Post Office.' said Doctor Llewellyn.

'They don't have spies on The Post Office' said Rod.

By way of explanation he added:

'The Post Office is not yet fully part of The New Enterprise Culture. They are a backward looking organization. As yet they have not fully grasped the opportunities that are available. They have an attitude problem. That Longhaired Bastard works for British Rail. He is under cover. He is a Post Office employee. But he is working for the Area Manager of British Rail' said Rod.

Doctor Llewellyn had heard enough.

'I've diagnosed your problem' he said.

'So what is my problem?' said Rod eagerly.

Doctor Llewellyn scribbled a certificate. He handed it over.

'That's your problem' he said.

Rod peered at the certificate.

'You're signing me off work for a month' he said.

Doctor Llewellyn nodded. Rod peered again at the certificate dubiously.

'Because I am suffering from paranoia. That means I'm nuts don't it?, he asked.

Doctor Llewellyn shook his head.

'It means you are suffering from a clearly recognized mental condition, probably brought on by strain' he said.

Rod thought about this for a moment.

'You mean I've got stress?' he said.

'Stress and paranoia' Doctor Llewellyn conceded.

Rod shook his head.

'I can't go sick with a mental condition. They expect me to have stress. If you don't have stress it counts against you. It goes on your record, they think you just don't give a shit, but I don't want it going round that I'm nuts' he said.

When he saw Doctor Llewellyn preparing to argue Rod asked in near desperation:

'Can't you just give me some tablets?'

Doctor Llewellyn seized his pen.

'Repeat prescription?' he asked.

Rod nodded.

'It's got to be better than being nuts' he said as he put the prescription away.

When he'd gone Doctor Llewellyn was thoughtful. An alarming notion struck him. Maybe Williams wasn't nuts. Maybe there were spies on every railway station. After all the public were regularly invited to spy on their neighbours and ring a hotline if they suspected someone was fiddling the social security. Naturally there was no such facility for those who thought someone might be fiddling their income tax. He considered the possibilities in the light of the general climate of the country and decided that on balance there probably was a spy on Derby Station, and the most likely holder of the office was the Long Haired Bastard of a Postman.

He punched the bell.

'Round two. Seconds out' he bellowed.

'I think Doctor Llewellyn's got stress' said an infertile woman.

'Who hasn't got bleedin' stress?' said the woman next to her.

The second patient looked like a walking ghost. He just about made it to the chair and didn't sit down so much as collapse. Doctor Llewellyn seemed to be faced with an inert mass.

'What's the problem Mr. Jenkins?' he asked.

Mr. Jenkins made an obviously painful effort to gather his faculties so he could speak.

'I'm knackered' he breathed and then seemed to slip into something akin to a coma.

Doctor Llewellyn looked at the notes. 'I see you work for The Post Office Mr. Jenkins,' he said.

Mr. Jenkins underwent something akin to a convulsion. His painfully exhausted frame stiffened with indignation, his eyes lit up and a volley of muffled sounds came from his lips. Doctor Llewellyn leaned forward straining to hear. He caught enough to get the general picture.

"Shaggin' Post Office … nothing but slave labour … shaggin' Gaffers … straight out of the shaggin' Gestapo … shaggin' Union … bunch of shaggin' wankers …. if the shaggin' public knew what was going on they'd be shaggin' up in shaggin' arms."

It began to look to Doctor Llewellyn as though what he now had to deal with was someone suffering from exhaustion, stress and an acute resentment. In other words a perfectly typical British worker. Mr. Jenkins was sufficiently inarticulate to make it likely that he read The Sun and voted conservative. It did seem odd that so many workers voted for a government that proudly proclaimed it had broken the unions, as indeed it had, and then complained that their Union was ineffectual.

However this was England where logic had long since been trodden ruthlessly underfoot.

Meanwhile here was Mr. Jenkins, who having got various things off his chest, had now resumed his previous coma like state, and looked a likely candidate for the Terminal Ward somewhere, always supposing of course he could be found a bed. One thing was perfectly obvious. Mr. Jenkins was not fit for work.

"I'm going to sign you off Mr. Jenkins" he said.

The response astonished him. Instead of looking gratified, as a man in his pitiable condition obviously should Mr. Jenkins looked horrified.

"I can't have time off" he protested.

"Why on earth not?" asked The Doctor.

"The bastards'll sack me" said Mr. Jenkins, and sat slumped in his chair, a picture of complete despair. The Doctor shook his head.

"This is a civilised country" he began. He got no further because the wraith sitting opposite him was shaking with what, to his relief, was not a seizure but laughter.

Mr. Jenkins took out a handkerchief and wiped his eyes.

He held his sides.

"Have you been working abroad Doctor?" he asked. "Surely you realise we are being governed by barbarians. At the bottom of the heap we're back in The Dark Ages."

Doctor Llewellyn thought this might be overstating the case, and was about to lodge a mild protest, when Mr. Jenkins cut him short.

"Look at the state of me" he said.

Doctor Llewellyn did so. Mr. Jenkins really did look awful.

"Do I look like a product of civilisation?" asked Mr. Jenkins.

Doctor Llewellyn didn't know what to say. What Mr. Jenkins looked like was something out of an apoplectic vision. He looked appalling.

"I look like The Picture of Dorian Grey. I'm like one of those poor sods you see lurking on the fringes of a medieval tapestry. I look like one of the undead" he concluded" and again slumped back in the chair, the brief flurry of animation seemingly having taken whatever life remained out of him.

Doctor Llewellyn felt he could be about to lose a patient to the undertaker.

"What you need Mr. Jenkins is rest" he said.

Mr. Jenkins nodded miserably.

"I'll sign you off for two weeks" said The Doctor.

Mr. Jenkins sat bolt upright. He shook his head violently.

"I can't take time off" he said.

"Why on earth not?" asked The Doctor, already knowing the answer.

"The bastards'll sack me" he was told.

"But … began The Doctor, but Mr. Jenkins cut him short. "Don't tell me this is a civilised country. It's wallowing in barbarism" he said.

"But you're obviously not fit for work" The Doctor protested.

"Of course I'm not fit for work. What's that got to do with anything? If I go sick it'll cost the bastards money, so they'll sack me. This is what they call improved industrial relations. It works. They found it very satisfactory in Russia. It's called slave labour" Mr. Jenkins concluded.

Doctor Llewellyn had heard enough.

"I'm not listening to this" he protested. We don't have slave labour in this country. Well not yet" he added.

"Would you accept being forced to work for nothing as a reasonable definition of slave labour? asked Mr. Jenkins, his eyes glittering in his emaciated dead white mask of a face.

Yes, but you don't work for nothing at The Post Office. You're paid wages. You get paid overtime" Doctor Llewellyn countered.

Mr. Jenkins sighed and shook his head, a gesture of infinite weariness. "Do you know how many hours a week I work for nothing?" he asked.

Doctor Llewellyn shook his head and waited to be told, wondering what horror was to be revealed to him.

"I work twelve hours a week for nothing" said Mr. Jenkins. Doctor Llewellyn didn't know what to say. For a few moments they sat regarding each other in silence. Mr. Jenkins spoke first. "I'm on delivery work" he said as though that explained everything. Doctor Llewellyn was still mystified. "Why would anyone work twelve hours a week for nothing?" he asked. "Just about all the workers in the Delivery Room work around ten to twelve hours a week for nothing" Mr. Jenkins replied. Doctor Llewellyn was even more mystified. "Wouldn't they rather be paid?" he asked. Mr. Jenkins nodded. He seemed to be slipping back into his near coma like state. He looked as though he needed the attention of the paramedics, a good whiff of oxygen.

"Do you know what time I start work?" asked Mr. Jenkins. The Doctor didn't. He realised he was being given an insight into the ugly truth hidden behind the tissue of lies and euphemisms that disguised the nature of contemporary life in the United Kingdom. "Four o'clock" said Mr. Jenkins. The Doctor wondered what time Mr. Jenkins had to get out of bed to start that early, but he held his peace. He knew more was to come. "I should start at half past five" said Mr. Jenkins. "But I can't possibly sort my walk in the time allowed. No-one can sort their walk in the time allowed. So we all come in early and work for nothing, which I think we agreed was an acceptable definition of what constitutes slave labour" he said.

"Why can't you prepare your rounds in the time allocated?" asked The Doctor. "Because a round that a few years ago would consist of one bulging bag of mail now consists of four, five or six bags of bulging mail" said Mr. Jenkins. "We used to be a drain on the public purse. Now we pay around a hundred and fifty million pounds a year to the government. This transformation has been achieved by the great motivator" said Mr. Jenkins.

"The great motivator? asked Doctor Llewellyn.

"Fear" said Mr. Jenkins. "There are millions of frightened people out there Doctor". "Then tell me this Mr. Jenkins countered The Doctor. "If things are so bad, and these people are, as you say, frightened, why are they voting for more of the same?"

"If I knew that Doctor I wouldn't be working as a shaggin' postman, and I wouldn't be sitting here looking like death warmed up" Mr. Jenkins replied. Doctor Llewellyn sighed.

"I'll tell you this though" said Mr. Jenkins, heaving himself upright with an obvious effort.

"Yes?" said The Doctor.

"Some of those poor benighted souls out there are so dim if they'd been Jews during The Holocaust and Hitler stood for re-election on his record they'd have voted for him. If The Sun told him to." said Mr. Jenkins.

"What paper do you read Mr. Jenkins?" asked The Doctor.

"I used to read The Guardian" said Mr. Jenkins.

"You've packed up The Guardian" said The Doctor.

A flash of irritation crossed Mr. Jenkins's face. Then he resumed his former passivity.

"Right now I'm too knackered to read anything" he said.

"Are you sure they'll sack you if I sign you off?" asked The Doctor.

Mr. Jenkins nodded. "They can't screw much more work out of people without actually using torture. What they're trying to do now is absolve themselves from the responsibility of providing statutory sick pay without actually admitting that's what they're doing. They'll achieve that by making people afraid to go sick. Regardless of what sort of condition they're in if people can actually walk they now come in to work. What with that and the hours of work done for nothing the managers' bonuses are going through the roof.

"How is staff morale?" asked The Doctor. "I keep thinking it can't get any lower, but it always somehow does." said Mr. Jenkins.

Doctor Llewellyn thought for a moment. Then he took up his pen. "Here's what we'll do' he said. Mr. Jenkins leant forward, a slight flicker of what could have been hope passed across his face.

"I'll say you've got a slight stress fracture of the ankle and should be engaged on indoor duties until this rights itself" said The Doctor.

Mr. Jenkins thought for a moment. Then he shook his head. "I've got a better idea Doctor. Tomorrow morning when I'm carrying three bags of mail down the stairs I'll stage an accident. I'll get it in the accident book. Then I'll come and see you again. That way if they try and sack me I'm covered. The accident will naturally be blamed on me, because they'll say I shouldn't have been carrying three bags down the stairs, but if I don't they'll accuse me of working to rule. No doubt you'll read in our splendid impartial press about wicked bolshie employees working to rule. What do they say they're doing?" he asked.

"Holding the country up to ransom" said The Doctor.

"And imposing intolerable burdens upon the employer, thereby destroying jobs. Don't forget that Doctor" said Mr. Jenkins.

He rose. "It's pretty rough being a worker in a neo fascist state" he said.

"Come come now. It's hardly that" said The Doctor.

"Give the bastards time Doctor" said Mr. Jenkins as he shuffled wearily out.

Doctor Llewellyn sat holding his head in his hands. That was how The Receptionist found him ten minutes later.

"Are you allright Doctor Llewellyn?" she asked.

"Do you know what it is out there?" he demanded.

"No" she replied.

"It's nothing but a shaggin' Gulag" said The Doctor. He punched the bell. "March in the next prisoner" he bellowed.

CHAPTER
SEVEN

The Strike

The workers didn't tamely submit. There were frequent strikes. What people found puzzling after one of the strikes on The Post Office was that the man arrested for disturbing the peace on the picket line wasn't a shop steward, he didn't even work for The Post Office, he was the tory voting landlord of the pub opposite the gatehouse. He was indeed guilty of shouting 'shagging scabs', and shaking his fist at the traitors who left other people to fight their battles and went into work, scabs and right wing martyrs. John Flaherty gave the strikers his enthusiastic support on what in the current climate of the country could be considered religious grounds. He backed the strikers for sound commercial reasons.

Despite the fact that every day provided fresh claims about the incredibly brilliant things being achieved under the conservative government, within the non existent confines of the free market, businesses were going under at a rate hitherto unknown. As the businesses they'd fought to establish and maintain were destroyed by the halfbaked theories of a bunch of idiots who for the most part, having married money, had never themselves run so much as a chip shop, they were informed this was an indication of how sound the notions of these imbeciles were, since now only the most efficient firms would survive. Remarkably none of these wantonly destroyed proprietors of what could have been perfectly sound businesses, were they not operating under conditions imposed by near lunatics, resorted to assassination. Instead they blamed the unions and continued to vote tory.

Naturally the pubs suffered along with everything else. The unemployed and the bankrupt couldn't afford much in the way of entertainment. John Flaherty's pub was teetering on the very brink of extinction. He knew that if his sales didn't show a marked improvement the brewery would close him down. He tried everything he could think of. He confined his wife to the back of the premises and engaged two good looking barmaids. He started offering snacks, he ran a darts team, all to no avail. Sales continued to plummet. Without doubt John was going under. And then there was a miracle. One night around ten o'clock to John's amazement his pub was full of postmen demanding pints. He and the girls set to, filling glass after glass. The demand for pints became more insistent and John had to get his wife to put in an appearance behind the bar. She was somewhat reluctant to do so, having been understandably peeved by the implied criticism of her that had led to her banishment to the rear of the premises. However she overcame her reservations when a good looking young postman eyed her with what she felt sure was admiration and said 'four pints of bitter darling'. When closing time came the view from the bar was of a riotous assembly fronted by a row of hands thrusting forward empty glasses and the air was full of cries for more ale. John decided that to close at this point would be like deliberately sinking the lifeboat and trusting yourself to the unruly elements, so he announced at the top of his voice: "Those who are in are in, and those who are out are out" A cheer went up. He locked the front door, closed the curtains, and resumed his place behind the bar.

No-one showed any inclination to go home. The postmen seemed like people released from an intolerable burden. They were enjoying life. As the till continued to ring merrily visions of bankruptcy began to fade. John was once again able to entertain hopes that he might be Chairman of the Licensed Victuallers Association. It was a happy prospect. He felt in such good humour that he even responded to invitations to 'have one yourself landlord' by drinking far more pints then was wise.

John looked round his bar with a broad beaming smile. Suddenly life was good. People were fine. Around three o'clock the drinking had slowed down and the previous roar of bellowed conversations and orders had diminished to a steady murmur. Suddenly someone said 'we'd best organise a shaggin' picket line. The delivery men will be turning up soon.'

John was a Daily Mail reader. Like everyone else in England he maintained he didn't believe a thing he read in the papers, and docilely swallowed every lie and distortion offered. He looked round his bar. It was a heartwarming sight. He'd gathered from snatches of conversation overheard that the postmen had walked out. He realised with some bemusement that his business, indeed his very life, was in the process of being saved by a bunch of militants. These lads and lasses were he would no doubt read holding the nation up to ransom. They were 'the enemy within', and here they were, God bless them, keeping him afloat. John was a man of honour. He had principles and he believed he should stick to them. He was actually a member of The Tory Party, but as he looked round the bar he knew who his friends at that moment were. A picket was quickly organised and set up outside The Post Office gates opposite. It rapidly swelled as the delivery men heard there was a strike and joined the picket. Remembering all he had read in The Daily Mail about bully boy tactics John kept his eyes open. What he saw was a bunch of amiable postmen laughing and joking and engaging in what used to be known as comradeship. John remembered that once there had been such a thing. Soon there were so many postmen around John's door that it was obvious no policeman would be able to get inside and do him for being open after hours. Indeed at five am he reasoned that they would have to frame a charge of opening before hours. At intervals he heard cheers and knew that yet another worker had joined the picket. By this time he had a better grasp of the issues involved than any of the local or national industrial correspondents would ever acquire, and knew that the main thing was that all the lads and lasses, his customers, were what with one thing and another 'shaggin' tittsed and bollocksed off'. It was John reasoned surely a great British tradition that whenever a group of workers felt sufficiently 'tittsed and bollocksed off' that they said 'shag this for a shaggin' lark' and voted with their feet. Eventually the lads who had originally walked out and were now well and truly pissed decided it was time to have a sleep. Gradually the pub emptied and John sat down to count the contents of the till. Tired though he was he made his plans for the day.

"We'd best lay on some grub for the lads" he told his wife. She agreed. "And we'd best make a contribution to the strike fund" he added. His wife was about to protest, but John gestured towards the impressive pile of money. His wife nodded.

"They seem an awfully nice bunch of lads and lasses" she said sounding somewhat puzzled.

The day brought sunshine and warmth. The demand for beer was heavy. Early on John made an alarming discovery. He was running out of beer. He rang the brewery. "I must have a delivery" he told them. "We can't deliver until next week' he was told. "Don't talk like a bloody fool. There's a strike on here" he shouted.

"Who's on strike?" asked The Man From The Brewery. "The Post Office" said John. "So there's no bloody mail" said The Brewery Man. "Who cares a sod about the mail?" said John. "I do. They're supposed to be providing a service" said The Brewery Man. John had had enough.

"I haven't rung you up to discuss the ins and outs of the bloody dispute. I want some supplies" he said angrily.

"If you wanted more beer you should have ordered it last week" said The Brewery Man who was increasingly getting up John's nose.

Indeed he was causing him to feel thoroughly tittsed and bollocksed off.

"How the bloody hell was I to know the lads were going to walk out?" he asked. The shaggin' Head Postmaster has just been on the shaggin' radio and he didn't shaggin' know. He's supposed to be running the place. If he doesn't know what the shaggin' hell is going on, how am I supposed to? Am I getting more shaggin' beer or not?" he demanded.

"Are they using bully boy tactics?" asked The Man From The Brewery. "No but I will be if you don't get some shaggin' beer down here double quick" John warned him. "Is there any violence?" asked The Brewery Man hopefully.

"No there is not. There is a carnival atmosphere. The sun is shining. The lads have cast off their chains for a day or so, they're in holiday mood. They're drinking steadily and I am running dry. Now are you going to send down more beer, or am I going to have to make a serious complaint to your superiors?" John asked.

The threat was sufficient. Muttering about succouring The Enemy Within The Jobsworth From The Brewery agreed to send more beer immediately. John rubbed his hands together in delight. He wondered if it might be a good idea to ask The Brewery to make a contribution to the strike fund. On balance he decided it probably wasn't. They did after all contribute massively to the tory party.

In a remarkably short time the new supplies arrived. A few postmen who had been sinking pints with great enthusiasm and were somewhat the worse for wear stopped the lorry before it drew level with the gates and proceeded to harangue the driver, urging him to turn round. The driver looked understandably confused. Fortunately John was outside at the time.

"No no no lads" he called. The postmen turned towards him puzzled. "It's the beer" he explained. By that time there was a row of postmen opposite The Post Office three or four deep on the pavement for at least a hundred yards. The word was passed down the line – "it's the shaggin' beer'. A great cheer went up. Startled faces appeared in The Post Office windows where the managers were filling in the day playing cards. As they appeared cries of 'wankers' rent the air. They hastily withdrew. The driver to his alarm was hauled from his cab. His fears were quickly stilled, and he found he was being slapped on the back, having his hand shaken and told he was without any question of doubt the best shaggin' driver in the whole of the shaggin' country.' The driver found this acclaim very much to his liking and clambered on top of his lorry to take a bow. Another cheer went up and bursts of clapping. The driver was lured into the bar, just for a quick half.

At that moment John's wife came in looking pale. "What's up duck?" he asked. "It's that bastard at The Royal Oak" she said. "What about him?" he asked. "He's having a happy hour from midday to one o'clock" she said miserably. "Is he" said John, not looking at all worried. "He'll take all our trade" said his wife. John shook his head. "He's got no chance. I've spoken to The Branch Secretary. The Union are making their headquarters in our back room. We will have a happy hour from twelve to three o'clock, and what is more I have pulled a few strings to get an extension. We do not close today. I've arranged for extra staff" he concluded.

His wife looked out at the thronged pavement. "I must say they're a jolly lot" she said. John nodded his agreement. "What's the trouble about?" his wife asked. "They're all bollocksed and tittsed off" he explained.

The Happy Hour was a riot. Beer was drunk at such a rate John began to wonder if he would have to call for yet another delivery. He noticed that The Driver was still drinking with a crowd of postmen who were still telling him what a shaggin' great bloke he was. He looked a really happy man. Recognition had come to him at last. Towards the end of Happy Hour there was a call from The Man From The Brewery. He wanted to know where The Driver was. John noted the driver's red face and inane grin. "There's a problem with the lorry" he said. "What's wrong with it?" asked The Man From The Brewery. The Driver was wobbling across the room. "Steering trouble" said John. "Let me speak to The Driver" said The Man From The Brewery. John was trying to think of an excuse when a terrific din started up outside. There were shouts of 'Scab Scab Scab'. The chorus rose to an earsplitting crescendo.

"Can't stop. All hell's broken loose" John yelled. "Is the lorry allright?" Asked The Man From The Brewery. "Shag the lorry" said John and rang off.

The people who according to your point of view were either exercising the sacred right to work or leaving others to fight the battle on their behalf were crossing the picket line. Two policemen arrived. "There's only supposed to be six pickets here" said The Sergeant. "That's all there are" The Branch Secretary assured him. "There must be two hundred here" said The Sergeant. "They're not pickets" said

The Branch Secretary. "If they're not pickets what are they?" asked The Constable. "Bystanders" said The Branch Secretary. "Scab Scab Scab" roared The Bystanders. "Seem to be a pretty partial bunch of bystanders" remarked The Sergeant. "We've got the public sympathy" claimed The Branch Secretary.

"He's right there Officer" said John, pushing his way through. The Bystanders stood back to make way for him. "Are you a picket?" asked The Sergeant. "No Officer" said John. "What's it got to do with you then?" asked The Constable. He read The Sun. He claimed the pop music coverage was outstanding. "It's still a free country isn't it?" countered John. "It's a shaggin' police state" shouted someone at the back. "Why aren't you doing that lot in there for drinking and driving?" shouted another man from the back, indicating The Managers. "Cos they're in with them" said another man. "The police always back the bosses" said someone else. "I've not come here for a political discussion" said The Sergeant.

"What are you here for?" someone wanted to know. "To see there is no breach of the law" The Sergeant told him. "Does that include shaggin' Gaffers driving when they're over the limit?" he was asked. "You're only allowed to have six pickets" said The Constable. "We've only got six" said The Branch Secretary. "See for yourself" he invited. Six men stepped forward wearing armbands.

"The rest of you clear off" said The Sergeant. "What for?" called someone. "So they can beat up the pickets with no witnesses" said another voice. "We're completely impartial" said The Sergeant. "Like you were in The Miners' Strike" called a bystander. "They thump you then charge you with assault" added another. "I am telling you to disperse" said The Sergeant. "Suppose we don't?" asked A Truculent Postman. "They'll surround us" said someone else. This sally provoked much laughter. The Sergeant began to feel that his position was not a strong one, and that it would be adviseable to be diplomatic.

"When I come back I want to see no more than six pickets" he announced and did his best to make a dignified exit followed by The Constable. "What about the shaggin' managers drink driving?" shouted someone. The Police kept on walking.

"Capitalist lackeys' howled a passing motorist. "Did you hear that Sarge?" asked The Constable. "I'm not deaf" replied his superior somewhat tersely. "That's a breach of the peace" said The Constable. "So's a brick round the ear'ole said The Sergeant.

"That lot want sorting out' said The Constable indignantly. "I dare say they do, but we're not doing it" said The Sergeant firmly. "Why not?" asked The Constable. "Because there's two of us and there's two hundred of them, and I'm not putting my arse between a load of pissed up postmen with a grievance and a bunch of poxy scabs" said The Sergeant. "What about the right to work?" asked The Constable with just a hint of truculence. "What about the right to sleep safe in your beds?" countered The Sergeant. The Constable looked puzzled.

"There's a lot of people who need us more than that bunch of freeloaders in there" said The Sergeant indicating The Post Office. The Constable held his peace, but he decided The Sergeant was a distinctly old fashioned copper, not attuned to the spirit of the age.

After four days there was no sign of an end to the dispute. The Branch Secretary and his officials were beginning to worry. Their members were not getting any money and they had bills to pay. Takings in the pub began to fall, but they were still way above what they had been before the strike. Some of the strikers were looking for casual work to tide them over. The heady enthusiasm of the beginning had hardened into a grim determination to stick it out. The night picket was now a mere six strong. The Sergeant and The Constable had come to regard them as their strikers and looked forward to having a cup of tea and a chat. It broke up the monotony of the shift. As the nights went by The Constable began to find his certainties being shaken. He still read The Sun but with a sense of incredulity which increased as the strike continued. He found it quite impossible to accept the paper's version of events, or its depiction of the strikers. He found he not only liked the strikers, he actually admired them. So far as he could see they had no chance of winning. The forces lined up against them were overwhelmingly strong and crushing them was regarded as a perfectly worthy aim. All they had was their spirit, their belief in the justice of their cause. He envied them their sense of comradeship. It began to appear to him that far from being a threat to liberty they were its defenders. The observations of several of his colleagues began to annoy him considerably.

John Flaherty had come to look upon the strikers as his customers and a number of the leaders as his friends. He reasoned that if these workers had not elected to stand and fight he would by now have been reduced to the indignity of having to apply for state benefits. When The Post Office's Chief Executive appeared on television giving a highly selective and slanted version of the issues at stake John found himself hissing him as heatedly as the most splenetic postman. "I hate that oily bastard" he confided to The Branch Secretary. "So do I" said The Branch Secretary. He took a pull at his pint. "But he's our biggest asset. Any fool can see he's an utter liar" he explained. John nodded. It was relatively quiet in the bar so John decided he might as well have a stroll over the road and watch the scabs coming out of the office. The booing was by now a matter of routine and lacked the passion that was apparent in the early stages. One scab was sufficiently emboldened to stick up two fingers as he went by. It was questionable whether the gesture annoyed John, The Branch Secretary or The Constable the most. "That lad wants sorting out" said The Constable. "Shall we do him for a breach of the peace Sarge?" he asked hopefully.

The Sergeant shook his head. "Why not?" asked John. "I'd love to, but it would be a waste of time. The Courts support the other side" he said. "What about British Justice?" asked The Constable. "Yes. What about British Justice?" John echoed. "What about Father Christmas?" countered The Sergeant. He nodded at The Pickets. "These blokes have as much chance of seeing Santa as they have of getting a fair deal in a British Court." Seeing John and The Constable preparing to demur he turned to The Branch Secretary. "Am I right Branch Secretary?" he asked.

"Too bloody true you're right" affirmed The Branch Secretary.

"Anyone for coffee?" called The Picket who was presiding over the camping stove. "Will you join us Sarge?" asked The Branch Secretary. "I thought you'd never ask" replied The Sergeant eagerly taking the proferred cup.

The Constable was still fuming over The Cheeky Scab. "That prat wants a good smack in the gob" he declared.

"You're not an Agent Provocateur are you?" asked The Branch Secretary with a grin. "No you silly sod, I'm Church of England" said The Constable.

John Flaherty produced a bottle of whiskey from his pocket. "Anyone want a shot of this?" he asked. Cups were thrust towards him, including The Sergeant's. The Constable decided it was a good time to unquestioningly follow his superior's example and hastily took a gulp of coffee to make way for the dram. The Sergeant grinned happily. He raised his cup. "Here's to you lads. Don't let the rotten bastards grind you down" he toasted. He took a draught with relish. He looked at The Constable. "Sometimes you talk sense" he told him. The Constable looked somewhat taken aback. He still felt annoyed by The Insolent Scab.

"That effer wants a good smack in the gob" he said. The Branch Secretary nodded his head. "He's getting a bit cheeky. A smack in the gob would be good enough for him" he said. The rest of the pickets were in agreement. "The shagger wants tar and feathering" said one. There were other less charitable suggestions as to what the shagger deserved, all of which struck John Flaherty as having much merit. "He'd better not stick his nose in my pub when this is over" he declared. "He don't drink" said one of the pickets. John was thoroughly disgusted. "A shaggin' scab and a shaggin' teetotaler" he gasped. "And he's a shaggin' Notts Forest supporter" said another picket.

"Is there no limit to this man's perfidy?" said The Sergeant.

The Branch Secretary had a far away look in his eyes. "I'd do six months if I could smack that prat in the gob" he declared. A number of pickets also said they'd consider the penalty worth paying. The Branch Secretary sighed heavily. "The trouble is you'd lose your job" he said sadly. Everyone nodded.

That night John Flaherty found sleep difficult. He had a lot on his mind. The next evening John watched from his upper window as The Scabs crossed the picket line. The Cheeky Scab went through with both fingers raised. John's eyes narrowed. At the end of the shift The Scabs emerged. The Cheeky Scab had both fingers raised and an infuriating smirk on his face. This complacent self satisfied smirk changed to a look of acute pain as John Flaherty's fist connected with his nose and was followed instantly by a second fist ramming into his gob. The Cheeky Scab stepped backwards and was promptly tripped by an alert picket.

"What happened?" asked The Sergeant, who had seen perfectly well what had happened. "He fell over" said The Constable happily. The Cheeky Scab clambered to his feet. "I've been assaulted" he complained. "Oh yes" said The Sergeant. "What are you going to do about it?" demanded The Scab. "If you feel you've cause for complaint you must follow the correct procedure" said The Sergeant. "I suppose a punch on the nose and one in the gob is cause for complaint" said The Cheeky Scab.

The Sergeant got out his notebook. "Were these blows in your opinion delivered with malicious intent?" he asked. The Cheeky Scab looked dumbfounded. "What else could they be?" he asked. "It could have been horseplay" said The Constable. "Look at it" demanded The Cheeky Scab sticking his thumped visage under The Sergeant's nose.

The Sergeant looked completely unimpressed. "I've had worse than that from my missus" he said with an sir of finality.

The Cheeky Scab pointed an accusing finger at John Flaherty. "It was him" he said. The Sergeant looked at John. "What do you say in answer to this accusation sir?" he asked with his pen poised. John drew himself up straight. "I am a member of The Conservative Party" he said. "Well there you are then" said The Sergeant and returned the book to his pocket.

The Cheeky Scab stood with his mouth hanging open. "Is he allowed to thump me because he's in The Conservative Party?" he asked. The Sergeant considered the matter. "No-on's actually passed a law to that effect, but on balance I think it is likely that a court would uphold the right of a self employed member of The Conservative Party to thump a postman" he said. "That's shaggin' disgusting" spluttered The Cheeky Scab. "Things have indeed come to a pretty pass" agreed The Sergeant. "Nothing wrong with Victorian values" said The Constable. "I'll write to Edwina" said The Cheeky Scab. "You can write to bloody Cilla Black for all I care" The Sergeant told him.

There the matter would have ended were it not for the unknown presence of a photographer looking for ammunition that would enable the tabloids to crucify the strikers. In due course John appeared on a number of front pages obviously thumping The Cheeky Scab with considerable relish. "Left Wing Bully Boy Assaults Working Postman" shrieked the headlines. The Sergeant and The Constable continued to maintain that they'd seen nothing, their attention having been drawn elsewhere at the vital moment, but with the evidence lying on the mat in millions of homes John could do little else but plead guilty, not forgetting to enter a plea of mitigation on the grounds that he had been under great stress.

He was fined and invited to resign from his branch of The Conservative Party. Unionists from miles around flocked to his pub to drink the beer and shake his hand. John had a photograph of the incident blown up and put in pride of place in the bar. The Brewery did not approve but John had an argument they could not combat. "Will you look at the shaggin' takings" he said. The Brewery Manager knew when to hold his peace.

"I'll tell you something else" John said. The Brewery Manager listened intently. John pointed to the photograph. "Next time there's a strike I'll be doing my best to get another one up to match that" he said. The Brewery Manager thought he really ought to say something to the effect that The Brewery deplored violence, but decided that business was after all business, and kept quiet.

CHAPTER
EIGHT

The Cricket Club

Rod Williams sat in his office. He never left it now unless he had to. He was not a happy man. It seemed to him that the entire working class were crushed, reduced to spineless compliance, except for those working under his control. He glanced at the closed circuit television and shuddered. George appeared heading towards The Railway Institute for the first pint of the evening. It was six thirty. The Institute had just opened. George glanced at the camera and stuck up two fingers. With shaking hands Rod got out one of the pills the doctor had assured him would ease his feelings of tension and anxiety and swallowed it with much difficulty.

'Be positive' he told himself.

He stuck two fingers up to George. He knew he would be confronted by the spectacle of George either going to the Institute fast, or strolling back from The Institute all night. Only the cry 'last orders please' would end the torment. And when George came back for the last time, looking insufferably contented, the Bellowing Maniac would start the late night show outside his window.

He'd heard the performance so many times that a number of the lines were familiar and he found himself joining in. To his alarm he found he was howling bits of Treasure Island and The Ghost Train at the most embarrassing moments. The Area Manager had been giving him strange looks. He knew there were informers on The Station. There had to be. It was now the sort of country where narks thrived. He did his best to cope. He had some literature from Alcoholics Anonymous sent round to the Mail Porters' Room. The Repertory Company then improvised a sketch about an Alcoholics Anonymous meeting, he felt sure for his particular benefit. Apart from him everyone said it was brilliant.

In near desperation he demanded of The Post Office Managers that they order George to keep out of The Institute and was told they already had, only to be told by George that they 'weren't shagging up his social life' Rod mulled that one over for a fortnight. After hours of painstaking thought he came to a conclusion.

'It's not his shaggin' social life, it's his shaggin' job' he reasoned. He accosted The Post Office Manager to that effect. The Post Office Manager nodded sympathetically. He was beginning to feel that a special department should be opened just to deal with George. He got out George's file. It was very heavy. He plonked it down on the desk.

'We are keeping a record' he said with a somewhat defensive air.

'Never mind about keeping a record. Get rid of the bastard' Rod demanded.

The Post Office Manager was leafing through the file.

'Here it is' he said. 'Record of interview with George Sampson, conducted by Len Grant, that's me, on the 14th April. That was last month.'

'I know when it was' said Rod. He was beginning to think that all The Post Office people, management included, took him for a first class prat.

The Post Office Manager read laboriously.'

'I opened the interview by pointing out to Mr. Sampson that drinking on duty was now an offence under the requirements of the railway by laws. I said he had been informed of this on many occasions, verbally and in writing.

He said: 'Where's the effin' union Rep?'

I said there was no need for a Union Rep as this was purely informal.

He replied: 'Pull the other effer.'

'I said there was no need to take that attitude.' He said: 'You are not effin' up my effin' social life.' 'I said it is not your effin' social life, it is your effin' job.'

The Post Office Manager closed the file. Rod looked puzzled.

'Is that it?' Is that as far as it goes?' he asked. The Post Office Manager looked puzzled.

Rod was beside himself. 'What's wrong with the bloody Post Office? You've told him it's not his effin' social life, it's his effin' job and he's still over the effin' road effin' drinking' he fumed.

'It's not as simple as it seems' said The Post Office Manager.

Rod's blood pressure went up several points. 'How much more simple can it get?' he exploded.

'It's gone up to Region' said the Post Office Manager mysteriously.

'Region' echoed Rod, suddenly looking frightened.

All Dim Managers were terrified of Region. The very mention of Region caused the colour to flee from their cheeks. It was like the KGB so far as they were concerned. To Management Region represented terror. It was one thing investigating other people, but when Region got involved someone was likely to start investigating you. And then of course there were the informers. Suddenly Rod found he was in agreement with The Post Office Manager. It was not so simple as it had at first seemed. Just when he thought he had finally fixed George it was all turning sour.

The Post Office Manager leaned forward. So did Rod.

'We've asked for a ruling' The Post Office Manager confided.

Rod was impressed. The Post Office Manager looked gratified. Since Rod seemed sympathetic he decided to expand somewhat. Rod took a tablet. The Manager got out his fags. He offered one to Rod. Rod declined. The Manager lit up, took an appreciative puff, coughed, and continued.

'The thing is you see George says because he has to work such crappy hours he hasn't got an effin' social life, so he has to have his effin' social life while he's at work. He says even an effin' convict has some sort of an effin' social life. It could look bad for the corporate image you see' he said.

Rod could scarcely believe his ears. He felt a hot flush coming on. He stood up.

'It's a bastard madhouse' he stormed.

'We know that mate' said The Post Office Manager.

'The Post Office is complete crap' raged Rod.

The Post Office Manager smiled smugly.

'Maybe. But we've got a better image than British Rail' he told Rod.

Rod was stung. 'I don't deal in images, I deal in substances' he said.

At this point the postman known as the Longhaired Git came in. On hearing Rod's words he perked up.

'You deal in substances mate?' he asked. Rod nodded.

'Just the man I want, I need some substances. What have you got?' The Longhaired Git asked. Rod practically ran back to his office. He arrived just in time to see George coming back to do a train. George stuck two fingers up at the camera. Rod glanced at the clock. George was half an hour early. Rod immediately wondered why and feared the worst. He sat trying to think of some possible reason why George should have abandoned the attractions of The Institute early. He had a lot on his mind. For a start he was half inclined to report The Longhaired Git for trying to purchase substances from a Station Manager.

After much agonizing he decided against it. It was probably an elephant trap. Best leave it for now he told himself. He headed for the sanctuary of the Executive Toilet.

'I'll keep an eye on the bastard' he told himself as he made his way along the corridor. Then he paused as a chilling thought struck him. 'Maybe that Longhaired Bastard is the one that's keeping an eye on me' he said.

Sitting on the executive toilet Rod fought the temptation to write obscenities about the Post Office on the wall. He had to be careful. He was worried. Something was up. What on earth would induce George to leave the Institute with its gaming machines and subsidized beer and return to The Station long before his train was due? With the truly alarming prospect of Region becoming involved he didn't dare do anything other than commute between the executive toilet and his office. A happy thought struck him. Perhaps the bastard Post Office would send all its stuff by road and he'd finally be rid be rid of them, including their so called managers who seemed to swill even more beer than the postmen. It seemed highly likely. They had after all not long before amid a flourish of trumpets declared themselves to be an environmentally friendly organization, and everyone knew that was management speak for introducing a policy of pouring yet more shit into the atmosphere and further fucking up the ozone layer, in order to save money which they would then waste in various profligate ways.

What had actually lured George from The Institute was cricket. Something roughly akin to cricket was being played on the car park outside the rest room with a tennis ball and a length of wood. The Player King was attempting to make contact on the ball with the piece of wood. He was not having much success. George scoffed.

'Bloody hopeless' he said.

The Indian and West Indian taxi drivers parked outside The Midland Hotel were even more derisory, restraining their jeers with some difficulty. What they were witnessing was a travesty of the much-loved game. After some ineffectual groping The Player King began to get wood on ball by dint of playing straight. The taxi drivers no longer felt inclined to jeer, started to watch keenly, and became merely critical. The Player King's footwork left something to be desired. Soon to his obvious delight The Player King square cut. The ball bounced off a car bonnet and landed amid the taxis. It was lobbed back to the bowler. Then The Player King cover drove and the ball, gathering pace, sped along the ground and disappeared. The taxi drivers began to edge closer. Suddenly what they were witnessing was recognizably cricket, not a very high standard, but cricket nonetheless. They were interested.

Ten minutes later Sylvester, a muscular West Indian who was more interested in playing cricket than driving a taxi, had the piece of wood in his hand and was beginning to get the feel of it. A voice called from the front of the rank.

'Sylvester there's someone here that wants to go to The Great Western Hotel.'

'Well I ain't stopping him' said Sylvester as he stared down the wicket, reminding himself of the necessity of keeping his head perfectly still.

'But it's your turn' the voice persisted. Sylvester was exasperated.

'There's plenty of taxis aren't there? Can't you see I'm beginning to play an innings?' he said.

Such is the power of the imagination that Sylvester was no longer outside Derby Station waiting to do some cabbing. He was in the middle at Sabina Park with the tropical sun beating down and thousands of eyes on him, watching him dig The West Indies out of trouble. When the train came and with it the interval Sylvester reckoned he was on fifty two not out. He had survived a few shouts for lbw, but he thought so far it had been a chanceless innings, played with resolution and a distinct touch of class.

There was an irritating interruption when some dismal earthbound spirits had insisted he take a fare and had practically thrown him behind the wheel. With great reluctance he was then persuaded to drive a singularly unfortunate traveler to an outlying suburb. Such was his anxiety to get shot of his fare and resume his triumphant innings that he drove like a man in the grip of diabolic possession, while his passenger sat white faced in the back, was flung from side to side, and occasionally found himself scrabbling round frantically on the floor.

'Don't worry about a thing' Sylvester urged as he hurtled round a sharp bend with screaming tyres.

'I've got my eye well in Skipper' he added.

The hapless passenger was completely mystified as to why he was being addressed in this manner and was too terrified even to attempt a protest. When to his amazement and relief he found he was not in Casualty but had arrived at his destination, Sylvester grabbed the fare, and drove off far too quickly for the nerve shattered passenger to get his number. Sylvester's return journey was accomplished in an even shorter time than the outward trip and he was back in good time to resume his innings.

His second fifty was spectacular. The cars, the taxis, five passersby, The façade of The Midland Hotel, platforms one to six and the marshalling yard were all peppered. When the postmen had to go to service trains, and play had to stop, Sylvester calculated he was on 152 not out. He was so elated he went across to the pub and had a few pints. Then he had a few more. Finally after he'd climbed into five taxis that weren't his, he had to admit he wasn't fit to drive, and was driven home by an Indian taxi driver of advanced years who had witnessed the innings and now regarded Sylvester with something akin to awe.

When they arrived at Sylvester's house the Indian was keen to be on his way, but Sylvester would have none of it. He wanted to share his triumph.

'Azza' he said.

The Captain of India, Mohammed Azharuddin; was entrancing cricket lovers in Derbyshire with displays of silky, wristy elegance which contrasted sharply with the brutal front foot bludgeoning that was now far more common, and therefore it was by this name that Sylvester addressed his new found friend. He beamed at Azza.

Come in and have a drink. Meet my wife Mabel. You'll see how proud she'll be when she hear what I done' he predicted.

Azza had been married a long time and somehow doubted whether Mabel would be overjoyed to see her husband arriving home in this state. He doubted also whether she would regard the display of batting, excellent though it had been, as an acceptable substitute for driving a taxi and earning money. They didn't accept runs at the checkout in the supermarket: Sylvester was way beyond such mundane considerations. Azza entirely understood the big man's elation and had no wish to see him brought sharply down to earth, but there was nothing he could do. Sylvester at last, after much ineffectual poking with his key, opened the door and ushered Azza in.

Mabel was in the front room. To Azza's relief she looked amiable. Sylvester made the introductions. Mabel didn't look particularly surprised at his condition.

'Have you had a good evening?' she asked.

'Woman I have had a triumph' Sylvester told her.

Mabel looked pleased. Azza felt uneasy. He felt this was the calm before the storm.

'We got quite a few bills coming due. We need all the money we can get' said Mabel.

Sylvester nodded idiotically, a broad grin spreading from ear to ear. Mabel beamed at him.

'Well come on' she encouraged. 'Don't keep me in suspense. How much did you make?

Sylvester stood up proudly.

'I made one hundred and fifty two' he said.

Mabel was truly delighted.

'Not out' Sylvester added and sat down.

'What?' Mabel's voice was suddenly sharp. 'You made what?' she repeated, as her grinning husband sat waiting complacently for his commendation.

'One hundred and fifty two not out' said Sylvester savouring every syllable of the great score.

With a dangerous calm which terrified Azza but seemed to have no effect on Sylvester. Mabel eyed her errant husband.

'You made one hundred and fifty two not out' she said, articulating each word with a chilling clarity. Sylvester was too far gone even to sense danger. He nodded.

'I would have made a double century but the bloody train come in and all the bowlers had to buggeroff' he said.

Mabel raised one hand to her temple, a gesture so eloquent it rendered words unnecessary, but Azza knew that nonetheless the words would come. She remained holding this pose for what seemed like an eternity while Sylvester sat there, grinning vacuously and dreaming of further inspiring exploits in the middle. Mabel folded her arms and eyed her errand spouse.

'You bloody stupid big pillock' she said.

Sylvester was in a world of his own.

'You should have been there' he said.

Mabel nodded her agreement.

'I should have been there. You're not fit to be out on your own' she told him.

Sylvester picked up the poker. Azza stirred uneasily. Sylvester peered over his left shoulder.

'I cut, I glanced, I pulled, I hooked and I drove all round the wicket. I broke three windows in The Midland Hotel and one of the balls is at Crewe now on the back of a goods train. Women, I was inspired,' he said.

'Gimme that bloody poker' shrieked Mabel. Sylvester did as he was told. Mabel was obviously debating whether or not to bend the poker round Sylvester's ear. He backed away. Mabel advanced gripping the poker firmly.

'Inspired. You're not inspired. You're bloody demented' she said as she continued her relentless advance. Sylvester looked worried. He held up a hand deprecatingly.

'Mabel, let's sit down and discuss this' he suggested.

Mabel shook her head.

'Is that what I'm supposed to tell the man from the Building Society when he wants to know what's happened to the payment on the house?' she asked.

Sylvester tried a little bluster.

When the man from the bloody Building Society makes one hundred and fifty two not out against a varied attack then he can come here asking stupid bloody questions', he said.

Mabel was not impressed.

'Sit down Sylvester she said.' He did so. Mabel gazed at him steadily. Sylvester shifted in his seat.

'Tomorrow night Sylvester do you know what you're going to do?' she asked. Sylvester nodded. Mabel looked pleased.

'That's right. You're going to work a double shift to make up for the money you didn't earn tonight' she told him.

Sylvester shook his head.

'I'd like to Mabel, but I can't' he said, looking slightly apprehensive.

'And why not? Mabel asked. Sylvester edged towards the door.

'Tomorrow night your husband has got plans' he said.

'Such as?' said Mabel.

Sylvester folded his arms. He gazed past Mabel with a strange faraway look in his eyes. Already he was beginning to savour the sweet prospect of another triumph at the wicket, out there in the middle, bathed in glory. He beamed at his beloved wife.

'Tomorrow night Mabel, you are coming with me to Derby Station, and you are going to watch me take all ten wickets' he told her.

The sheer effrontery took Mabel aback. She thought momentarily about the lines 'for better or worse, richer or poorer' and gave up. She looked at the beaming Sylvester with a weary tolerance.

'Sylvester, when are you ever going to grow up?' she asked.

The next night the complaints started to come in. The postmen were in trouble, the railwaymen, what few of them were left, were in trouble, and the taxi drivers were in trouble. All this trouble naturally meant The Managers were in trouble as well.

Rod Williams sat at his desk trying to decide if things were going in his favour, or if he should start thinking in terms of exhibiting unmistakable signs of mental strain and going for the medical discharge. It was tricky. It seemed obvious that the postmen were in the shit, including George. The railwaymen were in the shit, including the uppity Sean. Furthermore the taxi drivers were in the shit. He was delighted that so many of these turbulent swine were in the shit. The trouble was he could well be in the shit with them. Basically his problem was that his meagre brain simply couldn't cope with so much shit coming from so many directions. He was out of his depth.

He hadn't had a good night's sleep since he'd heard Region were involved in the saga of George's effin' social life, and now things had taken a definite turn for the worst. He had a letter on his desk from The Manager of The Midland Hotel. Its contents caused Rod to break out in a muck sweat. An Important Personage staying at The Midland had complained. Scenes had been enacted beneath his bedroom window that had heretofore only been witnessed in Bedlam. Rod creased his brow. Which bloody Region was Bedlam? he wondered. A grinning maniac had been brandishing a lump of wood, and dispatching missiles in every direction while he howled in triumph. The Hooligan Chief was apparently a taxi driver. His accomplices were a motley crew of postmen, railwaymen, trainspotters and taxi drivers. Blind panic gripped him as he read on. Was anyone in charge at Derby Station? Or was mere anarchy loosed upon the world?

CHAPTER
NINE

Ten Wickets

Rod gazed at the letter as though he feared it might leap up and savage him. After a few hours, during which he made a number of visits to his beloved executive toilet, he'd grasped two facts, neither of which provided him with any comfort. The first was the buck had stopped at his desk. The second was that he had to get rid of the bastard before it finally did for him.

He decided against any attack on George. There was the matter of the issue being taken up at Region and he didn't want to be accused of victimization. With any luck he'd be able to precipitate such an avalanche of shit that George would be swept away. He'd make his first attack on the taxi men. They were not part of an organization with mysterious and daunting upper reaches where strange denizens lurked waiting to demolish Managers who were unlucky enough to come to attract their attention. The taxi men did have a representative. He was forever writing letters to the local paper complaining about authority.

He struck Rod as being a bolshie sort of bastard who needed sorting out. Rod rang him up. He even sounded a bolshie bastard.

'This is Rod Williams, Manager of Derby Station;' said Rod, full of piss and importance. It did sound good. Music to his ears. Manager of Derby Station. However the bolshie bastard was not impressed.

'So?' he said.

Rod was thrown off course somewhat. This man appeared to be lacking in the essential quality of deference Rod felt deflated. His call began to seem just a little silly. However he now had no course open but to press on. He did so with a sinking heart. He attempted bluster.

'One of your guys here is a maniac. There's been a very serious complaint from an Important Person staying at The Midland Hotel. Did you know you had a maniac down here?' he asked.

'What do you expect for two pound fifty an effin' hour? Bloody Einstein? said The Taxi Rep and rang off. Rod stared into the mouthpiece.

'Thank you for your co-operation' he said and replaced the receiver. He bristled indignantly.

'I'll sort this out' he vowed. The phone rang. He picked it up. It was The Police. There had been a complaint. Someone had been driven round Derby at dangerously high speed by a maniac. It was a taxi driver working from the Station Rank. Rod seized his pen. Now he was getting somewhere. A civil prosecution would show them who was in charge.

'What's the number?' he asked.

'We don't know. He drove off too fast for the complainant to take a note, but we have a description of the driver' said The Policeman.

Rod recovered from his momentary disappointment.

"Right. Let's have it' he said with his pen eagerly poised.

'He's a big black bugger' said The Policeman.

'Is that all you've got?' asked Rod.

'With white teeth' added The Policeman.

'I'll make enquiries' Rod promised. He looked a little more cheerful. That thing much beloved of Dim Managers was beginning to take shape. A pattern was starting to emerge. He might not be Inspector Morse but he was beginning to make connections. There had been a complaint about a Maniac brandishing a club outside The Midland Hotel. There had been an additional complaint about a Maniac driving a taxi at a dangerously high speed. That meant there was either one Maniac or two Maniacs. If there was one Maniac it had to be the same Maniac. His face contorted with the effort of concentration. 'It's either one guy or two' he told himself. 'Either way I know where to look' he added and out of his office heading for the Cab Rank.

Poor benighted Would Be Travellers asked about trains and were brushed aside.

'Not my department' he said.

'Don't you work for British Rail?' asked someone who obviously knew nothing about the managerial revolution.

'Not any more. No such thing' said Rod.

'This Station is a bloody disgrace' said the Benighted Would Be Traveller.

'It is not a Station. It is a Profit Centre' Rod told him.

'Why are the toilets closed?' asked a man with crossed legs.

'Vandals' said Rod and left him to work that out.

He marched up to the cab drivers.

'Now then' he bellowed. A driver pointed at Rod and tapped his forehead. Rod ignored him. He launched into an attack.

'One or maybe two of you guys is a Maniac. I have had a very serious complaint from The Midland Hotel about a Maniac brandishing a club and hitting balls in all directions. There has been another complaint about a Maniac driving a taxi like a Maniac. What I want is a confession.' He said.

The drivers stared at him wondering if he'd finally gone right over the edge. Rod grinned nastily.

'If I don't get a confession The Police will be round here examining your vehicles and you could find yourselves off the road. Right who's the guilty one?' he asked. There was a silence.

'I'll give you one minute' said Rod sensing he had the advantage.

Sylvester stepped forward.

'I'm the bloody Maniac' he said.

A split second later Azza stepped forward.

'I'm the Bloody Maniac' he said.

Rod stared from one to the other. He'd been right all along. There were two of the bastards. He smirked in delight. It was a triumph. Management had once again prevailed over the rabble. Suddenly all the drivers were marching towards him bellowing 'I'm The Bloody Maniac.'

A taxi stopped just before it entered the Station concourse. The driver leapt out and bellowed 'I'm the Bloody Maniac.' His passenger looked as though he believed him. Rod was aghast. How could undoubted triumph turn to utter catastrophe in the merest blink of an eyelid.? Nothing could be worse than this. Then another blow struck him and he reeled.

He heard the hated voice of The Player King on platform one.

'I'm Spartacus' it rang out.

The taxi drivers held their clenched fists aloft and to a man howled: 'I'm Spartacus.'

The once benighted but now thoroughly infuriated passenger who couldn't find out where his train went from and was still trying to find an open toilet appeared beside Rod.

'I'm Spartacus and if you don't open the bleedin pisshouse I'm going to piddle up the wall right outside your office he threatened.

'That goes for me too' said another Irate Passenger.

Rod recognized defeat when he looked it right in the eye. All he could do was retreat.

'I'll get the key' he promised meekly.

As he retraced his steps towards his office, feeling rather as Napoleon must have done on his way back from Moscow, he heard it again, what had become for him the most dreaded of all sounds.

'Hee haww! Hee haw! Hee haw!

It echoed inside and outside the Station. He opened the toilet. Someone had written on the wall in large letters.'

ROD WILLIAMS IS A STUPID PRICK

The Irate Passenger showed no mercy, no generosity in victory. He stared at the letters then at Rod.

'Are you Rod Williams?' he asked.

'Rod nodded miserably.'

'I thought as much' said The Irate Passenger.

Sylvester sat in his cab, Mabel beside him.

'Well what do you think of that?' he asked.

She gazed at him fondly.

'Sylvester Malone you're a big stupid bastard and I'm proud of you' she told him. Sylvester looked gratified. Mabel looked happy. Then she noticed Sylvester was longingly fingering a cricket ball in the glove compartment. She removed his hand and firmly closed the drawer.

'I think you'd best lie low for a bit. Until the heat dies down' she said.

Sylvester nodded. There was no hurry. He'd take all ten wickets another time.'

CHAPTER
TEN

Wrongful Arrest

When Rod Williams heard there was a postal strike he was a happy man. He raised grateful eyes heavenwards. "Thank you God" he said. He hoped the strike would go on for ever. The prospect of not having to see George filled him with a sense of well being. He would be able to strut round the station and glory in the sense of power. His dignity would be unassailed. He felt as though a great weight had been lifted from his shoulders. All he had to do was avoid passengers, remember to take his stress tablets, and do his deep breathing exercises. Doctor Llewellyn had mentioned the possibility of referring him to a psychiatrist, but he was wary of proceeding on the basis that he was nuts. It did suggest that his problems were being taken seriously, and he reminded himself that lots of Hollywood stars had analysts, and spoke openly of the fact, but then he thought they were probably all nuts, and if they had to cope with George they'd be barking in no time. On balance he thought it was best to keep taking the tablets.

The Leprauchan came in. "There's a bloke kicking in the door of the bog" he said with an air that made it obvious he considered the problem was Rod's. "What's up with the guy?" asked Rod. "He wants a piss" said The Leprauchan. "Can't he read the notice. Closed for cleaning" said Rod. "He's going to complain" said The Leprauchan. "Let him" said Rod. "He's on his mobile now" said The Leprauchan with gloomy satisfaction.

"Mobile phone! Jesus H Christ! Get that door unlocked" said Rod. "And straighten your tie" he added as The Leprauchan left the office clutching the bog key. Apart from that early alarm the day was blessedly peaceful and Rod had none of the sense of foreboding he usually experienced as the hour neared when the Poxy Post Office would descend upon the station.

He sat in his office with his feet on the desk looking at the internal television screen, monarch of all he surveyed, a complacent smile spreading across his fat stupid face. Then he had a shock. His smile became a fixed grimace. He stared aghast at the screen. He decided he would take up Doctor Llewellyn's suggestion and put himself in the hands of a psychiatrist for he was surely hallucinating. He could see George heading for the station. Moreover George was in uniform. George stuck up two fingers at the camera as usual and went out of range. "It can't be" muttered Rod. Ivor, The West Indian Platform Manager, came in. Seeing Ivor's look of bafflement he added "Shaggin' George. He's on strike". "They're all on shaggin' strike. One hundred per cent" said Ivor. "I've just seen Shaggin' George" Rod insisted. "Where?" asked Ivor. "Up there" said Rod pointing to the screen. "All this shaggin' technology is crap" said Ivor. "It's probably an old film" he added and left Rod to his musings.

He peered out of the window. No sign of George. There were only the usual disconsolate knots of passengers trying to find someone to tell them about trains, and trainspotters contentedly strewing rubbish all over the platform. Reassured somewhat Rod resumed his seat. He steeled himself to look at the screen. It was empty. Some suspicious looking characters were poking around among the parked cars, but that was nothing to do with him. He breathed a sigh of relief. Ivor was probably right. It was gremlins on the screen. Suddenly he sat bolt upright. It was there again. He could see George standing in front of the camera. He was grinning provocatively. He turned and made his way towards The Railway Institute. Then he was gone.

The Leprauchan came in. "Shall I lock up the Shitehouses?" he asked. Rod was staring at the screen. "Shall I lock up the Shitehouses?" asked The Leprauchan again. Rod pointed at the television screen with a shaking hand. "Shaggin' George" he whispered. The Leprauchan looked at the screen. "Shagall there" he said. With difficulty Rod took his eyes from the screen and focused on The Leprauchan. "I've seen Shaggin' George. I've seen The Shagger twice. He shaggin' came and then he shaggin' went" he said. The Leprauchan backed towards the door. "He's on shaggin' strike" he said, eyeing Rod and preparing to leave the office in a hurry if he showed any signs of becoming violent.

Out on the platform The Leprauchan was confronted by an Angry Passenger. "Where's The Station Manager?" he demanded. "He's in his office, but I wouldn't go in there if I were you" said The Leprauchan. "Why not?" asked The Angry Passenger. "He's seeing Banquo's Ghost" said The Leprauchan. "What's wrong with these bloody people?" said The Angry Passenger to anyone who might be listening, but no-one was. He stormed into Rod's Office. "Now just you look here" he began before Rod stopped him in mid sentence. "Look at that, look at that" screeched Rod as he staggered to his feet with his eyes starting from his head, pointing at the television screen. The Angry Passenger stopped dead in his tracks appalled at the spectacle before him. Rod clutched him by the arm. "Look" he insisted. The Angry Passenger considered escape, but hysteria gave Rod the strength of a genuine maniac and he was imprisoned. He turned to the screen. "Did you see it?" demanded Rod.

The Angry Passenger was suddenly anxious to placate Rod. "Yes yes I see it" he said completely mystified. "The shaggin' bastard is there again" gasped Rod. The Angry Passenger, who was by now The Thoroughly Frightened Passenger, tried to watch the screen with one eye, while keeping the other on Rod.

Rod was taking a pill. The Thoroughly Frightened Passenger wondered what it contained. "My doctor wants to refer me to a psychiatrist" Rod confided. The Thoroughly Frightened Passenger wasn't sure how he should respond. Fortunately Rod continued. "But I'm not nuts" he declared. The Thoroughly Frightened Passenger did his best to look convinced. Rod turned his desperate gaze full upon him. "Do I look like a guy who's nuts?" he asked. "No no" The Thoroughly Frightened Passenger assured him.

Suddenly Rod leapt to his feet and flinging out a shaking arm pointed at the screen. "Look at that" he ordered. The Thoroughly Frightened Passenger did as he was bid. He became even more alarmed when he realised there was nothing to see. He was being asked to gaze at a blank. Rod slumped back in his chair.

"The bastard's not there" he whispered. "Did you see him?" he asked. "Well actually no" said The Thoroughly Frightened Passenger. "I wasn't nuts when I came here" said Rod. The Thoroughly Frightened Passenger wanted to leave but found his legs wouldn't move. But that shagger could have driven me nuts" said Rod.

The Thoroughly Frightened Passenger resolved that in future under no circumstances would he venture onto a railway station. "Shaggin' George, he drinks like a shaggin' horse" said Rod. The Thoroughly Frightened Passenger edged his way to the door. "Is there an Enquiry Office?" he asked. "Sure there is" said Rod as he gazed fixedly at the screen. "Where is it?" asked The Thoroughly Frightened Passenger. "Opposite" said Rod. "When does it open?" asked The Thoroughly Frightened Passenger. "You'll have to ask them" said Rod. The Thoroughly Frightened Passenger decided to give up. He went back onto the platform and confronted The Leprauchan who at least was small and looked docile enough.

"The Station Manager is barking mad" he said angrily. "Sure we all know that" said The Leprauchan.

"You can't have a lunatic in charge" said The Thoroughly Frightened Passenger who now he was no longer in imminent danger felt his ire rising again. "Ah now that's a policy matter" said The Leprauchan. "You can't just accept it" said The Angry Passenger. "What else can I do?" asked The Leprauchan. Seeing The Angry Passenger looked entirely unconvinced and obviously expected some action on his part he explained his position further. "I'm just a shaggin' menial, I keep me nose clean and wear my servitude with an air of pride" he said.

"Don't you try to take the piss out of me" said The Angry Passenger. "Are you a first class passenger sir?" asked The Leprauchan. "What's that got to do with it?" said The Angry Passenger. "Well you see sir in the current climate no-one wearing a railway uniform can take the piss out of a gentleman holding a first class ticket" said The Leprauchan.

The Angry Passenger was about to take The Leprauchan's number when he spotted The Sergeant and The Constable. He was rich enough to feel the police were his friends, indeed they were his servants. He hailed them. "Sergeant". The Sergeant and The Constable approached eyeing him warily. He was well dressed and looked and sounded like the sort who could cause trouble, perhaps played golf with other people who could cause trouble.

"Can I help you sir?" said The Sergeant. He managed to sound as though he actually wanted to be of assistance. "There's a maniac on the station" said The Angry Passenger. "Whereabouts sir?" asked The Sergeant. "In The Manager's office" said The Angry Passenger. "Would the gentleman in question by any chance be The Station Manager sir?" asked The Sergeant. "You've got a maniac running things" said The Angry Passenger. "He's got problems sir, but I wouldn't go so far as to say he was a maniac" said The Sergeant.

"He's in there seeing things. Things that aren't there" protested The Angry Passenger. "It's the executive stress you see sir" The Sergeant explained. "He suffers from executive stress" confirmed The Constable. "I suffer from executive stress, but I'm not seeing things" said The Angry Passenger. "There's a lot of it about" said The Sergeant. "He says his doctor wants to refer him to a psychiatrist" said The Angry Passenger. The Constable snorted. "Take more than a psychiatrist to sort him out" he said. "He shouldn't be out on his own" said The Angry Passenger.

"Ah well you see sir that's the policy of your government. Care in the community." said The Sergeant. "This not how the policy is supposed to work" protested The Angry Passenger. "They're supposed to go and stay with their families" he added, appealing to The Constable. "Makes it very difficult for us sir" said The Constable noncommittally. "He keeps on about Shaggin' George" said The Angry Passenger again.

As soon as he mentioned Shaggin' George he suspected he was talking to two more men who were undergoing care in the community. The Sergeant and The Constable were overcome by uncontrollable laughter, and in no time at all were reduced to holding each other up while they spluttered helplessly.

"We know all about Shaggin' George sir" said The Sergeant. "Don't we Reginald" he said to The Constable. "If you've got a few hours to spare sir we'll tell you a bit about Shaggin' George" said The Constable. "Shaggin' George sir is what you might call a real loveable rascal" said The Sergeant. "He's a character" said The Constable. "Shaggin' George sir is what you might call one of the yeoman of England" declared The Sergeant.

The Angry Passenger thought he really must stop this litany of praise for Shaggin' George. "There's a poor sod in there says Shaggin' George has driven him nuts" he said.

"Two questions involved there sir" said The Sergeant. "Which are?" said The Angry Passenger. The Sergeant thought for a moment. "The first question is, is he shaggin' nuts? The second question is, if he is shaggin' nuts is it Shaggin' George's fault?

"I don't know if it's Shaggin' George's fault, but The Shagger is obviously shaggin' nuts" said The Angry Passenger. The Sergeant was about to raise such matters as the burden of proof when Rod Williams rushed out of his office waving his arms frantically.

He screamed out: "The Shagger's back. The Shagger's back. I can see him. Come and see for yourselves" and rushed back into his office. The Angry Passenger looked triumphantly at The Sergeant. "I rest my case" he said smugly. The Sergeant looked at The Constable.

"Did you observe any foam on his lips?" he asked. The Constable shook his head. "Then at least it's not rabies. If it was rabies we could probably shoot The Shagger, but now as it's obviously merely a mental disorder we'll have to go and investigate. Follow me" said The Sergeant. The door to Rod's office was wide open and they entered cautiously. Rod didn't notice them. He was staring at the television transfixed.

"You see Sergeant. He's demented" hissed The Angry Passenger. You could be right sir" breathed The Sergeant. "What do you mean, could be? What else could it be? He's barmy" insisted The Angry Passenger.

"I think he might have had a visitation" said The Sergeant. Rod came out of his seeming trance and turned to the group in the doorway. "The Shaggers gone again" he told them. "He was there a moment ago. I saw him. He knew I was here. He stuck up two fingers like he always does. Then he disappeared."

"Who are we talking about Rod?" asked The Sergeant.

"Shaggin' George" said Rod turning back and gazing intently at the screen. "He's on strike. He's not working. He's not there, but I keep seeing him" he moaned.

"Is this a dagger I see before me, the handle towards my hand?" said The Leprauchan. "Never mind the Agatha Christie" fumed Rod.

Before The Leprauchan could deliver a short lecture on English literature Rod let out a howl of triumph and pointed at the screen. "Look. There's the bastard. There he is. Shaggin' George!" he howled.

Everyone stared at the screen. A postman appeared briefly, stuck up two fingers and disappeared. The Angry Passenger looked puzzled. "Is that it?" he asked. Rod nodded. "That's him. I knew I'd seen him" he said. "So what's all the fuss about?" asked The Angry Passenger.

"The Shagger shouldn't be there" said Rod. "Why not?" asked The Angry Passenger. "Because he's on strike" Rod explained. Then something happened that caused all the other occupants of the room to back away in alarm. A glimmer of intelligence momentarily lit up Rod's pudding of a face.

"I've got it" he said triumphantly. "Well you hang onto it Rod" said The Sergeant. "That's right. You might not be able to get another one" said The Constable. "The shaggin' shagger is shaggin' scabbing" spluttered Rod, almost overcome by a combination of delight and indignation. "He's supposed to be on strike and he's shaggin' working. Typical! He never shuts up about trade unionism and The Shaggin' Labour Party, but when it comes to the point he's not prepared to put his principles before his beer money" he told them.

"Don't you support the right to work!" asked The Angry Passenger. "I've got the bastard. I'll do him for being over the limit when he's on duty" howled Rod. The Sergeant and The Constable burst into laughter. "The bugger won't piss in the bottle" said The Sergeant. "Or blow in the bag" added The Constable.

"Don't you support the right to work?" asked The Angry Passenger. "I've got the bastard. I'll do him for being over the limit when he's on duty" Rod said. "What is the limit?" asked The Angry Passenger. "He can't have a drink twenty four hours before he comes on duty" said Rod. "When's he supposed to drink then? asked The Angry Passenger. "That's his problem" said Rod dismissively as he put on his hat. "Follow me" he ordered and charged out of the office.

"Oh Gawd!" said The Sergeant. "I'd best go and lock up the pisshouses" said The Leprauchan and sidled off. The Sergeant, The Constable and The Angry Passenger followed Rod. They watched him march up to George who was standing on the edge of the platform gazing towards London. Rod accosted George. "I have reason to believe you have been drinking" he said. "So what?" said George still gazing towards London. "You realise it is expressly forbidden to drink on railway premises while on duty" Rod began when George stopped gazing towards London and transferred his attention to the destination indicator over their heads.

"Look at that. The shagger's forty five minutes late. I might as well go over the road and have another" he said, not looking too grieved at the prospect. Rod barred his way. "You are not going back over the road. "You're coming to my office" he said. "What for?" asked George. "Samples" said Rod. "And if I decline?" asked George. "You can't decline" said Rod. "You mean I have no choice. I'm going to be forced?" asked George. "That's right" Rod nodded. "So it's three to one and I'm being forced" said George. "That's right" said Rod.

"You shall have your samples. Give me the bottle and I'll adjourn to the pisshouse" said George. The Leprauchan reappeared. "I've locked up the pisshouses" he said and promptly disappeared again. "Come with me" said Rod and set off back to his office. George dutifully followed him with The Sergeant, The Constable and The Angry Passenger bringing up the rear.

Once inside Rod's office George blew in the bag with an eagerness that should have aroused suspicion. He then seized a bottle, looked at Rod and said: "Kindly direct me to the executive Shitehouse." "You are not of executive status" Rod told him. "Do you want a sample or not?" asked George. Rod considered a moment. "Then he grinned nastily. "Make the most of it. You'll soon have to get used to using a chamber pot. Slopping out" he said. "You heard that?" George asked The Angry Passenger. He nodded and George looked satisfied.

George seemed to be in the executive toilet for rather a long time and refused to answer questions as to his well being. Rod began to look slightly less happy. "It would be just like the bastard to hang himself in the executive toilet" he muttered. When the point was reached at which it seemed it would be necessary to break down the door George appeared and presented his sample with the air of one bestowing a benediction.

The Sergeant was looking sad. "I'm afraid you'll have to come with us George, you're way over the limit" he said. "Not driving am I?" said George. "No George you're not driving" said The Sergeant. George turned to The Constable. "Haven't been causing an affray have I?" he asked him. The Constable said he had not "Co-operated haven't I?" he asked them both. They nodded their heads. "Then what am I charged with?" asked George sounding genuinely puzzled.

Before The Sergeant or The Constable could speak Rod broke in. "Drinking on shaggin' duty. That's what you're charged with" he brayed.

"Then I'm not guilty" said George. "You're way over the shaggin' limit" said Rod. "Yes I know" said George. "Then what the shaggin' hell are you talking about? You haven't got a shaggin' leg to stand on" said Rod.

"I've had about nine pints" said George. "Sympathisers bought me several. When I go back to work I expect I'll have to buy my own" he said smiling affably at Rod. Rod looked startled. His fat face crumpled somewhat. "What do you mean when you go back to work? You're working now. You're shaggin' scabbing" he said. George shook his head. "You should know me better than that. I'm no shaggin' scab. I may be a shaggin' gambler and a shaggin' pissartist but I'm no shaggin' scab" he said.

"But you're in uniform" Rod gasped. "What are you doing in uniform?" he asked beginning to look very worried. "It'll all come out in court" said George. "What court?" said Rod. "The court you'll have to attend to answer charges of libel, assault, wrongful arrest and being a tosser" said George. "You can't sue me" said Rod. "I think you'll find I can" said George happily. "You see I am an official picket" he added. "The law allows me to picket doesn't it?" he asked The Sergeant. With some difficulty The Sergeant managed to suppress a guffaw. "It does indeed George" he said. "There'll be no scabs on this station, drunk or sober" said George and left.

The Angry Passenger looked at Rod. "Are you really a manager?" he asked. Rod nodded miserably. He shuddered as he looked up at the screen. George was there again. His mouth was moving. Rod stared at him in horror. "What's he saying?" he asked plaintively. "The workers united can never be defeated" The Leprauchan told him. Rod pulled himself together with an obvious effort. He straightened his tie and looked at The Angry Passenger.

"What can I do for you sir?" he asked. "Don't bother. I'll ask George" said The Angry Passenger.

Rod winced. On the screen before him he was confronted with the stuff of nightmares. George and The Angry Passenger stood side by side sticking their fingers up. Then they left and headed towards The Railway Institute.

"They're going for a goddam drink" said Rod. "They are" The Leprauchan confirmed. "I'll tell you something else" he added. "What's that?" asked Rod. "George won't be paying" said The Leprauchan.

Rod put on his cap and set off towards the executive toilet. Reasoning he would stay in the bog for the forseeable future The Leprauchan decided to try out the managerial chair. He was just settling down comfortably when he heard an earsplitting scream. A moment later an ashen faced Rod Williams stood trembling in the doorway trying to speak. He gestured towards the executive toilet and staggered off towards it. Cautiously The Leprauchan followed him. Rod stood before the open door of his sanctuary.

"Look. Just look what that shagger's done" he implored. The Leprauchan peered in. His mouth fell open. The walls were covered in graffiti, all lewd and all directed towards The Area Manager." Get some shaggin whitewash. If anyone sees this The Area Manager will crucify us" said Rod. "Where do you expect me to get shaggin' whitewash this time of the shaggin night?" responded The Leprauchan.

He had another look at the walls. "You don't need whitewash" he said. "What else can I use?" asked Rod desperately. "What you need is a couple of cans of petrol and a box of matches" declared The Leprauchan. Rod's eyes lit up with a glimmer of hope. "You mean set light to the station?" he asked. The Leprauchan shook his head. "No. Set light to yourself" he said. Rod sat slumped in despair. He began to wonder if it might be a good idea to go back to Canada.

CHAPTER
ELEVEN

The Ghost Squad

The Longhaired Git sat on a barrow smoking a substance that might have been plain tobacco, or might have included something on the banned list. Warnings about him had started to appear on the bog walls. He decided it was time to clarify his position. He stood on the barrow. "I am not a spy working for The Area Manager of the railways" he said. Some Would Be Passengers pricked their ears up. Rod Williams stood behind a pillar straining to hear. The Longhaired Git continued his statement.

"The statements written about me on the bog walls are incorrect" he claimed. Rod felt encouraged. Someone shared his suspicions and had gone public. He knew that in an age of an unprecedently mendacious press the bog wall was regarded as having the authority and veracity once accorded to the BBC News. The Longhaired Git was by now really getting into his stride.

"If I find out who is spreading these malicious lies I shall not hesitate to sue" he declared.

Rod was outraged. "Cocky little bastard" he hissed to himself. He caught the eye of a Gormless Looking Trainspotter. "Who does the sonofabitch think he is? - a bloody Cabinet Minister?" he asked. The Trainspotter looked aggrieved. "There's shagall to spot nowadays" he complained. Rod impatiently turned away, anxious to hear what else The Longhaired Sonofabitch would have to say. "What sort of a station do you call this?" asked The Gormless Spotter. Rod spared him a pitying glance. "You should try and keep abreast of the times" he said. The Gormless Spotter looked puzzled. Feeling momentarily charitable now that he was faced with someone undeniably his mental inferior, Rod explained. "This is not a station. This is now a profit centre" he said. "Is that why you've closed the buffets and locked the bogs?" he was asked." That's to save costs" said Rod. "Why not get rid of the trains altogether?" said The Gormless Spotter. "That is an option" Rod assured him.

"I'm not saying there isn't a spy on the station" said The Longhaired Git. "All I am saying is it's not me" he added with the air of one who had said all he had to say on a particular subject.

Rod was entirely unimpressed by this denial. The threat of legal sanctions confirmed him in his view. The Longhaired Sonofabitch was The Spy. Suddenly Rod started as though someone had rammed a sharp object into him. He heard George's hated voice. "The shaggin' Area Manager has got shaggin' eyes and shaggin' ears all over the shaggin' station" he said in a tone that defied anyone to contradict him. No-one did. "He's right" said Joe. He glanced up at the steps where he was as usual hoping his mates might appear. "It could be the shaggin' Ghost Squad" he suggested. George nodded agreement. "They do shagall else" he said.

"The whole Station is riddled with Common Informers" said a stentorian voice. It came from behind The Guardian and Rod knew it was The Player King. "Oh Jezus" he thought. "The bastards'll all be doing donkey noises in a minute. Just when The Master Cutler is due in" he added. He decided it was a good time to retreat to the executive bog.

In the womblike seclusion of the executive bog he thought about what he had heard. It did nothing for his executive stress. "That guy who sounds as though he's swallowed a megaphone may be nuts, but he's not stupid" he mused. He sat reading the appalling things George had written on the bog wall about The Area Manager during his recent brief arrest, and wondered how many more layers of paint would be needed before they were entirely hidden. He decided to follow The Player King's assertion through to its logical conclusion. He then clutched his brow in horror. "If that mad old bastard is right then every goddammed sonofabitch on this goddamed shaggin' station could be a spy" he told himself. He had noticed there had seemed to be a lot of railway and Post Office personnel using the 'phone boxes lately. Perhaps they were all ringing up their Control.

Meanwhile The Longhaired Git hadn't entirely satisfied his hearers. He tried a different tack. The Branch Secretary swears blind The Union's phone is bugged" he said. This revelation produced an immediate and enthusiastic response. "Electronic surveillance, the curse of the age roared The Player King. "There's cameras and microphones everywhere" said George.

"We've come a long way from the twitching lace curtains" said The Player King. "The old girl opposite me hasn't" said Joe. "Industrial espionage. That's the thing to be in now" said The Player King. "Or sabotage" added George. "That's it. If you can't run your own business you shag up someone else's" said Joe.

The Longhaired Git took a contemplative draw on whatever it was he was smoking. "If I could find out who's writing those things about me on the wall of the Shitehouse then we'd know who the spy really is" he mused. The group looked somewhat puzzled. "Don't you see?" said The Longhaired Git. Heads were shaken. "Whoever is trying to drop me in it is trying to draw attention away from himself" he explained.

"The classic diversionary tactic" said The Player King. "It's sometimes advisable for those living in glasshouses to throw a great many stones" he added and turned back to the study of The Guardian.

"You can't believe a thing you read in the papers" said Joe. The television is no better" said George. "Believe the worst and you can't go far wrong" said The Player King. This declaration met with universal approval, and since The Player King's voice carried to every corner of the station, and with a favourable wind, to the concourse as well, heads were nodded far away as people heard their own sentiments expressed.

Joe peered hopefully up the steps. He was no longer absolutely sure that he'd actually recognise The Ghost Squad if they happened to turn up. "Anybody heard anything about the redundancies?" he asked. No-one had. The redundancies were spoken of as a fact whether or not there was any likelihood of there ever being any. "They don't need to pay for redundancies, the bastards just keep sacking blokes" said George bitterly. "They call it good house keeping" said The Player King.

Why would anyone want a spy here?" asked The Longhaired Git. "Empire building" The Player King told him. "Then why should a postman be a spy for the railways?" asked The Longhaired Git. "Nothing is ever as it seems" said The Player King. "Oh yes it is" countered Joe. "Enlighten me" invited The Player King.

"It seems as though my mates, The Shaggin' Ghost Squad, aren't here and they're not." said Joe. "Has anyone seen them lately?" asked The Player King. "They're shaggin' aliens" said Joe. The Player King put down his Guardian. "There is something unearthly about them. They somehow contrive to sign the attendance sheet without being seen. Their signatures mysteriously appear but where are they? Perhaps we should report them as missing. Get the police to issue descriptions" he suggested.

"I reckon they've got second jobs" said George. Joe snorted. "Second jobs! Those idle bastards! Don't make me laugh!" Joe sat down looking as though he would never laugh again. Paddy drove up on the tractor. "Anyone seen the shaggin' Ghost Squad?" he asked. Hollow laughter was all the reply he got. "They must be some bloody where. They've signed on" said Paddy. "You mean their names have been written" said The Player King. "I mean they've bloody well signed on" said Paddy. "Have you seen them?" said The Player King. "No. I haven't bloody seen them. Didn't I just ask if any of youse had seen them?" said Paddy.

"Have you considered forgery?" asked The Player King.

"I've considered every form of crime" said Paddy. "It's possible The Ghost Squad are just that" said The Player King. "What do you mean just that?" asked Paddy. "They may have shuffled off this mortal coil" said The Player King. "Alas poor Ghost Squad, I knew them well" he boomed. "You mean the shaggers could be dead?" asked Paddy. "They might as well be" said Joe.

"Will we have to get a wreath for them?" asked George. "I'm paying shagall for them" declared Joe indignantly. Then he cheered up as a thought struck him. "Perhaps someone's murdered the shaggers" he said. "Ghosts, murderers, spies, lunatics. Is there no-one normal working on this station?" asked Paddy as he headed back towards the relative sanity of the shed.

"What was that you said about people living in glass houses?" asked George.

The Player King rose to his feet. "It is truly a mad mad world my masters" he declaimed. "It's a shaggin' nuthouse" said Joe with a kind of gloomy satisfaction. "Now then what about the shaggin' Ghost Squad?" he asked, addressing his question to anyone disposed to answer.

"What about 'em?" responded George.

"Should I report the shaggers missing?" said Joe. "Keep the shaggin' Gaffers out of it" said George. There were nods of agreement.

"That's all very well" said Joe. Anticipating an objection to the concensus everyone listened intently. Joe sensed he had an attentive audience and decided to make them wait. He walked a few paces away from the group and then turned round to face them. "Suppose it turns out the useless shaggers have been dead six months" he said. George considered the proposition. "Then they'll have decomposed by now" he said.

Joe nodded impatiently. "Yes yes" he said tetchily. "But when the shaggin! coroner examines them he'll say the shaggers died six months ago" he continued. "So?" asked George.

"So the shaggin' gaffers will say shaggin' Joe has done the shaggin' job on his own for six shaggin' months" said Joe.

He looked at the unresponsive group with exasperation. "You don't get it" he said. The Player King nodded approvingly at Joe. "I get your drift. Management will argue that if you've done the job for six months, aided only by two corpses, you may as well carry on. They'll see yet another chance to make money by flogging a willing horse. The Ghost Squad will cease to exist even as a spectral presence" he concluded.

"We'll lose two more shaggin' jobs" said George angrily.

The Player King beckoned the postmen towards him and looked round with a furtive and conspiratal air. "We know management will go to any lengths to balance their budget, secure their bonuses, get promotion" he said in a penetrating but low voice. The group nodded their assent.

"As the pressure increases so the remedies will become ever more desperate" The Player King continued. Everyone looked puzzled, "Perhaps they're disposing of workers who they deem to be surplus to requirements" he said.

"You mean they're murdering the shaggers?" screeched Joe, absolutely horrified. "Human life is cheap" said The Player King. "What about the shaggin' union?" asked George. "We've got no shaggin' union" said Joe. "Shaggin' management can do what they like" said George.

A man sitting nearby was scribbling furiously on a pad. He put his pen away and strolled over to the group. "We live in strange times" he said, addressing The Player King. "To be sane is to stand condemned" said The Player King. "Shaggin' right" said Joe. "Sinister forces are at work" said The Man With The Notebook. "Evil is in the ascendant" intoned The Player King.

"I couldn't help overhearing your concern as to the whereabouts of The Ghost Squad" said The Man. "Tell me about them" he asked. Joe needed no second invitation. The Man's shorthand was thoroughly tested as Joe poured forth countless tales of the iniquity of The Ghost Squad. When Joe paused for breath The Long Haired Git took over and recounted the saga of the official spy on the station. The Man was obviously very interested and was keen to make sure he had all the facts right. After The Man left on the London train the group forgot about him.

Two days later Joe was astounded to see The Ghost Squad coming down the steps. He was about to ask where they'd been for the last six months when they cut him short.

"Have you seen this shagger?" demanded Arthur, angrily waving a newspaper under Joe's nose. "What shagger?" said Joe. "The shaggin'

Sun" bellowed Len, also waving a copy under Joe's nose. "Have you read it?" said Arthur. "If you'd stop waving it about I would" Joe told him.

"Look at it" bellowed Len. Joe caught a glimpse of a headline. "Where are The Ghost Squad?" "You stupid old sod" howled Len. "I was halfway through the story. I was enjoying it. Then I found I was in it. You stupid old effer" he said, white faced and shaking with rage. "Let's have a look" said Joe. "They've spelt my name wrong" he complained.

"You've dropped us right in the shit" said Arthur.

"If you're in the shit it's your own fault" said Joe stoutly.

"What did you want to go talking to the shaggin' press for?" said Len. "I haven't talked to the shaggin' press" protested Joe. "What do you think you are? A shaggin' filmstar?" spluttered Len.

"I haven't talked to the shaggin' press" said Joe, beginning to get annoyed. Before Len and Arthur could assail him again with these accusations he decided to beat them to the punch. "And where the shaggin' hell have you been?" he asked. "We've been here" chorused The Ghost Squad. "Shagoff!" said Joe derisively.

"I'm surprised at you dropping your mates in the shit" said Len. "Mates!" echoed Joe. "What mates? I've not seen you for six months".

"We've been around" said Arthur. "On the gaming machines" added Len. "Gaming machines! Where? Shaggin' Las Vegas?" asked Joe.

"There was no call to shop us to the shaggin' Sun" said Len. "I haven't shopped you to the shaggin' Sun" said Joe. "Well we're in the shagger" said Arthur. "And it's down to you. It says so here" said Len. "You can't believe what you read in that shagger" Joe replied.

"It's here look. Joe Adams, aged fifty two, married with two children" said Arthur pointing to the passage. "Joe was near to tears as he told our reporter he feared his mates might have been murdered by a cynical management seeking to cut costs" read Len. "Did you actually come out with that crap?" asked Arthur.

"There's a funny atmosphere here now. No-one trusts anyone any more" Joe told them. "We know The Gaffers are twats" said Len. "But they haven't started murdering us yet" said Arthur.

"How was I supposed to know that?" asked Joe. He glanced towards the platform steps and saw The Gaffer rushing down. He was brandishing a newspaper like a club. "We're all in the shaggin' Sun" he howled. "You've made me look a complete shaggin' idiot" "How's that then?" asked Joe. "It says I don't even know if my staff are alive or dead. They make me out to be a complete prat" said The Gaffer.

"What are you getting onto me for? I don't run the shaggin' Sun" said Joe. "You've dropped everybody right in the shit. There's hell to pay" shouted The Gaffer. "How many times have I told you there's supposed to be three blokes on this door?" Joe asked.

The Gaffer was gradually turning purple, veins were beginning to stand out on his forehead. He pulled himself together with an obvious effort. "If you didn't like the shaggin' way I was shaggin' running things you only had to shaggin' tell me" he howled. A number of Would Be Travellers abandoned their examination of the screens and gave The Gaffer their undivided attention.

"I did" Joe countered.

"When?" bellowed The Gaffer.

"Every time you came out of the pub" said Joe.

"I don't remember that" declared The Gaffer.

"I don't suppose you remember telling me to shagoff either" said Joe.

"Don't you accuse me of telling you to shagoff" said The Gaffer.

"The truth hurts" said Joe, and as a mischievous afterthought, he added "especially when it's in print". "Don't you go reporting me to the shaggin' Sun" gasped The Gaffer, his empurpled visage immediately paling at the thought of further exposure in the scandal sheet.

"My conscience is clear. I can't speak for other people" said Joe. The thought crossed The Gaffer's mind that if it weren't for the near certainty of the matter appearing in due course in The Sun he'd take great pleasure in thumping Joe. He decided to try a different tack.

"Do you want to hear what The Head Postmasters says?" he asked.

"Not particularly" Joe told him. The Gaffer decided to tell Joe anyway.

"He says he doesn't dare come down here" said The Gaffer.

"Oh yes" said Joe noncomittaly.

"Do you want to know why?" The Gaffer asked, still hoping to arouse Joe's sense of inquisitiveness.

"My conscience is clear" said Joe. He noticed with satisfaction some Would Be Passengers nodding in approval. The public sympathy was plainly with him.

"The Unions needed sorting out but when they start murdering blokes to save costs that's going too far" said a Prosperous Looking Man to the Would Be Traveller next to him.

"It's not official Post Office policy is it?" asked his neighbour.

"Good heavens no" said The Prosperous Looking Man. "It's a matter of a wink and a nod. No-one is actually going to admit anything. Have all the Do Gooders up in arms" he said.

"Far too many of these people have never had to run a business" replied his neighbour. "No room for sentiment in business" said The Prosperous Looking Looking Man. "And The Post Office is showing a handsome profit" said his neighbour. "Exactly. Can't make an omlette without breaking a few eggs" said The Prosperous Looking Man. "Looks bad when it gets in the paper though" said his neighbour. "Bad public relations" said The Prosperous Looking Man.

"I'll tell you why" said The Gaffer. He felt he was getting nowhere but could see no option other than to persist.

"Do you have to? I've got work to do. Can you see three men on this door?" said Joe.

"No I can't" admitted The Gaffer.

"Have they gone walkabout again?" asked Joe.

"They're being interviewed on national bleedin' television" howled The Gaffer. "I'd like to see that" said Joe.

"You stay where you are" The Gaffer told him. "It's all a bloody nightmare, and it's all your fault."

"At least it's good publicity" said Joe.

"The Head Postmaster won't come down here" began The Gaffer.

"He says if he does come down here he'll personally murder the lot of us. Not to save costs. Purely for the pleasure" he ended.

"Who's upset him then?" asked Joe innocently.

"You're trying to work your ticket aren't you?" accused The Gaffer. Joe was about to make an angry retort when to his amazement The Gaffer was suddenly transformed from a purple faced wild eyed maniac into a picture of smiling benignity. "Any problems you get Joe, you know you can speak to me any time. My door is open day or night" he said at the top of his voice.

The reason for this astonishing change soon became apparent. The Ghost Squad were descending the stairs accompanied by a camera crew. Joe rubbed his eyes in disbelief. His first thought was that he was witnessing a scene from a forthcoming film, but he was soon disabused. Intense scrutiny confirmed that it was indeed Len and Arthur who were coming towards him looking as though they could scarcely contain their enthusiasm for the task ahead. They leapt into the brake and began heaving out bags, ignoring Joe's attempts at protest.

"You have a breather Joe" said Len. "Take it easy mate. Us young 'uns have to help you old fellers" said Arthur. Joe was about to tell the pair of them to shagoff when The Director broke in. "Fling 'em off lads" he called. Len and Arthur continued heaving bags out of the brake and onto nearby barrows. Nobody took any notice of Joe until The Director decided he wanted a change of angle, and Joe was immortalised on film. Immediately The Gaffer put his arm around Joe's shoulders, the picture of brotherhood and benign command.

"Piss off you two faced shagger" hissed Joe. The Gaffer ignored him. He faced the camera. "I understand Joe. As you get older it gets harder" he said, smiling so odiously Joe felt tempted to smack him one on television.

The Director was delighted. "Great stuff, great stuff. The new spirit of British industry" he said. Len and Arthur continued heaving out bags, sweat pouring off their brows. When Joe attempted to stop them he was led away by two members of the production team and told not to shagup The Director's vision. When the brake was empty its bare spaces were lovingly captured by the camera, and, at The Director's instigation, Len and Arthur indulged in the most puerile triumphalist antics. The train meanwhile pulled out.

"Great television" said The Director. "And now we'll follow these bags on their way to be sorted" he declared. "No you shaggin' won't" Joe told him.

"Why not?" asked The Director "Because they're supposed to be on that shaggin' train just going round the shaggin' bend. Until you stupid buggers arrived I was chucking them on. Then these two useless shaggers came and started flinging the buggers off" said Joe.

For perhaps the only time in his life The Gaffer showed he was made of the stuff of management. "Not to worry" he told The Director. "We'll film another barrow. "No-one will know any difference" he said triumphantly.

"Shaggin' typical" said Joe.

CHAPTER
TWELVE

George

George was in the shit. There were no two ways about it. He was in it up to his neck. The Manager sat at his desk gazing at a report. He liked what he saw. Not even George could get out of this one. George had failed to turn up for the parcel train. The case against him was absolutely watertight. Every brake had been closely examined. There had been no sign of George. George had been over in The Railway Institute. There were witnesses. For George this could be the beginning of the end. He had been ordered to report to the office. The Manager was looking forward to the encounter. This time it was all going to be different. The door opened and George walked in. The Manager smiled at him.

'Sit down George' he said.

George did so. The Manager decided to let George sweat. He pretended to be closely studying the report. He had no doubt that this would cause George to become anxious. George took out his paper and turned to the racing page. The Manager shot a surreptitious glance at him. George was completely engrossed in the runners and was busily markings nags that would carry his hopes. The Manager's confidence began to evaporate just a little. George was still in the dock with no semblance of a defence, but he was not behaving as he should be. He decided to launch the attack.

'Right George' he said, fixing George with what he believed was a keen penetrating glance. Unfortunately it was wasted. George was studying form. He couldn't make his mind up between Naughty Lady at three to one and Caught Napping at evens. The trouble was he really fancied them both. The Manager cleared his throat nervously.

'George' he said in a far milder tone than he intended.

George looked up. Just as The Manager was about to speak George beat him to it.

'Just a minute' he said, and carefully drew a large circle round each of the horses, The Manager felt he now had no choice but to go for the all out onslaught. Any subtlety would be wasted on George. Mere pinpricks would not shake him. He wouldn't even notice. Bazookas would be needed to even shake George's seemingly invincible composure. The Manager began to wonder if the bloke who had conducted the weekend course on main management he had been made to attend knew what he was talking about. Had he actually ever had anything to do with men? Probably not. Certainly not with any like George. He swallowed hard.

'Right George' he said, trying to sound firm and in command.' It was no use. He had an uncomfortable feeling George wasn't altogether with him. He gripped the report as though it were a crucifix and George a thirsty vampire.

'I've got a report here' he said.

'I can see that' said George.

'You weren't on the parcel train' said The Manager.

George was poking about in his inside pocket. The Manager wondered if he had prepared a written statement. So far as George was concerned The Manager might as well not have been there. He felt precious control was slipping away. Indeed he wondered if he'd ever had it in the first place. He watched George and wondered what on earth he was doing. George produced a red pen, looked at it critically, rejected it and put it back. Next he took out a green pen, held it poised over the racing page for a moment, seemed to have reached some sort of decision, then changed his mind and put that back too. Then he brought out an orange pen, hesitated for a moment, then made up his mind and marked four emphatic stars beside one of the runners. He then folded the paper up and put it in his pocket. The Manager had by this time entirely forgotten what he had been told at The Weekend School.

'I've got a report here' he said.

George turned his attention to him with an obvious effort.

'You weren't on the parcel train' said The Manager.

He waited for George to deny the charge.

'No I wasn't' said George.

The Manager waited. He remembered they'd told him on the course it was a good technique to wait. The theory was that the poor sod being interviewed would be unable to stand the accusatory silence, and would panic and blurt out something that would be damaging to him. The Manager had no doubt the theory was not only sound but proven in practice. The trouble was George. Obviously nobody had told George about the theory. He sat and gazed steadily at The Manager. They sat like this for to the Manager seemed an eternity. Then to his intense relief George spoke.

'If that's all I'll get back to work' he said and stood up. He was at the door before The Manager pulled himself together.

'Sit down George' he said.

'What for?' asked George.

'I've got a report here' said The Manager.

He knew that somehow it had all gone wrong. He wondered if perhaps he could get rid of George and start again, but he knew that was out of the question. He had to try and redeem the situation.

'Why weren't you on the parcel train?' he asked.

George shook his head and sighed. The Manager was by now clutching at straws.

'Do you want The Union Rep here?' he asked. This was hell. George wasn't even taking the matter seriously. The presence of The Union Rep would surely add a touch of much needed gravity to the proceedings. George shook his head.

'What do I want the Union Rep for?' he asked.

The Manager was not very bright, but he was bright enough to be feeling by now thoroughly stupid.

'Because you weren't on the parcel train' he repeated, and realized he was going to have to ask George again why he hadn't been on the parcel train. He was beginning to think he must sound like a parrot.

'What's that got to do with The Union?' asked George.

The Manager felt he should not be sidetracked into attempting an explanation of the role of The Union, of which he had only the most rudimentary grasp. He remembered the man who conducted the course telling him The Union was crap, and that didn't seem likely to prove particularly helpful at the moment.

'So you don't want The Union Rep' he said.

George sat silent. The Manager took his silence for assent. He was about to return to the attack when George stood up.

'If you think I should have The Union Rep I'll have The Union Rep' he said.

The Manager was getting rattled.

'I didn't say you should have The Union Rep' he protested.

'Yes you did' said George.

'No I didn't. I asked if you wanted The Union Rep' countered The Manager.

'What's it say in The Minutes?' asked George.

'What Minutes?;' asked The Manager, completely baffled.

'The Minutes of this Meeting' said George.

'This is not a Meeting' said The Manager.

'Oh yes it is' insisted George. 'It's a Meeting between you and me and there should be Minutes' he added.

'This is not a Meeting' shouted The Manager and thumped the desk.

'If it's not a Meeting, then what the effin' hell is it?' said George.

'It's a shaggin' interview' said The Manager.

George leant forward thrusting his face into The Manager's.

'It makes no difference if it's a shaggin' Meeting or a shaggin' interview, there should be a proper record of the shaggin' proceedings. Otherwise it's just my shaggin' word against your shagger' he told him.

The Manager leapt to his feet practically incoherent with fury. He jabbed a furious forefinger at George.

'Why weren't you on the shaggin' parcel train? he asked.

'If you're making accusations I want the shaggin' Union Rep here' said George.

'You weren't on the shagger. We looked up and down it from one shaggin' end to the other shagger' screamed The Manager.

'You admitted it' he added.

'Does it say that in The Minutes? asked George.

'There aren't any Minutes' howled The Manager.

'It's time you learnt to follow shagging' procedure' said George and swept out.

The Manager picked up his chair and flung it across the room. He picked it up and was beating his desk with it when there was a knock on the door and Rod Williams walked in.

'Bloody wasps' he said by way of explanation, replaced his chair and sat behind his desk.

'I've just seen George going over to The Institute' Rod Williams began. The manager unceremoniously cut him short.

'I don't want to hear anything about George' he said.

'It seems to me that guy does what the shaggin' hell he likes' protested Rod Williams and walked out leaving The Manager fuming. He cheered up a little when he remembered he had a notice to pin up forbidding the practice of playing cricket outside the Station. Being a Manager had its consolations. You had to put up with the antics of prats like George, but you could make people do things they didn't want to, and stop them doing what they did want to. That was how you did your bit towards making Britain great again. People like George were the trouble. They would insist on standing between the nation and its date with destiny.

Rod Williams sat staring at the closed circuit tv. He was waiting for the return of George.

George appeared in the doorway of The Institute and began to cross the busy road. Rod watched hopefully. Perhaps the speeding traffic would solve his problem. George reached the pavement intact. Rod shook his head sadly. As George approached the camera Rod stuck two fingers up and waited for George to do the same. Instead George flung his coat wide open in the manner of a flasher and continued on his way. Rod was outraged.

'Two can play at that game. You wait till next time' he threatened.

He sat himself down at his desk and considered his next move.

George meanwhile faced the military commander's nightmare. He had to engage the enemy on two fronts. Furthermore he had had a bad run on the machine and was looking for someone to lend him five pounds to tide him over until his fortunes took a turn for the better. Under the circumstances he thought it advisable not to approach The Manager. George always steered well clear of the room. Unless he had to go there he never went in.

Some years ago he had been quietly studying the racing page when the Manager came in and he found himself landed with a job that had cropped up unexpectedly. It was a classic instance of someone being in the wrong place at the wrong time. He was determined that he would not make the same mistake twice. He looked round for someone who might lend him the fiver.

Ronnie was standing on the platform looking at a man speaking into a mobile phone. Among the mail porters people speaking into mobile phones always aroused feelings of near universal contempt.

'Look at that prat' said Ronnie.

George did so. He wasn't remotely interested and couldn't understand why anyone should have feelings about a prat speaking into a mobile phone one way or the other, but he wanted to get into Ronnie's good books. It was degrading. He understood a little what it must be like to be a Chancellor of the Exchequer having to go and butter up the incompetent toerags on the IMF. He looked at The Prat With The Mobile Phone.

'Friggin' idiot' he said and hoped this was sufficiently condemnatory.

'He's been on that for twenty minutes' said Ronnie, glaring at The Prat.

George didn't want to listen to Ronnie droning on about The Prat droning on the mobile phone so he came straight to the point.

'How are you fixed?' he asked.

Everyone knew that when George posed this question it wasn't an enquiry as to the current state of their lives. It was plainly understood to be a request for a loan. Ronnie continued to glare at The Prat.

'Shagoff' he said.

Normally at this stage George would attempt to touch the heartstrings with an account of his misfortunes at whatever form of gambling he had been indulging in, but on this occasion with Ronnie in such an intransigent mood there was obviously no point. He felt life was dealing him some pretty poor cards. If the bloody machine had come up with two sodding lemons the way it should have done he'd have been over the road buying someone a beer, not trying to tap this miserable old bleeder for a fiver. The fact that everyone knew perfectly well that the life of a gambler was full of ups and downs was precious little consolation. There was no escaping the grim reality, lately there had been a lot more downs than ups. Still there was always The Lottery on Saturday. Once he won that he could tell them all to bollocks.

Millions were now sustained throughout increasingly desperate weeks by the thought that when their numbers came up on Saturday they would be in a position to tell all sorts of people to bollocks. It gave them all just a glimmer of hope, a tantalizing possibility that better things might just lie ahead.

Meanwhile George sensed danger. He wasn't by nature apprehensive. His talent for self justification was like a suit of armour. George had never been wrong. However he did realize that the managements of both The Post Office and British Rail were out to get him.

The knowledge that he was a marked man didn't disconcert him unduly. He didn't intend to allow them to interfere with what he persisted in regarding as his social life. The Union Man had suggested that it might be a good move to seek the assistance of The Welfare Officer on the grounds that he had a drink problem. George thought this was a singularly stupid idea. So far as he was concerned the only problem he had with drink was the price. The Union Man tried to convince him that trouble was looming and it was always a good idea to have The Welfare Officer on his side.

'He's a wanker' George told him.

'I know he's a wanker. That's why he got the job' said The Union Rep.

'So what good will he do me?' George wanted to know.

The Union Rep felt that not only had George virtually no grasped on reality, he'd also got no real appreciation of tactics.

'He's never done anybody any friggin' good' he said.

He could see George was completely unimpressed with his argument. He attempted to clarify.

'When you're in the shit you plead personal difficulties Trouble with the Missus, trouble with the kids, money problems, drink problems, trouble with the car, you're suffering from acute depression, you think you might be a woofter, you've got piles, anything you like, but if you haven't been to see The Welfare Officer and had a good snivel, the bastards say you're lying' he explained.

'I'm not cutting out my drinking for any effer' said George.

The Union Rep gave up at that point. He'd just have to play it by ear and hope for the best, but he did begin to fear George could prove to be a lost cause. Perhaps when it came to the crunch the best course might be to point out how completely irrational George's behaviour had been over a number of years and plead insanity.

'That's it. I'll say the bastard's barmy' he said to himself.

Since George obviously was barmy this had to be a good defence. The Prat With The Mobile was still on the platform. He put his mobile down while he poked about in his briefcase. The Union Man sat down beside it. It was still on. He listened intently. The sound of a hymn could be heard distinctly. The Union Rep got up and walked away. It somehow seemed the decent thing to do. At times it seemed to him as though the entire nation was cracking up. Perhaps that was the price for the restoration of national greatness.

'Compared to some of these poor sods George is reasonably normal' he told himself.

Meanwhile The Post Office Manager sat staring at his report. He was in what could only be described as a right state. He was suffering from an acute sense of injustice. He also wanted to kill George. George had missed the train but so far the only one who seemed to be in the squelchy stuff wasn't the man who'd admitted to being guilty to unauthorized absence from his designated place of duty, it was the bloke who'd quite correctly tried to heave the book at him.

'He's guilty and I'm in the shit' he said out loud as The Union Man walked in.

The Union Man had decided on a pre-emptive strike. If George wouldn't help himself he would have to prepare the ground for him. He looked as grim and anxious as he could.

'I think we may have a problem with George' he began.

The Manager's jaw dropped. He wondered what on earth could possibly be coming next. He still wanted to kill George. It was hard for him to think about anything else. He looked enquiringly at The Union Rep. The Union Rep sighed heavily, giving the performance of a lifetime.

'Poor George' he said.

'Poor George my shaggin' arse' responded The Manager.

The Union Rep shook his head sadly and again sighed heavily. Sometimes it paid to overact.

'You don't know the half of it' he said.

'I know he missed the shaggin' parcel train' said The Manager.

The Union Rep ignored this diversion.

'I can't deal with this' he said.

'Deal with what?' asked The Manager irritably. He'd just about had enough of this.

The Union Rep continued, again ignoring The Manager's intervention.

'It's beyond my capabilities. It needs a professional man' he declared.

Curiosity overcame irritation and The Manager found himself intrigued despite himself.

'What's the problem?' he asked.

The Union Rep knew that he had what in fishing terms would be called a nibble. He leaned forward, glancing momentarily over his shoulder as though he feared to be overheard.

'Of course this is not to go beyond these four walls, it's strictly between you and me' he said lowering his voice.

The Manager leaned forward.

'You can rely on my discretion' he assured The Union Rep.

The Union Rep managed with difficulty to keep a straight face. He knew perfectly well that anything told in confidence to this particular Manager would be all over the office in no time.

'The problem is … ' He began.

At that point Rod Williams flung the door open. He ignored The Union Rep and glared at The Manager.

'George is a flasher' he bellowed.

The Manager turned pale. This really was a problem. He didn't know how to respond to this. He'd been rudely thrust into the realm of the unknown. What was the line at Region? Was he supposed to exhibit outrage or sympathy? So far as he could make out the current practice was to persecute people doing their job well and conscientiously and award them everything short of capital punishment for the most minor transgressions, and at the same time bend over backwards to accommodate all sorts of useless tossers, and for all he knew deviants. It was all somewhat beyond his powers of comprehension so he looked noncommittal.

The Union Rep was somewhat taken aback. He'd often said that nothing George did would surprise him, but flashing was not a charge he'd expected. He simulated outrage and rounded on Rod Williams.

'Are you accusing my member George of being a flasher?' he roared.

'He is a Goddamed Flasher' Rod roared back.

'What proof have you got?' demanded The Union Rep.

'It's on the bastard television' Rod told him.

Guffaws of mirth came from the room. Postmen and a few postwomen waiting for the arrival of the next parcel train were finding this heated exchange highly diverting.

'George is a flasher' said one.

'He's been waving his willie at the television' said another.

In no time at all the story was all over the station and its environs. Within ten minutes the story had grown to the extent that George had several convictions and had been recommended for chemical castration. All the railwaymen, all the postmen and all the cab drivers knew that George was a compulsive flasher. Soon everyone in The Institute knew as well. When George was invited to confirm or deny the rumours he was so furious he stormed out with his pint glass on the counter barely touched. As he made his way along the platform heading for The Manager's office various railwaymen and postmen flung their coats open at him and cried 'Whaaay'. George was not amused. He charged into The Manager's office.

Rod Williams, The Post Office Manager and the Union Rep were trying to establish the facts. The Longhaired Git had invited himself in and was telling Rod Williams he needed to loosen up as he was clearly repressed, probably as a result of faulty potty training.

'There was nothing wrong with my potty training' protested Rod.

'What if George is a flasher? So what?' The Longhaired Git was saying as George entered.

'I am not a flasher' shouted George.

'Oh yes you are' countered Rod.

'George wants to see The Welfare Officer' said The Union Rep.

'Fuck The Welfare Officer' said George spluttering with fury.

'I've got positive proof. It's all there on the television' said Rod triumphantly.

The Post Office Manager decided that since it was his office he should at least appear to be conducting the enquiry.

'George are you a flasher?' he asked.

For a moment it looked as though George was going to hit him. He was incoherent with rage.

'It's all there on the film' said Rod again.

The Post Office Manager had a flash of inspiration.

'We'll go and watch the film' he said.

Rod Williams shook his head.

'That film will be at Region Headquarters first thing tomorrow morning' he said.

George's face turned from scarlet to a shade nearer purple. He shot a look at Rod Williams that caused him to step back hastily.

'And there'll be a letter from my shaggin' solicitor on your desk first thing tomorrow morning' he said and charged out slamming the door.

Rod Williams was astounded.

'Did you hear what that cheeky bastard said?' he asked.

The Union Rep was secretly delighted.

'It's obvious George needs help. It should have been spotted long ago' he said.

'George wants shafting' The Manager bridled.

'We want The Welfare Officer and The Nurse' said The Union Rep.

Meanwhile some raucous comments could be heard coming from the room.

'It pays to advertise' was one that caused The Union Rep to supress a smile.

Suddenly there was a cry:

'Train on one'

Everyone piled out onto the platform. The Manager, The Union Rep and Rod Williams followed.

As the train pulled in postmen and railwaymen provided a guard of honour. Coats were flung open and cries of 'Whaaay and What about that then?' echoed round the station. Suddenly there was just one place in the world where Rod longed to be. He made his way disconsolately to the Executive Toilet. The Post Office Manager was trying to assess his situation in the light of the latest developments. He rather feared he was way out of his depth. The course in man management hadn't covered this sort of situation. Missing a parcel train was one thing, flashing was an altogether different category of offence. He didn't like the idea of George having his solicitor poking his nose in. There was no knowing where all this would end. One thing he was sure of was that he didn't want the brains from The Area Manager's Office or Region poking their noses in. He couldn't understand Rod Williams' apparent eagerness to expose Derby Station to an examination by people who had the power to make life thoroughly uncomfortable for them all. He sought out The Union Rep.

'We don't want all these sods from Area Office and Region down here stirring it up. We can sort out our own problems' he said.

The Union Rep pretended to be considering the proposition.

'I think George needs help' he said.

The Manager swallowed hard.

'The Welfare Officer' he suggested.

The Union Rep nodded.

'Agreed' said The Manager.

The Welfare Officer was a docile twat and didn't know his arse from his elbow. His overriding concern in life was not to upset anyone important. So far he had succeeded in achieving this humble aim. The Union Rep had a word with George.

'You're seeing the Welfare Officer' he told him.

'I'm not seeing that wanker' George insisted.

'George do us both a favour. See him. Spin him a yarn. Tap him up for a fiver' The Union Rep urged.

The prospect of borrowing the fiver did the trick. George agreed to see The Wanker. The Union Rep felt the defences were being constructed and he was reasonably happy. He was also curious.

'Tell me George. Why did you miss the parcel train?' he asked.

'I was on the black' said George.

The Union Rep looked bemused.

'You can't come off the snooker table when you're on the black" said George with the air of one uttering a truth so obvious it should not be necessary to state it.

'Did you pot it?' asked The Union Rep.

George shook his head.

'I missed the shagger' he said.

'That's why I need to borrow a fiver' he added hopefully.

The Union Rep grinned at him.

'Seeyuh George' he said as he made his way to the exit.

CHAPTER
THIRTEEN

Media Strategy

The Branch Secretary had managed to run the gauntlet of the media massed outside the office and was sitting behind his desk wondering whether there was the slightest possibility he might be able to get the deplorable hacks weaned off their obsession with The Ghost Squad and direct their spotlight onto the plight of the mass of his members. The Assistant Branch Secretary came in and sat down. "It gets more like Pinewood Studios every day" he complained.

"They're a bloody nuisance" said The Assistant.

"They could do some good. If they'd just sort their priorities out" declared The Branch Secretary.

The Assistant snorted derisively. "Some bloody hopes" he said.

The Branch Secretary warmed to his theme. "It's sheer Maxim Gorky here and all they want to film is Carry on Postman" he said.

If anyone else starts singing Postman Pat I won't be responsible for the consequences" said The Assistant.

At the moment the phone rang. The Branch Secretary answered it. After a few moments he replaced the receiver. The Head Postmaster wants a meeting" he said. "What about?" asked The Assistant.

"He didn't say" said The Branch Secretary.

"Didn't you ask?" said The Assistant.

"He sounds peculiar" said The Branch Secretary.

"So what's new?" asked The Assistant.

"Let's go and see" said The Branch Secretary.

They made their own way down to The Head Postmaster's office and knocked on the door.

"Come in" howled an agonized sounding voice.

They entered and glanced at each other in some alarm.

The Head Postmaster was hitting his executive chair with a cricked bat. He appeared to be beside himself. "Bastard! Bloody bastard" he hissed as he whacked the shining leather.

"If you're busy we can always come back" said The Branch Secretary, eyeing the bat with some alarm.

"When I find out which of the bastards it is he'll wish he'd never been born" said The Head Postmaster, giving his chair another whack.

"Are you introducing corporal punishment into the discipline code?" asked The Assistant.

"That's no way to treat a cricket bat" The Branch Secretary admonished him.

"The press are going to crucify me" said The Head Postmaster. "It's no good complaining to me" replied The Branch Secretary. "You should get onto The Press Council" added The Assistant. "What good will that do?" asked The Head Postmaster.

"None" said The Branch Secretary.

"There's a traitor here" said The Head Postmaster.

"There's a what?" said The Assistant.

"A traitor" repeated The Head Postmaster.

The Union Men glanced at each other somewhat nonplussed. The Assistant decided to seek clarification. "Are we talking here in terms of offences threatening the security of the realm?" he asked.

"You what?" said The Head Postmaster.

"Is some bugger likely to find himself facing the headman's block?" asked The Branch Secretary.

"He would if I had my way" replied The Head Postmaster.

"Who is this poor sod?" asked The Assistant Secretary.

"I don't know" said The Head Post Master.

"Why not?" asked The Branch Secretary.

"The underhanded swine won't come out into the open" said The Head Post Master.

"You can hardly blame him" said The Assistant Secretary.

"What exactly has this bloke done?" asked The Branch Secretary.

"He's dropped us all right in the shit" replied The Head Post Master. "We've been in the shit for years" replied The Assistant.

"Ever since this government came in" said The Branch Secretary. The Head PostMaster looked as though he'd like to fetch him one with the bat. "We need to issue a statement" he said.

"What for?" asked The Branch Secretary. "Because we're in the shit" explained The Head Postmaster, somewhat tetchily. "We must stand together" he added by way of further explanation.

"You mean solidarity?" asked The Assistant Secretary.

"Yes, exactly" said The Head Postmaster eagerly.

The Union Men exchanged glances. Then they stood up.

"I can see no point in prolonging this meeting" said The Branch Secretary.

"Sit down" ordered The Head Postmaster.

"What for?" asked The Branch Secretary.

"We have to present a united front against the common enemy" said The Head Postmaster. The Union Men did not look impressed.

"I know we haven't always seen eye to eye" The Head Postmaster said.

"That's very true" said The Branch Secretary.

"You see. We have common ground" said The Head Postmaster.

"If you call seven unresolved disputes common ground, we have" said The Branch Secretary.

Before The Head Postmaster could reply The Assistant Secretary spoke. "Can we be quite clear about something?" he asked. "What?"

said The Head Post Master. "Just who is this common enemy we're supposed to stand against?" The Assistant Secretary asked.

The Head Postmaster looked round as though he feared eavesdroppers. He leaned forward. The Union Men waited.

"The bloody media" hissed The Head Postmaster.

The Branch Secretary gazed at him in disbelief.

"You mean all this fuss is about that bloody shower out there" he said.

The Head Postmaster nodded. "Someone is feeding them information" he said.

"Oh yes" said The Branch Secretary noncomitally.

"There is an informer in the office" said The Head Postmaster. The Union Men stood rooted to the spot with their mouths open. Seeing he had their attention at last he warmed to his theme.

"I am going to be exposed" he told them.

"Is there a shortage of news?" asked The Assistant Secretary.

"Some irresponsible bastard has told them my staff are dropping dead like flies" The Head Postmaster said.

"That's common knowledge isn't it?" said The Branch Secretary.

"They've been on the 'phone" breathed The Head Postmaster.

"Who?" chorused The Union Men.

"The Sun" said The Head Postmaster, looking as though he was tempted to cross himself.

"You're not going to be on page three are you?" said The Assistant Secretary.

"It's no laughing matter" The Head Postmaster told him severely.

"It seems funny to me" The Assistant Secretary retorted.

"They door stopped me this morning" The Head Postmaster confided.

"Did they manage to catch you looking shifty?" asked The Branch Secretary.

"I was fetching in the milk" said The Head Postmaster.

"Should have sent your wife" said The Assistant Branch Secretary.

"You can laugh now. They'll come for you next" The Head Postmaster told him.

"My life's an open book" said The Branch Secretary.

"I've got nothing to hide" said The Assistant primly.

The Head Postmaster tightened his grip on the bat handle.

"I shan't hesitate to sue" he declared.

"Litigation's an expensive hobby" The Branch Secretary told him.

"How much is a man's good name worth? asked The Head Postmaster.

"A damn sight more than you can afford" said The Assistant brutally.

"That bloke Carter Ruck charges about four hundred pounds an hour" said The Branch Secretary. The Head Postmaster turned pale and put down the bat.

"I hope you don't expect us to have a whipround to cover your costs" said The Assistant.

"I don't have to have Carter Ruck" protested The Head Postmaster.

"It's not compulsory agreed The Branch Secretary.

"But all the top rascals have him" objected The Assistant.

"I'm not a bloody rascal" said The Head Postmaster looking very annoyed.

"Is your wife standing by you?" asked The Branch Secretary.

"I haven't done anything wrong" said The Head Postmaster.

"That's what they all say" said The Assistant in a very rude tone.

"I'm getting fed up with you" The Head Postmaster told him.

"I never asked to come here" said The Assistant.

"What exactly is this highly esteemed organ accusing you of?" said The Branch Secretary.

Before The Head Post Master could reply The Assistant cut in, using a most censorious tone.

"I hope it's not sexual deviation" he said.

"So do I. The working class are very puritanical" added The Branch Secretary.

"They expect a man in your position to set an example" said The Assistant.

"I am not on trial here" protested The Head Postmaster.

"The cleaners will want overtime" said The Assistant.

"They will indeed" said The Branch Secretary.

"That's your budget gone down the pan" said The Assistant.

The Head Postmaster felt as though he was careering down with no brakes towards something decidedly unpleasant.

"What will the cleaners want overtime for?" he asked, not really wanting to know the answer.

"They'll be spending hours cleaning things about you off the bog walls" The Assistant told him with obvious satisfaction.

"If you think The Sun's bad you wait 'till our Shitehouse Poets get going" said The Branch Secretary.

"They won't worry about Carter-Ruck" said The Assistant.

The Head Postmaster flung down the bat and raised his fist. The Union Men thought they were about to be subjected to a crude assault and leapt to their feet, but The Head Postmaster merely banged his fist on the desk top.

"I am not being accused of sexual deviation" he bellowed.

"So what's the charge?" said The Assistant.

"It is not a charge. I am not being prosecuted. It is an accusation" said The Head Postmaster.

Seeing The Union Men were obviously expecting him to continue The Head Postmaster leaned forward. Eager to hear the revelation The Union Men also leaned forward.

"They're going to accuse me on page one of killing off my staff, under the headline of "The Butcher of Derby" said The Head Postmaster.

"Is that all?" asked The Assistant incredulously.

"What are you wittering on about?" You've got nothing to fear" said The Branch Secretary.

"You'll get promoted" said The Assistant.

"And most likely a mention in the New Year's Honours list" added The Branch Secretary.

"This is no laughing matter" said The Head Postmaster indignantly.

"Who's laughing?" asked The Assistant Secretary.

"They asked me how many postmen had died suddenly and unexpectedly in the last year" complained The Head Postmaster.

"What did you tell them?" asked The Branch Secretary.

"I said I didn't know" said The Head Postmaster.

Thinking The Branch Officials were looking at him reproachfully he added with the slightest touch of bluster.

"Well do you know?"

"I stopped counting after the first half dozen" said The Assistant.

"They made this office sound like something out of Uncle Tom's Cabin" complained The Head Postmaster.

"And we can guess who's cast as Simon Legree" said The Assistant.

"Not like Postman Pat is it" said The Branch Secretary.

"Some bastard's shooting his mouth off" said The Head Postmaster.

"You can hardly hope to keep the deaths quiet" The Branch Secretary pointed out.

"Things are pretty bad, but we don't have people disappearing yet" added The Assistant.

"It's all the fault of that bloody Ghost Squad" said The Head Postmaster.

"It's surely a question of where the buck stops" said The Branch Secretary.

"Are you saying I'm to blame?" asked The Postmaster.

"You're in charge aren't you?" said The Assistant.

"It's not my fault we have to keep producing more and more profits" for the bloody government" said The Postmaster furiously. "I never voted for the bastards" he added.

"It's amazing how they keep getting back in though no-one ever votes for them" said The Branch Secretary.

"I'm not responsible for those blokes deaths" said The Postmaster.

"Don't tell me. Tell their widows" The Branch Secretary told him.

"The Post Office is a caring employer" said The Head Postmaster. The Union Men burst into laughter.

"How can you say that?" gasped The Assistant Secretary as he wiped the tears from his eyes.

"It says so in the policy statement" asserted The Head Postmaster.

With an obvious effort The Branch Officials pulled themselves together. Watching them The Head Postmaster steeled himself for an attack. It came first from The Assistant. Glaring at The Head Postmaster he asked him:

"If you're a caring employer how come we've got a death rate rivalling The Burma Railway?" he asked.

"It's not that bad" protested The Head Postmaster.

The Branch Secretary took up the attack.

"How does it happen that the spiralling rate of sudden deaths coincides with the new work schedules, and the continual policy statements telling us how much The Post Office cares about us?" he asked.

Before The Head Postmaster could attempt an answer The Assistant fired another question at him.

"What do you do with a bloke who can't stand the strain and goes sick?" he asked.

The Head Postmaster opened his mouth but was too slow. The Branch Secretary got in first.

"You threaten to sack him" he accused.

"We've got recognised procedures" said The Head Postmaster.

The Branch Secretary was beginning to look very angry.

"You've got men in their fifties and instead of allowing them to ease off you're piling more and more burdens on them, subjecting them to severe physical and mental strain, you threaten them with the sack when they go sick, and when you've worked them to death you say you're not responsible" he said.

"And you have the bloody cheek to turn up at their funerals" added The Assistant.

"If you manage to kill me off I've told my wife no member of Post Office management is to attend my funeral" said The Branch Secretary.

The Head Postmaster looked genuinely shocked.

"That's a terrible thing to do" he said.

"It's a terrible state of affairs we have here" retorted The Branch Secretary.

"And we don't want a bunch of hypocrites shedding crocodile tears at our funerals" said The Assistant.

"So I'm barred from your sendoff as well am I?" asked The Head Postmaster.

"Too right you are" said The Assistant.

"Then I'll wish you good morning" said The Head Postmaster.

The Union Men rose to their feet. The Head Postmaster pointed threateningly at them.

"Don't forget you've both signed the Official Secrets Act" he said.

"There aren't any secrets left here are there" said The Branch Secretary. The Union Men then left the office.

CHAPTER
FOURTEEN

Emergency Meeting

The Branch Secretary had called an emergency meeting. This did not surprise any of the local officials. They were used to operating in a state of continual crisis and being summoned to confer at a moment's notice. What did cause some puzzlement was the chosen venue.

"Why are we meeting in the pisshouse?" asked a Section Secretary.

"What's up with the Union Office?" asked his Chairman.

"It's a matter of security" said The Branch Secretary.

Seeing the Branch Officials looked decidedly irritated he added. "I think we may have bugs in the Union Office."

"Well send for shaggin' Rentokil" said an official.

"I mean electronic devices" said The Branch Secretary.

"Electronic devices. Don't talk like a twat" said a man who had only came onto the Union to sort out his own job and wasn't having much success even in that limited aim.

"This isn't Russia you know" said another official.

"No it isn't conceded The Assistant Secretary.

"They've stopped doing it there" said The Branch Secretary.

"So they've started doing it here instead" said The Assistant.

"What the same effers?" asked someone.

"They're the same everywhere" said his mate.

"Everything we say gets back to management" complained The Branch Secretary.

"Shaggin' good job. Eff'em!" said The Truculent Man.

"We know the phone's bugged" said The Branch Secretary.

"Is that why you keep blowing a whistle down it?" asked someone who rarely spoke.

The Branch Secretary nodded.

"Can we have a code word so we know when you're going to do it?" he was asked.

"Then with a bit of luck we won't all go deaf" said The Truculent Man.

"I know they're listening" said The Branch Secretary.

"How?" he was asked.

The general feeling was that this was all a bit far fetched.

"When I blow the whistle now a voice comes on the line and shouts 'never touched him ref'" said The Branch Secretary.

"They're taking the piss" said The Truculent Man.

"That's why we're holding the meeting here" said The Branch Secretary.

"Am I to put in the minutes that the meeting opened in the piss house on the second floor? asked The Notetaker.

"Yeah. And when you list those present don't forget to mention the bloke having a crap in trap two" said The Truculent Man.

I've thoroughly checked this meeting place and it is secure" said The Branch Secretary.

"No electronic devices?" said The Truculent Man.

"Run all the taps" said The Branch Secretary. The officials decided to humour him and turned on all the taps.

"Now flush all the bags" said The Branch Secretary.

Entering into the spirit of things the officials began to flush all the bogs.

"There you are. That will frustrate any would be eavesdroppers" said The Branch Secretary looking very pleased with his precautions.

"I dare say it will but since you've started blowing shaggin' whistles down the phone half of us are practically Mutt and Shaggin' Jeff so we can't hear either protested an official.

"Watch my lips" said The Branch Secretary.

"Oh bollocks" retorted The Protester.

"Let's get started" said The Truculent Man.

"Is the notice hanging on the door?" asked The Branch Secretary.

"Closed for cleaning" confirmed The Assistant.

The Branch Secretary motioned them in closer.

"The eyes of the media are upon us" he began.

"Have you closed the pisshouse to tell us that?" asked The Truculent Man.

The Branch Secretary ignored him.

"The Head Postmaster is going paranoid" he continued.

"He's not the only one" retorted The Truculent Man.

The University Dropout raised a hand diffidently.

'If I might make a few observations' he said.

'Oh Keerist here we go!' Educated Phucking Idiot! Said The Truculent Man.

'The issue here is the very nature of sanity' said The University Dropout.

'Is this on the record?' asked The Notetaker.

The Truculent Man snorted explosively.

'We'll put in a motion for conference on the nature of sanity. It'll probably go down to a card vote' he said.

'Precisely' said The University Dropout.

The man on the brink of going Mutt and Jeff as a result of The Branch Secretary blowing whistles down the phone cupped a hand to his ear.

'I'm not quite sure I've got the hang of this' he confessed.

The University Dropout was only too pleased to enlarge upon his theory.

'This is the matter that lies at the very heart of all our concerns" he said.

The Truculent Man was getting redder and redder in the face.

'Do you mean to shaggin' tell us we're all up here in the shaggin' piss house on the shaggin' second floor to discuss the nature of sanity?' he asked.

'It's just like The Caine Phucking Mutiny' said a voice from somewhere.

'I think there may be something in this' said The Branch Secretary.

'There's something in this said the burglar as he stuck his hand in the pisspot' said The Truculent Man.

However it was obvious that the meeting was intrigued by what The University Dropout had to say. Seeing that he had the attention of the officials he warmed to his subject.

'Sanity can never be more than a matter of opinion' he said.

'Bollox!' said The Truculent Man.

"We're trying to have an intelligent discussion here" The Branch Secretary told him.

Feeling emboldened The University Dropout fixed The Truculent Man with a challenging stare and asked him:

"Would you for instance say The Prime Minister was sane?"

"Of course she phuckin' isn't sane" answered The Truculent Man.

The entire meeting erupted at this point and everyone present went on record with highly uncomplimentary opinions as as to the state of The Prime Minister's mind.

"But a lot of people think she's not only sane, but she's absolutely brilliant as well. Why is that?" countered The University Dropout.

"They're as barmy as she is" howled someone.

"That's obvious, you don't need to go to university to see that" said The Truculent Man.

"She's got maniac's eyes" said The Man Who Was Verging On Mutt And Jeff.

"If she was a bloke she'd be an axe murderer" said The Assistant Secretary.

"Since we're being governed by someone who missed her vocation as an axe murderer what does that tell us? asked The University Dropout indicated.

"Buggered if I know" said The Branch Secretary.

Someone who rarely spoke raised his hand. The University Dropout indicated he was to speak.

"She's chucking everyone out of the funny farms to prepare for her succession" he said.

The Truculent Man spotted a flaw in the logic and furiously pounced upon it.

"Bloody hell! If she's a homicidal maniac and she's looking for someone to take over when she actually starts foaming at the mouth she'll open shaggin' Broadmoor" he said.

"Fook that" said someone in hushed tones.

'I think we're rather getting away from the point here' said The Branch Secretary.

'If I knew what the point was I'd be able to tell you if I agree with you' said The Truculent Man.

'We're not discussing lunacy in the general sense' said The Branch Secretary.

'Is this on the record? asked The Minute Taker.

'What are we discussing then?' asked The Truculent Man.

'I think we need to decide whether or not The Head Postmaster is cracking up' said The Branch Secretary.

'And going barmy' added The Assistant.

'He's been barmy for years' said The Truculent Man.

'He's threatening to invoke The Official Secrets Act' said The Branch Secretary.

'What for? Has some shagger been talking to the Russians?' asked someone.

'Selling secrets?' The Man On The Verge Of Going Mutt And Jeff asked.

'He says someone is talking to the press' said The Branch Secretary.

This revelation was greeted with a chorus of guffaws.

'What's he on about? Every shagger is talking to the press' said The Truculent Man.

'He says we're in the shit' said The Branch Secretary.

Everyone looked mystified. The University Dropout broke the silence.

'What's new. We've been in the shit for years' he said.

'He doesn't care about that. What worries him is that he's right there in the shit with us. Only he's in it a bit deeper' said The Assistant.

'Phuckin' great' said The Truculent Man.

'Let's hope he sinks altogether' said a voice in the corner.

'He thinks The Sun are going to make him look a right prat' said The Branch Secretary.

The meeting broke up into disorder again as everyone was overcome with paroxysms of mirth. When they'd recovered themselves somewhat The Truculent Man spoke.

'It doesn't take The Sun to make him look a right prat' he chortled.

'He's done it himself every day since he's been here' said The Man Going Mutt and Jeff.

'He wants us to present a united front said The Branch Secretary.

There were gasps of incredulity.

'The cheeky shagger' said The Truculent Man.

'That's what we thought' said The Assistant.

At that point two or three men headed for the door.

'Where are you going?' asked The Branch Secretary.

'To the newsagents' he was told.

'What for?' he asked.

'To order a copy of The Sun' said the man nearest the door.

'I wouldn't wipe my arse on that phuckin' thing' said The Truculent Man.

'I'm not going to wipe me arse on it. I'm going to read the shagger' was the response.

'It's anti Union.' protested someone.

'It's anti every phucker but if it's going to make Shagnasty look a prat for the benefit of ten million readers I'm not missing it' said the man and left.

'That's a bloody fine attitude' said The Assistant Secretary.

Everyone agreed.

'Nip after him and tell him to tell the newsagent to order several hundred more copies' he added.

A messenger duly set off.

'The reason I've called the meeting' The Branch Secretary began. He got no further as The Truculent Man interrupted.

'At phuckin' last' he said.

'We need to develop a media strategy' said The Branch Secretary. The Truculent Man's jaw sagged. He was plainly taken aback. He looked about from face to face but saw no-one who looked likely to be able to enlighten him. He rushed towards the cubicles and dashed from one to another flushing the lavatories. Then he returned to face the puzzled looks of the group:

'Security' he said.

'What?' said the man whose faculties had suffered as a result of having whistles blown down the mouthpiece.

'Can someone tell me just what the fuck a media strategy is and why we have to have one?' asked The Truculent Man, sounding as though he had just about had enough.

'Point of order Mr. Chairman' said an official.

'Who's supposed to be chairing this shambles?' asked The Assistant Secretary.

'You are' The Branch Secretary told him.

'What's the point of order?' asked The Assistant severely.

'The Educated Idiot raised the matter of the nature of sanity. So far as I know we haven't come to any conclusion' said The Point of Order Man.

'I'm ruling that matter out of order. This meeting has been called to deal with one subject only' said The Assistant hastily.

'And what the shaggin hell might that be' asked The Truculent Man.

'Media strategy' said The Branch Secretary.

'We have to have one to protect ourselves' added The Assistant.

'What like Polaris?' said someone.

'Kin' ell!' spluttered The Truculent Man.

'We'll have fookin' peace women camping outside the office' said Mutt and Jeff.

The door opened and a Shifty Looking Postman entered.

'These pisshouses are closed for cleaning' said The Truculent Man.

'You're not cleaners' said The Shifty Looking Postman.

'I'm a cleaner' said The Cleaners' Representative.

'Then what are all the rest of them doing here,' asked The Shifty Looking Man.

'What is this? Twenty shaggin' questions?' said The Truculent Man.

'This looks to me like a conspiracy' said The Shifty Looking Man.

The Cleaning Rep picked up a mop.

'What are you going to do with that?' asked The Shifty Looking Man.

'If you don't phuckoff out of it he's going to hand it to me and I'm going to shove it up your arse' said The Truculent Man.

'Threats of violence eh!' said The Shifty Looking Man looking absolutely delighted.

'I think we should go to Whitby this year' said The Branch Secretary.

Everyone including The Shifty Looking Man, looked nonplussed.

'We must seek new challenges' said The Branch Secretary.

'Yes we must' said The Assistant, not having a clue what he was agreeing to, but seeing the necessity of showing a united front before a stranger.

'Time we tried some deep sea fishing' added The Branch Secretary.

'What's wrong with the tookin' river,' asked The Truculent Man, determined to have a confrontation, no matter what the subject.

'So you're The Fishing Club are you' said The Shifty Looking Man with a nasty sneer.

'And this is a private meeting' said The Assistant.

'So kindly fuck off' said The Cleaning Rep.

Mutt and Jeff was staring hard at The Shifty Looking Man.

'What's your job mate?' he asked.

'Postman' said The Shifty Looking Man.

'What section?' asked Mutt and Jeff.

The Shifty Looking Man started to look worried.

'He's a bloody imposter said The Cleaning Rep raising his mop in a manner that suggested he was no longer going through the actions of cleaning the floor.

The Shifty Looking Man backed towards the door. The Truculent Man stood in his way.

'What's your game sunshine?' he asked.

'Would you mind standing out of my way' said The Shifty Looking Man.

The Shifty Looking Man turned round looking for another exit. The University Dropout seized him by the lapels.

'I know who this is. It's that slimy twat from The Sun' he said.

He began to shake the Shifty Looking Man like a terrier that had hold of a rat.

'Your effin' paper is a disgrace' he said as he continued to shake The Shifty Looking Man'.

'I wouldn't wipe my arse on it' said The Truculent Man prodding him with a bony forefinger.

'That's assault' said The Shifty Looking Man through rattling teeth.

'It's an insult to the intelligence' said The University Dropout.

'And the Bingo's crap' said Mutt and Jeff.

'I'll have you all for assault. Wait till my Editor, hears about this' blustered The Shifty Looking Man.

'Impersonating a postman is a very serious offence" said The Assistant Secretary.

The University Dropout continued to shake The Shifty Looking Man with relish.

Suddenly, he shoved The Shifty Looking Man into the arms of The Cleaning Rep.

'Hold onto him' he instructed.

'I might catch something' protested The Cleaning Rep.

'I think the bloody little ferret is wired up' said The University Dropout.

'Search the Wanker' said The Assistant.

Despite his struggles The Shifty Looking Man was subjected to a search and it was discovered that he was indeed wired up.

'There you are you see. Electronic devices everywhere' said The Branch Secretary triumphantly, his warnings amply justified.

The bugging device was handed round.

That belongs to The Sun' said The Shifty Looking Man.

'And that uniform belongs to The Post Office' said The University Dropout.

'Let's debag the bastard' said The Truculent Man.

The Post Office uniform was removed forcibly while The Shifty Looking Man uttered baleful threats as to what Mr. McKenzie would do whom news of this outrage reached him. The Branch Secretary looked at the unprepossessing specimen in front of him.

'You wouldn't think such a wretched little weasel could be so dangerous' he said.

'We definitely need a media strategy' assented The Assistant.

'Naked we come into the world and naked we go out' said The University Dropout.

The Truculent Man grinned in sheer delight.

'Too bloody right we do' he agreed.

'Strip the bastard' said The Dropout.

'Tar and feather his willie' said Mutt and Jeff.

'You'll be hearing from my solicitors' howled The Man From The Sun.

'Oh no we won't. If you complain about us we'll report you for masquerading as a postman, and when the Police find Postman 423 bound and gagged, you'll be right in the shit.

'He's not bound and gagged' protested The Man From The Sun.

'He will be when he's discovered. He'll have to back us because he's right in the shit, just like you. Aiding a felony is what he'll be accused of, and he'll lose his job for certain' said The Dropout.

The Truculent Man gazed at The University Dropout in admiration.

'Brilliant. We'll strip the wanker stark bloody naked and sling him out into the street' he said. He turned to The Dropout.

'The sooner you stand for The Executive Council the better' he told him.

The Man From The Sun was duly stripped and his clothes slung into a plastic bag.

Mutt and Jeff gazed at him critically.

'He's not exactly God's gift to women is he' he observed.

Despite his continuing protests, pleas and threats The Man From The Sun was taken downstairs and thrown naked out into the street.

The Union Men gazed out of the window as The Man From The Sun wandered along stark bollock naked. He didn't really seem to know where he was going. A policeman approached him. He was detained. He pointed accusingly up at the window. The policeman did not seem to be interested. The Man From The Sun was led off.

'That's the way to deal with the rotten fuckers' said The Truculent Man.

The Branch Secretary thought for a moment. Then he delivered his verdict to the meeting.

'It's not entirely what I'd call a coherent media strategy. But it'll do for a start' he declared.

CHAPTER FIFTEEN

The Naked Truth

Rod Williams sat at his desk staring apathetically at the wall. The appearance of The Ghost Squad and the subsequent invasion by the media had thrust him into the limelight in a way he found thoroughly disturbing: He did not want to be a media personality. He wanted to be a minor dictator operating within his own small clearly defined territory. He did not welcome publicity and its accompanying public scrutiny. He looked back nostalgically to the days when all he had to worry about was George, The Post Office, The Spy On The Station, the occasional Bolshie Passenger and the dreaded possibility of coming to the attention of some strange power at Region. Now he found the eyes of the world upon him. He sighed heavily and shook his head sadly.

'At least things have got bad as they can possibly get' he told himself as he switched his gaze to the television screen. The Master Cutler drew into platform one and suddenly there they were, the upper crust. Platform one was full of Executives. Rod gazed at them with something like affection. There were the achievers, the wealth creators, the elite who would leave the country if Labour ever got into power.

Rod was feeling very flat and cast down as he reached for his bottle of uppers. He took one and thought he felt better. Then his eyes practically started from his head and he began to search frantically for his bottle of downers. He gulped one down and gazed transfixed at the screen. A man was pushing his way through the mobile phone carrying executives. Rod closed his eyes for a moment hoping that what he saw was some sort of optical illusion. He hoped in vain.

Sean the Leprauchan, who was wearing a smart uniform this week as he was acting in a minor managerial capacity, walked in. Rod pointed at the screen.

'Will you look at that. There's a stark bollock naked bastard on Platform One' he said in a tone that verged on the hysterical.

Sean glanced at the screen.

'Nudity is a form of statement' he told Rod.

Rod took his hat off the hook, threw it on the floor, and jumped on it.

'You're The Acting Deputy Assistant Under Manager and all you can do is talk crap' Rod bellowed.

Before Sean could point out that Acting Deputy Assistant Under Managers did not talk crap Rod's mobile crackled into life and Ivan's voice came on:

'Rod. Rod. Are you there Rod?'

'Yes. I'm here' answered Rod.

'I've got a guy on platform one with a problem' said Ivan.

'What's his problem Ivan?' asked Rod as he stared at the answer to his question on the screen.

'He got no clothes. He stark bollock naked' said Ivan.

'Who is he?' asked Rod.

'How the phuck do I know? He got no means of identity' said Ivan.

'Ask him' instructed Rod.

He watched the screen as the man spoke excitedly to Ivan, his discourse accompanied by much gesturing.

The phone crackled.

'Are you there Rod?' asked Ivan:

'Of course I'm shaggin' here' said Rod.

'He says he's an ace reporter from The Sun newspaper' said Ivan.

'Ask him where he keeps his pen' suggested Sean.

Rod's furious retort was cut short as Ivan came back on the line.

'Rod I think he's some sort of nutter. He says three women bundled him into a car, said they found the page three girls an affront to womanhood, stripped him stark bollock naked, raped him, stole his money, took his pen and his mobile phone and slung him out in the road. It sound like wishful thinking to me.'

'This will do wonders for our tv ratings' said Sean.

'This is not going on television' said Rod.

'You tell them that' said Sean pointing to the camera crew eagerly closing in on Ivan and The Stark Bollock Naked Man. Ivan turned and beamed at the camera.

'Ivan'll be phoning all his friends telling them to look out for him on the six o'clock news' said Sean.

'No-one's supposed to speak to the media without clearance from Region' said Rod.

'What are you supposed to do when there's no-one from Region about and someone thrusts a microphone at you?' asked Sean.

'Say no comment' Rod replied.

'Sir I disagree with every word you utter, but I will defend to the death your right to say it' said Sean and swept out to carry on with his duties as an Acting Deputy Assistant Under Manager.

Meanwhile out on platform one Ivan was playing a blinder. He stood resolutely in front of The Stark Bollock Naked Man with his arms flung wide.

'This man is not in a fit state to appear on television when minors are watching' he said firmly.

A microphone was thrust at the cowering figure behind him.

'Why are you streaking?' he was asked.

'I am not streaking. I have been attacked by sinister forces seeking to destroy the precious freedom of the press upon which all our liberties ultimately depend' he claimed.

'He been raped' said Ivan with a broad grin. 'And they took his mobile phone' he added.

'Can you describe your assailants?' asked a reporter.

'Three beautiful young women' said The Stark Bollock Naked Man.

'It's wishful thinking. I reckon he's supposed to be having care in the community. That means it's all our responsibility' said Ivan.

'Are you a fantasist?' asked another reporter.

'No I am not. I'm a Sun reporter' replied the Stark Bollock Naked Man indignantly:

'Then you are a fantasist' said someone else.

At the mention of The Sun a buzz went round the crowd that had now gathered.

'Can I have your autograph please?' asked a middle aged woman.

The Stark Bollock Naked Man signed her book. Paddy drove up on the tractor. He applied the brakes and look in the scene. He began to sing.

'Oh the King is in the altogether
The altogether the altogether
He's altogether as naked as the day
That he was born'.

The rowdier element took up the song. The noise got louder. The Stark Bollock Naked Man lost his nerve and decided to make a run for it. He set off towards the entrance hall with the camera crew in hot pursuit and an ever increasing gang of onlookers following after. Rod Williams was horrified. He went to the cupboard and took out a dirty mackintosh and a trilby hat. Feeling comfortingly anonymous he followed the throng.

There was pandomonium in the vestibule. People were pushing through the gates trying to get off the station while others were coming in on their way out for the night. The Stark Bollock Naked Man was caught in the middle. He sprinted over to the ticket office.

'Single to London' he panted.

The clerk said: 'Forty seven pounds sixty two pence.'

'That's bloody extortionate' said The Stark Bollock Naked Man.

'Do you want the ticket or not?' asked The Clerk.

'I'll have it' said The Stark Bollock Naked Man.

'Put your money there' said The Clerk indicating the turntable.

'It's in my wallet' said The Stark Bollock Naked Man.

The Clerk looked up at The Stark Bollock Naked Man and then peered over the edge of the counter.

'Is this a bloody windup?' he asked suspiciously.

'I've been raped and robbed' said The Stark Bollock Naked Man.

'I think he mean he been robbed and raped, said Ivan appearing suddenly at The Stark Bollock Naked Man's elbow.

'We take most credit cards' said the Booking Clerk.

'Where do you think he going to keep his credit cards?' asked Ivan.

'Do you really want me to tell you?' asked The Booking Clerk, by now beginning to enjoy the diversion.

'Not when innocent children are watching the television' said Ivan primly.

'There he is' shouted someone and The Stark Bollock Naked Man turned and saw the camera crew hearing down upon him. He sprinted past them, found his way off the station was blocked and headed back onto platform one.

In the Post Office section The Dim Manager was presiding over a team talk. He held the briefing paper in front of him, reading with some difficulty.

'You've all got to look smart?' he said. The postmen stared at him gloomily.

'Why have we got to look smart. We're fookin' postmen not fookin' male models' said Joe.

The Dim Manager consulted the paper moving his lips laboriously.

'Look smart, act smart he read.

Joe looked entirely unconvinced.

'What's that fooker supposed to mean?' he asked.

'I don't write the phucker I just read the phucker out' answered The Dim Manager.

Joe was feeling particularly pissed off and would not be mollified.

'We're supposed to look to you for guidance' he said.

The Dim Manager referred again to his briefing.

'There's some cheap tickets going for the Pink Coconut on Wednesday night' he said.

'That's a lot of phucking use. We're all stuck here' snorted Joe.

The Dim Manager was getting tired of Joe. He was about to tell him off when George piped up.

'How are we supposed to look smart when we're working our bollocks off and sweating buckets?' he asked.

'Half the bags are shitty' said Joe.

'You've all got to wear ties' said The Dim Manager.

'What to chuck shaggin' bags about?' said Mike.

'Any man not properly dressed is to be sent home' The Dim Manager read laboriously, but not without a certain satisfaction.

'Well shag me' said Joe.

'Ties are to be of sober design and colouring' went on The Dim Manager.

'I don't believe this shagger' muttered someone to no-one in particular.

'Any questions?' said The Dim Manager in an aggressive tone which made it quite plain that enquiries were not required.

The door was flung open and The Stark Bollock Naked Man entered. He sat down in a vacant chair.

'That's Paddy's chair mate' said Joe.

The Dim Manager stared open mouthed. 'Don't stand there catching flies. Ask him where his shaggin.' tie is said Mike.

'You have to wear a tie mate. Otherwise the shaggers send you shaggin' home' explained Joe.

'Are you some sort of Kissogram mate,' asked Mike, The Union Man.

Joe snorted. 'We know there's some right queer effers here but this is bloody ridiculous' he said.

'Is the meeting closed?' said George getting up ready to go over to the Institute and his first beer of the evening.

'I've been raped' said The Stark Bollock Naked Man.

'You'd best see the Police' said The Dim Manager anxious to get this embarrassment out of his jurisdiction.

'Hang on hang on. I want to hear about this' said Joe.

George sat down and leaned forward. All eyes were on The Stark Bollock Naked Man.

'I thought it were women what got raped' said a puzzled voice.

The Stark Bollock Naked Man shook his head. 'Not always' he said.

'Who was it?' asked The Union Rep.

'There were three of them' said The Stark Bollock Naked Man.

Joe looked appalled. 'What blokes?' he said in a horrified tone.

The Stark Bollock Naked Man shook his head. 'Women' he breathed.

'You've been raped by three women?' asked Joe his voice rising in disbelief.

Paddy flung the door open and came in full of excitement.

'There's a Stark Bollock Naked Man running round the station' he yelled.

'Shut up you twat. Sit down and listen' instructed Joe.

'That's him there' said Paddy.

'We can see that' said Mike.

'He's been raped' said Joe.

'By three women' added The Dim Manager wondering if he should include this incident in his report as to the response from the Team Briefing.

'They said it was a political statement' said The Stark Bollock Naked Man.

'Three women?' said Paddy in sheer disbelief.

'Three beautiful young women' said The Stark Bollock Naked Man.

Joe leaned forward. 'Are you boasting or complaining?' he asked.

'It was an outrage' said The Stark Bollock Naked Man.

'Three of 'em? said Paddy again.

'How many more times. 'Three of them' said The Stark Bollock Naked Man.

'All at once?' asked Paddy.

'No you soft twat. One after the other' said Joe.

'You've got no idea' Mike told Paddy.

'I'm only trying to establish the facts' said Paddy.

'I think that winds it all up then' said The Dim Manager backing hastily towards the door.

'Just a minute. There's something I want to bring up' said Joe.

The Dim Manager looked at his watch.

'Can't it wait?' he asked.

'No it can't. Sit down' said Joe.

The Dim Manager reluctantly did so.

'What is it?' he asked.

'It's The Shaggin' Ghost Squad' said Joe.

'What about The Shaggin' Ghost Squad?' asked The Dim Manager:

'Do the shaggers work here or not?' asked Joe.

'They're on the duty lost' said The Dim Manager evasively.

'I know that shagger but where are they? They're no use to me on the duty list' said Joe.

The Dim Manager opened his mouth but Joe continued his attack before he could speak.

'I'm not shaggin' Arnold Schwarzengger you know' said Joe.

'I know that' said The Dim Manager.

'It's fookin' preposterous' said Joe.

The Dim Manager's mouth dropped open.

'It's fookin' what?' he asked.

'Fookin' preposterous' Joe told him.

'What's that fooker?' said The Dim Manager edging towards the door.

He reached the door as Rod Williams entered. Before he could speak The Player King who had been dozing quietly through the team briefing as usual spoke.

'If we're going to discuss The Ghost Squad I fear we are entering into a decidedly nebulous area' he said and closed his eyes again.

'Never mind the shaggin' Ghost Squad. At least they've got some clothes on wherever they are. There's some bastard running round the station stark bollock naked said Rod: His gaze fell upon Stark Bollock Naked.

'That's him. He's there'.

'Where?' said Joe.

'Sitting right there' said Rod.

'Are you sure it's him?' asked Paddy.

'Sure I'm sure. Look for yourself. The bastard's got no soddin' clothes on' said Rod.

'Can you describe the man you saw?' asked Paddy.

Rod looked puzzled and exasperated in equal measure.

'The thing is you see what Paddy is suggesting is that there could be an epidemic' said The Player King, keeping his eyes firmly closed.

George stared hard at Rod's attire.

'Why are you going round in that dirty mac?' he asked suspiciously.

'Look bloody smart. Wear a bloody tie or we'll send you home. He's stark bollock naked and the Station Manager is disguised as a tramp. I'm off for a bleedin' pint' said George and left slamming the door.

'The shagger's at it again. Drinking on shaggin' duty' protested Rod.

'Don't talk fookin' preposterous' said The Dim Manager.

'I have to get to London' said Stark Bollock Naked.

'If you think you're going to London dressed like that Buddy you can think again' said Rod.

'I've been raped' protested Stark Bollock Naked.

'Don't give me any of that crap' said Rod.

'You might not be interested but I want to hear about this' said Paddy.

'And I want to know where the shaggin' Ghost Squad are' said Joe.

'Human Resources will be issuing a statement' said The Dim Manager.

'And what might Human Resources be?' asked Joe.

'How the phuck do I know?' said The Dim Manager.

The Player King sat up straight and opened his eyes. He stood up. 'Of the Human Resources, for The Human Resources, and by The Human Resources' he said.

Rod and The Dim Manager gazed at each other in total incomprehension.

'Some Human Resources should be put against the shaggin' wall and shaggin' shot for the shaggin' things they do to the shaggin' English language' said The Player King, and then sat down and closed his eyes again. He leaned back in his chair and placed both hands behind his head. He indicated the Stark Naked Man.

'Surely the obvious thing to do is take this poor player who struts and frets his hour upon the stage and turns up stark bollock naked on Derby Station to the wardrobe' he said.

A glimmer of intelligence momentarily lit up The Dim Manager's face.

'Fookin' stores' he said.

'You talk like a fookin' twat' said Joe.

The Dim Manager waited for further statements from Joe. Joe's mouth remained firmly shut. The Dim Manager felt he'd best ask why he had been talking like a fookin' twat.

'Why am I talking like a fookin' twat?' He asked.

'Cos you can't do anything else' said Joe.

'The shaggin' stores are only open once a shaggin' week now. Didn't you know that?' snorted Paddy. The Dim Manager shook his head.

'You know shagall' Paddy told him.

'I'm not wearing Post Office uniform' said Stark Bollock Naked fearing prosecution for impersonating a postman.

'You're in no bloody position to pick and choose' said Paddy.

'Take him to C and A' said Joe.

'I want to hear about these three bloody women' said Paddy.

'It was terrible' said Stark Bollock Naked.

'Some people are never satisfied. It seems to me you've had a much more interesting evening than I've had' said Paddy.

'It was a political statement said.' Stark Bollock Naked.

'What Party would they be in then?' said Paddy.

'Where did this alleged outrage occur' asked The Player King.

'They bundled me into a car on The Midland Road. I thought they wanted directions' said Stark Bollock.

'The story is so positively bizarre it could conceivably be true' said The Player King.

'Do you reckon so?' said Joe.

'I would not dismiss the story out of hand' said The Player King.

'It was the mobile phone that did it' said Stark Bollock Naked.

"And the Filofax" he added.

'Proceed' instructed The Player King. Paddy was all attention. 'Bee Jasus this is better than listening to train announcements' he said.

'They said the mobile phone and the Filofax were symbols of man's domination over women' said Stark Bollock Naked.

'So basically what you're saying is they dragged you into the car, tore the clothes off you, pinched your belongings and gave you a bloody good seeing to because you had a mobile phone and a Filofax" said Paddy.

'And they said I was a mate chauvinistic pig' said Stark Bollock Naked.

Joe looked at The Dim Manager. 'Right then. So you can't tell me when I can expect to see The Shaggin' Ghost Squad doing a bit of work?' he asked.

The Dim Manager opened his mouth. Human.' he began.

Joe cut him short. 'Don't give me any of that Human Resources crap' be said, picking up The Dim Manager's mobile phone. The Dim Manager looked puzzled. 'Have you got a Filofax?' Joe asked.

The Dim Manager nodded. 'Let's be having the phucker then' said Joe, heading towards the door.

'Where do you think you're going?' asked The Dim Manager.

'I know where I'm going mate. I'm going to Midland Road' Joe told him.

'Afterwards they told me they were making a political statement' said Stark Bollock Naked.

'Why are you going to Midland Road Joe?' asked Paddy.

'Can't you guess?' said Joe.

Paddy shook his head. 'You're a thick prat' Joe told him. 'I might be a wrinkled old shagger, but the light's not too good and it might be my lucky night. There might be some more birds driving round looking for a chance to make a political statement', said Joe and swept out.

"Come back here" bellowed The Dim Manager.

'We must all do whatever we can to facilitate the political process' said The Player King.

The Dim Manager rushed to the door and shouted at Joe's back.

'You tell those tarts that mobile phone and the Filofax are shaggin' Post Office property' he instructed.

CHAPTER
SIXTEEN

CONSEQUENCES

The Branch Secretary sat in the Union Office reviewing the situation. 'I'm not sure if stripping that slimy bastard stark bollock naked was a good idea or not he remarked to The Assistant Secretary.

'Seemed a good idea at the time' said The Assistant.

'It did' agreed The Branch Secretary. 'But it set in train events over which we had no control' he added.

'Really set the cat among the 'pigeons' said The Assistant.

'The trouble is we let the bloody Head Postmaster off the hook' said The Branch Secretary. The Assistant nodded.

Events had indeed taken a wholly unexpected turn. When The Sun heard that their star reporter was wandering round Derby stark bollock naked, and claimed to have been robbed and raped by three militant feminists, The Editor immediately lost interest in The Head Postmaster on the grounds that there was blood and snot to the story but no sex. The Butcher of Derby story was spiked. Instead Sun readers were treated to a lurid account of the ordeal suffered by the reporter, whose one purpose in life was to seek out the truth, no matter what the cost, and bring it before Sun readers. The story was accompanied by a series of photographs of barely clothed young women who it was stated could look like one of the avenging harpies who had caused the star reporter to suffer such indignities.

Page three girls were required to issue statements to the effect that they were not feminists and had no need to ravish men.

This story was dragged out over several days and progressed from a lie to an extravaganza. The outcome was that in various police stations across the land, particularly in areas with a preponderance of Sun readers, stark bollock men started turning up claiming to be the latest victim of the ruthless ravishers. Station Sergeants did not appreciate the amount of paper work this caused, and an already hopelessly overstretched police was obliged to at least go through the motions of an investigation, just in case one of these bizarre allegations might be true.

When the number of men claiming to have been robbed and ravished was equalled by women confessing to the crime, and countless others informing on rivals in love, several Chief Constables began to consider the possibilities of early retirement.

Furious debates opened up based on the assumption that the indignities inflicted on the star reporter had in fact occurred, with some groups maintaining that this dramatic event was a sign that women were no longer prepared to be submissive doormats, and that this was an encouraging trend, and others asserting equally vehemently that it was surely a sign of desperation. At the height of the furore a renowned lady academic caused a sensation by declaring that the three women involved in the original incident were victims of male domination.

The sales of portable phones and soared and Filofaxes women driving along minding their own business complained that men on the pavement were eyeing them suggestively.

The Dim Station Gaffer became reconciled to being without his portable phone and Filofax as Joe paraded up and down Midland Road for a week until three young women who had lost their way going round the inner ring road stopped to ask for directions. Thinking his moment had arrived Joe climbed into the car assuring them he was prepared to struggle a bit. To his dismay he was called a silly old sod and tipped out into the road. His faith in the veracity of The Sun never recovered from that disappointment and he switched to The Daily Mirror.

Meanwhile The Ghost Squad were nowhere to be seen and since Joe had apparently joined them, the other postmen were having to cover the trains. Complaints to The Dim Manager produced nothing but vague tales of policy statements from region concerning the status now held by The Ghost Squad.

Paddy was beside himself. 'The Effin' Eejet says they're media personalities. Those two useless shaggers. They're media personalities' he fumed.

'I heard they'd got an agent' said Walter.

'Probation Officer more like' spluttered Paddy.

'It looks rather as though history has given us our brief moment of fame and passed on' intoned The Player King.

'You mean it's back to shaggin' business as shaggin' usual?' asked Paddy.

'The spotlight has moved elsewhere. The chroniclers of our times are seeking out new diversions for the populace' replied The Player King.

'They can seek out the shaggin' Ghost Squad as long as they like and they'll not find 'em' said Joe morosely, as with little hope and against expectation and experience he gazed once more towards the steps down which it was not altogether impossible The Ghost Squad might appear.

"How the hell do they get away with it?' asked Paddy.

'When no other explanation for the inexcusable comes to mind always suspect The Freemasons' said The Player King.

You mean they're somewhere with their trousers rolled up to their knees and a cucumber up the arse?' said Joe.

'Very likely' confirmed The Player King.

'Well I hope it's a bloody big cucumber' said Paddy.

'If Lady Bracknell had known about that she'd never have had cucumber sandwiches' said Sean The Leprauchan.

'Perhaps they'll both be found in a mailbag' said The Player King.

'A mailbag!' snorted Joe. 'Those bastards have never been near a mailbag' he said.

'Except when the bloody camera crew was here, and then you couldn't keep the bloody eejets away from the shaggin' mailbags' recalled Paddy.

The Union Man looked serious. 'There's bound to be some shite flying around after this bloody farce' he said.

'What's The Gaffer say?' asked Joe.

Before The Union Man could answer there was an explosion from Paddy.

'It's no use asking that friggin' eejet. Call him a Gaffer! You'd get more sense talking to my bollocks'. The group agreed that Paddy's bollocks were intellectually superior to The Gaffer and everyone felt instantly happier.

Blissfully unaware that his mental faculties had been condemned of hand The Dim Manager sat in his office trying to work out whether he was right in the shit and could expect summary dismissal, or at best demotion, or whether he was in clover and could look forward to rapid advancement. After a great deal of agonising and unaccustomed introspection he decided that having lost at golf to The Head Postmaster over the weekend would just about top the scales in his favour. If he was nothing else he was without doubt an accomplished and dedicated brownnoser.

There was a knock on the door and Rod Williams walked in. He sat down uninvited and stared at The Dim Manager. The Dim Manager waited for him to speak. Rod continued to stare at him. The Dim Manager hoped Rod's twitch wasn't contagious. At last Rod spoke.

'Heard anything from Region?' he asked.

'Not a shaggin' word' said The Dim Manager.

'Me neither' said Rod.

'It's early yet' said The Dim Manager, comforting himself with the thought that his defeat at golf was as good an insurance as it was possible to have.

'Maybe it'll all blow over' said Rod.

The Dim Manager shook his head dolefully. 'There'll be a load of shit flying around', he said.

Rod nodded glumly. In his heart he knew the day of reckoning had to come.

'The thing is who's it going to stick to,' said The Dim Manager.

'There's no shaggin' Ghost Squad on my staff' said Rod, not liking The Dim Manager's tone.

'The Ghost Squad didn't write obscene material about The Area Manager in the Executive Shitehouse' said The Dim Manager.

'No. That was shaggin' George' said Rod.

'If you're going to make unfounded accusations against one of my staff I think he ought to be here to defend himself' said The Dim Manager.

'The least said about the Executive Shitehouse the better' said Rod. The Union Rep walked in. 'Who's making accusations,' he said glaring at Rod. Rod glared back. He didn't want The Union involved.

'No-one's making accusations' he said.

The Union Rep looked at The Dim Manager. 'He says George wrote on the wall of the Executive Shitehouse' said The Dim Manager.

To Rod and The Dim Managers's surprise The Union Rep shrugged his shoulders. 'The Wall of The Executive Shitehouse is history' he told them.

Rod looked profoundly relieved. The wall of The Executive Shitehouse had haunted his dreams for weeks. He hoped with all his being that The Union Rep was right.

The Union Rep turned his attention to The Dim Manager. 'Just where are The Ghost Squad? The blokes really would love to know' he said.

'They're not the only shaggers' said The Dim Manager.

'You don't know either' said The Union Rep somewhat taken aback by this frank confession of ignorance.

'I've been told not to ask' said The Dim Manager.

The Union Rep gazed at him in amazement. 'Are they phuckin' Freemasons?' he asked. It was a wild shot but he could think of nothing else.

The Dim Manager spread his hands in a gesture of helplessness.

'I'm phucked if I know where they are?' he admitted.

'They're at the shaggin' Lodge aren't they,' said The Union Rep. He was gettin very annoyed. 'Phuckin' golf and phuckin' Freemasonery' he snorted.

'Nothing wrong with golf' said The Dim Manager defensively.

'What about walking round with your trousers rolled up and a cucumber stuck up your arse?' said The Union Rep.

'We do not have cucumbers stuck up the arse in my Lodge' said Rod indignantly.

'Oh you're one are you? I might have guessed' said The Union Rep.

'Are you the bloody Gaffer or not?' he asked The Dim Manager.

'Do they really have to stick cucumbers up their arses?' asked The Dim Manager. He'd been sounded about joining a Lodge lately and had been assured that membership would more than compensate for lack of ability. It was tempting but he didn't much care for the idea of a cucumber up the arse.

'You can sort the cucumbers out later with him' said The Union Rep indicating Rod.

'We do lots of work for charity' protested Rod.

'I want something sorted out' said The Union Rep.

'There's shagall I can do' said The Dim Manager.

'You must have some idea what's happening' said The Union Rep.

He looked expectantly at The Dim Manager. The Dim Manager blinked first.

'There is a rumour they're getting jobs on the public relations side' he said.

The Union Rep sat down. 'It's got to be true. It's cucumbers up the arse. Nothing makes sense otherwise' he said.

'What can you do?' asked The Dim Manager.

'We'd best all get down the allotment, Sainsbury's is closed' said The Union Rep.

This suggestion left The Dim Manager looking puzzled.

'We need The Sun back here' said The Union Rep.

'You can't talk to the press' said The Dim Manager.

'Want to bet?' said The Union Rep.

'You've signed The Official Secrets Act' said The Dim Manager.

'The Official Secrets Act does not cover cucumbers up the arse' said The Union Rep and stormed out.

Rod looked horrified. His twitch intensified. He looked appealingly at The Dim Manager.

'The Sun won't come back here will they?' he asked.

'They will if they hear about cucumbers up the arse' said The Dim Manager.

Rod blanched. He stood up, or rather staggered to his feet. He looked round desparately. 'Gotta take a tablet' he muttered and left.

'Soft sod!' said The Dim Manager.

George looked in. 'How you fixed?' he said without preliminary gambits.

'Phuckoff!' said The Dim Manager:

"You wait till you need a favour' said George and left.

The Dim Manager was beginning to think things were going his way. He decided he didn't need The Freemasons. He wanted to steer clear of scandal and he didn't particularly want a cucumber up his arse.

The Union Rep made his way over to the Union Office where he found The Branch Secretary and The Assistant discussing tactics.

'We can't just lurch from moment to moment. The Branch Secretary was saying.

'What else can we do? asked The Assistant, reasonably enough.

'We need a goal, a long term aim' said The Branch Secretary.

'We want the bloody Sun back' said The Station Rep.

'They don't care about our blokes dropping dead, like bloody flies' said The Assistant.

'Of course they don't. They're anti trade union' said The Station Rep.

'That one we stripped stark bollock naked is' said The Secretary.

'They're not interested in blokes being worked to death. They will be interested in Freemasons going round with their trousers rolled up and cucumbers up the arse' said The Station Rep.

'Think we've got Freemasons here?' asked The Branch Secretary.

'How else can the bloody Ghost Squad get away with it all the time?' said The Station Rep.

'There are some bloody funny handshakes in this building' said The Assistant.

The Branch Secretary shook his head. "We can't take on the poxy Freemasons' he said.

'Why not?' asked The Station Rep.

'We haven't got the resources' The Branch Secretary told him.

The Station Rep and The Assistant Secretary looked decidedly unconvinced.

The Branch Secretary attempted to explain: 'If we take on a Secret Society we're liable to get snuffed out' he said.

'What terminated?' said The Assistant.

'The Branch Secretary nodded.'

'Unexplained accidents' said The Station Rep.

'Exactly' said The Branch Secretary.

'No-one's going to bother about a few more postmen popping their clogs' said The Assistant.

'At the rate our members are dying I doubt if anyone would even notice' said The Branch Secretary.

'The trouble with a Secret Society is you just don't know who's in it' said The Assistant.

The Branch Secretary sat in silence for some moments apparently deep in thought. Then he spoke. 'We must lower our sights' he said.

The Station Rep and The Assistant looked puzzled.

'Remember Al Capone?' The Branch Secretary asked.

'Did he have cucumbers up his arse?' asked The Assistant looking puzzled.

'He may have had for all I know. Remember how they first got him?'

'Income tax' said The Assistant.

'We can't expose the rotteness and corruption of the ruling class. They'll close ranks, so we'll just have to do what we can, in a small way' said The Branch Secretary.

'And what might that be?' asked The Assistant.

The Branch Secretary looked at The Station Rep. 'What's your immediate aim?' he asked.

The Station Rep. thought for a moment. 'I'd like to get the shaggin' Ghost Squad working their bollocks off on platform six' he said.

'I don't really see those two dim sods as members of a Secret Society' said The Assistant.

'They don't have to be' said The Branch Secretary.

The Station Rep and The Assistant again looked puzzled. The Branch Secretary leaned intently towards them. 'How do you progress on The Post Office?' he asked.

'Bumsucking' said The Assistant and The Station Rep simultaneously. The Branch Secretary nodded agreement.

'Exactly. You don't do anything to upset anyone above you. Sycophancy is a religion. It's the management culture in a word' he said.

'So how does that help us?' asked The Assistant.

'Let's suppose someone has been protecting The Ghost Squad due to a misunderstanding. Someone entirely wrongly thinks they have powerful friends at court, only nobody knows who they are'.

'You mean it's not a conspiracy. It's a cockup?' said The Assistant.

'Exactly. It's all one almighty big cockup.' said The Branch Secretary.

'So what do we do?' asked The Assistant.

'We implement our media strategy' said The Branch Secretary.

'What you mean we somehow manage to find the bastards and strip 'em stark bollock naked?' said The Assistant with considerable relish.

'Nothing so crude' said The Branch Secretary.

'What then?' asked The Station Rep.

'We issue a press release' said The Branch Secretary.

'Had we better go to the bogs and turn on all the taps?' said The Assistant. The Branch Secretary nodded and went out. The others followed him.

Two nights later the gang were slogging away on the parcel train on platform six. Paddy drove up on the tractor. 'No sign of those two shaggin' eejets I see' he remarked.

'If they ever do turn up we won't recognise the useless sods' said Joe. The Station Rep. had a little smile playing around the corners of his mouth.

Joe was incensed. 'I don't see what there is to shaggin' laugh at' he said.

'You will' said The Rep.

The cheeky shaggers do what they shaggin' well like' said Paddy:

'They're taking the piss' said Joe.

'Phuck me! the age of phuckin' miracles isn't phuckin' past' said Paddy. He pointed to the steps. Joe stared in disbelief, The Ghost Squad were coming down the stairs. They looked absolutely furious.

'If I find out who's dropped us in the shaggin' shit he's a dead shagger' said Len. 'Dead shaggin' meat' added Arthur.

'You cheeky twats' said Paddy.

'Are you staying?' asked Joe.

'Don't you start taking the piss' said Len:

'Only if you're stopping for a bit you can start chucking some of these off' Joe told him. 'They're mail bags' he added helpfully.

The Ghost Squad started flinging bags off. They both looked absolutely murderous.

'Will you be here every night now like?' Joe wanted to know:

'It's shaggin' victimisation' fumed Arthur:

'What's the effin' Union going to do about it?' asked Len.

'About what?' said The Union Man.

'Some rotten bastard shopped us to The Sun' said Len:

'Why what have you done?' asked Paddy.

'They said someone sent an anonymous note saying the reason we weren't on the Station was because we were in The Masonic Hall with cucumbers up our arses' said Arthur.

'And is it true?' said Paddy.

'You can't work properly with a cucumber stuck up the arse' said Joe.

'We haven't got cucumbers up the arse' said Arthur.

'If you say so' said Joe.

'So why are you here exactly?' The Union Rep asked.

"Cos the rotten shaggin' Sun threatened to have an exposure, They said they'd pry into every murky corner, find out who the perverts were and expose them. They said they wouldn't hesitate to name names" said Arthur.

"And some sod at Region has told management to shite on us from a great height" said Len.

"If we put a foot wrong, we're shaggin' finished" Arthur added.

Joe rubbed his hands together. "Fucking brilliant" he cried.

"We'd better not find any discarded cucumbers round here" said The Union Rep.

"I can't believe this is happening" said Joe.

"Neither can we" said Len.

"Back to a full staff. Just where have you fuckers been for the past twenty years?" said Joe.

Rod Williams appeared at the foot of the stairs. The Player King hailed him.

"Good evening mister Station Master" he said.

"Good evening" said Rod.

"We are living through very strange times" said The Player King.

"Things look normal to me" said Rod.

"Depends entirely on your idea of normality" said The Player King. He then turned to the group.

"One thing is perfectly obvious" he told them.

"And what might that be?" asked Paddy.

"Someone high up in this organisation is indeed going round with a cucumber stuck up his arse. The question is will we ever find out who it is?' he said.

CHAPTER
SEVENTEEN

The Return to Normality

'I've called this meeting to ensure we all know what the priority is' said The Head Postmaster.

The Union Men who had been summoned en masse stared at him blankly. There was an awkward pause.

'And what might that be?' asked The Assistant Secretary.

'We must all work together' said The Head Postmaster.

'What for?' asked The Branch Secretary.

'To effect a resumption of normality' said The Head Postmaster after a quick glance at the letter he had received from Region.

'To do what?' asked The Truculent Man.

'Effect a resumption of normality' said The Head Postmaster, speaking now with a little more confidence.

'And just what might that be when its a home?' asked The Truculent Man.

'We must have good industrial relations' said The Head Postmaster.

'Tell that to your Supervisors' said The Branch Secretary.

'According to your Government' The Assistant started to say before The Head Postmaster cut him short.

'Don't refer to my government, I never voted for them' he said indignantly.

'Incredible how they keep getting back in when no-one votes for them' said The Branch Secretary.

'I haven't asked you all come here for a political discussion' said The Head Postmaster.

'Have I been asked here?' said The Assistant innocently.

'Yes of course' said The Head Postmaster.

'I was under the impression I had been ordered to attend. Summoned' said The Assistant.

'Certainly not' said The Head Postmaster with a tight smile.

'So we're all here on a voluntary basis. To take part in a bridge building exercise?' said The Educated Fucking Idiot.

'Exactly' said The Head Postmaster, falling into the pit.

'In that case I'll wish you good morning' said The Educated Fucking Idiot, getting up and heading for the door.

'Where are you going?' asked The Head Postmaster.

'Out' said The Educated Fucking Idiot and left.

'Where's he gone?' said The Head Postmaster.

'Out' said The Truculent Man.

'Tell him to come back' ordered The Head Postmaster.

'You've just told him attendance is voluntary' said The Assistant.

'We all heard you' said The Truculent Man.

'Voluntary means you don't have to do it' said The Assistant.

'I know what voluntary means' said The Head Postmaster testily.

'Well then' said The Truculent Man who was beginning to look very aggressive.

'Right you all listen to me' said The Head Postmaster. He was beginning to get somewhat rattled.

'Is it still voluntary?' asked The Truculent Man.

'No it bloody isn't' said The Head Postmaster.

'We've had detente. Now he's bringing in the tanks' said The Assistant.

'It's in all our interests to have good industrial relations' said The Head Postmaster.

'Then tell your Gaffers to stop shaggin' the shaggin' blokes about', said The Truculent Man.

'We're facing stiff competition' said The Head Postmaster.

'Why don't you tell your shaggin' Supervisors to shag the competitors about instead of the blokes?' asked The Truculent Man.

'It's not as simple as that', said The Head Postmaster.

'Oh yes it is' said The Truculent Man raising his voice.

'Oh no it isn't' said The Head Postmaster, thumping the table with his fist.

'I always said this office was nothing but a pantomime' said The Assistant.

'Any more of that sort of talk and I'll order you out of the Meeting' said The Head Postmaster glaring furiously.

'First I'm ordered in, then I'm ordered out and that's your idea of building bridges' said The Assistant getting up and heading to the door.

'Come back here' howled The Head Postmaster.

'Will you make your mind up. Are you ordering me in or ordering me out?' asked The Assistant.

'They're all the shaggin' same. Power mad. Ever since that bloody mad woman has been in charge the whole shaggin' country has been full of shaggin' little Hitlers', muttered The Truculent Man.

'What did you say?' asked The Head Postmaster.

'I was just thinking' said The Truculent Man. 'I suppose we're still allowed to' he added.

'You can think what you like but keep your thoughts to yourself' said The Head Postmaster.

'Are you running a dictatorship or a democracy?' asked The Branch Secretary.

'Democracy doesn't come into this' retorted The Head Postmaster.

'Can we have that in writing?' asked The Assistant.

'We have to move with the times' said The Head Postmaster.

'I thought you wanted to go back to where we were before' said The Truculent Man, genuinely puzzled.

'Effect a resumption of normality' said The Assistant helpfully.

'That means going back to where we were surely' said The Truculent Man.

'Well yes and no' said the Head Postmaster, glancing furtively at the briefing from Region.

'Perhaps we should withdraw while you sort yourself out a bit' suggested The Assistant.

'You need to clarify your position in your own mind' said The Branch Secretary.

'I know exactly where I stand' claimed The Head Postmaster.

'Well would you mind telling us?' said The Truculent Man.

'We must have good industrial relations' said The Head Postmaster.

'Like we had before?' said The Branch Secretary.

'Yes?' said The Head Postmaster.

'Like we had before what?' said The Truculent Man.

'Before all this trouble' said The Head Postmaster.

'You mean before people found out what was going on?' said The Assistant.

'Before we were misrepresented' said The Head Postmaster.

'Back to the bloody Dark Ages' said The Branch Secretary.

'You've got an attitude problem' said The Head Postmaster.

'And you gave it to me' The Branch Secretary replied.

'This is just a waste of bloody time' said The Truculent Man standing up.

'Sit down' said The Head Postmaster.

'What for?' said The Truculent Man.

'We have to issue a joint statement'.

'Who says?' demanded The Truculent Man.

'Region' howled The Head Postmaster.

'Now we're getting to it' said the Assistant.

'Who runs this place? You or Region?' asked The Branch Secretary.

'How can we issue a Joint Statement? We have nothing in common', said The Assistant.

'We have to overcome our differences for the good of the Office' said The Head Postmaster.

'You mean you want us to get Region off your back' snorted The Truculent Man.

'I must remind you all that you've signed The Official Secrets Act' said The Head Postmaster.

'Are you threatening us?' demanded The Truculent Man.

'I'm just pointing out that the consequences of revealing official secrets could be very severe' said The Head Postmaster.

'What's the definition of an official secret?' asked the Assistant.

'Anything that shows up the bosses' said the Truculent Man.

'From now on all statements to the press will be officially sanctioned.' said The Head Postmaster.

'Or anonymous' said the Assistant.

'So this is what it's all about' said The Truculent Man.

'It's all to do with The Sun and cucumbers up the arse' said The Branch Secretary.

'It's a matter of observing commercial confidentiality' said The Head Postmaster.

'What about the right to know?' asked The Assistant.

'We don't want the Sun poking about here' said The Head Postmaster.

'We've got nothing to hide' said The Truculent Man.

'Neither have I' protested The Head Postmaster.

'Well someone's going round with a cucumber up his arse' said The Assistant.

'That's just supposition' said The Head Postmaster.

'There's no smoke without fire' said The Branch Secretary.

'You sound like a bloody Hanging Judge' said The Head Postmaster.

'Hanging's too bloody good for them' said The Truculent Man.

'Whoever this bloke is he should make a clean breast of it and ask to see the Welfare Officer' said The Assistant.

'For all you know it is The bloody Welfare Officer' said The Truculent Man.

'I won't have you coming in here making wild accusations' said The Head Postmaster.

The Branch Secretary leaned forward and gazed steadily at The Head Postmaster. 'Let's get down to specifics' he said.

The Head Postmaster brightened visibly. It seemed the Meeting was going to actually get somewhere after all. The status quo would be happily restored.

The Branch Secretary continued 'Supposing I actually find out which one of your Managers is going round with a cucumber up his arse and sell the story to The Sun, will I be judged to have endangered the safety of the realm?' he asked.

'You'll be straight off to The Tower' said The Assistant.

'You will be in breach of the Official Secrets Act and liable to prosecution' The Head Postmaster told him.

'Are you an authority on the Official Secrets Act?' asked the Assistant.

'Supposing it was me and I flogged my own story to The Sun? What about that?' asked The Truculent Man.

'You'd be charged with bringing The Post Office into disrepute.' said The Head Postmaster.

'There's nothing in my terms of contract that says I can't shove a cucumber up my arse if I want to' said The Truculent Man.

'So long as you wear a tie' added The Assistant.

'That's not the sort of image we wish to present' said The Head Postmaster.

'I should bloody well think not' said The Truculent Man.

'But where would he stand under the provisions of The Official Secrets Act?' asked The Branch Secretary.

'They'd have to do him surely' said The Assistant.

'I'm not sure' said The Head Postmaster.

'Well you'd better bloody well find out. I want to know where I stand', said The Truculent Man.

'Perhaps we should adjourn until this point is cleared up' said The Branch Secretary.

'Look this is all hypothetical' protested The Head Postmaster.

'So's the future' said The Assistant.

'No it isn't' said The Head Postmaster.

'Of course it is. It's bound to be' said The Assistant.

'What do you say?' the Head Postmaster asked The Branch Secretary.

'I'll have to consult the Area Officer' said The Secretary.

'Thank Christ for that! We've settled something' said The Truculent Man getting up.

'We've settled nothing' said The Head Postmaster.

'Yes we have. You're going to consult Region, we're going to see what the Area Officer says' said The Truculent Man.

'About what?' asked The Head Postmaster.

The Truculent Man sighed. 'About whether the future's hypothetical' he explained.

'Region know shagall' said The Assistant.

'Neither does the Area Officer' countered The Head Postmaster.

'Agreed' said The Truculent Man.

'Like I said we can settle our own differences. Keep it all in the family' said The Head Postmaster.

'We have to work within an agreed framework' said The Branch Secretary.

'Of course we do' said The Head Postmaster, brightening visibly.

'We have for instance to know where a bloke stands if he shoves a cucumber up his arse and sells his story to The Sun,' said The Assistant.

'So long as it's his own cucumber what's it got to do with anyone else?' said The Truculent Man.

'I still say this is hypothetical' said The Head Postmaster. 'After all' he added, 'you're not actually proposing to shove a cucumber up your arse, so where's the problem?'

'It's a matter of principle' said The Branch Secretary.

The Head Postmaster made a gesture of exasperation. 'Let me see if I've got this right. You're saying that shoving a cucumber up your arse' is a matter of principle?' he stated.

The Branch Secretary shook his head. 'The cucumber is not the point at issue' he said.

'Then what is?' demanded The Head Postmaster.

'The official reaction when he sells his story to The Sun' said The Branch Secretary.

'This is all entirely beside the point' declared The Head Postmaster.

'Is it?' said The Truculent Man.

The Head Postmaster nodded.

'Then what is the point?' asked The Branch Secretary.

'If any' added The Assistant.

'We are The Royal Mail' said The Head Postmaster.

'Have you brought us here to tell us that?' asked The Branch Secretary.

'We do not shove cucumbers up our arses' said The Head Postmaster.

'Not unless we're Freemasons' said The Truculent Man.

'We deliver letters' said The Head Postmaster.

'We know that' said The Assistant.

'Anyone spreading malicious rumours about other members of the staff will be in serious trouble' said The Head Postmaster.

'So you're declaring war on The Shitehouse Poets?' said The Truculent Man.

'Is that the priority?' asked The Branch Secretary.

'They've been writing that I'm a wanker for years' said The Assistant.

'Just how do you propose to put a stop to this?' asked The Branch Secretary.

'We're going to photograph the evidence' said The Head Postmaster.

'You're going to take photos of the Shitehouse walls?' said The Truculent Man incredulously.

'And then we're going to photograph the signing on sheets' continued The Head Postmaster.

'What's the point of that?' asked The Assistant.

'We will then send all the copies to London where a graphologist will compare the handwriting and establish who is the culprit. We will then take the appropriate measures' concluded The Head Postmaster triumphantly.

'You're going to shove a cucumber up his arse' said The Truculent Man.

'It's a shaggin' windup isn't it?' said The Assistant.

'We regard this as a very serious matter. There are laws of libel you know' said The Head Postmaster primly.

'If we didn't have so many shaggin' Gaffers they'd have something better to do' said The Truculent Man.

'You can't make unsubstantiated allegations in this country' said The Head Postmaster.

'You tell that to the bleedin' Sun' retorted The Branch Secretary.

'So now it's all coming out. This is the priority. We have to know who writes I'm a Wanker on the Shitehouse Wall' said The Assistant.

'And when you find out it's the cucumber up the arse, and you'll do him for bringing The Post Office into disrepute' said the Truculent Man.

'Correct' confirmed The Head Postmaster.

'Yes but suppose it's me. Suppose I'm writing I'm a Wanker on the wall, what then?' asked The Assistant.

'That's ridiculous' said The Head Postmaster.

'You mean the rest of this crap is rational?' asked The Branch Secretary.

'All staff are entitled to protection under the terms of the Agreement signed by the Union and Management' countered The Head Postmaster.

'And all this amounts to a resumption of normality?' said The Branch Secretary.

'Certainly it does. Provided both sides approach the matter in a spirit of goodwill, bearing in mind that the good name of The Post Office is of the utmost importance to us all' said The Head Postmaster.

'No-one will fookin' believe this' said The Truculent Man.

'I don't believe it. And I'm shaggin' well here' said The Assistant.

'You either embrace the future gentlemen, or you get left behind' said The Head Postmaster.

CHAPTER
EIGHTEEN

Business As Usual

Normality did not return to the Station without difficulties. The staff were assembled in the room with The Dim Gaffer glaring at them. He glanced at his guide notes for the team talk. They did not inspire confidence. He decided to go straight onto the attack.

'Right we've all got work to do' he started. Joe got up.

'Where are you going?' demanded The Dim Manager.

'I've got work to do. I can't sit around here' said Joe.

'Sit down' ordered The Dim Manager furiously. He glared round at the men.

'What's up with you?' asked Paddy.

'There's nothing wrong with me' said The Dim Manager.

'That's a matter of opinion' said Joe.

'I don't want any questions until the end' said The Dim Manager.

'The end of what?' asked Joe.

'You're being deliberately awkward' said The Dim Manager.

'No I'm not. I just want to know where I stand' said Joe.

'In regard to what?' asked The Dim Manager.

'I don't know' said Joe.

'That's what we're waiting to find out' said Len.

Insolence from one of The Ghost Squad was more than The Dim Manager was prepared to put up with.

'If you know what's good for you you'll keep your mouth shut' he hissed.

'Is that a threat?' asked the second member of The Ghost Squad, Arthur.

'Yes it shaggin' well is' said The Manager.

'I hope you've made a note of that' said Len to The Union Man.

'He's been told to crap on us from a great height' complained Arthur.

'Complain to your Lodge. I'm only a Union Rep' said The Union Man.

'Tell us about the shaggin' cucumbers' demanded Paddy.

'I don't want to discuss cucumbers' said The Dim Manager.

'I bloody do. I still don't know where these shaggers went for twenty years' said Joe.

'We were bloody here' howled The Ghost Squad in unison.

'Being shat on from a great height is victimisation' asserted Len.

'They wouldn't do this if we were shaggin' black' said Arthur.

'The Post Office pursues an anti discriminatory policy' said The Dim Manager.

'That's true' said Paddy.

The Dim Manager looked at Paddy with gratitude for this unexpected support.

Unfortunately Paddy hadn't finished. 'They treat us all like shite' he concluded.

'It's time the shaggin' Union did something' said Len.

The Union Rep had been told that in no circumstances was he to get involved in any dispute involving the Freemasons. 'It is not Union policy to venture into the unknown' was the actual declaration and he was left to make what he could of it.

'It is not Union policy to venture into the unknown' he told the meeting.

Everyone looked somewhat bemused.

'Does that mean they're on their shaggin' own?' asked Joe.

'Yes' said The Union Rep.

'Shaggin' great' said Joe.

'What happened to shaggin' solidarity?' demanded Len.

'I've a good mind to resign from the shaggin' Union' said Arthur.

The Union Rep. had been advised that Headquarters regarded The Ghost Squad as a likely source of embarrassment at a time when they were trying to do all they could to improve their image and he was to do whatever he could to get rid of them.

'I'm sure The Lodge can do far more for you than the Union can' he said.

'We're not in any bloody Lodge' said Arthur.

'You wouldn't catch me with a cucumber up my arse' said Paddy!

'They haven't caught us with cucumbers up our arse' said Len.

'Oh so you admit it' said Joe eagerly.

'We admit shagall. 'We're being shat on from a great height for no reason. It's shaggin' victimisation' said Arthur.

'I reckon the Freemasons are shiteing on them from a great height as well' said the Longhaired Git.

'In that case why don't we all join?' said Joe.

'Is the cucumber optional?' asked The Union Rep.

'I'm seeing my solicitor about this shagger. It's nowt but fookin' character assassination' fumed Arthur.

The Dim Manager looked round from face to face. Then he looked round again.

'Where's George?' he asked.

'It's Happy Hour at the Institute' said Paddy. It was obviously considered that no further explanation was called for.

'He's not allowed to drink on duty' protested The Manager.

'Don't tell us. Shaggin' tell him' retorted Joe.

The Dim Manager glanced at The Union Rep. The Union Rep had been told in no uncertain terms that so far as Union Headquarters was concerned George too was regarded as a constant source of embarrassment.

He decided to use a well worn tactic that had served him well in the past.

'George has got problems' he said.

'Why don't they shite on him from a great height?' asked Lon bitterly.

'Because he hasn't got a cucumber up his arse' said Joe.

'We've rather strayed from the subject matter' said The Dim Manager.

'Perhaps you could tell us what the subject matter is' said The Long Haired Git.

The Dim Manager glanced at his notes.

'We've got to have a resumption of normality' he told them.

Everyone including The Dim Manager looked puzzled.

'That's what it says here' said The Dim Manager somewhat defensively.

'Does it say what it means?' asked Paddy.

'It just says I'm to take whatever steps are required to ensure a resumption of normality' explained The Dim Manager.

'What Shaggin' EEjet wrote that?' asked Paddy snorting in disgust.

'Someone at Region' said The Dim Manager.

'Is that all it says?' asked The Union Rep.

'It says it's in all our interests' said The Dim Manager.

'They always say that when they're going to shaft us' said The Long Haired Git.

'What's it mean?' asked Joe.

'It means what it says' said The Dim Manager.

'What do they consider normal?' asked The Long Haired Git.

Joe opened his mouth to speak but The Dim Manager cut him short. 'I don't want to hear any more about blokes wandering round with cucumbers up the arse' he told him.

'Normality's what's usually happening isn't it?' challenged The Long Haired Git.

The Dim Gaffer didn't have a clue what he meant but thought it best to agree. He nodded.

'Then if blokes were wandering round with cucumbers stuck up their arse before, then a resumption of normality means they've got to go back to doing it, doesn't it?' he urged.

'I don't think that's what Region are referring to' said The Dim Manager.

'Why can't the shaggin' eejets say what they mean then?' asked Paddy.

'I'm willing to do my bit' said Joe.

'Glad to hear it' said The Dim Manager.

'Roll 'em up lads' said Joe.

'That's the spirit. Roll up your sleeves and get stuck into the job' said The Dim Manager.

Joe bent down and rolled up his trouser leg.

'This is all I'm rolling up' he said.

'Yes come on lads. If you can't beat the eejets it's best to join 'em' said Paddy and rolled up his trouser leg.

Despite protests from The Dim Manager the rest of the men rolled up their trouser legs and Joe insisted on climbing up onto the table. The rest of the staff with their trouser legs hitched as high as possible were joining Joe on the table when Rod Williams came in.

'I suppose you guys think this is shaggin' funny' he began.

'Who gave you permission to attend our Lodge Meeting?' demanded Joe.

Rod was taken aback: 'Well' he began.

'Speaking as The Lodge Master I'm ordering you out' said Joe.

Seeing Rod apparently rooted to the spot Joe clarified his instruction: 'Shagoff' he told him.

Rod turned meekly and left the room.

'That's got rid of that thick shagger' crowed Paddy.

'What do we do now?' asked Joe.

'We have to have a ritual' said The Longhaired Git.

The Dim Gaffer consulted his briefing sheet. There was nothing there about rituals.

'We need some shaggin' chicken blood' said Paddy.

'You're thinking of Black Magic' said The Union Rep.

The Dim Manager decided it was time to put his foot down.

'This is not a return to normality' he protested.

'It is for some of us' said Joe looking meaningfully at The Ghost Squad.

While Paddy was insisting on the need for chicken blood Rod Williams was scurrying along the platform seeking the sanctuary of his office. The Leprauchan was waiting for him.

'What do you want?' asked Rod.

'Will I be locking up the toilets?' asked The Leprauchan.

'Use your initiative' Rod told him.

'Is that a yes?' asked The Leprauchan.

'Don't bother me with petty details, I'm the big decision man' Rod declared.

'Whenever I'm near you I sense the whiff of power' said The Leprauchan.

'Being The Top Man carries a heavy burden' said Rod.

'Fortunately you've got broad shoulders' said The Leprauchan.

'Those Goddam postmen' spluttered Rod.

'What have they done now?' asked The Leprauchan.

'I thought they were just a bunch of good for nothing no hope labourers' said Rod.

'What else are they?' asked The Leprauchan.

'They're Goddam Freemasons. That's what the bastards are' Rod told him.

'Freemasons! That bloody shower!' The Leprauchan was plainly incredulous.

'I can hardly believe it myself'. If I hadn't seen it with my own eyes' said Rod his voice tailing off.

'Seen what?' asked The Leprauchan.

'They're holding a Lodge Meeting in their room' Rod told him.

'Never!' said the Leprauchan.

'I tell you I saw it with my own eyes' said Rod.

'That's astonishing' said The Leprauchan.

'And do you know who The Master is?' asked Rod.

The Leprauchan shook his head.

'Bloody Joe' said Rod.

'You're pulling my leg' said The Leprauchan.

'I wish I was' said Rod.

'Are you sure Joe is the top man?' asked The Leprauchan.

'You could have knocked me down with a feather' said Rod.

'Oh yes?' said The Leprauchan.

'There he was right before my very eyes standing on the table with his trouser leg rolled up to the knees. He ordered me out of the meeting' said Rod.

'I hope you told him to shagoff' said The Leprauchan.

'How could I do that?' asked Rod.

'Well you are the shaggin' Station Manager after all and he's nothing but a shaggin' Mail Porter.

'You don't understand' said Rod.

'No I don't' agreed The Leprauchan.

'A Station Manager may be a big job' started Rod.

'There's no shaggin' maybe about it' said The Leprauchan.

'But compared to the Master of the Lodge it's just peanuts' Rod explained.

'I still think you should have told him to shagoff' said The Leprauchan.

'It would not have been proper. Besides' said Rod.

'Besides what?' asked The Leprauchan impatiently.

'I recognised the voice of authority. Joe has to be pretty big in The Movement' said Rod.

'How the shaggin' hell can he be big in anything? He's just a shaggin' postman' protested The Leprauchan.

'I must admit I'm puzzled' Rod confessed.

'It must be something to do with The Bloody Mad Woman of Downing Street' declared The Leprauchan.

'That is no way to speak about The Prime Minister' Rod admonished.

'Sure everyone knows she's absolutely barking' snorted The Leprauchan.

'Possibly. But we have put her in charge' said Rod.

'So what does that make us?' The Leprauchan wanted to know.

'You tell me' said Rod.

'Victims of our own inadequacy' said The Leprauchan.

'You speak for yourself' said Rod.

'What action are you going to take?' asked The Leprauchan.

'In relation to what?' asked Rod.

'We're a profit centre aren't we?' said The Leprauchan.

'We're supposed to be' said Rod.

'Well then' said The Leprauchan.

Rod looked more than usually blank.

'If the bloody Freemasons are using The Station as a bloody Lodge surely they should be paying bloody rent' said The Leprauchan.

'You're right' said Rod.

'That's if they are Freemasons of course' said The Leprauchan.

'Of course they're Freemasons. What else could they be?' asked Rod.

'How many of them are there?' asked The Leprauchan.

'About twelve I guess' said Rod.

'That's what I thought. They could be a Coven' said The Leprauchan.

'You mean they're Goddamed witches?' gasped Rod.

'Anything's possible' asserted The Leprauchan.

'But they're blokes' protested Rod.

'So they're male witches' said The Leprauchan.

Rod was now completely out of his depth. 'Should I inform Region?' he asked.

The Leprauchan shook his head. 'If you tell Region the Royal Mail are running a Coven on the Station they might get the wrong impression' he said.

'You mean they'll think I'm nuts?' said Rod.

'The Leprauchan nodded.

'But Region don't know those bastards' Rod pointed out.

'There's only one thing to do' said The Leprauchan.

'What might that be?' asked Rod eagerly.

'Keep the situation under review' said The Leprauchan.

Rod looked round frantically. 'What about George?' he asked.

'What about George?' returned The Leprauchan.

'How am I supposed to tell my superiors I'm dealing with a pissed up male witch?' said Rod.

'The best thing to do with George is ignore him' said The Leprauchan.

Rod glanced up at the television. What he saw infuriated him. George was standing in front of the camera, grinning from ear to ear, and pointing down to his trouser leg which was rolled up to the knee.

'Look at that' shrieked Rod.

'I see it' said The Leprauchan.

'It's bloody George again. The Pissed Up Male Witch' said Rod.

'Ignore him. He's trying to attract your attention' said The Leprauchan.

'All the bastards are laughing at me. The Royal Mail think I'm just a shaggin' joke' complained Rod.

'You'll have to show the bastards different' said The Leprauchan.

'Yes but how?' wailed Rod.

'You must kill two birds with one stone. Shaft The Coven, The Lodge or whatever they are and show Region your mettle at the same time' urged The Leprauchan.

'Sounds great but how am I going to do that?' asked Rod.

'Take a Commercial Initiative' The Leprauchan told him.

'A commercial initiative' echoed Rod. He liked the sound of that. It suggested a hint of major league stuff.

'You get down to that room and you tell 'em' said The Leprauchan. Rod stood up, put his hat back on, straightened his tie and squared his shoulders.

'I'll tell the bastards' he said, and headed for the door. He then stopped and asked: 'Tell 'em what exactly?'.

'You grab hold of their Gaffer, tell him he can't shaft about with British Rail and you want the effin' rent' said The Leprauchan.

Rod looked a little doubtful. The Leprauchan decided he had to press home the point.

'Think in terms of extra revenue. That's the name of the game now' he said.

Rod nodded. 'You're right' he agreed.

'This could be the moment when the financial fortunes of British Rail were turned around for ever. And you could be enshrined as the man responsible. You could end up on the Board' said The Leprauchan.

'Me? On the Board?' said Rod.

'Think of the potential. These shaggin' postmen are probably running Lodges and Covens on every shaggin' Station in the country. And none of the shaggers are paying a penny' said The Leprauchan.

'It's a bloody scandal' said Rod. He marched through the door. The Leprauchan went and sat in the managerial chair.

'It feels good' he said contentedly. 'Somehow I don't think it'll be too long before my name is up on the door' he told himself. Then he stood up. 'I'm off duty in ten minutes. There's just time to lock up every pisshouse on the Station' he said and walked onto the platform with a sense of being part of a great and worthwhile enterprise.

CHAPTER
NINETEEN

The Return of the Media

The Head Postmaster was furious. The object of his wrath sat opposite him, shifting uncomfortably in his chair, heartily wishing himself elsewhere. He longed for the sanctuary of his office back at the Station. He was baffled. It was perfectly obvious he was right in the shit, but he had no idea why. The Head Postmaster was in such a state he was getting his words out with difficulty and his colour suggested that he might require the kiss of life at any moment. He kept waving a piece of paper up and down in front of The Dim Manager's face.

'Look at this shagger' The Head Postmaster screeched, quite beside himself. The Dim Gaffer attempted to do so, then recoiled in the face of a further furious attack.

'What the shaggin' hell is going on down there?' demanded The Head Postmaster.

The Dim Manager clutched at a straw. 'We've effected a return to normality' he said hopefully. He thought The Head Postmaster was going to strike him and got up hastily.

'Is running a Coven your idea of normality?' bawled The Head Postmaster.

The Dim Manager felt on safe ground here so he shook his head emphatically. He was still puzzled but thought there was a chance he might grasp what the trouble was and be able to put up some sort of a defence. There was just a faint glimmer of light. The Head Postmaster's next howl of anguish and fury snuffed out the light entirely. He was back in stygian blackness.

'Twelve bloody male witches and one of them a complete pisshead into the bargain' bellowed The Head Postmaster.

The Dim Manager began to feel even more uneasy. He shifted his position so that he would be able to make a run for it if it turned out that The Head Postmaster had become a Mad Axeman and came at him.

'What's the bloody explanation? What am I supposed to tell Region? Call yourself a bloody Manager?' howled The Head Postmaster.

The Dim Manager was by now in a state of sheer funk. He was beginning to think he was confronted by a raving lunatic. And the lunatic was in charge.

'It's a shaggin' nightmare' he muttered to himself.

'What did you say?' asked The Head Postmaster.

'I said it was a shaggin' nightmare' said The Dim Manager.

'No such luck' said The Head Postmaster. 'Your nuts are in the vice' he added.

The Dim Manager winced. The suspense was unbearable. He had to know just how bad the situation was. 'What's the problem sir?' he asked with a sickly attempt at an ingratiating smile. The reply was indeed the stuff of nightmare, but he realised there would be no waking up bathed in sweat and heaving sighs of relief. It was real.

'I've had a letter from shaggin' Region' said The Head Postmaster. These were the words all Dim Managers dreaded most.

'Who is this bloody Rod Williams?' asked The Head Postmaster.

The Dim Manager drew some solace from the fact that it seemed Rod Williams was in the shit with him. 'He's The Station Manager' he replied.

'Is he normal?' asked The Head Postmaster.

The Dim Manager began to think he had a bit of an inkling. This was all somehow connected with cucumbers up the arse. 'Hard to say. He's a bit of a loner' he said, deciding at this stage it would be best not to commit himself one way or the other.

The Head Postmaster took a tablet, breathed deeply for a while watched anxiously by The Dim Manager, then changed tack.

'Is there anything you want to tell me?' he asked.

The Dim Manager tried to think of something.

'Is there anything you'd like me to tell you?' he asked.

The Head Postmaster gazed keenly at him. The Dim Manager felt very uncomfortable.

'You say you've effected a resumption of normality?' said The Head Postmaster.

'Yes' said The Dim Manager, gallantly lying through his teeth.

The Head Postmaster nodded. The Dim Manager felt a little better.

'But of course one man's normality is another's perversion' said The Head Postmaster.

The Dim Manager had no idea what he was referring to but he didn't like the sound of this at all. He didn't want to admit he hadn't a clue what The Head Postmaster was talking about so decided to agree.

'It's in your interests to be perfectly frank' said The Head Postmaster. The Dim Manager spotted a trap. He didn't know a lot, but he knew only a bloody fool was completely frank.

'Honesty is the best policy' he said piously.

The Head Postmaster wondered if he really was a complete cretin or was acting a part. He took up the letter from Region again. The Dim Manager quailed.

'I'm sure there is a rational explanation' said The Head Postmaster.

He waited for The Dim Manager to give it to him. The Dim Manager sat glum and silent. The Head Postmaster decided to give him a little encouragement.

'This bloke Rod Williams wants stuffing' he said. The Dim Manager looked happier. He could agree with that.

'With a porcupine' he said.

'He's trying to shagup my budget' said The Head Postmaster.

The Dim Manager felt confident enough to ask a question.

'How can he do that?' he said.

'He's contacted his superiors and told them we're running additional businesses on the Station. They're after more rent' he said.

'That's a load of bollocks' said The Dim Manager indignantly.

'That was my first thought' said The Head Postmaster.

'What are we supposed to be doing?' asked The Dim Manager.

'Running a Lodge of Freemasons and a Coven of Witches' The Head Postmaster told him.

The Dim Manager was genuinely indignant.

'That's shaggin' ridiculous' he said.

The Head Postmaster looked absolutely delighted. He'd feared the worst, but now it looked as though his apprehensions were not justified.

'Lodge of Freemasons, Coven of Witches! They're not businesses' said The Dim Manager.

Doubt again disturbed The Head Postmaster. He now feared the worst.

'British Rail are threatening to send down a team of investigators' he said.

'Tell 'em to find out who keeps closing the pisshouses' said The Dim Manager.

The Head Postmaster did not think this a very helpful suggestion. He decided to appeal to The Dim Manager's better nature.

'If you have been dabbling in the Black Arts it might be a good idea to see The Welfare Officer' he said.

'I'm not dabbling in the Black Arts' protested The Dim Manager, who was again becoming alarmed lest he was closeted with a lunatic.

'It's easy to get drawn into these things. There was a programme on the television the other night. A man started for a bit of fun reading the tea leaves and ended up committing all kinds of bestiality' said The Head Postmaster.

'Am I being accused of shaggin' chickens?' said The Dim Manager.

'It has been suggested that on Wednesday night you were conducting a Satanic Ritual' The Head Postmaster told him.

'I was giving a bloody team talk. Same as I was told to' protested The Dim Manager.

'So this Rod Williams has got hold of the wrong end of the stick?' said The Head Postmaster.

'I'll sue the Shagger for all he's got' said The Dim Manager.

'Region wouldn't like that' said The Head Postmaster.

'What's it got to do with them?' asked The Dim Manager.

'They're not very pleased with us. I'm getting a lot of pressure' complained The Head Postmaster.

'I thought we were supposed to be the top office' retorted The Dim Manager.

'Performance wise we are' conceded The Head Postmaster.

'That's what matters isn't it?' said The Dim Manager.

'Not any more it isn't. It's the image that matters now. And they say ours is crap' said The Head Postmaster.

'All these bloody postmen popping their clogs doesn't help' said The Dim Gaffer.

'We were allright until the bloody media started poking their noses in and making things up' complained The Head Postmaster.

'Making things up?' queried The Dim Manager, dimly detecting some rewriting of history.

'Sheer fabrications?' asserted The Head Postmaster.

'What like bloody death certificates?' said The Dim Manager.

'My conscience is clear' said The Head Postmaster.

'I'm glad to hear it' said The Dim Manager.

'The Post Office is a caring employer' said The Head Postmaster.

'They call this place the Bloody Abbatoir' in town', The Dim Manager told him.

The Head Postmaster decided it was time to change the subject.

'So I can rest assured you're not running a Lodge of the Freemasons on the Station?' he said.

'Certainly not' said The Dim Manager.

'And you're not a Member of a Coven of Male Witches?' asked The Head Postmaster.

'Someone at Region has been watching too many horror movies' said The Dim Manager.

'So I can tell Region it's all nonsense and we won't be getting more attention from the tabloids' said The Headpostmaster.

'We don't want bloody Region poking about' said The Dim Manager.

'We can manage perfectly well without them' said The Head Postmaster.

'And we don't want the shaggin' Sun poking their noses in again either' said The Dim Manager.

'Don't forget the Official Secrets Act' The Head Postmaster said.

'I don't know any secrets' protested The Dim Manager.

'Commercial confidentiality is all the rage at Region' The Head Postmaster told him.

'So what does that cover?' asked The Dim Manager.

'Everything' said The Head Postmaster.

'Yes but who's affected?' asked The Dim Manager.

'You are' The Head Postmaster told him.

'Why pick on me?' asked The Dim Manager.

'It's not just you' said The Head Postmaster.

'Who else?' asked The Dim Manager.

'Everyone' said The Head Postmaster.

'Even The Shitehouse Cleaner?' asked the Dim Manager, not really believing what he was hearing.

'Especially The Shitehouse Cleaner' said The Head Postmaster.

'What does the shaggin' Shitehouse cleaner know?' asked The Dim Manager.

'The Shitehouse Cleaner is probably the best informed man in the Office' stated The Head Postmaster.

'So has he been sworn to silence?' asked The Dim Manager.

'He knows exactly where he stands. There'll be no trouble from him' said The Head Postmaster.

'What do you get if you get done under the Official Secrets Act?' asked The Dim Manager.

'Big trouble' said The Head Postmaster.

'Yes but what do you get' persisted The Dim Manager.

The Head Postmaster shrugged.

'Is it a set penalty? Like for pulling the communication cord?' asked The Dim Manager.

'It's entirely at the discretion of the authorities' said The Head Postmaster.

The Dim Manager looked appalled.

'So they can lock you up and throw away the key' he said.

'If it's considered to be in the national interest' said The Head Postmaster.

'Who decides that?' asked The Dim Manager.

'This may all seem barmy to you, but you must realise that there are some very clever people running this country' The Head Postmaster told him.

'You could have shaggin' fooled me' said The Dim Manager who was beginning to think that his first impression had been correct and The Head Postmaster needed a long rest.

'It's not how things seem to us. It's how things seem to them' said The Head Postmaster. 'So be warned' he added.

'Don't you worry about me. I'll keep my nose clean' said The Dim Manager.

'And tell that shower down the Station to keep their big gobs shut as well' said The Head Postmaster.

'I don't want to upset 'em. They may turn nasty and turn me into a shaggin' frog' said The Dim Manager.

'Don't forget. Make sure they know just where they stand! Commercial Confidentiality' said The Head Postmaster.

'And it's up to those brilliant shaggers running the country to decide what is a breach of the Official Secrets Act' said The Dim Manager.

'Exactly' said The Head Postmaster, delighted that his minion had apparently grasped the point.

'I'd best go and fill 'em all in' said The Dim Manager.

The Head Postmaster waved him away. The Dim Manager left the room. Once outside the shook his head in sheer disbelief.

'Phuckin'ell' he breathed and headed back to the Station.

As he walked onto Platform One the first person he saw was George. George was reading the racing page. A Would Be Traveller approached him.

'Excuse me postman' he said.

George looked up.

'Yes?' he enquired.

'Which platform does the London train go from?' asked The Would Be Traveller.

George opened his mouth to tell him when The Dim Manager stepped firmly between them and cut him short.

'Tell him shagall' he instructed.

The Would Be Traveller looked flabbergasted.

'What's going on here?' he asked.

'I am this man's Superior Officer' The Dim Manager told him.

'Well yes I dare say you are' said The Would Be Traveller.

'And I am giving this man a direct order' said The Dim Manager.

'To do what?' asked George.

'Nothing' said The Dim Manager.

'I'm doing that already. I've been doing it for twenty minutes. The train's late' said George.

'You carry on doing the shagger' The Dim Manager told him.

'And that's a direct order?' said George.

'It is' confirmed The Dim Manager.

'What is this crap?' asked The Would Be Traveller.

'It might seem like crap to you, it might seem like crap to me, and it certainly seems like crap to George, but it could look very different to certain people' said The Dim Manager.

'Is this Tosspot really your Superior Officer?' The Would Be Traveller' asked George.

George opened his mouth speak and then decided to enter into the spirit of things. He glanced at The Dim Manager for instructions.

'Tell him shagall' instructed The Dim Manager.

'But you've already told him' protested George.

'Yes and I could have dropped myself right in the shit' said The Dim Manager.

The Would Be Traveller decided to pretend he was enjoying the joke.

'Now come on mate, where does the London train go from?' he asked.

The Dim Manager fixed him with an accusing gaze.

'You just don't seem to realise what you're asking us to do' he said.

'Yes I do. I'm asking you to tell me where I can get the London Train' said The Would Be Traveller.

'It's not as simple as that' said The Dim Manager.

'Yes it is' said The Would Be Traveller.

'It might look simple from where you're standing, but the fact is you could be asking us to stick our heads in a noose' said The Dim Manager.

George and The Would Be Traveller looked equally puzzled.

'It could be a question of commercial confidentiality' explained The Dim Manager.

George and The Would Be Traveller stood with their mouths agape.

'George and I have signed the Official Secrets Act' said The Dim Manager.

'Isn't that right George?' he said turning to George.

'I'm saying shagall' said George. 'As per your direct order' he added.

'There are some very clever shaggers running this country' said The Dim Manager to The Would Be Traveller as though this somehow explained all.

'There are some right shaggin' idiots running this country' snorted The Would Be Traveller.

The Dim Manager nodded affably. 'You could be right' he conceded.

Before The Would Be Traveller could follow up his advantage The Dim Manager cut him short.

'But it makes no difference. Whether they're brilliant or complete bloody idiots makes no difference. They run things. They've got the power to decide to lock us up and throw away the key if we speak out of turn' he declared.

At this point Rod Williams arrived on the scene.

'Are you in charge of this Station?' asked The Would Be Traveller.

'I certainly am' said Rod Williams.

'Then perhaps you could tell me where I get the London train?' asked The Would Be Traveller hopefully.

'Are you intending to travel sir?' asked Rod.

'Tell him shagall' said George.

'It's like a shaggin' Bedlam here' complained The Would Be Traveller.

'I know that' said Rod.

'Then why the shaggin' hell don't you shaggin' well do something about it?' demanded The Would Be Traveller beginning to lose control.

'Steps are being taken' said Rod portentously.

'I'm glad to hear it' said The Would Be Traveller.

'We aim to serve' said Rod.

'What do you want me to do?' George asked The Dim Manager.

'Carry on' said The Dim Manager.

The Leprauchan hurried up. 'Will I be after closing the pisshouses before I go off duty sir?' he asked. He was currently studying the works of Sean O'Casey at his evening classes.

'The pisshouses should have been closed two hours ago' said Rod Williams.

'Why don't you brick 'em up?' asked George.

'If there is much more vandalism we might just do that' said Rod Williams.

'Can you tell me where I get the London train?' asked The Would Be Traveller.

Rod was about to tell him when The Dim Manager spotted The Ghost Squad on the opposite platform.

'Hey you two' he bellowed.

'You mean us?' asked Len.

The Dim Manager pointed to his mouth. 'I've got a direct order for you two' he said.

'We're being shat on from a great height' complained Arthur.

'Never mind about that shagger. Keep it shut' he instructed, again pointing to his mouth.

'I'm writing to my shaggin' MP' said Len.

'What for?' asked The Dim Manager.

'To ask him how he'd like being shat on from a great height' said Len.

'He probably is' said The Dim Manager.

'Now then sir the London train' said Rod.

'At last' breathed The Would Be Traveller.

'My latest information is' Rod began before The Dim Manager rounded on him.

'I'll be writing to my shaggin' MP and my shaggin' Solicitor' he told Rod.

'It's a free country' said Rod complacently.

'Is that what you think?' asked The Dim Manager.

Rod nodded.

'Well you'll soon find out shaggin' different' said The Dim Manager.

'This is a free democratic state. Mrs. Thatcher has set the people free' declared Rod.

'Who says so?' demanded The Would Be Traveller.

'She does' Rod told him.

'All the shaggin' time' said George.

'Have you signed The Official Secrets Act?' asked The Dim Manager.

'Of course I have. All railway employees sign The Official Secrets Act' said Rod.

'And what about commercial confidentiality?' asked The Dim Manager.

'What about it?' countered Rod.

'Do you know what it means?' asked The Dim Gaffer.

'There's nothing you can tell me about commercial confidentiality' said Rod.

'You wait till you upset the clever shaggers running this country' said The Dim Manager.

'Then you'll get shat on from a great height' said The Ghost Squad simultaneously.

'I told you shaggers to keep it shaggin' buttoned' said The Dim Manager.

'What do you mean shat on from a great height?' asked Rod, sounding just a little anxious now.

'Would one of you loons please tell me where I can get the London train?' asked The Would Be Traveller, not sounding at all hopeful.

'All it needs is a little careless talk and they'll lock you up and throw away the key' said The Dim Manager.

'Who said that?' asked Rod Williams.

'My Boss' said The Dim Manager.

'Who told him?' asked Rod Black.

'Region' said The Dim Manager triumphantly.

Rod turned pale.

'The London train … .anybody?' asked The Would Be Traveller.

The Leprauchan passed by on his way home. 'Sure sor and you'd be wanting Platform … ' he said until Rod Williams cut him short.

'Keep your mouth shut. Unless you want to be shat on from a great height' said Rod.

'Shat on from a great height is it? Sure that's shagall to me. Haven't I been shat on from a great height all me shaggin' life?' said The Leprauchan.

'At last! exclaimed The Would Be Traveller.

'Where would I get the London train?' he asked The Leprauchan.

'Platform six sir' said The Leprauchan.

'Thank you. Thank you very much. You're sure it's platform six?' asked The Would Be Traveller.

'Oh sure I'm sure sor. Sure you can see the shagger just going round the corner. It'll be in London in no time at all, but it looks as though you won't be on it', he concluded and left them.

'The Would Be Traveller turned to face them all.

'You bunch of shaggin' idiots' he said gazing at each in turn.

'Nothing we could do bud. Our hands are tied' said Rod.

'I will personally see to it that every one of you imbeciles is on the front page of every shaggin' crappy tabloid in the country' hissed The Would Be Traveller.

'We don't want to be in the papers' said The Dim Manager looking very worried. Then he brightened up.

'Still anything's better than being in a cell when those clever shaggers have thrown away the key' he said.

'We're already being shat on from a great height' said Len.

'And I'm in the clear. I'm following a direct order' said George happily.

'Commercial Confidentiality is no joking matter' said Rod.

The Player King entered. 'Tis true indeed. We can't be expected to have any brains. We are but hewers of wood and drawers of water. We do but follow the instructions of the Clever Shaggers' he said in his usual ringing tones.

'I think we're all in the clear. We've followed orders. We'll hear no more about this shagger' said The Dim Manager.

'I wouldn't bet on that' said George.

Suddenly The Dim Manager seized Rod Williams by the lapels. Rod was understandably alarmed.

'This is assault' he gasped.

'What's all this crap about me running a Freemasons' Lodge in the room?' demanded The Dim Manager.

'I was only doing my job' protested Rod.

'What telling lies about me?' asked The Dim Manager.

'All I did was report what I saw with my own eyes' Rod Williams told him.

'And what about this crap about us being a Coven of Male Witches?' asked The Dim Manager.

The Would Be Traveller pricked up his ears.

'I definitely saw a Masonic Ritual taking place in the premises you rent from the Railway' said Rod Williams.

'Masonic Ritual my shaggin' arse' said The Dim Manager.

'My shaggin' arse' said George.

'You taking the piss?' demanded The Dim Manager.

'No. I'm giving you support' said George.

'Are you telling me I didn't see Joe standing on the table with his trouser leg rolled up?' asked Rod.

'Don't forget the cucumber up his arse' Arthur reminded him.

'It's him who should be being shat on from a very great height, not us' said Len in an aggrieved tone.

'You keep out of this' said The Dim Manager.

The Ghost Squad muttered to each other and retreated to the edge of the platform where they stood looking resentful.

A thought suddenly struck Rod Williams. He grabbed hold of The Dim Manager.

'And while we're on the subject' he started.

'Are you just going to stand there?' The Dim Manager asked George.

'I'm acting under a direct order' said George.

'To do what?' said The Dim Manager.

'To do shagall' said George.

'That direct order no longer applies' said The Dim Manager, as Rod tightened his grip on his collar.

George shook his head. 'You can't cancel a direct order just like that' he said.

'Why not?' asked The Dim Manager.

'You have to follow procedure' George told him.

'He's bloody well choking me' protested The Dim Manager, as Rod Williams, the recollection of countless humiliations inflicted on him by The Post Office flooding back into his memory, shifted his grip to The Dim Manager's throat and began to increase the pressure on his windpipe.

'I'm sorry about that but my hands are tied. I can do nothing until the order is properly rescinded. And that means in writing' said George.

'That's shaggin' crap' The Dim Manager began to gasp, until he looked into Rod's infuriated eyes and realised he had every intention of choking him to death.

'Has anyone got a shaggin' pen?' he asked. He was handed a pen. He managed to get to a notice stuck on the wall with Rod grimly clinging to him and began to write.

'How many esses in rescinded?' he asked.

Rod Williams flung him away in disgust. 'You illiterate 'ass'ole' he hissed. The Dim Manager stood there gulping.

'You'll regret this' he told Rod.

'There's nothing you can do to me. I'm not afraid of witchcraft. I don't believe in that crap' said Rod.

'I am not a bloody Witch' said The Dim Manager.

'Oh yes you are. You'll be an incompetent Witch but you're a witch. You're all goddamed Witches' howled Rod.

The Dim Manager grasped Rod by the lapels. The Would Be Traveller took out a small camera and begin to shoot pictures.

Rod and The Dim Manager turned on him.

'You can't take pictures here' they said together.

'Who says so?' demanded The Would Be Traveller.

'British Rail Bye Laws say so' said Rod Williams.

'It's a matter of Commercial Confidentiality' added The Dim Manager.

'When two friggin' idiots of so called managers attempt to throttle each other on platform one of Derby Station they'll say it's a question of the Public Interest' said The Would Be Traveller.

'Commercial Confidentiality overrides the Public Interest every time' said Rod.

'Now that alas is very true' said The Player King.

'Have you signed The Official Secrets Act?' asked The Dim Manager.

'No' said The Would Be Traveller.

'Why not?' asked The Dim Manager.

'Because I'm not bloody stupid' The Would Be Traveller told him.

The Dim Manager looked at The Player King for guidance. The Player King shrugged.

The Would Be Traveller looked at Rod Williams.

'You say he's running a Freemasons Lodge on the Station and you want rent?' he asked.

'Say shagall' advised George.

'You can hardly deny it' said The Would Be Traveller.

Rod nodded miserably.

'And in your opinion he's also a Male Witch running a Coven here on the Station?' continued The Would Be Traveller.

'It's a load of bollocks' protested The Dim Manager.

The Would Be Traveller held up his hand.

'My Editor would like to know about the cucumbers up the arse' he said.

Rod and the Dim Manager turned pale.

The Ghost Squad brightened up and joined the group.

'Once they get their teeth into something they never let go' said Arthur.

'You'll never hear the last of those shaggin' cucumbers' added Len with a kind of gloomy satisfaction.

The Dim Manager felt like thumping them both, but realised it was not adviseable to do so with the camera at the ready.

'Cucumbers up the arse will be engraved on your headstone' said Len.

'There'll be a bloody row if it is' fumed The Dim Manager.

'What can you tell me about cucumbers up the arse?' The Would Be Traveller asked Len.

'He can tell you shagall' said The Dim Manager.

'What have you got to hide?' continued The Would Be Traveller.

'Have you got any ID?' asked Rod Williams.

'We've had a resumption of normality here. Write that shagger down' said The Dim Manager.

'You've resumed normality?' said The Would Be Traveller.

'We were instructed to. Right?' said The Dim Manager.

The rest nodded.

'So if you've resumed normality under orders things weren't normal before?' said The Would Be Traveller.

'You could say that' conceded The Dim Manager.

'You mentioned Witches' said The Would Be Traveller to Rod Williams.

Rod looked uneasy. He somehow didn't think Region were going to care much for this.

George sidled up to The Would Be Traveller. 'I've had a bad run on the machine. How are you fixed?' he asked him.

'I can lend you a fiver' said The Would Be Traveller. George looked delighted. 'You can't touch that money' said The Dim Manager.

'Why not?' asked George.

'It's tainted' said The Dim Manager.

'Does that mean they won't accept it at Sainsbury's?' said George.

The Dim Manager shook his head. George took the fiver and put it in his pocket.

'I'll just nip over the road' said George.

'You stop where you shaggin well are' said The Dim Manager.

'Is that a direct order?' asked George.

The Dim Manager nodded. 'It shaggin' well is' he said.

'You've got no idea how to handle men' George told him.

The Would Be Traveller went round handing out his card.

'I'll be staying at The Midland Hotel. If anyone wants to tell me anything there could be something in it for them' he said.

'If you'd told him what time the shaggin' London train went none of this would have happened' said George.

'Why don't you shagoff?' asked The Dim Manager.

'Is that a direct order?' asked George.

'Yes' said The Dim Manager.

'See you then' said George and disappeared round the corner.

Rod Williams looked round the depleted group.

'It's a good thing none of this will get into the papers' he said trying to look cheerful.

'How do you make that out?' asked The Dim Manager who was wondering whether he should stage a nervous breakdown there and then.

'None of this ever happened. It's all covered by Commercial Confidentiality and The Official Secrets Act' said Rod and stalked off to the Executive Toilet.

'Where did they find him?' asked Len.

'Montreal I think' said The Dim Manager.

'Haven't we got enough of our own wankers?' asked Arthur.

'You would have thought so' said The Dim Manager.

A gleam of intelligence suddenly lightened Len's face.

'Supposing we were all Male Witches? How much do you think they'd pay us?' he asked.

The Dim Manager thought for a moment. 'I don't know. But if it comes to that they can stick Commercial Confidentiality and The Official Secrets Act right up their arse' he said as the parcel train finally hove into sight.

CHAPTER
TWENTY

In the Same Boat

'I am being shat on from a great height'. The Head Postmaster having made his statement sat back and waited for a reaction. The Union Men stared at him blankly. After a while The Assistant responded: 'Welcome to the Club' he said, and got up preparing to leave.

'Sit down' said The Head Postmaster.

'Why is there more?' asked The Assistant.

'What line is The Union taking?' asked The Head Postmaster.

The Union Men stared at him in baffled silence. The Head Postmaster snorted indignantly. 'Surely you have an official position' he said.

The Branch Secretary spoke. 'It's a matter of making the best of things' he said.

The Head Postmaster waited for him to finish, then realised he had.

'Is that the best you can offer?' he asked.

'If you're being shat on from a great height there's not really a great deal we can do about it' The Branch Secretary told him.

'I want it to stop' said The Head Postmaster.

'I dare say you do' said The Assistant.

'It's high time we all got up off our knees' said The Branch Secretary.

'That's the sort of talk I was hoping to hear from you' said The Head Postmaster.

'Since when?' asked The Assistant.

The Head Postmaster ignored him and looked at The Branch Secretary.

'As I see it we're all in the same boat' began The Branch Secretary.

'All in the shite together' interrupted The Assistant.

'Exactly' concurred The Head Postmaster.

'All in the shite together, so we have a choice' said The Branch Secretary.

'What might that be?' asked The Assistant Secretary.

'We either let 'em pour more buckets of shite on us or we fight back" said The Secretary.

'Let's hit back' said The Assistant thumping the desk.

'Show the bastards what we're made of' said The Head Postmaster thumping his desk as hard as he could. Alarmed by the noise his Secretary nervously poked her head round the corner.

'What is it Miss Watson?' he asked.

'Are you allright?' asked Miss Watson.

'No I am not allright. I am being shat on from a great height' said The Head Postmaster.

'We're all being shat on from a great height. It's the way things are now. We just have to put up with it' said Miss Watson and closed the door.

'She's going to be a great help when they send in the troops' said The Assistant.

'Do you think it will come to that?' asked The Head Postmaster nervously.

'Bound to' said The Assistant. The Head Postmaster looked at The Branch Secretary seeking reassurance. None was forthcoming.

'They'll try to crush us.' said The Branch Secretary.

'By what means?' asked The Head Postmaster.

'Any means they think necessary' said The Assistant.

'Such as?' asked The Head Postmaster.

'Mounted police, troops, tanks' said The Branch Secretary.

'Surely not' said The Head Postmaster turning pale.

'Remember the Miners' urged The Assistant.

'But we're not the Miners. We're the Post Office. Postman Pat. We're cuddly. We're docile. No-one could turn us into hate figures to be squashed underfoot' protested The Head Postmaster.

'So were the Miners until they stood up for themselves, it was all how green way my valley' said the Branch Secretary.

'This is not Russia' said The Head Postmaster.

'No. Things are getting better there' said The Assistant.

'They're dismantling the apparatus of state tyranny there' said The Branch Secretary.

'And putting it into place here' said The Assistant.

'Surely it's not that bad' said The Head Postmaster.

'You come out of your Ivory Tower, you'll see how bad it is' said The Branch Secretary.

'Are you man enough to be clubbed down on the Picket Line?' asked The Assistant.

The Head Postmaster flinched. 'Surely it won't come to that?' he said.

'If you decide to take on the might of the State you have to take the consequences' said The Branch Secretary with a kind of grim satisfaction.

'But our stand is going to be non violent isn't it?' asked The Head Postmaster.

'We're going to be non violent. What the police are is another matter' said The Branch Secretary.

'We'd best stock up with marbles' said The Assistant.

'What do we want marbles for?' asked The Head Postmaster.

'To make the horses go arse over tit when they charge us' said The Branch Secretary.

'I won't have anything to do with cruelty to horses' said The Head Postmaster. 'My wife would give me hell' he added.

'I hope you and your wife feel the same way when you're being clubbed down from the saddle' said The Assistant.

'It won't come to that' said The Head Postmaster.

'I always thought you were out of touch with reality, but I never realied to what extent' said The Branch Secretary.

'You don't think the Police will just ask you to move along' said The Assistant incredulously.

'Give them half a chance and they'll ride you down' said The Branch Secretary.

'We're dealing with the British Bobby, not the brutal agents of tyranny' protested The Head Postmaster.

'You don't seem to understand. The Mad Woman of Downing Street has given these bastards bloody great pay rises, and license to batter enemies of the State. That is to say anyone who disagrees with her' said The Assistant.

'Haven't you heard about The Enemy Within?' said The Branch Secretary.

'That's not us' said The Head Postmaster.

'You speak for yourself' retorted The Assistant.

'You two paint a very grim picture' said The Head Postmaster.

'It's not all gloom' said The Assistant.

'It isn't?' said The Head Postmaster, sounding very dubious.

'There's a chance you could end up as a working class martyr' said The Assistant.

'The Che Guevara of the Midland Region' said The Branch Secretary.

'I'm not really looking for that sort of distinction' said The Head Postmaster.

'When you're lying outside the office in a pool of blood and those rotten shaggers are standing there jeering and beating their shields and having handfulls at you how do you think your men will react?' asked The Assistant.

'If they've got any sense they'll be running for it' said The Head Postmaster.

'You forget Solidarity' said The Assistant.

'That's all very well in Poland it's not the same here' said The Head Postmaster.

'My members will charge' said The Branch Secretary.

'What for?' asked The Head Postmaster.

'To snatch your remnants from amid the whirling hooves' said The Assistant.

The Head Postmaster got up and paced to and fro.

'Why can't we have a nice quiet orderly protest? Carry some placards, shout 'Maggie Maggie Maggie, Out Out Out' and then disperse?

'Because the bastards won't let us' said The Branch Secretary.

'The Miners had some orderly marches' said The Head Postmaster.

'They were high profile. She had to show some restraint because of all the public interest. No one gives a sod about us.' said The Branch Secretary.

'They'll be able to kick the crap out of us and no-one will be any the wiser' said The Assistant with a kind of grim relish.

'Then they'll charge us with assaulting the Police in the course of their duty' said The Secretary.

'Our Police aren't like that' insisted The Head Postmaster.

The Assistant guffawed. 'Of course they're not. When they see a Picket Line they just say 'Hello hello hello. What's going on here then?' he said with a marked curl of the lip.

'Then they kick the crap out of you' said The Branch Secretary.

'No honest man need fear the Thin Blue Line' said The Head Postmaster.

'It's the Thick Blue Line that's the problem', said The Branch Secretary.

'What about the placards?' said The Assistant.

'We need a good unifying slogan' said The Branch Secretary.

'I've got it' said The Head Postmaster.

The Union Men looked at him expectantly. 'What about, we're being shat on from a great height?' asked The Head Postmaster.

'You can't put that' protested The Assistant.

'Why not?' asked The Head Postmaster.

'You can't use swear words. You'll alienate the public' explained The Assistant.

The Head Postmaster looked at The Branch Secretary for support. He was disappointed. 'It's a matter of the Public Sympathy' said The Secretary.

'What does that mean exactly?' asked The Head Postmaster.

'It means that when the Police bend their truncheons round your ear the public sympathise with you' said The Assistant.

'That's a fat lot of use' spluttered The Head Postmaster.

'It's better than nothing' said The Assistant.

'The Poles had The Public Sympathy in nineteen thirty nine and much bloody good it did them' muttered The Head Postmaster.

'It turned out allright in the end didn't it' said The Assistant.

'No it didn't. They got shat on by the Russians' said The Head Postmaster.

'Serves the bastards right' said The Assistant with a vehemence that surprised The Head Postmaster.

'Why do you say that?' asked The Branch Secretary, also surprised at The Assistant's apparent fury.

'They didn't help the Jews when they had an uprising' said The Assistant.

'The same as we didn't help The Miners when they rose up' said The Branch Secretary.

'Hardly the same thing' protested The Head Postmaster.

'It's exactly the same thing. Divide and rule' said The Branch Secretary.

'If we make a stand surely The Miners will back us' said The Head Postmaster.

'Why should they?' asked The Assistant.

'It's a question of making common cause against the same enemy' said The Head Postmaster.

'It's too late. The Miners are finished. The Dockers are finished, the Public Sector Workers are all finished. There's only us left' said The Branch Secretary.

'And we were shagall to start with.' he added.

'How long do you think we'll last out?' said The Assistant.

'History repeats itself and we never learn' said The Branch Secretary.

The Assistant nodded glumly. 'He's right. It's too late. It's all over' he said.

'When they came for the Catholics I did nothing because I was not a Catholic. When they came for the Trades Unionists I did nothing because I was not a Unionist. When they came for the Jews I did nothing because I was not a Jew. When they came for me there was no-one left' said The Branch Secretary.

The Head Postmaster looked absolutely horrified.

'This is not what I wanted to hear' he said.

'Why does everyone in authority find the truth offensive?' pondered The Assistant.

'I wouldn't say that' said The Head Postmaster.

'Of course you wouldn't. It's the truth' said The Assistant.

The Head Postmaster felt he was being unfairly got at but decided not to pursue the matter. He decided it was time to call the meeting to order.

'Right gentlemen' he said in a tone that clearly demanded full attention.

The Union Men gazed at him expectantly, not quite sitting to attention, he noticed with gratification, but almost.

'So what have we decided?' he asked.

'I thought you were going to tell us' responded The Assistant, not very helpfully.

'I think we've made progress. We seem to be agreed on a number of points' said The Head Postmaster.

The Branch Secretary got out his pen. 'Let's note them' he suggested.

'Splendid idea' agreed The Head Postmaster.

The Assistant looked decidedly unimpressed. 'This is a waste of time' he said glumly.

The Branch Secretary ignored him.

'First point' he said as he prepared to write. He looked enquiringly at The Head Postmaster.

'We're all being shat on from a great height' said The Head Postmaster.

'Agreed' said The Branch Secretary and started to write. He looked up. 'How many tees in shat?' he asked.

'One' said The Head Postmaster.

'Two' said The Assistant, and immediately looked a lot more cheerful.

'We're talking about agreement and making common cause and we can't agree how many tees there are in shat' he said.

'There are bound to be some areas of dispute' said The Head Postmaster.

'But given the will we can arrive at a satisfactory compromise' said The Branch Secretary.

'How can you reach a satisfactory compromise?' asked The Assistant. 'There's either one tee shat or two. That's all there is to it. One of us is right and the other's wrong. You can't fudge it.'

'We'll vote on it' said The Branch Secretary.

'Yes that'll settle it' said The Head Postmaster.

'No it won't' said The Assistant.

'Why not?' asked The Branch Secretary.

'The vote will be inconclusive' said The Assistant.

'How do you know that?' asked The Head Postmaster.

The Assistant stood up. 'We'd best adjourn and reconvene with The Educated Shaggin' Idiot in attendance' he said.

'Sit down. We can manage without that shagger' said The Head Postmaster.

'We'll vote on a show of hands' said The Branch Secretary.

'It's pointless and I'm having shagall to do with it' said The Assistant.

'How can you object to a democratic vote?' asked The Head Postmaster.

'You say it's spelt with one tee, I say it's spelt with two. We cancel each other out' said The Assistant, speaking very slowly.

'And what about his vote?' asked The Head Postmaster pointing to The Branch Secretary.

'How can he vote? He admits he doesn't know. That's why the problem cropped up in the first place' said The Assistant.

'Then we refer to The Chairman for a casting vote' said The Branch Secretary.

'Who's the Chairman?' asked The Assistant.

'He is' said The Branch Secretary indicating The Head Postmaster.

'He's already had a shaggin' vote. He thinks there's only one tee in the shagger' said The Assistant.

'I don't think there's only one tee in the shagger, I know there's only one tee in the shagger' responded The Head Postmaster.

'He can't have a casting vote' he's biased said The Assistant.

The Branch Secretary put away his pen and sat lost in thought for a moment. The Head Postmaster and The Assistant looked at him hoping he was going to come up with a solution.

'It really is remarkable how history does repeat itself' said The Branch Secretary.

The Assistant thought this was an entirely irrelevant observation and was about to return to the matter of the tees when The Branch Secretary continued.

'They must have met very similar problems when they were drawing up the Communist Manifesto' he said.

The Head Postmaster was somewhat puzzled and didn't entirely follow the drift but thought it best to appear noncommittal.

The Assistant snorted: 'Are you saying Stalin and Lenin spent weeks arguing the toss about whether there was one tee or two in shat?' he asked.

'Or something very similar' said The Branch Secretary.

'This is getting more and more shaggin' ridiculous. We'll have to bring the Educated Shaggin' Idiot in' said The Assistant.

'I'm not bringing him here just to ask him how to spell shat' said The Head Postmaster.

'Have you a dictionary here?' asked The Branch Secretary.

'It's not just a question of spelling shat right, we're into the shaggin' Communist Manifesto as well now' said The Assistant.

'Perhaps they consulted the Czar' said The Head Postmaster to the Secretary.

'And he gave the wrong answer so they thought they might as well shoot him' snorted The Assistant.

'Quite possible' said The Head Postmaster.

'I'm putting a formal proposal to the Meeting' said The Assistant.

The Head Postmaster and The Branch Secretary looked at him expectantly. The Branch Secretary took out his pen again and prepared to write.

'I propose we refer the matter to arbitration' said The Assistant.

'Splendid idea' said The Branch Secretary as he wrote.

'Excellent. Provided it's not The Educated Shaggin' Idiot' said The Head Postmaster.

'I recommend that we put the matter before a Quorum of The Shitehouse Poets' said The Assistant.

'Are you taking the piss?' said The Head Postmaster angrily.

The Branch Secretary held up a deprecating hand.

'The proposal does have a certain logic' he said.

The Head Postmaster shook his head. 'It might have as you suggest a certain logic, but it is not practicable' he objected.

'Why not?' the Assistant wanted to know.

'Because we still don't know who The Shitehouse Poets are' explained The Head Postmaster.

'What about that Graphologist you got to examine the writing?' asked The Branch Secretary.

'You know bloody well what he said' The Head Postmaster retorted.

'Just remind us' prodded The Assistant.

The Head Postmaster gritted his teeth and determined not to let himself be unduly riled.

'All he could tell us was that the people who did the writing were mentally unbalanced' he said.

'We didn't need to pay a shaggin' Graphologist to tell us that' jeered The Assistant.

'Telling us they were mentally unbalanced didn't even narrow it down. There's hardly anyone left in the shaggin' building whos's not mentally unbalanced' scoffed The Branch Secretary.

'I refuse to accept that most of the staff are mentally unbalanced. Some of them are just putting it on' protested The Head Postmaster.

'What we need here is a psychiatrist on the staff' said The Branch Secretary.

'We don't need a psychiatrist. We've got The Nurse' said The Head Postmaster.

'She's not qualified to deal with mental illness' said The Branch Secretary.

'She can refer anyone suffering from mental illness to someone who is' said The Head Postmaster.

'Can we get back to the point?' said The Branch Secretary.

'Yes let's get back to the point' echoed The Head Postmaster.

'What is the point?' asked The Assistant.

There was a long pause. The Branch Secretary glanced at his notes. He shook his head wearily.

'Where were we?' The Head Postmaster asked him.

'We were trying to establish how many tees there are in shat' said The Branch Secretary.

'We've settled that. We're going to hand the matter over to a Sub Committee of Shitehouse Poets' said The Head Postmaster.

'Members of this Sub Committee to be chosen by an as yet undecided method' said The Assistant.

'Correct' said The Head Postmaster.

'That's settled then' said The Assistant. The Head Postmaster wasn't sure if he genuinely agreed or was taking the piss, but saw no point in prolonging the matter. He stood up. The Union Men looked at him and then at each other and after a slight pause stood up too.

'It's been a most productive meeting gentlemen. Thank you for your co-operation' said the Head Postmaster. The Union Men looked somewhat bemused. The Head Postmaster was determined to end proceedings on a high note. He fixed them with his eye. They waited intently.

'Time alone will tell gentlemen what we three have started here this day' he said. The Assistant opened his mouth but could think of nothing to say and closed it again. The Branch Secretary headed towards the door and they left quietly. Once outside The Branch Secretary shook his head in bewilderment.

'What was all that about?' he asked.

The Assistant shook his head.

'I'm shagged if I know. But one thing is certain. We should have had The Educated Shaggin' Idiot' with us' he declared.

CHAPTER
TWENTY ONE

Examining the Entrails

'The bourgeoise never make overtures to the proliteriat unless they're after something' said The Educated Shaggin' Idiot.

'We know that shagger' snorted The Truculent Man.

'Speak through the shaggin' Chair' remonstrated The Assistant Secretary.

The Educated Shaggin' Idiot ignored the interruption.

'So just what does The Head Postmaster want?' he asked.

The Truculent Man was ready with the answer. 'He wants shaggin'' he declared.

There was a murmur of assent from the Union Men present. Various suggestions were put forward as to what would serve their purpose. After some heated exchanges, during which The Branch Secretary began to despair of ever getting back onto the agenda, a compromise was reached and a cactus was decided upon. Throughout this debate

The Educated Shaggin' Idiot waited calmly and patiently to continue his analysis of the situation.

'I think it might help if we distinguish between what he deserves, which we've agreed is shaggin' with a cactus, and what he wants which is what we have to determine. 'Let's take it step by step' he proposed. The Union Men nodded their assent.

'We know he wants us to join him in making a stand. He says he's being shat on from a great height. What we have to decide is what's his motive in trying to get us out on a demonstration with him, and is he in fact being shat on from a great height, or is he just saying that because he wants to lure us into a trap?'.

'If he is being shat on from a great height he'll get no sympathy from me' said The Truculent Man.

'What is his problem?' asked The Educated Shaggin' Idiot.

'He's a Wanker' said a voice from the back.

'One possibility is that he is in fact experiencing the same problems that we are' continued The Educated Shaggin' Idiot.

'You mean we're Wankers too?' said the same voice from the back.

'Look mate this is serious' rebuked The Assistant Secretary.

The Voice from the Back took umbrage and bridled up.

'I might not have a shaggin' degree but I know a shaggin' Wanker when I see one' he asserted.

It was made apparent that this was the general feeling of the meeting. Everyone could recognise a Wanker instantaneously. The Educated Shaggin' Idiot refused to allow this display of willful obtuseness to shake his belief in the mentality of The Working Man and ploughed on resolutely.

He decided to narrow his range, stop dealing in wide general issues and get down to specifics.

'Let's take an example' he said.

There was a murmur of agreement. Everyone was keen to consider a particular case. Before the meeting could launch into an impassioned argument as to which particular case most demanded their attention The Educated Shaggin' Idiot cited the woeful condition of the Delivery Postman.

'What about The Delivery Men?' he asked.

'We might as well shoot the poor shaggers and put 'em out of their bleedin' misery' said The Truculent Man.

'If I was on delivery I'd shoot me shaggin' self' said a man who had hitherto remained silent.

'If you're on shaggin' delivery you've got no shaggin' time to shoot yourself' said another previously silent man.

This was what The Educated Shaggin' Idiot wanted to hear. Examples of the atrocities daily perpetrated by Management upon The Delivery Man came flying thick and fast. It did indeed amount to a most deplorable saga.

'They're putting in at least ten hours a week unpaid overtime' said The Truculent Man.

'Coming in ninety minutes before they start getting paid cos the deliveries are too bleedin' big' said someone else.

'Going out loaded up like shaggin' donkeys' said The Truculent Man.

'Four or five bags of shaggin' mail said another man.

'Using their own vehicles and petrol'.

'Running round'.

'Chased from pillar to post'.

The protests came from every corner.

'So how did all this come about?' asked The Educated Shaggin' Idiot.

'It's that Mad Cow in Charge' said someone.

The Educated Shaggin' Idiot shook his head.

'She merely paved the way' he said.

The Meeting looked puzzled. Then the Truculent Man smashed his fist down on the table.

'Improved Working Methods. That was the shagger that started all this' he roared.

A chorus of assent broke out.

'Perhaps you'd care to remind us for the record?' said The Educated Shaggin' Idiot.

The Truculent Man looked nonplussed.

'Just exactly what did Improved Working Methods mean?' asked The Educated Shaggin' Idiot.

'We all got shafted' howled another hitherto silent man.

'Remember that Cockney Shagger they sent down from Union Headquarters?' said The Truculent Man.

'Told us Improved Working Methods was the best thing since sliced bread' said The Assistant Secretary.

'Told us Branches were scrambling to get into it across the length and breadth of the country' said The Truculent Man.

'And they shaggin' were' howled a voice.

'Did we agree with it?' asked The Educated Shaggin' Idiot.

'I didn't agree with the shagger' declared The Truculent Man.

'But you voted for it' The Educated Shaggin' Idiot pointed out.

'Well yes I voted for it but I never agreed with it' said The Truculent Man.

'Why did you vote for it then?' asked The Assistant.

'Cos that Cockney Shagger they sent down from London told us we could either vote for it and get some bonus or Management would impose it and we'd get shagall' said The Truculent Man.

'We were forced into it' said another man.

'What was management's argument for bringing in Improved Working Methods?' asked The Educated Shaggin' Idiot.

There was a momentary silence while the men strove to recall the circumstances attending the introduction of Improved Working Methods.

An Elderly Man raised his hand. The Educated Shaggin' idiot nodded to him.

'The twisting bastards said the shaggin' mail was dropping off and we had to cut costs and save jobs' said The Elderly Man.

'The Lying Bastards' roared The Truculent Man.

The Educated Shaggin' Idiot looked pleased.

'Exactly. So they extended the walks and made The Delivery Men sort mail in between their deliveries. Then what happened?' he said.

'Instead of dropping off like they said it would the mail got heavier and heavier and the job got more and more like slave labour' said The Truculent Man.

'And?' asked The Educated Shaggin' Idiot.

'Then when Management had got the cuts they wanted and the deliveries had got bloody impossible so bloke's were killing themselves with strain and overwork they cancelled the bloody bonus scheme,' said The Truculent Man.

'And what was Union Headquarters response to this outrage?' asked The Educated Shaggin' Idiot.

'They told us Management had the right to cancel a Productivity Scheme at any time they wanted' said The Assistant Secretary.

'They can do anything they shaggin' well want to. There's five million unemployed out there and the shaggers know it' said The Truculent Man.

'And where do our local management stand in relation to all this?' asked The Educated Shaggin' Idiot.

'Now they're getting the bonuses our blokes are earning' said The Assistant Secretary.

'Our blokes are walking their legs to shaggin' stumps and those useless overpaid wankers are wittering on about executive stress' said an Embittered Man.

'And now The Head Postmaster complains he is being shat on from a great height and comes to us for help' said The Educated Shaggin' Idiot.

'Tell him to bollox' said A Man of Few Words.

'Can we vote on that?' said his Mate.

The Branch Secretary stood up. A chorus of groans went up.

'We don't want to hear any crap about tactics' said The Truculent Man.

The Branch Secretary was undeterred. He was determined to take a long term view.

'The Head Postmaster has offered us an olive branch. He has extended the hand of peace' he said.

'Howls of derision' greeted this statement.

'He can stick his olive branch right up his arse' said an Embittered Man.

'Right next to the cactus' said The Truculent Man.

'We need to think about this' said The Branch Secretary.

'You're right' conceded The Truculent Man.

The Branch Secretary was about to speak when The Truculent Man cut him short.

'I've thought about it and he can stick his olive branch and his hand of friendship right up his shaggin' arse next to the cactus' he said.

Some quite revolting suggestions as to what could accompany the hand of friendship, the olive branch and the cactus were made before the meeting calmed down.

The Educated Shaggin' Idiot held up his hand. The meeting looked at him expectantly.

'When someone appeals for help and that someone is an opponent what do you do?' he asked.

Suspecting a trap no-one said anything.

'You ask what he can offer in return' said The Educated Shaggin' Idiot.

'You mean put the screws on the bastard?' asked The Truculent Man.

'Make the bastard grovel' hissed The Embittered Man.

'Make him grovel and then give him shagall' said an Elderly Man.

'Don't turn him down flat. Keep him guessing' said The Branch Secretary.

'Tell him we've got his best interests at heart like he always tells us and then shaggin' well shaft him' said The Embittered Man.

'Like he's always done to us' said The Truculent Man.

'Just what does he expect us to do?' asked The Educated Shaggin' Idiot.

'There's shagall we can do' said The Truculent Man.

'We can't do shagall for ourselves never mind him' said The Embittered Man.

'That's defeatist talk brother' remonstrated The Assistant Secretary.

'Bollocks' said The Embittered Man.

The Assistant Secretary sighed and nodded.

'We need to consider our media strategy' began The Branch Secretary.

'Tell those bastards shagall' roared The Truculent Man.

'We'll get no help from those lying toerags' said The Embittered Man.

'We're on our bloody own' said The Truculent Man.

There was general assent to the proposition that the media were fossers and they were without allies.

'Let's go and see what the slippery old sod is up to' said The Truculent Man.

'See what he's got to say for himself' said The Assistant Secretary.

They found The Head Postmaster somewhat subdued. It seemed he had nothing to say for himself. As they filed into his office he gazed at them blankly. They stood in a half circle before him.

After a long silence he spoke.

'Anyone got a fag?' he asked.

The Truculent Man snorted. 'This is a non smoking building' he said belligerently.

'People get disciplined for smoking here' said The Assistant.

'One law for management another for the shaggin' workers' said The Embittered Man.

'They can't discipline me' said The Head Postmaster.

'What did I tell you? Do as they shaggin' like' said The Truculent Man.

'I've been on The Post Office since I was sixteen' said The Head Postmaster.

'So have I and if I light up they march me off the premises' said The Embittered Man.

'I don't know anything else. I don't know what to do' said The Head Postmaster.

The Educated Shaggin' Idiot looked baffled.

'Just what is going on?' he asked.

The Head Postmaster was turning purple.

'You want to know what's going on do you?' he spluttered.

'We all want to know what's going on' The Truculent Man told him.

'I'll tell you what's going on?' said The Head Postmaster. He paused, either for effect or to get a grip on himself. The Union Men waited eagerly.

The Head Postmaster sprang quivering to his feet. The Union Men instinctively stepped back. The Head Postmaster pointed in the direction of Birmingham.

'Those bastards at Birmingham are getting rid of me' he howled.

The Truculent Man gave a derisive snort.

'Don't talk like a prat' he admonished.

'I'm not talking like a prat. I'm telling you what's happening' protested The Head Postmaster.

'They can't shaggin' get rid of you' said The Truculent Man.

'Don't tell me. Tell them' said The Head Postmaster.

The Truculent Man would not modify his line.

'They can't shaggin' get rid of you' he said again.

'You can't shift a Head Postmaster' said The Branch Secretary.

The Assistant Secretary nodded his agreement and then said as an afterthought.

'Unless he's done something really gross' he said.

'Such as?' asked The Truculent Man.

'Shaggin' sheep' said The Assistant.

'Shaggin' sheep' said The Embittered Man.

The Head Postmaster felt he had to protest.

'I do not shag sheep' he said.

'I should hope not' said The Truculent Man.

'Shaggin' sheep is effall to what some of those buggers have got up to' said The Embittered Man.

'What are you suggesting?' asked The Head Postmaster.

'Malpractices' replied The Embittered Man.

'What malpractices?' asked The Head Postmaster.

'Filthy malpractices' replied The Embittered Man.

'We haven't come here to discuss sheep shaggin'. I don't want to pursue this line' said The Branch Secretary.

'You speak for yourself. I'd like to hear more about this' said The Truculent Man.

The Head Postmaster suddenly felt he didn't like the way The Union Men were staring at him.

'I'll see my solicitor' he said.

'What for?' asked The Truculent Man.

'To protect my good name' said The Head Postmaster.

'Innocent men don't need solicitors' said The Assistant Secretary.

'Bollocks!' said The Truculent Man.

'There's worse things than shaggin' sheep' muttered a man at the back.

'You what?!' roared The Truculent Man.

'There's worse things than shaggin' sheep' said The Man at the Back.

'Such as?' demanded The Truculent Man.

'Taking the bread out of kids' mouths' said The Man at the Back.

'Knocking off our shaggin' overtime' said another man.

'I had to knock off the shaggin' overtime. I had to keep within the shaggin' budget those rottem shaggers at Birmingham set me' howled The Head Postmaster.

'He was only obeying orders' hissed The Embittered Man.

'Was he only obeying orders when he shagged sheep' said a voice from the back.

'We don't know he shagged sheep' said The Assistant Secretary.

'We don't know he didn't' retorted the voice.

The Head Postmaster tried to locate his accuser.

'Who said that?' he asked.

'Baaaa!' Was the reply.

'I think this meeting is getting out of hand' said The Assistant Secretary.

'This is nothing to do with sheep' explained The Head Postmaster.

'If you say so' said The Truculent Man.

'I do say so' said The Head Postmaster.

'Then what is it to do with?' asked The Branch Secretary.

'They can't get rid of a Head Postmaster. He's like a Constitutional Monarch' said The Embittered Man. The shift from shagging sheep to the position of The Constitutional Monarch was a bit sudden for the mass of the meeting and all eyes turned to The Embittered Man. For further explanation.

He gazed back at them.

'You can't shift a Monarch without a revolution, bloodless or otherwise' he told them.

'He's right, you have to have a revolution' said The Truculent Man.

'Exactly!' said The Head Postmaster, thumping his desk.

'Have you gone daft?' asked The Embittered Man.

'No. It's those bastards at Birmingham who've gone daft' The Head Postmaster told him.

The Educated Shaggin' Idiot spoke tentatively.

'Are you saying there's been a revolution at Birmingham?' he asked.

'Yes and I'm the first bloody victim' howled The Head Postmaster.

'That's bloody stupid' said The Truculent Man. 'They can't shaggin' do that' he added.

'I knew they can't shaggin' do it but they shaggin' have' said The Head Postmaster.

'Alice in Wonderland' said The Educated Shaggin' Idiot and sat down.

'Is that your contribution?' asked The Truculent Man.

'This is enough to make Lenin turn in his grave' said The Educated Shaggin' Idiot.

'The poor shagger has never stopped turning in his grave' said The Embittered Man.

'It's positively unnatural said The Educated Shaggin' Idiot.

'So's shaggin' sheep' said the man who'd lost his overtime.

'Will you shut up about shaggin' sheep' howled The Head Postmaster and The Branch Secretary in unison.

'How can the people running things start a revolution?' asked The Truculent Man.

'Do you expect me to answer that?' said The Educated Shaggin' Idiot.

The Truculent Man thought a moment and then shook his head in obvious bafflement.

'They say there's no place for me in the bright new future' said The Head Postmaster.

'When's that going to start?' said The Embittered Man.

'It already has' replied The Head Postmaster.

'So what are we going to do?' asked The Educated Shaggin' Idiot.

'Whatever we do we must do it together' said The Head Postmaster.

'Baaaa!' came from the back.

CHAPTER
TWENTY TWO

Baa baa baa!

The grapevine had never worked better. Within two days it was all over the office that The Head Postmaster had been summoned to Birmingham, confronted by his accusers, faced with the evidence, and had been given early retirement on the grounds that he had been proven to be a sheepshagger. In three days it was all round the Midland Region. On the fourth day the news had spread all over England and Wales, and on the fifth calls were received from Scotland asking what was so unusual about the English being run by a shagger of sheep?

A number of people in the office said they had known all along and had wondered how long it would be before the facts came to light. The Postmaster was understandably furious and consulted his solicitor as to whether or not he could sue. His solicitor, a man made deeply suspicious by the nature of his work, eyed him warily. 'I take it there is no substance in these allegations' he said. 'None at all' The Postmaster assured him.

'Just who do you want to sue?' asked his solicitor.

The Head Postmaster was nonplussed. 'Surely there must be someone I can sue?' he asked plaintively. The solicitor shook his head. 'That's the trouble with rumour. It's unattributable' he sighed.

'Should I issue a statement?' asked The Head Postmaster.

'Saying what?' asked the solicitor.

'That I do not shag sheep' said The Head Postmaster.

'I think that might make you a laughing stock' advised his solicitor.

'I'm a laughing stock already' said The Head Postmaster, wondering just how he came to find himself in this deplorable plight.

'You'll just have to rise above it' said the solicitor.

The Headpostmaster wondered if the solicitor would have the nerve to charge him for this crap and made his way out. Seated in his office he was sure he could hear baaing coming from various directions.

He decided to consult The Union Men.

'What are we going to do?' he asked.

'We're going to do buggerall' said The Assistant.

'That's not a very constructive attitude' said The Head Postmaster.

'This is nothing to do with us' said The Branch Secretary.

'No man is an island' said The Head Postmaster.

'He is when he shags sheep' said The Assistant Secretary.

'This is a management matter. It's between you and Birmingham' said The Branch Secretary.

'It's between you and Birmingham' added The Branch Secretary.

'We can't interfere' said The Assistant.

The Head Postmaster looked decidedly unconvinced. The Assistant glanced at The Branch Secretary inviting him to enlarge. With some relish he did so.

'Management have been given the right to manage' he said.

'By The Mad Witch of Grantham' added The Assistant.

'When you were shafting us you thought she was brilliant' said The Branch Secretary.

'Now she's stuck it up you you expect us to spring to your defence' said The Assistant.

'But it's not fair' bleated The Head Postmaster.

'Was it fair when men nearing sixty had their workloads doubled and their earnings cut?' said The Branch Secretary.

'That never happened' retorted The Head Postmaster.

'Oh yes it did' said The Assistant.

'And there are death certificates, grieving kids and widows and headstones to prove it' said The Branch Secretary.

'How many times have you told us we have to modernise?' said The Assistant.

'Adapt or go under' added The Secretary.

'Cut away the excess meat' continued The Assistant remorselessly.

'Be competitive'.

'Price ourselves into jobs'.

'End restrictive practices'.

'I'd no idea you felt like this' protested The Head Postmaster.

The Union Men looked flabbergasted.

'Why didn't you tell me?' asked The Head Postmaster.

'We did shaggin' tell you' said The Assistant.

'Every shaggin' day' added The Secretary.

'I don't remember that' said The Head Postmaster.

'You mean you don't want to remember that' scoffed The Assistant.

'We have to look to the future' asserted The Head Postmaster.

'What future?' asked The Branch Secretary.

'Do you want to discuss hobbies?' asked The Assistant.

'We're facing a common enemy' said The Head Postmaster.

'Are you proposing an alliance?' asked The Branch Secretary.

'Yes' said The Head Postmaster.

'You've got buggerall to offer' The Assistant told him blurtly.

'Together we can restore goodwill to the office. Make this a happy place to work' said The Head Postmaster.

'Happy shaggin' place to work! snorted The Assistant.

'It's like The Third Shaggin' Reich' said The Secretary.

'I resent that' said The Head Postmaster.

'Do you think we like it?' asked The Assistant.

'Why are you so bothered anyway?' asked The Branch Secretary.

'You'll get a good settlement' The Assistant said.

'That's not the point' said The Head Postmaster.

'If money isn't the point what is?' asked The Assistant.

'That's all that matters now' said The Branch Secretary.

'And whatever happened to principle?' asked The Head Postmaster.

The Union men were convulsed with mirth.

'This is not a laughing matter' protested The Head Postmaster.

'How can you sit there and talk about principle?' The Assistant asked.

'I am a man of honour. My word is my bond' declared The Head Postmaster.

'We haven't come here to listen to your fantasies' said The Assistant.

'I'm a worker too you know' said The Head Postmaster.

'Not for much longer by the sound of it' said The Assistant.

'You could write to your MP' suggested The Branch Secretary.

'And much good it'll do you' said The Assistant.

'There must be something I can do' insisted The Head Postmaster.

'You could try talking to The Educated Shaggin' Idiot' said The Assistant.

The Head Postmaster clutched at the straw.

'He might be an idiot, but he's a clever idiot' he said.

'There's only one snag' said The Assistant.

'What's that?' asked The Head Postmaster.

'He thinks you're a prize wanker' The Assistant told him.

'I still can't see why you're bothered. Why not take the money and run? After all it's what everyone does nowadays'.

'I don't want a dishonourable discharge' said The Head Postmaster.

'It won't be a dishonourable discharge. It'll be on medical grounds', said The Assistant.

'That'll be the official line, yes, but everyone will know that's not the real reason' said The Head Postmaster.

'Sheepshaggin' will never stand up in court' said The Assistant.

The Head Postmaster turned pale.

'Who's talking about court?' he asked.

'The Shitehouse Poets for a start' said The Branch Secretary.

'They're worse than the tabloids' said The Head Postmaster.

'Some of the writing is better' said The Assistant.

'I'm not interested in their prose style' said The Head Postmaster.

'We neglect the arts in this country' said The Branch Secretary.

The Assistant produced a piece of paper from his pocket and smoothed it out.

'I thought you might like to hear this' he said.

'Hear what?' asked The Head Postmaster.

With obvious relish The Assistant Secretary said.

'This is the tale of a rotten creep

Who spent his time shagging sheep

When asked what he'd done

He said so far I've shagged twenty one'.

Asked what he proposed to do

He said I think I'll make it twenty two'.

Then he said and now I'll go and shag a Guernsey cow

The Assistant beamed.

'There are twenty five verses all told' he said.

'What's your wife say about all this?' asked The Branch Secretary.

'She's gone to her sister' said The Head Postmaster.

'She's very highly strong' he added defensively.

'Let's hope it doesn't get into the papers' said The Assistant.

'The Head Postmaster turned pale.

'There's no fear of that' he said without a lot of conviction.

'You don't really have a lot to worry about' said The Branch Secretary.

'Apart from the Animal Rights maniacs' said The Assistant.

'If they decide to make an example of you … ' said The Branch Secretary shaking his head dolefully.

'But I haven't done anything' protested The Head Postmaster.

'We know that, but do they?' said The Assistant.

'I'll issue a statement' said The Head Postmaster.

'You can't do that' said The Branch Secretary.

'It'll give substance to the allegations' said The Assistant.

'You're trying to keep it quiet', The Branch Secretary said.

'There's nothing to keep quiet' said The Head Postmaster.

'We know that shagger' said The Assistant.

'What's that got to do with anything?' asked The Branch Secretary.

'The facts don't matter any more' said The Assistant.

'This is the age of illusion' declared The Branch Secretary.

'Economic miracle, improved industrial relations, people set free, unions handed back to the members, Britain great again', it's all bollocks,' snorted The Assistant.

The Head Postmaster was a Conservative voter and opened his mouth to protest but The Branch Secretary cut him short.

'The reality is the economy's bollocksed, the North Sea oil is wasted, the country's a shabby mess, the diseases of poverty are back, the Unions have been castrated and Britain is an ugly laughing stock, but the truth is buried under a mountain of lies' he said.

'Get off your bloody soap box' said The Head Postmaster.

The Branch Secretary opened his mouth but this time The Head Postmaster cut him short.

'If you want to rant and rave you can shag off to Hyde Park Shaggin' Corner but I won't have it in my shaggin' office' he shouted. The Branch Secretary leapt to his feet.

'If you're not shaggin' man enough to face the shaggin' truth I'm wasting my shaggin' time talking to you' shouted The Branch Secretary.

'What do you know about the shaggin' truth?' howled The Head Postmaster.

'I live with the shagger every shaggin' day' The Branch Secretary yelled back.

'You're in a world of your own' The Head Postmaster bellowed.

'Why don't you join The Sheepshaggers' Union and get them to fight your case?' The Branch Secretary howled and stormed out slamming the door.

'You've upset him' said The Assistant Branch Secretary.

'Upset him! I'll suspend him!' bellowed The Head Postmaster.

'If that's going to be the line you can suspend us both' shouted The Assistant and stormed out banging the door. The Head Postmaster rushed after him.

'You'll leave when I tell you to' he shouted.

'Bollocks' said The Assistant Secretary without even turning round.

'And bollocks to you too' howled The Head Postmaster. He turned round to find his Secretary, Miss Watson, looking at him with much disapproval.

'A man in your position should not be shouting bollocks down the corridor' she chided.

'He got my rag' complained The Head Postmaster.

'He probably intended to' said Miss Watson.

'Well he's going to wish he hadn't' said The Head Postmaster.

'You'd best sit down and have a cup of coffee' Miss Watson told him.

Meekly he sat down. Suddenly the fire died out in him and he felt very vulnerable and very alone.

'I think I'm finished Miss Watson' he said in a very subdued tone.

'Nonsense!' said Miss Watson briskly.

'There's no place for the likes of me in the new order' said The Head Postmaster.

'If it comes to that you'll go out with your head held high' Miss Watson assured him.

'But these rumours … ' started The Head Postmaster.

'No-one really believes then' said Miss Watson.

'It's all becoming part of the legend' said The Head Postmaster.

'In a few weeks time it will all be forgotten' said Miss Watson.

'I don't want to retire' said The Head Postmaster.

'Then you must make a stand' said Miss Watson.

'How?' asked The Head Postmaster.

'First of all you must repair your alliances' Miss Watson told him.

'I haven't got any alliances said The Head Postmaster.

'Then make some' said Miss Watson and left.

The Head Postmaster sat at his desk and tried to think. He considered the possibility of making a direct appeal to the people like other beleaguered leaders had done, but after some thought decided against the idea.

'Those bastards wouldn't want to know. All they care about is their overtime' he told himself. Then he came to a decision. He rang The Chief Inspector.

'Tell The Educated Shaggin' Idiot to report to my office' he instructed.

'We don't want that Shagger as a shaggin' manager. He's bad enough as a shaggin' postman' protested The Chief.

'We need shaggin' brains' said The Head Postmaster.

'We've done without shaggin' brains all this time why do we suddenly need them now?' asked The Chief.

'The old times are over. It's all different now' said The Head Postmaster.

'Not so far as I'm concerned it isn't' said The Chief.

'There's no place for unreconstructed dinosaurs' said The Head Postmaster.

'And there's no room for sheepshaggers' retorted The Chief.

The Head Postmaster slammed the the phone down and stormed out of his office. He kicked open the door of The Chief's office. A number of Managers were sitting round drinking tea.

'What do you mean there's no room for sheepshaggers?' demanded The Head Postmaster.

A couple of Managers choked on their tea. The Chief remained calm.

'It was merely an observation' he said.

'If you've got anything to say come out and say it' shouted The Head Postmaster.

'If it's an offence to discriminate against sheepshaggers I withdraw' said The Chief.

'You've read the instructions from Human Resources in Birmingham. We don't discriminate against minorities' said The Head Postmaster, somewhat piously.

'All right, fine. Sheepshaggers are in. We'd best get some more and make sure we're up to our quota or we'll get a bad press' said The Chief Inspector.

'I blame the shaggin' Union for all this' said a stupid looking Dim Manager with a pot belly and acne.

'It's a bloody farce' said another stupid looking Dim Manager with a beer belly and a red nose.

The Head Postmaster looked enquiringly at him.

'All you have to do here is say you've got a drink problem, you shag sheep and you want to see The Welfare Officer and no-one can touch you' he said.

'This is all news to me' protested The Head Post Master.

'You want to come out of your office occasionally' The Chief Inspector told him.

'Just what is the official line on sheepshagging?' asked an earnest young Acting Dim Manager, anxious to ingratiate himself with his superiors.

'There is no official line on sheepshaggin' said The Head Postmaster. 'It's never been an issue' he added.

'I remember when all we did was handle letters' said an Older Dim Manager.

'If somebody shagged sheep it was his own business' said The Chief Inspector.

'Just so long as he did his job' said Elderly Dim Manager.

The Head Postmaster shook his head in exasperation.

'We're in an entirely new era. We're a modern corporation. We've got new dynamic thrusting management at the top' he said.

'They're a bunch of wankers' said The Older Dim Manager.

'Well yes I know but what they say goes' said The Head Postmaster. 'There's shagall I can do about it' he added defensively.

'You can tell 'em to get phucked!' said The Elderly Dim Manager.

'And that's just what they'll tell me at the Job Centre when I go looking for work' The Head Postmaster retorted.

'Why doesn't the shaggin' Union do something about it?' asked The Dim Manager with a pot belly and acne.

'Don't mention the shaggin' Union to me' spluttered The Chief Inspector.

'We used to be one big happy family' said a Dim Manager who was renowned for living in a world of his own.

'Every day it's some new bollocks' complained The Dim Manager with the pot belly and red nose.

'We have to be forward looking. We can't spend millions on a new modern logo and be known as a bunch of stick in the muds and sheepshaggers' said The Head Postmaster.

'So long as people get their mail they don't give a sod if we're sheepshaggers or not' maintained The Dim Manager with the pot belly and acne.

'Birmingham aren't pleased with us' said The Head Postmaster.

'So what?' said The Dim Manager with a pot belly and rednose.

'So they're going to sort us out' The Head Postmaster told him.

'How?' asked Acne.

'By getting rid of me for a start' The Head Postmaster said.

'They can't do that' said The Chief Inspector.

'According to them they can' said The Head Postmaster.

'They can do what the shag they like said The Elderly Dim Manager'.

'Can I count on your support?' asked The Head Postmaster.

'For what?' asked The Chief Inspector.

'My stand against Birmingham' The Head Postmaster replied.

'What are you going to do?' asked The Elderly Dim Manager.

'I'm going to fight' said The Head Postmaster.

'Just like the shaggin' miners' said Acne.

Red Nose snorted, 'Just like the shaggin' miners, the dockers and the shagger print workers' and every other shaggin' he said.

'What'll you do? Mount a picket?' asked The Chief Inspector.

'A Mass Picket' breathed The Acting Manager.

'You're not allowed more than six' said The Head Postmaster.

'You'll never get six' The Chief Inspector told him.

'The police will thump you with clubs and then arrest you for assaulting them' said Red Nose.

'I don't want any trouble I'm six months off my pension' said The Elderly Dim Manager.

The Head Postmaster looked at them all in disgust. He decided on one last appeal:

'Haven't you got a set of bollocks between the lot of you?' he asked.

They all looked resentful and shifty. He realised he would have to look elsewhere for assistance.

'Find The Educated Shaggin' Idiot' and send him to my office immediately' he instructed and walked out slamming the door.

'What's he want The Educated Shaggin' Idiot for?' asked Acne.

'Is he in the shit?' asked Red Nose hopefully.

'Let's hope so' said The Elderly Dim Manager glumly.

'That bugger's fireproof' said The Chief Inspector.

His eye lit upon The Acting Dim Manager.

'Don't just sit there. Go and find the shagger' he told him.

The Acting Dim Manager leapt to his feet.

'Right Chief I'll find him. And when I find him I'll tell him you want to see him'.

'Bloody hell! I don't want him you pillock. Tell him The Head Postmaster wants to see him right away'.

The Acting Dim Manager left the office mouthing the message.

'Christ he's thick' said Red Nose.

'Is he a Freemason?' asked Acne.

'He walks as though he's got a cucumber rammed up his arse' said The Elderly Dim Manager.

The Chief Inspector was furious.

'Don't start stirring it up about the bleedin' cucumbers' he told them all. They looked puzzled.

'We've got enough coping with the sheepshaggin'' he explained.

'I blame it all on television' said The Elderly Dim Manager.

CHAPTER
TWENTY THREE

The Global Context

The Branch Secretary was standing on a chair reaching up to stick a drawing pin in the corner of a map of the world as The Assistant entered.

'Grab a chair and hold up the other end would you?' he asked.

The Assistant Secretary did as he was requested.

'What's this?' he asked.

'What do you think it is?' responded The Secretary.

The Assistant peered from one side to the other, then from top to bottom.

'It's a map of the world' he said.

'Correct' said The Branch Secretary.

'So why is it on the wall and what have you done with the Derby County fixture list?' asked The Assistant.

'Would you mind handing me one of those little flags?' said The Secretary.

The Assistant sighed and climbed down from the chair. He picked up a little flag and handed to The Secretary.

The Secretary stuck it onto the map. He glanced down at The Assistant.

'Do you know what this really is?' he asked.

The Assistant felt he had had enough of this interrogation.

'It's the Mona Shaggin' Lisa' he said.

'Wrong' said The Secretary.

'Go on, surprise me' said The Assistant.

'It's the battlefield. This is where it's all happening' The Secretary declared with the kind of satisfaction expressed by someone who has thought long and hard and finally come up with the answer.

'Where else could it be shaggin' happening?' asked The Assistant.

The Secretary ignored him and pursued his own line of thought.

'I know whose behind all this?' he claimed.

'So do I. It's the bloody Chief Inspector. He's always been a bastard' said The Assistant.

'It's not him' said The Secretary.

'Then who is it?' said The Assistant.

The Secretary got down from the chair. He went across to the door, opened it and peered out. Then he closed the door quietly and sat at his desk. He beckoned The Assistant closer. The Assistant sat opposite him and leaned forward. The Branch Secretary leaned forward also.

'It's Coca-Cola' he said.

The Assistant gazed at him blankly. Then a glimmer of understanding came to him:

'You're taking the piss' he said.

'I'm deadly serious' said The Branch Secretary.

'Shagoff! You're taking the piss' The Assistant insisted.

'Look at the map. All the answers are there. It's Coca Cola' said The Branch Secretary, somewhat excited now.

The Assistant shifted his chair further back. He thought for a moment and could come up with only one explanation.

'If you've had enough and you're going for medical discharge there's no need for all this' he said.

The Branch Secretary looked blank. The Assistant shifted his chair back towards the desk.

'Ask to see The Welfare officer' he said.

'Why should I ask to see The Welfare Officer?' said The Branch Secretary, completely nonplussed.

'Tell him you've got a drink problem and tensions in the home'.

'There are no tensions in my home' The Secretary assured him.

If you get a farmer to lodge a complaint that you've been shagging his chickens. You'll probably have to sign a gagging order.

'I don't want a medical discharge' said The Branch Secretary.

The Assistant got up and put his chair between him and The Branch Secretary.

'Then just exactly what are you after?' he asked.

'I went to call an Emergency Branch Meeting' The Secretary said.

The Assistant Secretary held up his hands palms forward.

'Now don't let's be hasty. Let's think about this' he urged.

'I've thought about nothing else for weeks' said The Secretary.

'Perhaps it would be better if you did think about something else for a bit' suggested The Assistant.

The Branch Secretary leapt to his feet and grabbed a ruler. The Assistant Secretary leapt hastily back, but The Secretary ignored him and went to the map.

'See this?' he said, pointing to the flag he'd just stuck in.

'Yes' gulped The Assistant.

'That's us' said The Secretary.

'Yes?' said The Assistant.

'And what's our situation?' asked The Secretary.

'Continually in the shit' answered The Assistant.

'Exactly' said The Secretary. He peered closer at the map, then located the spot he wanted and pointed at it with the ruler.

'That's Columbia' he said.

'Is it?' said The Assistant.

'The people are right in the shit there. Human rights don't exist. Unless you're a Drag Baron.

He pointed again. 'Do you know what this is?' He asked.

'The bottom right hand corner' said The Assistant.

'It's Australia. It's pretty grim there too'.

'Are you going to take up a collection?' asked The Assistant, groping in the dark.

'This is Vietnam. They've been shafted for decades. Now we cross over to Europe. It's beginning to happen there. The people are getting shafted there as well. It's the same everywhere. Now this is the United States; The Mafia, The CIA the Pentagon …'

'And Coca Cola' interrupted The Assistant.

'You've made the connection' said The Secretary in delight.

'So the Americans are shafting everyone so that Coca Cola can corner the market' said The Assistant.

'That's it' said The Secretary.

'But why are they doing it?' asked The Assistant.

'Because they're maniacs' said The Secretary.

'It's a disgrace but what can we do?' asked The Assistant.

'Expose them' said The Branch Secretary.

'Can we do that?' said The Assistant.

The Branch Secretary went and stared intently at the map.

'All the odds are stacked against us. They've got the CIA, the Mafia and The Pentagon, plus the Drug Barons and unrestricted capital. Then there's M15, M16, The SAS, The City and The Mad Witch of Grantham. It's a formidable lineup,' he sighed.

'Don't forget all the poxy papers and the tv stations and the radio' The Assistant reminded him.

'And what do we have?' asked The Branch Secretary.

'We've got the Shitehouse walls' replied The Assistant.

The Branch Secretary looked absolutely delighted.

'You're right. That's where we'll write the truth' he said.

'You mean it's going to be The Sun varies the Shitehouse walls?' asked The Assistant.

'The truth always starts in a small way' said The Branch Secretary.

'I suppose you're right. We've got to start somewhere' conceded The Assistant.

The door was flung open and The Truculent Man marched to.

He stared at the wall.

'What have you done with the shaggin' Derby County fixture list?' he demanded angrily.

'I've filed it' said The Branch Secretary.

The Truculent Man snorted indignantly and glared at the map of the world.

'What's this shagger? Are these the new shaggin' deliveries?' he demanded.

'It's the shape of things to come. You start your delivery in London Road and finish in Saigon' said The Assistant.

'That's about the size of it. They've turned us into a bunch of effin' coolies' complained The Truculent Man.

'That's what they're after. They want a globe serviced by coolies' The Branch Secretary told him.

'What do you mean that's what they're after? It's what they've got. The walks are bloody scandalous' said The Truculent Man.

'You've seen nothing yet' The Branch Secretary told him.

'I've seen plenty mate' bridled The Truculent Man.

'What we've had so far is just Phase One' said The Branch Secretary.

'Well they can shove Phase Two up their arse' said The Truculent Man.

The Branch Secretary grabbed the ruler and went over to the map. 'You see here?' he asked, pointing excitedly.

'What?' asked The Truculent Man.

'This is Vietnam' said The Branch Secretary.

'Shag Vietnam' said The Truculent Man.

'That's exactly what they want you to say' The Branch Secretary told him.

'Who?' asked The Truculent Man.

The Branch Secretary located Washington. The Truculent Man looked puzzled.

'The White House, The Pentagon, The Mafia The CIA and Wall Street' said The Branch Secretary. The Truculent Man looked if anything more bemused. The Branch Secretary pointed at London.

'Ten Downing Street, MI5, MI6, Special Branch, The SAS' he said.

'Don't forget The Mad Witch of Grantham' The Assistant reminded him.

'May she rot in hell!' exclaimed The Truculent Man.

Amen said The Assistant.

'The Devil may be a bit of a bastard but I wouldn't wish her on him' said The Branch Secretary.

'Why not? He's on her side' said The Truculent Man.

The Branch Secretary nodded. 'You're right. We'll add The Devil to the list of our opponents' he said.

'But we've got God on our side' claimed The Assistant.

'And a lot of good He is' said The Truculent Man.

'He needs to get on the ball' said The Assistant.

'Right. So where does all this leave us?' asked The Branch Secretary.

'Up Shit Creek without a paddle' The Truculent Man told him.

'Correct. But I believe that Coca Cola can be beaten' said The Branch Secretary.

The Truculent Man went and examined the map closely.

'Where does Coca Cola come into this?' he asked.

'Coca Cola's piss' said The Branch Secretary.

'I know that' said The Truculent Man.

'So the only way they can sell it all over the world is by killing off the competition' The Branch Secretary explained.

'Then they have to drink Coca Cola cos there's shagall else' said The Assistant.

The Truculent Man stood staring at the map. Then he turned round.

'Are you telling me that what it comes down to is the Yanks have butchered more people than Hitler because Coca Cola is piss?' he asked.

The Branch Secretary thought a moment:

'Basically that's it' he said.

'Supposing shaggin' Hitler had won the shaggin' war?' asked The Truculent Man.

'Then we'd have all been drinking some German piss' said The Assistant.

'It's a global shaggin' madhouse' said The Truculent Man.

'That's exactly what it is' agreed The Branch Secretary.

The Truculent Man thumped the desk.

'So what are we going to do about it?' he demanded.

'Inform the people' said The Branch Secretary.

'Write the truth' said The Assistant.

'Where?' said The Branch Secretary.

The Truculent Man thought a moment. Then a gleam came into his eye.

'On the Shitehouse walls' he shouted.

'On the Shitehouse walls' shouted The Branch Secretary.

'Where are we going to write the truth?' demanded The Assistant.

'On the Shitehouse walls' bellowed The Branch Secretary and The Truculent Man.

A nervous looking Dim Manager appeared in the doorway:

'What do you want?' bellowed The Truculent Man.

'Can you blokes stop bellowing about the Shitehouse walls. They can hear you all over the building' said The Dim Manager.

'Let 'em' bellowedf The Truculent Man.

The Dim Manager disappeared shaking his head.

The Truculent Man turned to The Branch Secretary and The Assistant.

'Now then. We'll buggerup Coca Cola, but first we've got trouble here. The Educated Shaggin' Idiot' is in with The Head Postmaster' he said.

The Branch Secretary was indignant.

'He'll be trying to pick his brains' he said angrily.

'It's great isn't it. He's got no brain of his own and when he wants to use one he has to turn to one of our blokes. The only brain available belongs to a shaggin' postman' said The Truculent Man.

'We'll soon see about this' said The Branch Secretary heading out of the door.

'Wait for us' called The Assistant.

The Branch Secretary hammered furiously on The Head Postmaster's door.

'Come' said a voice.

The Union Men stormed in. The Head Postmaster looked alarmed.

The Educated Shaggin' Idiot was sitting with a glass in his hand. The Branch Secretary was outraged.

'What are you drinking?' he demanded.

'Coca Cola' said The Educated Shaggin' Idiot.

All three Union Men gave indignant snorts. The Branch Secretary snatched the glass from The Educated Shaggin' Idiot's hand. He handed it to The Truculent Man.

'You know what to do with that' he said.

The Truculent Man emptied it over the potted plant.

The Head Postmaster got to his feet looking furious. The Branch Secretary pointed an accusing finger at him.

'That piss is stained with the innocent blood of millions' he told him.

The Head Postmaster sat down in a heap. The Branch Secretary rounded on The Educated Shaggin' Idiot.

'I didn't expect to find you fraternising with the enemy' he told him.

'I was brought here' said The Educated Shaggin' Idiot.

'You were coerced?' said The Branch Secretary.

'I was' said The Educated Shaggin' Idiot.

'Nonsense!' blustered The Head Postmaster.

'The Chief Inspector told me I could either come here or be suspended' said The Educated Shaggin' Idiot.

The Head Postmaster looked decidedly uncomfortable.

'You might well look shifty' said The Truculent Man.

'Why don't you get a pair of jackboots and a shovel helmet?' asked The Branch Secretary.

'No need to buy them. You can borrow The Chief Inspector's' said The Assistant Secretary.

Throughout these heated exchanges The Educated Shaggin' Idiot maintained his customary composure. He glanced across at The Head Postmaster:

'Do you by any chance have any drinks that aren't hopelessly compromised and stained with the blood of millions?' he asked innocently.

The Head Postmaster thought for a while, then got up and went to the drinks cabinet.

'I'm not sure' he admitted. He turned to The Branch Secretary:

'Is there anything here that a man of conscience can drink?' he asked.

'Just so long as it's not Coca Cola' The Branch Secretary told him.

'I'll have a lager if no-one objects' said The Educated Shaggin' Idiot.

The Head Postmaster handed him a can of lager. The Educated Shaggin' Idiot sat sipping it. The Truculent Man sat glaring at The Head Postmaster.

'I wouldn't mind one of these' he said.

'Nor me' said The Assistant.

The Head Postmaster sighed and got up.

'Perhaps I'll run a country pub when they've got shot of me' he said.

He brought across some cans and put them on the table, indicated that The Union Men were to help themselves and took one for himself. For a while no-one spoke. Then The Truculent Man broke the silence:

'Got any peanuts?' he asked.

'The Head Postmaster snorted in annoyance, he was just beginning to enjoy his drink.

'Anything else you want? Shall I get in a couple of strippers?' he asked.

'That would be the best thing you'd done since you've been here' The Truculent Man told him.

'They'd love that in Birmingham' said The Assistant.

'Especially if it got in The Sun' said The Truculent Men.

The Branch Secretary decided it was time he asserted himself decisively.

'Just what is on the agenda for this meeting?' he asked.

'This is not a meeting' protested The Head Postmaster.

'We've got a quorum' said The Assistant.

'If it's not a shaggin' meeting what is it?' demanded The Truculent Man.

'It's a consultation' said The Head Postmaster.

'Concerning what?' asked The Truculent Man.

'That's none of your business' said The Head Postmaster.

'If that's your attitude I might as well have this last can' said The Truculent Man, leaning over and helping himself to a can of lager.

'Finish it outside' said The Head Postmaster.

'If he leaves we all leave' said The Branch Secretary.

'I never asked you to come here in the first place' returned The Head Postmaster.

The Union Men rose to their feet. When The Educated Shaggin' Idiot also rose The Head Postmaster changed his tune.

'Don't let's be hasty. Sit down' he said as he strode purposefully over to the drinks cabinet.

'I'm sure we can find common ground somewhere' he claimed as he handed round more cans.

The Union Men gratefully seized their cans and sat down again.

'Is this a truce?' asked The Truculent Man.

'An interlude in the war' said The Educated Shaggin' Idiot.

'We're all up against The White House, The CIA, The Pentagon, M15, M16, The SAS, The City, Wall Street, The Foreign Office and The Mad Witch of Grantham' said The Branch Secretary.

'May she rot in hell' said The Truculent Man.

'All I care about is getting that shower in Birmingham off my back' said The Head Postmaster.

'Birmingham are just a tool of all those other bastards' said The Branch Secretary.

'If you say so' said The Head Postmaster.

'What you need is a global strategy' said The Branch Secretary.

'Will that help me shaft those sods at Birmingham?' asked The Head Postmaster.

'Possibly. In any event it'll mean you understand what's going on' replied The Branch Secretary.

'I know what's going on? They're shafting me' said The Head Postmaster.

'You are now a fully accredited member of the human race' said The Assistant.

'What's that supposed to mean?' asked The Head Postmaster.

'Ninety eight per cent of humanity are being shafted by the other two per cent' said The Branch Secretary.

'That's bloody socialist propaganda' jeered The Head Postmaster.

'Is it socialist propaganda you're being slung out by a bunch of squirts with third class degrees who haven't been with the firm for more than a year or so and you've done thirty years?' asked The Assistant.

'That's all a misunderstanding' said The Head Postmaster with not very much conviction.

'And is it socialist propaganda that snivelling little gits who know sodall about the job are being put in authority over blokes like you who've spent your life learning the ropes?' said The Assistant.

The Truculent Man raised his hand. The Head Postmaster looked at him.

'Well? What's your contribution?' he asked.

'Is there any more booze?' asked The Truculent Man.

'Look in the cabinet' said The Head Postmaster.

The Truculent Man got up and went over to the drinks cabinet. He turned accusingly towards The Head Postmaster.

'There's sodall there' he complained.

'Well I apologise. If I'd known you were coming I'd have laid on a barrel' said The Head Postmaster.

'What are we going to do then?' demanded The Truculent Man. The Head Postmaster sighed. He drew out his wallet.

'Nip over the road and get a crate' he said.

The Truculent Man grabbed the note.

'What am I? The bleedin' goofer?' he asked and left.

The Head Postmaster turned to The Branch Secretary.

'Now tell me. Why do I need a global strategy?' he asked.

'Because these bastards at Birmingham have got one' said The Branch Secretary.

'Elaborate' said The Head Postmaster.

The Branch Secretary launched into an analysis of the global realities, laying particular stress on the crimes committed in the name of Coca Cola.

'That's bloody outrageous' said The Head Postmaster.

The door was flung open and The Truculent Man marched in with a crate of beer.

'Is this where the demob party is?' he asked.

'Good thing your desk's always empty' said The Assistant as the crate was dumped in front of The Head Postmaster.

'I can't stand clutter' retorted The Head Postmaster.

'You'll need to get the tops off a bit quicker when you're running that country pub' said The Truculent Man.

'I'm doing my best' protested The Head Postmaster.

'You'll have to do better. Remember you're now competing with some downtrodden little sod pulling pints in Saigon' said The Assistant.

'I've got the edge. That downtrodden little sod hasn't got a global strategy' said The Head Postmaster.

'Nor have you. That's probably why you're being shat on from a great height' retorted The Truculent Man.

'Welcome to the Club' intoned The Assistant Secretary.

'We should organise a demonstration, get all the downtrodden sods out onto the streets' said The Truculent Man.

'All carrying banners saying 'We are being shat on from a great height' said The Educated Shaggin' Idiot.

'Shat opens of the world unite' suggested The Assistant.

Various suggestions for slogans depicting the plight of the legions of the shat upon were put forward while the contents of the crate were disposed of. After a while The Truculent Man looked round aggressively:

'This shagger's empty' he said holding up his bottle.

'Well get another one. What's the matter with you?' said The Head Postmaster crossly.

He reached for his wallet but The Branch Secretary stepped him. He held up his hand and rose to his feet.

'Kin' ell!' muttered The Truculent Man.

'This is a symbolic gathering' began The Branch Secretary.

'Siddown for Chrissake!' urged The Truculent Man.

The Branch Secretary ignored him.

'This is a symbolic gathering' he repeated.

He appeared to lose his thread for a moment and fell silent. Then he resumed.

'We are gathered here, representatives from both sides of industry, drinking together in a spirit of comradeship and unity and solidarity, and why?'

'Because he's paying?' said The Truculent Man indicating The Head Postmaster.

'Because we all have one thing in common that unites us and that is …'

'We're all being shat on from a great height' said The Assistant.

'Correct. We are all victims. And who is responsible for our suffering?' asked The Branch Secretary.

'The Mad Witch of Shaggin' Grantham' shouted The Truculent Man.

'Indeed. But what is she?' asked The Branch Secretary.

'A Shaggin' Evil Cow' bellowed The Truculent Man.

'Right again. But she is no more than an agent of … who?'

'Coca Cola!' howled The Head Postmaster.

'We're all being shat on from a great height so that everyone has to drink that piss' shouted The Branch Secretary, his face by now red.

'If people only knew what was happening?' howled The Head Postmaster.

'We're going to tell them' shouted The Branch Secretary.

'How?' bellowed The Head Postmaster while grabbing another bottle and to his great disgust finding it empty.

'We're going to write the truth?' said The Branch Secretary.

'They'll never print it' said The Head Postmaster.

'That's why we're going to write it and print it' said The Branch Secretary.

'Where' demanded The Head Postmaster.

'On the Shitehouse walls bellowed The Union Men in unison.

The Educated Shaggin' Idiot looked quietly pleased.

'More beer' said The Head Postmaster again reaching for his wallet.

The Branch Secretary rose again and held up his hand. The Assistant was examining the bottles hopefully holding each one up to the light in case it still had some beer in it.

'We're being shat on from a great height together, we're drinking together, we're standing together, we'll pay together' he declared.

Everyone clapped. Then there was a pause while The Branch Secretary waited expectantly. Finally realisation dawned. The Truculent Man looked astonished.

'You mean you want us to pay?' he said.

The Branch Secretary nodded in confirmation. The Truculent Man sighed deeply and got out his wallet.

'Is this to do with the global strategy?' he asked as he handed over his note.

'It most certainly is' The Branch Secretary confirmed.

'Then I don't think much of it' said The Truculent Man as he collected all the contributions and went off to get another crate.

CHAPTER
TWENTY FOUR

Come Landlord Fill The Flowing Bowl

The Head Postmaster's office was getting very crowded. Several crates of beer were lined up against one wall and the people in the room were doing their best to drink them all. Miss Watson had at first wandered in and out shaking her head and tut tutting while urging caution but The Head Postmaster was way beyond such craven considerations.

'Have a drink Miss Watson. We all have to let our hair down occasionally' he said, but Miss Watson was having none of it.

'Someone has to keep a clear head' she said primly.

'Let me tell you about Coca Cola' said The Head Postmaster.

'Some other time' said Miss Watson and returned to her office.

'That woman is an absolute jewel' said The Head Postmaster.

'She is. She's Post Office through and through. Real Post Office Rock' said The Chief Inspector, unaccustomedly amiable after drinking a few bottles.

'We've got to have a global strategy Chief' The Head Postmaster told him.

'What for?' asked The Chief.

'To shaft those sods at Birmingham' said The Head Postmaster.

'In that case I'm all for it' said The Chief.

'And Coca Cola' said The Head Postmaster.

'Coca Cola?' echoed The Chief looking mystified.

'They're linked.' said The Head Postmaster.

'Coca Cola and those sods at Birmingham?' said The Chief.

The Head Postmaster nodded solemnly. The Chief looked at The Head Postmaster's nearly empty glass. He looked round the room and his gaze fell on The Educated Shaggin' Idiot.

'What about The Educated Shaggin' Idiot?' he asked.

'He's on our side' The Head Postmaster told him.

'I'd sooner he was with those sods at Birmingham' said The Chief.

'He's got the brains' said The Head Postmaster.

'We don't need brains. We're shaggin' management' said The Chief.

'I didn't realise' said The Head Postmaster.

The Chief had no idea what he was talking about.

'It's a bit late in the day to start realising now. You're bloody near retirement' he said.

The Branch Secretary looked round at what seemed to him to amount to a bacchanalia. He turned to The Assistant.

'This is no bloody way to launch a global strategy' he complained.

'Of course it isn't' said The Assistant.

He pointed out The Truculent Man who was holding up an obscure Dim Manager by the lapels while he explained a point to him.

'Look at him. Is that any way to win hearts and minds?' he asked.

The Branch Secretary glanced across.

'He's a good man as far as he goes' he said indulgently.

'He means well' conceded The Assistant.

'You know what's missing here?' said The Secretary.

'Are we regarding this impromptu pissup as the official launch of The Global Strategy?', said The Assistant.

'We might as well' said The Branch Secretary.

'You're not going to make a speech?' asked The Assistant looking worried.

'We need the press' said The Branch Secretary.

'You are going to make a speech' said The Assistant.

'How can you have a significant launch without the media' reasoned The Branch Secretary. The Assistant nodded vaguely and made his way over to The Truculent Man.

'Have you got a moment?' he asked.

The Truculent Man reluctantly removed his hands from The Obscure Dim Manager's lapels and nodded.

'The Assistant indicated The Branch Secretary who was standing on his own deep in thought.

'He wants to bring in the media?' said The Assistant.

'What now?' said The Truculent Man looking round at the redfaced company.

The Assistant nodded. Realisation dawned on The Truculent Man's face.

'He wants to make a shaggin' speech' he said.

The Assistant Secretary nodded.

'Why is he never satisfied till he's up on his feet making a twat of himself?' asked The Truculent Man.

'What are we going to do?' said The Assistant.

'Speak to The Educated Shaggin' Idiot' said The Truculent Man decisively.

The Assistant Secretary sighed heavily. He made his way over to The Educated Shaggin' Idiot who was sitting down with a glass of beer looking somewhat bemused.

'I still have no idea why I'm here' he told The Assistant. The Assistant looked round the thronged room. 'This is all bloody weird' he said.

'Surreal' said The Educated Shaggin' Idiot.

'Some of these shaggin' gaffers have always looked as though they've been painted with a thick brush by Piccasso' said The Assistant.

The Educated Shaggin' Idiot looked round and shook his head wearily.

'This is the managerial class. This country can't possibly survive' he said.

The Assistant Secretary looked around him.

'It doesn't bloody deserve to' he said.

'Amid the drunken babble they saw The Branch Secretary waving his arms about and his lips moving.

'What the bloody hell is he doing?' asked The Educated Shaggin' Idiot.

'I think he's making a speech' said The Truculent Man.

'No-one's taking any notice' said The Educated Shaggin' Idiot.

'That won't stop him' said The Truculent Man.

'Talk to him. Shut him up' said The Assistant.

'He'll take no notice of me' said The Educated Shaggin' Idiot.

As they were wondering what they could possibly do The Chief Inspector took a hand. He marched up to The Branch Secretary:

'What the shaggin' hell do you think you're doing?' he asked.

'What does it look as though I'm doing?' countered The Branch Secretary.

'Making a right prat of yourself' said The Chief.

'Well someone's got to' said The Branch Secretary somewhat ambiguously.

'It doesn't always have to be you' The Chief told him.

'You're nothing but an office boy for Coca Cola' said The Branch Secretary and stalked away.

The Chief stared after him open mouthed.

'What's all this bollocks about Coca Cola?' he asked himself.

He spotted a Dim Manager and collared him.

'What's all this bollocks about Coca Cola?' he asked.

'I don't know Chief' answered The Dim Manager.

'Well bloody well find out' said The Chief.

'How am I supposed to do that?' muttered The Dim Gaffer.

He went wandering off round the room.

'What's all this bollocks about Coca Cola?' he asked another Dim Manager.

'Shagoff' said The Second Dim Manager.

'Shagoff yourself you fat shagger' replied The First Dim Manager.

The Dim Manager found himself facing a somewhat disgruntled Branch Secretary.

'What's all this bollocks about Coca Cola?' he asked somewhat aggressively.

'You want to know about Coca Cola?' replied The Branch Secretary.

Before The Dim Manager could reply The Branch Secretary started telling him about Coca Cola.

'It's the FBI, the CIA, the White House, the Pentagon, the Mafia and Wall Street. Then it's Ten Dawning St., The Foreign Office, The SAS, MI5, MI6, the Media, The City and The Mad Witch of Grantham'.

'I vote for her' said The Dim Manager.

'It's thanks to bloody idiots like you that Coca Cola are establishing The Fourth Reich' said The Branch Secretary and walked off.

'If it's anything like The Third Reich they had some good ideas' said The Dim Manager to himself.

He sought out The Dim Manager with A Pot Belly And Acne.

'What do you know about Coca Cola?' he asked.

'Shagall' said The Dim Manager With A Pot Belly And Acne.

'They're trying to establish The Fourth Reich said The Dim Manager.

'The sooner the shaggin' better' said The Dim Manager With A Pot Belly and Acne.

'That's what I think' said The Dim Manager.

'All these poxy Dogooders want sorting out' said The Dim Manager with a Pot Belly and Acne.

The Chief cornered The Dim Manager.

'Right. What have you found out?' he asked.

'They're forming The Fourth Reich to shaft the poxy Doogooders' said The Dim Manager.

The Chief looked thoughtful. He looked at The Dim Manager.

'Good work' he told him and went across to where the beer was.

The Dim Manager felt really pleased with himself. Promotion appeared to be beckoning. He did vaguely grasp that he was living in an era in which being stupid was no handicap and he also dimly discerned that under a Fourth Reich creeps like him would prosper.

The Branch Secretary meanwhile was thinking that extreme circumstances call for extreme measures.

'What this country needs is a bloody revolution' he said to the man standing next to him.

This happened to be The Misfit Manager, a man who did not suffer fools gladly, was not deferential to his superiors and didn't like the way things were going.

'We should have had that shagger years ago' he agreed.

The Branch Secretary realised that here was an ally within the citadel. He was about to launch into a tirade about Coca Cola when The Misfit Manager got in first.

'They're shagging up the entire world just so MacDonalds can make people eat shit and underpay their staff' he fumed.

'It's not MacDonalds' said The Branch Secretary shaking his head.

'You don't believe all this crap about defending freedom?' said The Misfit Manager his lip curling in scorn.

The Branch Secretary shook his head in vigorous denial.

'MacDonalds are no more than bit players. The real villains are Coca Cola' he said.

'What makes you say that?' asked The Misfit Manager.

'Come and sit down. I'll explain' said The Branch Secretary drawing him aside.

Meanwhile The Truculent Man was having a spot of bother with The Dim Manager With A Pot Belly And Acne. They had never got on and over a period of twenty years had had various troublesome encounters. Moreover they were both more than usually aggressive as a result of drinking more than their share of the beer.

'You've allways been a useless shaggin' wanker. That's why you're still a shaggin' postman' said The Dim Manager with A Pot Belly And Acne.

'The reason I'm still a postman is because I don't want to be associated with tosspots like you' said The Truculent Man.

'You haven't got the brains to be a shaggin' Manager' said The Dim Manager With A Pot Belly And Acne.

The Truculent Man's eyes bulged and he went an alarming colour.

'Brains!' he exploded. His voice rose above the din and everyone turned to see what had caused this roar of anger and indignation. The Truculent Man was too furious to marshal his arguments and remained silent with his face thrust into that of The Dim Manager With A Pot Belly And Acne. For a moment the scene was frozen, then the din picked up again and people continued their conversations.

'You've got no shaggin' ambition' said The Dim Manager With A Pot Belly And Acne.

'And you've got no shaggin' integrity' said The Truculent Man.

The Dim Manager With A Pot Belly And Acne looked puzzled.

The Truculent Man looked triumphant. 'You don't know what integrity is do you?' he said.

The Dim Manager With A Pot Belly And Acne was nonplussed. He thought desparately for a rejoinder, then came up with one.

'You're a wanker' he said.

The Truculent Man felt he had won the argument and was happy. He beamed contentedly.

'Those two seem to be getting on like a house on fire' remarked The Chief.

'You're like all the rest of the Union blokes. You're all talk. You do shagall' said The Dim Manager With A Pot Belly And Acne.

'Is that right?' said The Truculent Man grinning and nodding.

'Yes' said The Dim Manager with a pot belly and acne.

The Truculent Man trod on his foot and then punched him. The Dim Manager With A Pot Belly And Acne. went down and lay on the floor motionless. Still smiling The Truculent Man pointed at him.

'Look at this pissed up prat!' he guffawed. 'He never could hold his beer' he continued grinning round.

'If he can't take it he shouldn't drink it' said The Chief.

'No point being on The Post Office if you can't lift heavy shaggin' bags and hold your shaggin' ale' said The Truculent Man. There was a chorus of assent.

'He never could do either' said The Chief.

'Should have been sacked when he was a postman' said The Truculent Man.

'We won't go into that' said The Chief.

'Should have been sacked when he was a higher grade Postman' said The Truculent Man.

'We won't go into that' said The Chief.

'Should never have taken the useless effer on in the first place' said The Misfit Manager.

'I can't argue with that' said The Chief.

'He's not dead is he?' asked someone as The Dim Manager With A Pot Belly And Acne remained motionless. The Truculent Man looked a little worried.

'Wave a docket under his nose. That'll bring him round' said The Assistant Secretary.

'There's no call to take the piss. Show some respect. He could be dead' said The Dim Manager With A Red Nose.

'No such shaggin' luck' said The Misfit Manager.

The Dim Manager With A Pot Belly And Acne got shakily to feet. His eye fell on The Truculent Man. He pointed at him.

'He shaggin' well hit me' he accused.

'Bollocks you fell over' said The Truculent Man.

'I fell over because you shaggin' hit me' said The Dim Manager With A Pot Belly And Acne.

'Did you shaggin' hit him?' asked The Chief.

'Did I bollocks' said The Truculent Man.

The Dim Manager With A Pot Belly And Acne looked round hoping for support.

'He shaggin' hit me. That's shaggin' assault that is' he wailed.

'Don't talk like a shaggin' idiot. If he shaggin' hit you that's assault. We all know that shagger' said The Misfit Manager.

'He's pissed. Breathlyse the prat' suggested The Truculent Man.

'I hope he's not driving home in that condition' said The Branch Secretary piously.

At least half a dozen pissed up Managers who had every intention of driving home rounded on The Dim Manager With A Pot Belly And Acne.

This demonstration of mass hostility from his peers caused The Dim Manager With A Pot Belly And Acne. to quail. He attempted to justify himself but he was rattled.

'I'm not worse than the rest of you' he faltered.

That caused another eruption of self righteous wrath.

'Don't you suggest the rest of us are as bad as you. We haven't fallen over' The Chief told him.

'I don't mean you Chief' he said with a positively grovelling air of false humility that was so nauseating it provoked more outpourings of scorn from Managers and Union Men.

'He's a bloody disgrace. Gets pissed, falls over, and then accuses me of chinning him' said The Truculent Man.

'I think you'd better apologise' said The Misfit Manager.

'Who to?' asked The Dim Manager with acne and a pot belly.

'Him' said The Misfit Manager indicating The Truculent Man.

The Dim Manager With A Pot Belly And Acne stood there dumbfounded. His mouth opened and closed with no sound. He looked appealingly at The Chief. There was no comfort to be found there. The Chief gazed back at him bleakly. He shook his head in bafflement.

'I'm supposed to apologise to the shagger who shaggin' well hit me' he said bitterly.

The Head Postmaster wagged an admonitory finger at him.

'Watch your language in my office' he told him.

The Chief also rounded on him.

'Watch your shaggin' language in The Head Postmaster's shaggin' office' he said.

'Show some shaggin' respect' said The Assistant Secretary.

The Dim Manager With A Pot Belly And Acne turned furiously and was about to unleash a torrent of abuse at The Assistant Secretary when he realised he was surrounded by an entirely hostile circle and desisted. Biting his lip he swallowed hard and held his tongue.

'My shaggin' solicitor's going to have something to say about this shagger' said The Truculent Man, managing to look aggrieved.

'We don't want any shaggin' solicitors brought into this' said The Chief.

'That's up to me' protested The Dim Manager With A Pot Belly And Acne.

'We don't want our dirty washing dragged through the courts' said The Head Postmaster.

'We've got enough trouble with the sheep shaggin'' muttered someone.

The Head Postmaster glared round. The Chief tried to locate the source of the comment. He suspected The Misfit Manager but he gazed back at him innocently. The Chief decided an investigation would not yield the culprit.

'We'll have no talk of sheepshaggin' here' he said.

There were murmurs of what he took to be assent. The Head Postmaster held up his head for silence. He cleared his throat. The Chief nodded encouragingly. The Head Postmaster began to speak:

'We're bound to have our little differences' he said.

The Dim Manager With A Pot Belly And Acne thought a right hander to the jaw followed by a threat of legal proceedings was rather more than a little difference but decided to hold his peace.

'. ... but it's important to remember the things that bind us together' continued The Head Postmaster.

Everyone nodded sagely while trying desperately to think of what those things were.

'.... Common interests' said The Chief.

The Branch Secretary was puzzled.

'Is he talking about Derby County?' he asked.

'Buggered if I know what he's talking about' said The Misfit Manager.

'Do you suppose he knows?' asked The Assistant Secretary.

'If he does it's the first time' replied The Misfit Manager.

'I think you've got an attitude problem' grinned The Assistant Secretary.

The Misfit Manager grinned back at him.

'I've always had an attitude problem. Since all this shaggin' everyone about started it's got worse' he said.

'You were a right little sod when you were a telegraph boy' recalled The Assistant Secretary.

'Those were the days' said The Misfit Manager.

The Head Postmaster was getting nicely into his stride.

'Common interests' he repeated, feeling this phrase had a certain resonance, 'the need to close ranks to face a common enemy' he said.

Suddenly everyone was all ears wondering if he was going to identify the common enemy who was buggering everything up.

The Head Postmaster took a swig from a handy bottle.

'We face a truly formidable foe' he told them.

He then wondered what to say next and fell silent. There was an awkward pause.

The Earnest Young Dim Acting Manager thought it was time to put his oar in?

'Who is the enemy sir?' he asked looking at The Branch Secretary.

'It's not me' said The Branch Secretary.

'Coca Cola' said The Head Postmaster. Everyone waited for him to expand upon this pronouncement but he had no intention of doing so.

The Chief thought it expedient to follow the official line.

'Coca Cola you pillock! I should have thought you'd have known that. Don't you know shagall?' he said to The Earnest Dim Young Acting Manager, who was wishing he had kept his mouth shut. No-one else was prepared to speak for fear of looking like a bloody fool and silence reigned for a while. This was broken by The Truculent Man who felt it was his day.

He pointed at The Dim Manager With A Pot Belly And Acne.

'I want an apology' he bellowed, The Dim Manager With A Pot Belly And Acne choked and spluttered on his beer.

'You can bollocks' he bellowed.

The Chief was furious.

'How many more times do I have to tell you no swearing in the Head Postmaster's office?' he asked.

'Pissed up, foul mouthed and not man enough to apologise' said The Truculent Man.

Murmurs of assent went round the room. In desperation The Dim Manager With A Pot Belly And Acne appealed to The Secretary of the Managers' Union.

'What's the Union going to do about this?' he asked with an attempt at belligerance. The Secretary of the Managers' Union was having nothing to do with it.

'This is not a Union matter' he said dismissively.

The Dim Manager With A Pot Belly And Acne opened his mouth to protest but The Chief cut him short.

'Watch your language' he warned.

The Truculent Man scented victory.

'Am I going to get an apology or not?' he demanded.

The Chief glared at The Dim Manager With A Pot Belly And Acne.

'Apologise' he told him.

The Dim Manager With A Pot Belly And Acne glared back at The Chief his face slowly turning a deep crimson.

'I apologise' he said, the words all but choking him.

The Chief nodded approval and The Dim Manager With A Pot Belly And Acne stood grinding his teeth while The Truculent Man grinned infuriatingly at him. The Dim Manager With A Pot Belly And Acne felt well nigh unbearable sense of grievance but worse was to come. The Assistant Branch Secretary spoke.

'Tell him you're a wanker' he demanded.

The Dim Manager With A Pot Belly And Acne opened his mouth and was going to tell The Assistant Branch Secretary to Shagott, but he saw The Head Postmaster and The Chief nodding his approval at The Assistant Branch Secretary's request and knew there was to be no escape.

'I'm a wanker' he said.

The Head Postmaster was delighted.

'Excellent. Well done' he said.

Everyone looked puzzled.

'That's what we need in the fight against Coca Cola gentlemen. Self knowledge' he said nodding happily as he reached for another bottle.

CHAPTER
TWENTY FIVE

The Aerosol Spray is Mightier than the Sword

Rod Williams sat at his desk chewing his fingernails. He was once more a worried man. Lately things had been looking better. There had been a kind of ceasefire in effect on the station. Nothing had been formally agreed, none of the problems resolved, but somehow both sides had drifted into a kind of tacit trace. George continued to go over to the Institute, sticking his fingers up at the tv as he did so, and also on his return, but despite George the tensions that had been so apparent had slipped back beneath the surface. Rod no longer found it necessary to lock himself in the Executive Toilet and The Doctor had reduced his medication.

Doctor Llewellyn was greatly relieved not to be confronted with the spectacle of Rod twitching uncontrollably opposite him nearly so often and was toying with the idea of writing a paper on the treatment of executive stress. His surgery was however still full of white faced postmen who collapsed into the patients' chair and with the greatest difficulty managed to inform him they were completely knackered. Painstaking enquiries had enabled him to form a clear impression of the way delivery postmen were being forced to work, and he let them know in no uncertain terms that he was surprised they were still alive, and made it perfectly clear to them that if they continued to work in this way they would rapidly place themselves entirely beyond the reach of medicine. Whilst this was without doubt a perfectly sound diagnosis it did absolutely nothing for the state of mind of the persecuted delivery men.

'It's no good coming to me, I can't help you. If you're going to carry on working like this all I can advise is insure yourself heavily, see The Parson and try and make sure you got a better deal in the next life. Not to put too fine a point upon it, the fact is the bastards are killing you' he told one particularly broken man.

The delivery man gazed at him and shook his head hopelessly.

'It all started with what they called improved working methods' he managed to gasp out.

Doctor Llewellyn nodded. 'The usual pattern using euphemism to disguise atrocity' he said.

The Delivery Postman sat slumped in the chair looking as though his spirit had already moved on. Doctor Llewellyn hadn't had a patient actually expire in the consulting room and didn't want this one to set a precedent.

'Are you there Mr. Jenkins?' he asked.

'Only just' breathed Mr. Jenkins.

'It's bloody disgraceful' said Doctor Llewellyn.

'It's the same all over the country, but she's put the Great back into Britain' said Mr. Jenkins with an attempt at a derisive chuckle which left him looking nearer death than ever.

'My wife's threatening to leave me' confided Mr. Jenkins.

The Doctor didn't know what to say

'She's had enough of living with a zombie' Mr. Jenkins explained.

The Doctor shook his head sadly

'I'd threaten to leave her but she knows I'm too knackered to go anywhere' said Mr. Jenkins.

'I'm signing you off' Doctor Llewellyn told him.

Mr. Jenkins looked horrified.

'You can't do that. The bastards'll sack me' he protested.

'No they won't. We'll give the bastards something to think about' said Doctor Llewellyn as he wrote out a sick note. He handed it to Mr. Jenkins.

Mr. Jenkins looked at it closely. Then put it nearer to his eyes as though he couldn't believe what he saw.

'Executive Stress! You've put Executive Stress!' he said.

Doctor Llewellyn nodded. Mr. Jenkins shook his head wearily.

'But I'm a shaggin' postman,' he said:

'And I'm a shaggin' Doctor and I'm saying you're suffering from Executive shaggin' stress and should not work for a month. That'll give the bastards something to think about' said Doctor Llewellyn.

Mr. Jenkins sat for a moment looking at the certificate. Then he put it carefully into his wallet. He grinned at The Doctor.

'Executive Stress. Nice one Doc. You're right they won't know what to make of this shagger' he said rising to his feet. He paused for a moment in the doorway.

'When the uprising comes Doc. I'll put in a good word for you' he said and left.

'When the uprising comes I'll be leading the shagger' said Doctor Llewellyn to himself. He punched the bell.

'Send in the next poor downtrodden exploited sod!' he yelled.

Meanwhile Rod Williams at the Station was getting intimations once again, someone was writing on the Shitehouse wall, that all was not well, and he was rapidly going to pieces.

The Post Office's Dim Manager was his usual sympathetic self.

'You want to pull yourself together. We're all suffering from Executive Stress but we have to learn to cope with it' he said.

'It's terrible' said Rod.

'You've seen shagall yet' The Dim Post Office Manager told him.

'I've seen shaggin' enough' said Rod.

'It's nothing to do with me' said The Dim Post Office Manager.

'I thought you were supposed to be The Manager' said Rod.

'My blokes are all in the clear' said The Dim Post Office Manager.

'What about that Longhaired Git?' asked Rod.

The Dim Post Office Manager shook his head decisively. Rod was convinced The Post Office had something to do with it.

'What about George?' he asked.

The Dim Post Office Manager immediately became defensive. He always did when George was mentioned.

'What about George?' he said.

'You tell me' said Rod Williams.

'I'm having shagall to do with George. It's the best way' said The Dim Post Office Manager.

'He's one of your shaggin' blokes you can't just pretend he doesn't exist' protested Rod.

'You just watch me' said The Dim Post Office Manager.

'It seems to me you've no idea as to the gravity of the situation' said Rod Williams.

The Dim Post Office Manager snorted derisively.

'You're making a lot of fuss about shagall' he said.

'For a start it's sheer vandalism' said Rod.

'You can't expect people not to write on Shitehouse walls' The Dim Post Office Manager told him.

'That's a very negative attitude' said Rod.

The Dim Manager shrugged. He wasn't really in the slightest way interested in the Shitehouse walls and thought Rod should have better things to concern himself with.

The Leprauchan knocked and entered. He was carrying a bucket and was streaked with white paint.

'I've done what you said. I've painted over the walls of the Platform One Shitehouse thereby obliterating all traces of the offending graffiti. Some passengers are complaining because they've got paint on their clothes'.

Rod looked worried.

'Are they first class passengers?' he asked anxiously.

The Leprauchan shook his head. Rod looked relieved. He turned to The Leprauchan.

'I told you to paint the walls of the Platform One Shitehouse, not paint yourself. Go and get cleaned up' he said.

The Leprauchan shook his head.

'I haven't finished yet. I've come for more paint' he told Rod. Rod looked furious.

'Those Goddam postmen and taxi drivers are going to start that cricket crap again. You're going to paint the bastards a sightscreen' he accused.

'While I was obliterating all traces of the offending graffiti from the walls of the Platform One Shitehouse someone was covering the walls of the Platform Six Shitehouse. I think what we have here is an ongoing situation' said The Leprauchan.

Rod Williams blanched. He turned to The Dim Post Office Manager. The Dim Post Office Manager shrugged his shoulders:

'Shagall to do with me' he said dismissively.

Rod turned to The Leprauchan.

'I think you're right. This is organised. We're not dealing with a shambolic deranged nut. It's a Goddam conspiracy!'

'We could be being targeted by Moscow' said The Dim Post Office Manager.

'Do you think so?' Rod asked before he realised The Dim Post Office Manager was taking the piss.

'You sit there taking the piss. You won't think it so funny when the Goddam bastards are marching all over you' said Rod.

'It seems to me … … ' The Leprauchan began, taking a seat. Rod cuts him short.

'I don't want you sitting there giving me your analysis of the situation. Get your arse over to Platform Six and paint that poison over before someone sees it' he said.

The Leprauchan sighed wearily and got to his feet. He picked up his bucket and stood looking at Rod.

'What are you waiting for? I've given you an order. Carry it out' said Rod.

'Would you mind unlocking the paint?' said The Leprauchan.

'What are you looking up the shaggin' paint for?' asked The Dim Post Office Manager. Rod ignored him. He unlocked the cupboard. The Leprauchan filled his bucket. Rod returned to his desk and unlocked a drawer. He then relocked the paint cupboard. He took a piece of paper from the desk drawer, relocked the drawer, and passed the paper to The Leprauchan.

'Sign there' he said. The Leprauchan signed. The Dim Post Office Manager shook his head in wonder.

'Kin'ell!' he muttered to himself. Rod glared at him. 'You amaze me. You're in the middle of a war zone and you don't even know it' he said.

The door was flung open and George stormed in. He had white paint all over his uniform.

'Get out of my office' shrieked Rod.

George was spluttering in fury. He pointed to various splashes of paint on his uniform.

'Look at this' he shouted.

'Look at what?' countered Rod. The Dim Post Office Manager was edging towards the door. The performance with the keys had persuaded him that Rod was likely at any moment to commit an axe murder, and he didn't much fancy dealing with an irate George. George pointed to the various white patches on his uniform.

'Are you shaggin' blind as well as shaggin' stupid?' he roared.

'What do you expect? You're in a War Zone' Rod told him.

'It's to be expected is it?' said George.

'Sure it's to be expected' said Rod Williams. Then he added: 'There are no innocent bystanders in war.'

'Sure he's right there. It leaves its mark on us all' said The Leprauchan. George appeared to calm down:

'On all of us?' he asked.

Rod and The Leprauchan nodded. George grabbed The Leprauchan's bucket and brush. He painted a white line from The Leprauchan's forehead to his navel. Then he turned to Rod. Rod backed off.

'Get him off me' he demanded of The Dim Post Office Manager.

'Shagall to do with me' said The Dim Post Office Manager as he left.

'You're in a War Zone' said George as he slopped paint at Rod.

A passenger entered. He was covered in streaks and smears of white paint.

'Are you The Station Master?' he asked Rod.

'Well yes and no' said Rod evasively.

'I'm covered in white paint' said the passenger.

'You're not the only shagger' said The Leprauchan.

George turned to the passenger and indicated Rod.

'It's his shaggin' fault. He's a useless shagger. If he can't do the shaggin' job he should shag off back to shaggin' Canada' he said.

'I want to make a complaint under the terms of the Passengers' Charter' said The Passenger.

Rod looked longingly towards the Executive Shitehouse. Unfortunately both George and The Passenger blocked his route.

'I don't think we've got a copy of that. I could probably get one from Birmingham, but it might take some time' said Rod.

'I've got one' said The Passenger.

Rod's spirit sank. He was not having a nice day. Not only was he covered in paint, he was now confronted by an Uppity Bastard Who Knew The System.

'I think you'll find the Charter is solely concerned with punctuality of trains' Rod said in a voice which entirely lacked conviction.

'I think you'll find my case quite definitely comes under the heading 'or other matters' said The Uppity Bastard Who Knew The System.

Rod had no idea of how to deal with this. He knew he should under no circumstances admit culpability but he just couldn't cope with Uppity Bastards Who Knew The System. He turned hopefully towards The Leprauchan.

'My colleague Mr. Mulligan is something of an authority on The Charter' he said.

The Leprauchan felt strongly tempted to say he was just the shaggin' odd job man and leave Rod to squirm in the shite, but the opportunity to demonstrate his superior intellect was more than he could resist. He beamed at The Uppity Bastard Who Knew The System.

'You're obviously familiar with the terms of The Charter but in time of war national considerations prevail and we all have to sacrifice some of our individual privileges' he said.

Rod was not impressed. At the same time it struck him that he'd better see about getting the Cocky Little Bastard shifted since he was obviously dangerous. Unfortunately The Uppity Bastard Who Knew The System recognised crap when he heard it.

'That's simply obfuscation' he said.

The Leprauchan was nonplussed. None of his Workers' Educational Association classes had dealt with obfuscation. Fortunately George came up with a definition.

'It's bullshit' he said.

The Uppity Bastard Who Knew The System nodded:

'Absolute bullshit' he confirmed.

Rod thought he might yet be able to save the situation.

'This is definitely a war zone' he declared.

The Uppity Bastard Who Knew The System looked at The Leprauchan.

'So Sitting Bull here is all ready for battle is he?' he said indicating the paint down The Leprauchan's face.

'This Station's a shaggin' shambles' said George.

'I can see that' said The Uppity Bastard Who Knew The System.

'I'm meeting my performance targets' wailed Rod.

'Bollocks! The shaggin' trains are all over the place. Half the time you don't even know where the shaggers are!' snorted George.

'We know where you are' howled Rod.

'And what's that supposed to mean?' asked George.

'Getting a skinful of beer at the Railway Institute' said Rod.

'You be sure of your facts before you start making accusations' said George.

The sheer effrontery of this took Rod's breath away. Realising there was no point in trying to reason with George he decided to appeal to The Uppity Bastard Who Knew The System's sense of patriotism.

'Everything here may look normal … .' he began.

The Uppity Bastard Who Knew The System looked round at the three paint covered men.

'You call this normal?' he interrupted.

'They're hidden in the shadows' said Rod.

'Who?' asked The Uppity Bastard Who Knew The System.

'The people who are trying to overthrow our system' answered Rod.

'What system?' asked The Uppity Bastard Who Knew The System.

'Our way of life' Rod told him.

'Explain yourself' said The Uppity Bastard Who Knew The System.

'Commies' said Rod.

'Bollocks! They're all shaggin' working class conservative here' said George derisively.

'It's not working class conservatives writing that stuff about Coca Cola on the Shitehouse walls. It's Commies' Rod retorted.

The Uppity Bastard Who Knew The System became impatient.

'I realise a majority of the English people are now teetering on the verge of insanity, but what I'm hearing here beggars belief. You're saying the graffiti on your walls is the work of a communist cell?' he asked.

Rod nodded. 'They're accusing Coca Cola of war crimes and genocide' he said, his eyes like saucers.

The Uppity Bastard Who Knew The System gazed at Rod with plain contempt.

'You're hopeless. Not only do you not know where half the shaggin' trains are, you don't even know what's written on your Shitehouse walls. It doesn't accuse Coca Cola of war crimes and genocide. It says American and British foreign policy since the end of World War Two have been responsible for more murder, torture, maiming, rape and starvation than Hitler. And it is entirely correct' he concluded.

The Leprauchan nodded.

'He's right. That is what it says. And it says Coca Cola is the beneficiary of all this murder and genocide. I think it must mean Coca Cola is such piss you have to commit mass murder before you can get people to drink it' he said.

Rod didn't hear a word The Leprauchan said. He was staring whitefaced at The Uppity Bastard Who Knew The System. This was far worse than anything he had ever dreamt was possible. He wondered what he had done that such a dire fate should befall him. To be confronted with An The Uppity Bastard Who Knew The System was bad enough. To be faced with An The Uppity Bastard Who Knew The System with Left Wing Leanings was beyond endurance. He picked up the telephone and dialled.

I want an appointment with Doctor Llewellyn tonight' he said. He sat chewing his fingernails.

'My name is Rod Williams. This is not a laughing matter. Executive Stress is not a joke' he told The Receptionist who broke into uncontrollable titters when she heard his name.

'I'll lodge a complaint about you under the terms of The Patients' Charter' he shouted and rang off before she could reply.

The Uppity Bastard Who Knew The System shook his head in sheer disgust.

'I'm not pursuing my complaint under the terms of the Passengers' Charter' he said.

Rod looked gratified and beamed in delight. However his smile soon faded.

'I'm going to ring The Sun's 'Prat Line' said The Uppity Bastard.

'Sure he's been on that three times already' said The Leprauchan.

'The thick shagger went up to London and they gave him a little cup' said George.

The Uppity Bastard Who Knew The System went to the door. He turned and gazed bleakly at Rod.

'That writing on your Shitehouse wall isn't by a communist cell. It's ordinary blokes who've had enough of the whole rotten system. With any luck before too long the whole rotten edifice will come tumbling down and useless dim wankers like you will be buried under the rubble' he said and stalked out.

There was a long silence which was eventually broken by The Leprauchan.

'He might have been a bit of an anarchist but you could tell he was a gentleman. He spoke very well' he said.

Rod sat with his head in his hands: He felt he couldn't get as far as The Executive Shitehouse.

CHAPTER
TWENTY SIX

The First Shot

The Station Union Man stood in the Platform Six Shitehouse rubbing his hands together in delight. He turned to Paddy.

'What about that then Paddy?' he asked indicating the wall.

'I can't say I'm surprised. The English eejets murder millions wherever they go, but I'm shocked about Coca Cola' Paddy replied.

'This could be the start of great things' said The Union Man.

'What, this writing on the Shitehouse wall?' said Paddy looking puzzled.

'Paddy all great movements begin with something tiny, the merest suggestion of a whisper, and it grows until it's a mighty hurricane sweeping all before it, and when you look back you realise that nothing was ever the same after that first murmur' said The Station Union Man.

Paddy looked dubiously at the wall.

'I suppose you could be right' he conceded.

Rod Williams peered round the entrance, then stood in the doorway.

'Caught you in the act' he said triumphantly.

'What are you wittering about?' said Paddy.

'I knew if I kept watch I'd catch the guilty men' said Rod.

'I hope you're not shaggin' accusing me of shaggin' writing on the shaggin' Shitehouse wall' said Paddy indignantly.

'Bluster will get you nowhere' Rod told him.

'I'm not listening to this crap' said Paddy and attempted to leave. Rod blocked his way:

'Get out of the shaggin' way' demanded Paddy. Rod stood his ground and he and Paddy began to wrestle in the doorway.

A Would Be Traveller appeared. He attempted to get by. As he went to go left Rod and Paddy lurched that way. He went to go right they lurched in front of him again. The Would Be Traveller got angry and grabbed Rod. Rod thought it was The Station Union Man coming to Paddy's assistance and grappled with The Would Be Traveller. After much heaving and huffing and puffing and muffled exclamations The Would Be Passenger managed to break free. Rod was horrified to realise he had been setting about a typical representative of that enshrined species Middle England, impeccably clad in a suit and wearing a garish tie that made it look as though a drunk had puked across his shirt front.

'I do apologise sir' said Rod, grovelling and cringing in the the most nauseating way imagineable. 'I thought you were a Union Man' he said by way of explanation.

'So when you see a Trades Unionist you set about him do you?' said The Would Be Traveller.

Rod stood there yammering and stammering and wringing his hands in an agitated manner. The Would Be Traveller lost patience.

'Get out of the way man' he said and pushed past. He entered The Shitehouse and had a pee while he read the graffiti. He remained reading for some time. Then he turned to The Union Man.

'Things have come to a pretty pass in this country when the only place you can read the truth is on the Shitehouse walls' he said bitterly. Rod was standing outside trying to work out what to say. He was terrified lest The Would Be Traveller report him to Region. He knew there would be no sympathy for someone who had laid hands on a Would Be Passenger without first making sure he wasn't the sort of person who actually mattered, that is to say someone who could make trouble for the authorities, as this Would Be Traveller obviously could, and who was very likely the holder of a first class ticket as well. Rod worshipped the powerful, but he did much prefer dealing with the long suffering poor who never complained no matter what the official provocation, be it closed waiting rooms, closed toilets or no seats due to the fact that eighty per cent of the train was first class and most of the carriages empty.

Rod decided to take the bull by the horns. He entered the Shitehouse with a show of bravado. The Would Be Traveller was still gazing at the wall. Rod approached him, sure of his ground.

'I realise that is an affront to all decent people and I am having those responsible arrested and charged' he said.

'You're a shaggin' eejet' said Paddy.

'I've caught you redhanded' said Rod.

Paddy ignored him. He turned to The Would Be Traveller.

'You'd think the shaggin' English had enough shaggin' eejets of their own without shipping some more shaggers in from Canada' he said.

'Did you write this?' asked The Would Be Traveller.

'Do I look like the sort of man that goes round writing on Shitehouse walls' said Paddy.

The Would Be Traveller had a good look at Paddy and apparently decided he did not look like the sort of man who went round writing on Shitehouse walls. He turned to The Station Union Man.

'Did you write this?' he asked.

'He wrote it all right. I've caught him redhanded' said Rod.

The Would Be Traveller gestured for Rod to keep quiet, but Rod was not to be silenced. He pointed accusingly at The Union Man.

'He's the Goddamed Union Man. They're supposed to be moderate, but they're not. They're nothing but a bunch of Goddam Communists, and there's the evidence right there on the Goddamed wall' howled Rod.

'Why are you so sure it's these two?' asked The Would Be Traveller.

'I've been watching this place from my office and I saw them go in. When they didn't come out I knew they were up to no good, so I came over and I caught them' said Rod triumphantly.

'Just what exactly is your function?' asked The Would Be Traveller.

Rod looked mystified, his stupid face creasing with the effort of trying to think.

'What's your job?' asked The Would Be Traveller.

Rod puffed himself up, straightened his tie and pulled down the peak of his cap.

'I am The Station Manager' he said proudly.

The Would Be Traveller looked astounded. He stared at Rod for a moment or two. Rod stood grinning like an idiot. Paddy stood behind him tapping his forehead.

'You're The Station Manager and you spend your time spying on the Shitehouse. Haven't you got anything better to do?' demanded The Would Be Traveller.

'I've got plenty to do but this has top priority. It is a matter of national security' claimed Rod.

'Writing on the Shitehouse wall' scoffed Paddy.

'What's written there is terrible' protested Rod.

'It certainly is' said The Would Be Traveller.

'It says Britain and The United States have murdered more people than Hitler and Stalin put together' said Rod.

The Union Man pointed to a passage halfway down the wall.

'It also says this can be confirmed by consulting official records' he said.

'Everything written there is just plain wrong' claimed Rod.

'Paddy peered at a section.

'It says here Rod Williams is a wanker. That's true' he chortled.

The Union Man glanced across at Rod.

'I think we might have a problem here' he said.

'You've got a problem. I'm in the clear' said Rod.

'Someone seems to have been in that trap for a long time. I think they may have died' said The Union Man indicating a closed cubicle door.

Rod hoped that if someone had died in the Platform Six Shitehouse it was one of the unemployed. He hammered on the door.

'Anyone in there?' he yelled.

There was no reply.

'It's empty' said Rod.

'Then why is it shaggin' locked?' asked Paddy.

'You've got a corpse in there brother' said The Union Man.

'We'd best kick the door in' said Paddy.

They heard the sound of muffled voices coming from inside the cubicle. Rod hammered on the door.

'What's going on in there?' he demanded.

'Mind your own shaggin' business' said a voice from behind the door.

'It is my shaggin' business' claimed Rod.

'And who the shaggin' hell might you be?' asked a second voice.

'There's two of them in there' gasped Rod in horror.

'You come out of there or I'll fetch the Police' he threatened.

'All right all right. We're coming out' said a voice.

The door opened and The Ghost Squad came out.

'What were you doing in there?' asked Rod.

'Keeping out of the way' said Len.

Arthur looked at The Would Be Traveller.

'We're being shat on from a great height' he told him.

Len nodded glumly.

'It used to be great. We never bothered nobody and nobody bothered us. Now it's terrible' he told The Would Be Traveller.

'Why?' asked The Would Be Traveller.

'We're being shat on from a great height' said Arthur as though that explained all. The Ghost squad walked out of the Shitehouse. Rod chased after them and peered round.

'They've disappeared' he said.

'Of course they have. They may be being shat on from a great height but only when anyone knows where they are' said Paddy.

'Rod stared at the graffiti. A glimmer of an idea seemed to be stirring in him. His face creased grotesquely with the effort.

'Do you suppose they wrote that?' he asked.

'They may have written Das Capital' as well' said The Union Man.

'It's as much as those ignorant shaggers can do to write their names' said Paddy.

'They could be sleepers' said Rod.

'They're that allright, especially when there's work to be done' said Paddy.

'No no. I mean Moscow could have planted them. They could be Agents' Rod said.

Paddy could scarcely believe his ears.

'You don't seriously think that Russia would employ a couple of useless shaggers like them do you?' he said.

Rod was about to argue the point when Ivan The West Indian walked in. Grinning from ear to ear Ivan pointed to the writing on the wall.

'I see the latest edition of The Shitehouse Gazette is out on time' he said, obviously thoroughly delighted.

'It's not funny' said Rod.

'No it's not, it's shaggin' hilarious' chortled Ivan.

'Shouldn't you be on Platform One' said Rod pointedly.

'I should, but I had to come over here to find you. There's a guy wants to see you'.

'What's he want?' asked Rod.

'He wants speak to The Head Man' said Ivan.

'Is he a customer?' asked Rod.

'I think he might be. He's waving round a copy of The Passengers' Charter' said Ivan grinning happily at Rod's obvious discomfort.

'Who keeps handing that round? It's not supposed to be for public consumption' said Rod.

'It's probably the same bloke who keeps writing the truth about those bastards at The Foreign Office on the Shitehouse walls' said Ivan.

'That is not the truth. It's all lies' said Rod.

'If you say so' said Ivan.

'This is The Free World' said Rod.

'I thought it was the Platform Six Shitehouse' said Paddy.

Rod glared at the graffiti. He turned to The Station Union Man.

'I don't know who wrote this, but I'm sure The Post Office is at the bottom of it he said. The Would Be Traveller sighed heavily.

'I trust that man is unique' he said.

Ivan shook his head sadly.

'He ain't unique. He's typical. We've got thousands of the shaggers. They're everywhere. And they keep getting promoted' he said.

The Would Be Traveller turned to The Station Union Man.

'What happens to a country where incompetent imbeciles keep getting promoted?' he asked.

'It ends up with abysmal pensions, a buggered up health service, chaotic transport, the return of the diseases of poverty and corruption at every level of government' said The Station Union Man.

'And everyone shrugs their shoulders and says what can you do?' said The Would Be Traveller.

Meanwhile Rod Williams had managed to dodge the irate customer flourishing a copy of The Passengers' Charter and gained the sanctuary of his office. He peered cautiously out of the window. Everyone on the platform looked perfectly docile. He couldn't tell which one had a copy of The Charter.

'That's what's so frightening. They all look normal, just like everyone else' he muttered. Then he began to think about the witches coven that used the Mail Porters' Rest Room as its headquarters and he felt he must take a couple of the tranquillisers without which he could no longer function.

Ivan strolled in.

'There's a group of people wandering round The Station. They've all got copies of The Passengers' Charter. They say they're The Society for Raising The Awareness of Citizens' he said.

Rod clutched his brow in horror.

'More Commies!' he howled.

Ivan shook his head.

'They're not Commies. Basically they're a bunch of sad sods with nothing better to do', he said.

Rod nodded in agreement.

'You're right. Goddam Nosey Parkers. Why can't they let things rest? Everyone's perfectly happy, things are just drifting along and then they have to start going round agitating, stirring people up and telling them about their rights. If people don't know they've got any rights they don't bother about them. That Charter should be withdrawn' he declared.

Ivan was having none of this.

'You haven't thought it through. Read The Shitehouse Wall man. It's all there. It all comes down to Coca Cola. If they could come up with a decent product we wouldn't have to blow people to buggery to make them buy it. When you look at the facts you can see every time the Americans invade a country and blow everyone to buggery it's so they can give them back their rights, that's what they tell us and we're so stupid we believe them. They can't say we're propping up this horrible dictator because he's on the payroll of Coca Cola and they run America along with the Mafia. They say we've reduced the people to the Stone Age to restore their rights. It's all there on the Shitehouse Wall man' concluded Ivan.

Rod was truly horrified. He gazed at Ivan for a long time trying to grasp the enormity of what he'd said. Then a manic gleam came into his eye.

'Someone should blow that Goddamed Shitehouse to Kingdom Come' he said.

CHAPTER
Twenty Seven

The Warning

The Station Union Man, Paddy and Joe were sitting on a barrow on platform six when The Dim Station Manager came up to them. He looked round anxiously. Then he spoke to The Union Man.

'We've got a problem' he said.

'I won't be responsible for George said The Union Man.

'It's not George. It's Rod Williams, said The Dim Manager.

'What about him?' asked The Union Man.

'He's gone shaggin' bonkers' said The Dim Manager.

'He's always been shaggin' bonkers' said Paddy.

'He wants to blow up the Shitehouse' said The Dim Manager.

Paddy looked across to The Shitehouse. Then he stood up and edged away a little.

'This Shitehouse?' he asked.

'How many Shitehouses are there?' said The Dim Manager.

'There's one on platform one, one in the middle and one on six' Joe answered.

'Well he definitely wants to blow this one up' and for all I know he might be planning to blow up them all' said The Dim Manager.

The Union Man thought the news over. Joe looked towards him.

'What's the shaggin' Union say about this?' he asked.

'Blowing up Shitehouses is not normal behaviour' said The Union Man.

'If he's mad he shouldn't be here running things, he should be in The Meadows' said Joe indignantly.

'So what are you going to do?' The Union Man wanted to know.

'Strictly speaking it's a railway problem' began The Manager when Joe interrupted.

'If you happen to be sitting on the Shitehouse when the mad shagger blows it up it'll be your problem' he said.

'That'll shift your piles' said Paddy.

This wasn't the sort of line The Dim Manager wished to follow and he decided he'd best call for order.

'This is no laughing matter. What are we going to do?' he asked.

The Union Man shrugged.

'You're The Manager. It's up to you' he said.

The Dim Manager had no idea how to deal with the situation. He looked round at the group hopefully.

'Any suggestions?' he asked.

None were forthcoming. He was about to return to his office when George came striding along the platform. As always George came straight to the point.

'That mad shagger is going to blow up the shaggin' Shitehouse. What are you going to do about it?' he demanded.

'What do you expect me to do about it' asked The Dim Manager.

'Evacuate the shaggin' station and call the police' said George.

'What about the mail?' said The Dim Manager.

'Shag the mail' said Joe.

'What about my shaggin' bollocks flying at two hundred feet over the shaggin' station?' demanded Paddy.

'It might not come to that' said The Dim Manager.

'Suppose it does. What'll he get? A letter of apology?' said Joe.

'He'll get proper compensation' said The Dim Manager.

'I don't want proper compensation. I want me bollocks' said Paddy.

'Everybody knows about it. It's all over The Railway Institute' said George.

'I'm in a difficult position' said The Dim Manager, in a vain attempt to gain the sympathy of the group.

Joe gazed at him balefully.

'We expect a decision. We don't want that Ghost Squad bollocks all over again' he told him.

'The trouble is there's no evidence. It's all hearsay' said The Dim Manager.

'Once he's demolished the Shitehouse you'll have all the evidence you want' said George.

'How far does a blown up Shitehouse go?' asked Joe.

'What are you looking at me for?' demanded Paddy.

'You're from the land of flying Shitehouses' said Joe.

'It depends how much explosive he uses. If he uses enough it could go as far as Chesterfield' said George.

The Dim Manager spotted Ivan on platform one.

'Ivan. Can I have a word?' he called and went over.

George turned to The Union Man.

'Where's the Union stand on all this?' he asked.

'Blowing up Shitehouses definitely comes under the heading of extra Parliamentary activity and The Union supports the rule of law' said The Union Man.

'Exploding Shitehouses won't do a lot for British Rail's image' said George.

'British Rail regret the late arrival of the nine twelve due to the Station Manager at Derby taking it into his head to blow up the platform six Shitehouse' said Paddy.

'It's like being in a bloody Hitchcock film working here' said George.

The Leprauchan came along with a bucket of paint and headed for the Shitehouse.

'I wouldn't go in there if I were you Sean' said George.

'Why not?' asked The Leprauchan.

'Your Great Leader is going to blow it up' said George.

The Leprauchan put down his bucket and sat on the barrow.

'I've seen this coming for a long time' he said. Then he turned on George:

'You've got a lot to answer for' he told him.

'You can't blame me. It's not my fault he's gone shaggin' bonkers' said George.

'It was you that drove him bonkers' said The Leprauchan.

'And The Ghost Squad. They drove everyone bonkers' said Joe.

'He was bonkers when he arrived here. He's always been bonkers. It's just that it shows more now. It's modern life. It's driving everyone bonkers. Some show it more than others. Some people drink, some write on Shitehouse walls and some blow Shitehouses buggery. It's modern life' George told them.

'It'll take more than modern life to drive me bonkers' said Joe.

The Leprauchan nodded and picked up his bucket.

'George's right. Modern life is more than flesh and blood can stand' he said and headed towards The Shitehouse.

The Union Man rose to his feet.

I doubt it Rod has the slightest idea of how you go about blowing up a Shitehouse' he said.

'But I bet he knows a man who does' said Paddy.

'I'd best alert the Railway Police. That's if they haven't heard already' said The Union Man and made his way over to platform one.

An Irate Would Be Traveller stopped him outside The buffet.

'Where's The Station Manager?' he demanded.

'In his office learning to prime fuses' said The Union Man.

'I'm going to give him a rocket' said The Irate Would Be Traveller.

'Don't do that for Chrissake! We're trying to keep explosives away from him' said The Union Man, glancing back over his shoulder.

The Irate Would Be Traveller looked round and managed to find a bench. He sat down to think things over.

'There's some very peculiar people about nowadays' he said to the woman sitting next to him. She got up hurriedly and walked away. The Irate Would Be Traveller decided the best thing to do was keep his mouth shut and get off the station at the first opportunity.

George wasn't satisfied with the way the situation was being handled.

'It's no good just drifting. We need to get something sorted out. I'm going to go and talk to the shagger' he said.

'Don't go in that office. You might as well walk into the Bates Motel' warned Joe.

'Someone's got to do something' said George and strode purposefully down the platform towards the bridge.

'He's always been a daft bugger' said Joe.

On platform one The Irate Would Be Traveller caught sight of George, didn't like the look of him, and pretended to be deeply immersed in his newspaper.

George flung open the door of Rod William's office.

'Is that right you're going to blow up the Shitehouse?' he demanded.

'I'll do whatever has to be done' said Rod.

'Are you going to blow up the Shitehouse or not?' said George.

'If it's necessary to blow up the Shitehouse in order to save civilisation and preserve democracy that is what I will do. The Prime Minister is prepared to press the nuclear button in order to save humanity. I am prepared to blow up the Shitehouse' said Rod.

'If she presses the nuclear button there'll be no need for you to blow up the Shitehouse' George pointed out.

'Every man of goodwill must make a contribution' countered Rod.

Having to his own satisfaction established that it wasn't a mere rumour and that Rod Williams did in fact have every intention of blowing up the Shitehouse George felt it incumbent upon him to dig deeper.

'What have you got against the Shitehouse?' he asked.

'It has been violated' said Rod.

This reply left George floundering somewhat.

'I'm not with you' he confessed.

'Someone keeps writing terrible things on the walls' said Rod.

'You mean that stuff about Britain and America being responsible for the deaths of more than Hitler and Stalin together?' said George.

'It's all lies' said Rod.

'No it's not, it's all true. All you have to do is add up the figures. The Americans are imperialists and that's just another name for butchers' said George.

Rod winced. 'It may be true that some people have been called upon to make the ultimate sacrifice, but they did not die in vain' he said.

'They didn't make a sacrifice. No-one consulted them. They were blown to buggery. And we're all to blame' said George.

'You've been brainwashed' Rod told him.

George decided it was futile to try and reason with Rod about the crimes committed in order to advance the commercial interests of Coca Cola, and wondered if an appeal to his civic sense might work.

'In any case you can't blow up the Shitehouse' he said.

'Why not?' asked Rod.

'It's the one feature of architectural interest left after the refurbishment of the buildings. There's a preservation order on it' claimed George.

'I didn't know that' confessed Rod.

'Bear it in mind. An awful lot of important people are interested in conservation' advised George.

Rod looked impressed.

'I sure don't want to be taken for a vandal' he admitted.

'If you want to make a point why don't you blow up WH Smith's?' suggested George.

'Would that achieve anything?' said Rod doubtfully.

'The oxygen of publicity' said George.

Outside the office George saw The Union Man and The Dim Manager.

'It's allright. I've talked him out of it' he told them.

They both looked relieved:

'Thank Christ for that!' breathed The Dim Manager.'

'He's going to blow up WH Smith's instead' said George and went off to The Railway Institute.

The Dim Manager creased his brow trying to remember what they'd taught him on his latest weekend course in Management Techniques in the modern age.

'I think the best thing will be if I monitor the situation' he said.

'The Union Man nodded. 'Put in a report and keep a copy' he advised.

Seeing The Dim Manager looking puzzled he added:

'Cover your arse'.

The Dim Manager grinned.

'Not much point if my arse is flying at five hundred feet over the town centre, but I'll take your advice' he said.

'With or without your arse it's always best to have the paperwork in order' said The Union Man.

After this touch of excitement the shift proceeded in the usual routine manner until around eleven pm when The Dim Manager hurried over to platform six.

'Every shagger off the station' he bellowed waving his arms about.

'What's up?' asked Paddy.

'I've had a call from the police ordering me to evacuate the Station' said The Dim Manager.

'That's good enough for me' said Joe and started to walk off.

'What about that final bag?' said The Dim Manager.

'What about my shaggin' arse flying over Chesterfield?' countered Joe.

The Dim Manager thought briefly about the possibility of his own arse accompanying Joe's flying over Chesterfield and promptly forgot about the bag.

The Railway and Post Office staff were gathered in the Foyer with the trainspotters and a handful of would be travellers. Rumours were flying thick and fast.

'There's a bomb in the Shitehouse' said a trainspotter.

'I heard they were going to blow up WH Smith's' said a second trainspotter.

'It's the IRA' said a Would Be Traveller.

'It's not the shaggin' IRA, it's the shaggin' Station Manager' Paddy told him.

Hearing Paddy's accent the Would Be Traveller moved away sharply.

'He says the shaggin' Station Manager is going to blow the whole bloody station up' he said indicating Paddy.

'He won't do that shagger. He's too frightened of what Region might say' Ivan assured him. This made sense to Paddy.

'We could all be barking up the wrong tree here' said Paddy.

When he felt he had the attention of the crowd he expounded his theory.

'This could turn out to have more to do with the reunification of Ireland than Rod Williams going stark raving mad' he said.

'It's not me who's stark raving mad. It's that maniac writing on the Shitehouse wall' said Rod Williams arriving on the scene looking full of piss and importance.

'Are you the man who's going to blow up his own station?' asked The Irate Would Be Traveller.

'I will do what has to be done' said Rod.

The Irate Would Be Traveller took that to mean yes. At that point the Police Explosives experts arrived on the scene.

'This is the man you want' called out The Irate Would Be Traveller pushing Rod forward.

'Take your hands off me. I'm The Station Manager' Rod protested.

'He's a bloody Mad Bomber' said The Irate Would Be Traveller. 'History may be written in our drops of blood' he added.

Ivan arrived on the scene.

'Tell 'em where it is Rod. No one think any the worse of you' he urged. He turned to the Policeman.

'Things have been getting on top of him lately' he explained.

The Policeman took out a portable phone.

'This might not be political Sergeant. We could be dealing with a Mad Bomber here' he said.

Rod Williams nodded eagerly.

'That's right. A Mad Bomber' he said.

'Best not say anything' advised Ivan.

'Why not? It's a free country' said Rod.

'Maybe it is and maybe it isn't' said Ivan.

'This is The Free World. I've got my rights' declared Rod.

'I'm not very interested in your rights at the moment mate' said The Policeman.

'Can I have your number?' said Rod.

'No' said The Policeman.

'You're entitled to know the arresting officer's number under the terms of The Felons' Charter' said The Long Haired Git.

'Have you got a copy?' called Rod as he was hustled off.

Ivan shook his head. 'It could be we seen the last of him' he mused.

'No such luck' said The Long Haired Git.

'Who's in charge now?' asked George.

'I suppose I am' said Ivan.

'Well you'd best make an announcement. Let people know what's going on' said George.

'If I knew I would' Ivan told him.

'Stand up on the bench there and put everyone in the picture' said Paddy.

George and Paddy lifted Ivan up onto the bench and Paddy called for order.

Facas were turned expectantly towards Ivan. He gulped.

This is Ivan Johnson your Acting Station Manager. British Rail regrets the unavoidable delay to your journey due to the fact that a maniac says he's going to blow up the toilets. Normal service will be resumed as soon as possible and we hope you've had a nice day' he said.

CHAPTER
TWENTY EIGHT

The Investigation

Ivan was talking to a group of postmen and railwaymen on platform one. 'The fact that they ain't found it don't necessarily mean there ain't no bomb' he declared.

'Where do you think it is then?' asked The Leprauchan.

'You're asking the wrong man' said Ivan.

'If anyone knows it's that mad shagger' said George.

'The Police cleared him' said Ivan.

'He knows more than he's saying' said Paddy.

The Ghost Squad were sitting side by side on an empty barrow like a pair of bookends.

'This job's bollocksed' said Len.

'Completely shagged up' said Arthur.

'I used to look forward to coming to work' claimed Len.

Joe snorted.

'When did you ever come to work?' he asked.

The Ghost Squad ignored him.

'Now we're being shat on from a great height and bombed to buggery as well' said Len.

'And all we're trying to do is provide a public service' said Arthur.

'When they come to write the history of the Post Office it'll be told then' said Len.

'What where you two shaggers were for ten years and how you got away with the shagger?' asked Joe.

'How the blokes who were struggling to keep the mail moving were treated' said Len.

'Shat on from a great height' said George.

'Shat on from a great height' said The Ghost Squad in unison.

Ivan was looking puzzled.

'What I don't understand is how come he's back here in charge. When he was led off under arrest I thought the next we'd hear was that he was in an Institution' he said.

'They don't put 'em in Institutions now, they sling them out,' said George.

'Turn them loose onto the streets' said Joe.

'Put them in charge of British Rail Stations' said The Long Haired Git.

'What's his Doctor say?' asked Paddy.

'Keep that shagger out of my surgery' said Ivan.

'That's a bloody fine attitude' said Len.

The Union Man looked round cautiously. He beckoned the group in closer.

'In future be careful what you say in front of Rod' he told them.

'What for? He's shaggin' harmless' said George.

The Union Man glanced round again.

'I think he may have been recruited' he said.

'Who'd recruit that twat?' said George.

'The Secret State' said The Union Man.

'What shaggin' 007 and all that shaggin' bollocks' said Joe.

'I hope they haven't licensed the useless shagger to kill' said Paddy.

'I think they may be using him as an informer' said The Union Man.

'Who exactly are they?' asked The Longhaired Git.

'I've no idea. MI5, MI6, Special Branch, God knows!' said The Union Man.

'Why would those shaggers be wasting their time spying on us? Is that all they've got to do?' asked Joe indignantly.

'I think it's all to do with the writing on the Shitehouse Wall' said The Union Man.

'There have been some peculiar looking blokes hanging round there lately' said Paddy.

'I think I saw Sean Connery' said Joe, who refused to take any this seriously.

'If there's one thing the Fascists fear it's the alternative press' said The Long Haired Git.

'Is that what The Shitehouse Wall is then? The Alternative Press?' asked Len.

'Certainly it is' said The Long Haired Git.

'But we've got a Conservative Government and The Mad Witch of Grantham has set the people free' objected Len.

'Who said so?' asked Joe.

'She did' answered Len.

'Well then' said Joe.

'They're out to crush all resistance. They won't rest until we're on our hands and knees' said The Union Man.

'I don't know about the rest of you but I've been on my hands and knees for years' said Paddy.

'I remember when all you had to worry about was your mate shopping you to the Gaffers' said Len looking at Joe.

'Now you have to worry about the shaggin' Station Manager shopping you to the bloody Tonton Macoute' said The Longhaired Git.

'The Bloody Who?' asked Arthur.

'I thought James Bond was supposed to be a good bloke. Protecting us, not shaggin' persecuting us' protested Joe.

'We're The Enemy Within' said The Union Man.

'What are we supposed to have done?' asked Ivan.

'Nothing, but she's got to blame someone' said The Union Man.

'Course she has. She can't just say I've shagged it all up. I'm a bloody silly cow' can she?' said Paddy.

'I wish we could put the clock back' said Len.

'You can forget that shagger' Joe told him.

'I'll never vote for 'em again' said Arthur.

'Do you suppose any of these spooks will help us load the trains?' asked The Longhaired Git.

Meanwhile The Dim Manager had been summoned to Rod Williams office. He'd been given a direct order that he had to liaise with British Rail so he had to go but he wasn't very happy. He thought it quite possible that Rod was about to become overtly violent so he took a Dim Acting Manager with him in the hope that if someone was to be thumped The Acting Manager would be the one. The Dim Acting Manager was too stupid to realise he was being set up as a decoy and felt highly flattered to be taking part in a meeting at this level. Rod Williams might be certifiable but he was in charge of a major British Rail Station.

'This is just an ordinary routine meeting' lied The Dim Manager as they made their way along the platform. When they reached the office The Dim Manager politely stood back to allow The Acting Dim Manager to go first. Rod Williams greeted them cordially.

'Come in gentlemen, come in' he said, waving them to seats.

Eyeing him warily The Dim Manager took a seat, surreptitiously measuring the distance to the door with one eye as he did so.

'Sit down, sit down' said Rod.

'We are' said The Dim Manager.

Rod nodded affably. Then he consulted the sheet of paper in front of him.

'There's only one item on the agenda' he began.

'What's that then?' asked The Dim Manager.

'Shitehouse security' said Rod.

The Dim Manager didn't know what to say so he sat and waited. Rod looked at him expectantly.

'Is there anything you wish to say?' he asked.

'No' said The Dim Manager.

'Region are very concerned about the continuing problem with the graffiti' said Rod. The Dim Manager couldn't see what all the fuss was about.

'You should employ Shitehouse Attendants' said The Dim Manager.

'Employ Shitehouse Attendents' echoed The Acting Dim Manager.

'You need effective surveillance' said The Dim Manager, quoting a phrase he'd heard at one of his weekend schools. The Leprauchan knocked and walked in.

'What do you want?' asked Rod brusquely.

'More paint' said The Leprauchan.

'What for?' asked Rod.

'He's struck again' said The Leprauchan.

Rod didn't need to ask who had struck. Nor did The Dim Manager.

'It's the Shaggin' Phantom' he said.

'Is it the usual stuff?' asked Rod.

The Leprauchan nodded.

'He's employing the classic revolutionary tactic. The same message continually repeated' he said.

'That won't fool anyone' said Rod.

'It's got a lot of people talking' said The Leprauchan.

'Pity they've nothing better to do' said Rod.

'And the sales of Coca Cola are right down' said The Leprauchan.

Rod began to look worried. The Leprauchan continued to drive in the nails.

'The Committee are considering a ban at The Railway Institute' said The Leprauchan.

'What good will that do?' asked The Dim Manager.

'Accompanied by a Press Release' said The Leprauchan.

'Who'll print that?' asked Rod.

'No doubt in a little while I'll be painting over it on The Shitehouse Wall' said The Leprauchan.

'Why don't you just leave it for a while and see what happens?' asked The Dim Manager.

'They're trying to warp peoples' minds. We have to fight back' said Rod.

'It's me with me pot of paint and brush against the Forces of Darkness' said The Leprauchan.

'Stick at it Picasso' said The Dim Manager rising to go.

Rod also rose and beamed at the Post Office men.

'If you find any problems cropping up don't hesitate to call on me' he said.

Once they were safely out of the office The Dim Manager turned to The Acting Dim Manager.

'Thank Christ we're safely out of there' he said.

'He seemed a very nice chap' said The Acting Dim Manager.

'He's a shaggin' lunatic. I don't know why they've let him come back here. There's something very peculiar going on' said The Dim Manager.

Rod got The Leprauchan to sign for the paint. Then with an affected casualness he asked:

'What was it you said you were?'

'A Jack of all Shaggin' Trades' answered The Leprauchan.

'And what was it you said you were up against?' asked Rod.

The Leprauchan thought for a moment:

'The Forces of Darkness. It's only a figure of speech' said The Leprauchan.

'It's the truth' said Rod.

'The truth is written up on the Shitehouse Wall. Only the guilty have to fear it' said The Leprauchan.

When The Leprauchan had left Rod wrote his name on a piece of paper and locked the paper in his desk drawer. He felt certain he was doing his bit to protect the way of life of the Western World. A thought struck him:

'There could be a decoration in this' he mused.

The Dim Manager was in his office talking to The Union Man.

'It's bloody unnerving. He sits there beaming at you with a sort of glassy look in his eyes. He's not really there' he said.

'Is he still talking about blowing up the Shitehouse?' asked The Union Man.

'He's not talking about it anymore, but he could still be thinking about it' said The Dim Manager.

'Let's hope he makes a major ballsup and gets promoted out of here' said The Union Man.

'How mad do you have to be to get promoted?' asked The Dim Manager.

'Absolutely barking' The Union Man told him.

'Do you think he actually would blow up the Shitehouse?' asked The Dim Manager.

'You know what he keeps saying. I'll do whatever has to be done' said The Union Man.

'Yes but will he actually do it?' persisted The Dim Manager.

'If he thinks the forces of darkness are closing in and blowing up the Shitehouse is going to drive them back he'll do it' said The Union Man.

The Dim Manager sat thinking about this for a bit. He couldn't make a lot of sense about the situation. Somehow things were just getting out of control. A thought struck him:

'You know when they interview these shaggers at Birmingham?' he said.

The Union Man nodded.

'Do you suppose one of the questions they ask is if they're prepared to press the button and blow up The Shitehouse?' he asked.

The Union Man sat pondering a while. This was a possibility he hadn't considered. His first instinct was to dismiss the idea out of hand. It was simply too bizarre. However when he stopped to consider the idea it rapidly began to seem perfectly logical.

'I think that's probably the question that decides how far they can go up the ladder' said The Union Man.

'But that's shaggin' crazy' said The Dim Manager.

'Of course it's shaggin' crazy. That's the whole shaggin' point' said The Union Man.

'I'm not with you' said The Dim Manager.

'We're not prepared to make a bloke Prime Minister until he's told us he's prepared to press the bleedin' nuclear button and blow us all to buggery, otherwise we think he's not strong enough to defend us' said The Union Man.

'That's right' said The Dim Manager.

'So it that's the orthodox view the likelihood is that in every organisation they're only prepared to advance maniacs who're willing to be Shitehouse blasters' said The Union Man.

'Kin' ell!' said The Dim Manager.

'Can you make any sense out of it all?' asked The Union Man.

'No I shaggin' can't' said The Dim Manager.

'Nor me' said The Union Man.

'I'll tell you what though' said The Dim Manager.

'What?' asked The Union Man.

'I'm going to send a memo to The Chief and say we should go on an emergency footing,' said The Dim Manager.

'What would that entail?' asked The Union Man.

'We'll change the number on the security lock and we'll have sand bags all round the bleedin' Shitehouses' said The Dim Manager.

CHAPTER
TWENTY NINE

The Phoney War

'I want you to put together a really strong team Chief' said The Head Postmaster.

The Chief thought about the people he had available and wondered how on earth The Head Postmaster expected him to assemble a team that was not merely laughable. He sat facing The Head Postmaster looking glum.

The Chief's misery was apparent to The Head Postmaster.

'I do realise we have problems with Human Resources' he conceded.

'I've only got one bloke with a brain and he's bloody bolshie' complained The Chief.

'We've always managed in the past' said The Head Postmaster.

'We're managing now' said The Chief.

'Of course we are' The Head Postmaster agreed.

'So what's this strong team for?' asked The Chief.

'British Rail are taking the matter of station security very seriously. They've formed a sub committee to deal with it and we have to have input' explained The Head Postmaster.

'Are they still flapping about bombs?' asked The Chief.

'They're giving it the highest priority' said The Head Postmaster.

The Chief shook his head in exasperation.

'It was a bloody hoax. Someone's taking the piss' he said.

'A lot of people are worried' said The Head Postmaster.

'I've had this memo from our bloody idiot down there' said The Chief.

'What does he say?' asked The Head Postmaster.

'He seems to think there's a good chance his arse could end up flying over Chesterfield' replied The Chief.

'It may all be nonsense but we have to show that we're a caring employer' said The Head Postmaster.

'But we're not. We don't have to be. There's millions unemployed. We can do what we like' said The Chief.

'Fortunately we're responsible enough not to abuse power' said The Head Postmaster. The Chief thought there was no point in responding to this piece of self deception.

'Does this team have to actually do anything?' he asked.

'They have to come up with ideas?' The Head Postmaster told him.

'We don't promote blokes with ideas. We try and sack 'em' said The Chief beginning to look exasperated.

'We don't just promote idiots' said The Head Postmaster.

'I thought that was the policy. Idiots and brown nosers' said The Chief.

'A few people with minds of their own are bound to slip through the net' said The Head Postmaster.

'Not if I have anything to do with it' retorted The Chief.

The Head Postmaster began to realise he could expect no sympathy from The Chief. It was time to indulge in a little power politics.

'We must have some able management representatives to balance the Union input' he said.

The Chief looked horrified.

'How did the bloody Union got into this?' he asked.

'Can't keep them out' said The Head Postmaster.

'Why not?' asked The Chief.

'Have to present a united front against the common enemy' The Head Postmaster replied.

This was too much for The Chief.

'They are the shaggin' enemy' he said furiously.

'Study your history Chief' said The Head Postmaster, looking infuriatingly snug.

'I don't need to read my history, I can see what happens here' protested The Chief.

'You have to look beneath the surface of events Chief' said The Head Postmaster.

'The surface is bad enough. I don't want to go poking about underneath' The Chief said.

The Head Postmaster stood up, The Chief thought the meeting was over and stood up too, but The Head Postmaster motioned him to sit down. Sighing he did so. The Head Postmaster took a large trophy from the top of the drinks cabinet and brought it over to his desk. He put it in front of The Chief.

'This is what it's all about Chief' he said.

'What, fishing?' asked The Chief, thoroughly mystified.

The Head Postmaster gazed steadily at The Chief.

'Yes' he said.

The Chief thought there must be more and waited, but when it became obvious The Head Postmaster had finished he got up:

He paused in the doorway.

'I'm glad we had this talk Chief. It's been most valuable' said The Head Postmaster and then sat gazing at the trophy.

'Perhaps he really has been shaggin' sheep' said The Chief to himself on his way back to his own office. Back in his own realm The Chief quickly decided that sheepshaggin' was neither here nor there, orders were orders and he started to plan out the management team to take the field. It was not an easy task.

'I've got no-one with half a brain' he complained. Then a happier thought struck him.

'But it doesn't matter. British Rail are just as thick as we are' he said and started to pencil in names.

At the Station The Dim Manager was in his office talking to The Union Man.

'They've set up this joint meeting, the Post Office and British Rail to plan strategy. The Chief Inspector is putting together a high powered team' said The Dim Manager.

'You mean he's sending a few tosspets down here because he wants them out of his way for a bit' said The Union Man.

'That's about the size of it' agreed The Dim Manager.

'Who's taking the chair?' asked The Union Man.

'Rod Williams' said The Dim Manager.

'Bloody hell!' said The Union Man.

'What's up?' asked The Dim Manager.

'We're having a meeting to discuss station security and the bloke who's in The Chair is the same shagger that's threatening to blow up the Shitehouse. That's except when he decides he'll blow up W.H. Smith' instead' said The Union Man.

'It's shaggin' crazy, but what can you shaggin' do?' asked The Dim Manager.

'He keeps on about the safety of the realm and the need for constant vigilance. 'What films has he been watching?' asked The Union Man.

'He's never in his office. He spends all his time staring at the writing on the Shitehouse wall' complained The Dim Manager.

'Is it executive stress?' asked The Union Man.

'Remember when it used to be ulcers?' said The Dim Manager.

Ivan knocked and walked in.

'Anyone seen The Station Manager?' he asked.

'Have you tried The Shitehouse?' asked The Dim Manager.

'I don't like to keep going in there. People have started to stare at me' said Ivan.

'No wonder the shaggin' papers won't print the shaggin' truth' said The Union Man.

'Good thing they shaggin' don't' said The Dim Manager.

'The truth is a potent weapon' said The Union Man.

'We don't want if in the wrong shaggers' hands' said The Dim Manager.

'You're right there' said Ivan.

'Just so long as the bloke who's got the power doesn't go dolally' said The Dim Manager.

Ivan thought about this.

'We've got a bloke here who's dolally all right. The thing is, has he got the power?' he asked.

'I shaggin' hope not' said The Dim Manager.

'Suppose some bastard sells him explosives?' said The Union Man.

'No-one would be irresponsible enough to sell explosives to an obvious lunatic' said Ivan.

'The British government do on a regular basis' countered The Union Man.

'I ain't talking about politicians. I'm talking about human beings' replied Ivan.

'Do you suppose we'll ever get back to normal?' asked The Union Man.

'I can't even remember what normal is' replied Ivan.

'That woman has got a lot to answer for' said The Union Man.

Ivan crossed himself.

'Sometimes I think maybe there is a God and He sent her to punish us for something we done' said Ivan.

'We're all here for a purpose' said The Union Man.

Ivan put a finger to his lips.

'Whatever you do don't say that to Rod. He thinks he's been sent here to blow up Shitehouses he warned.

'See you in the meeting' said The Union Man.

To no-one's surprise the meeting was a complete shambles! It was doomed from the moment an attempt to have Rod Williams removed from The Chair failed because The Dim Managers and The Union Men were unwilling to join forces. Seeing his challengers in disarray Rod beamed happily.

'There is one item on the agenda and that is Shitehouse security' he announced.

The delegates sat there looking sullen and resigned.

The Union Assistant Secretary put up his hand. Rod nodded affably at him.

'Point of Order Mr. Chairman. This Meeting should deal with security in a general sense, not limit itself to the Shitehouse' said The Assistant.

Murmurs of agreement were heard round the table. Rod shook his head.

'The threat is directed specifically to the Shitehouse. That's what we have to deal with' said Rod.

'You're going to look a right wanker if while you're guarding the Shitehouse they blow up the Buffet' said The Station Union Man.

'I don't think they're interested in The Buffet' said Rod.

'Somebody should blow it up' said The Dim Manager with a pot belly and red nose.

'That's not a very constructive attitude' Rod told him.

'Who exactly are we dealing with here?' asked The Assistant Secretary.

'Anti social elements' said Rod.

'I suppose threatening to blow up Shitehouses is anti social behaviour' said The Branch Secretary.

'But what's the motive?' asked The Assistant.

'Publicity' said Rod.

'For what?' asked The Branch Secretary.

'I don't know' said Rod.

'If they've got a gripe why don't they put in a complaint. Use the Passengers' Charter' said The Station Union Man.

At the mention of The Passengers' Charter Rod winced.

'I somehow don't think they're motivated by dissatisfaction at our performance' he claimed.

The Dim Manager with a pot belly and a red nose lit a cigarette.

'The station is now officially classified as a no smoking zone' said Rod.

The Dim Manager with a pot belly and red nose snorted indignantly.

'Tell that to the shaggers who are going to blow up the Shitehouse' he said.

'If they smoke while they're blowing up The Shitehouse they'll be in serious trouble' said Rod.

'I don't believe this shagger' said The Dim Manager with a Pot Belly and Red Nose as he furiously stubbed out his cigarette.

'Have you got any proposals?' asked The Branch Secretary, beginning to feel this farce should be terminated as quickly as possible.

Rod put on his reading glasses and peered at the sheet of paper in front of him.

'We do have a number of options' he said.

'And what might they be?' asked The Assistant Secretary.

'We could close the Shitehouse, but that might cause problems under the terms of The Passengers Charter' said Rod.

Everyone agreed that this would most likely prove to be the case.

Rod peered again at his sheet of paper.

'We could mount a guard outside The Shitehouse and search customers before we let them into The Shitehouse' said Rod.

'But that will cause complaints under the terms of The Passengers' Charter' said The Station Union Man.

'And we do not have the Human Resources available' Rod added.

'So that option is out' said The Assistant.

'Therefore it's not an option' said The Branch Secretary.

Rod nodded and again referred to his sheet of paper. Before he could speak The Misfit Manager who had been taking no apparent interest in the proceedings interjected.

'How much more of this crap is there?' he asked testily.

Rod ignored him. He ran his finger down his piece of paper.

'We could extend the surveillance system to cover the Shitehouse' he said.

The Dim Manager was having none of this.

'You can't put the shaggin' Shitehouse on shaggin' tv' he protested.

There was general agreement that putting the Shaggin' Shitehouse on tv was not acceptable. Rod waited for the din to die down. He again ran his finger down his piece of paper. Before he could speak The Misfit Manager glared at him.

'Have you thought about closing down the shaggin' station altogether?' he asked.

'Yes' said Rod and carried on examining his paper. He read laboriously:

'Bearing in mind that the bomber is always likely to get through, providing he is determined enough, and bearing in mind the fact that we could be dealing with fanatics, the best option could be to limit the damage as much as possible!'.

He looked round the table to see what sort of reaction there was. No-one seemed to know quite what to make of it.

The Branch Secretary decided to ask for clarification.

'In practical terms just what does that entail?' he asked.

'We put sandbags all round the Shitehouse' said Rod.

The Dim Manager looked round. Everyone looked somewhat nonplussed. He decided to look on the bright side.

'If it means my arse won't end up flying over Chesterfield I'll vote for it' he said.

The Union Men conferred together in hushed tones. Then The Branch Secretary cleared his throat.

'We're glad to see that management is treating the matter of staff safety seriously and we'll support the proposal' he said.

Rod looked most gratified. He looked at the bottom of his sheet.

"There only remains the matter of cost. How much are you prepared to contribute?" he asked.

The Dim Manager spoke up.

"Cost shouldn't come into it" he asserted.

At this sheer heresy everyone, even The Misfit Manager, looked aghast. The Dim Manager put forward his justification.

"How do you put a price on your arse?" he asked.

CHAPTER
THIRTY

The Reckoning

The Head Postmaster was very annoyed.

'I don't care how many thousand feet that Dim Overseer's arse is when it passes over Chesterfield. I don't care if it flattens the crooked spire. I've got no money in my budget for sandbagging Shitehouses' he yelled.

The Chief Inspector was not very sympathetic.

'I knew no good would come of this' he said.

The Head Postmaster was having none of it.

'We're all geniuses with hindsight' he retorted.

'You've painted yourself into a corner' said The Chief.

'Not me. It's that team of halfwits you assembled' said The Head Postmaster.

'I was only obeying orders' said The Chief.

'There's no need to take the piss' The Head Postmaster told him.

'Just stating the facts' said The Chief.

The Head Postmaster knew when it was time to move on.

'No point in raking over the embers. We have to deal with the situation as it is' he said.

'So what are you going to do?' asked The Chief.

'My hands are tied. I've got no funds for sandbags' said The Head Postmaster.

The Chief shook his head.

'You know what those bastards at Birmingham are like. They're looking for any excuse to get shot of me' said The Head Postmaster.

'It's not going to look very caring if it comes out you're not prepared to spend a bit of money to stop loyal workers' arses flying over Chesterfield' The Chief pointed out.

The Head Postmaster nodded glumly.

'You're right. It'll look bad. It's bound to come out. But I've got nothing in the budget' What can I do?' he said.

'You'll have to cut something else' said The Chief.

The Head Postmaster saw just a glimmer of hope. He looked gratefully at The Chief.

'You're right Chief. It's a question of spending priorities! he said.

'All you've got to do is find something that's less important than stopping The Station Staff's arses flying over Chesterfield' The Chief said.

'That bloody lot at Birmingham don't care how many arses go flying over Chesterfield. All they bother about is figures, balance sheets' said The Head Postmaster bitterly.

'I remember when people mattered' said The Chief.

'It's no use looking back Chief' said The Head Postmaster.

'The bastards will never be satisfied. There'll never be enough cuts for them' said The Chief.

'You're right Chief. The trouble is they've got The Mad Witch of Grantham egging them on. This is all down to her. If those arses end up at ten thousand feet above the crooked spire it'll be her responsibility' said The Head Postmaster.

'No it won't. The likes of her are never responsible for what goes wrong' said The Chief bitterly.

'I voted for her' said The Head Postmaster.

'So did I' said The Chief.

'I'll never vote for her again' The Head Postmaster vowed.

'Nor me' said The Chief.

The Head Postmaster lowered his voice.

'No one knows I voted for her' he said.

'It's best to keep quiet about it' said The Chief.

'I put up a vote Labour poster in my window' confessed The Head Postmaster.

'A wise precaution' The Chief told him.

The Head Postmaster shook his head sadly.

'It doesn't say a lot for the British. All over the world people are dying for what they believe in and we vote for someone we're ashamed to admit we support' he said.

'It's all to do with survival' said The Chief.

'I'll be lucky if I even manage that' The Head Postmaster said, suddenly looking very depressed.

'If they get shot of you I'll be next' predicted The Chief.

'Surely not' said The Head Postmaster looking shocked.

'They're getting rid of all the existing management. They want to put their own people in' said The Chief.

'You're right. It's all planned. Somewhere there's a nasty spider sitting spinning his web and making us helpless so he can eat us when he's ready' said The Head Postmaster.

The Chief nodded glumly. That was exactly how the position looked to him.

'And while he's sitting there planning my destruction what am I doing?' said The Head Postmaster.

The Chief looked puzzled.

'I'm scratching my head wondering where I can find the money to pay for sandbags to go round the Station Shitehouse' said The Head Postmaster, looking the very picture of exasperation.

'It's a diversionary tactic' said The Chief.

The Head Postmaster got up and wandered round the room. He picked up the Fishing Club Trophy and gazed at it. Then he returned to his desk. He looked like a man who had found the solution to all his problems.

'I know what I'm going to do Chief' he said.

The Chief waited. The Head Post Master smiled contentedly.

'That bastard sitting spinning his web will have to come and get me. I'm stopping here. I'm going to play for time' he said.

The Chief thought about it for a while. Then he nodded approval.

'That's the best plan. Play for time you never know your luck. The bastard might decide to shaft someone else and forget about us' said The Chief.

'He might forget about me, but I shan't forget about him' said The Head Postmaster.

'We could get lucky. The shagger could die' said The Chief.

'That's a terrible thing to say Chief' admonished The Head Postmaster. Then a happy thought struck him.

'Someone might shoot the shagger' he said.

'We can but hope' said The Chief and returned to his own office happier than he'd been for some time.

The Branch Secretary was not happy. He saw trouble looming.

'Some evil shagger is sitting in the middle of his web plotting our downfall' he told The Assistant.

'That was achieved by the Mad Witch of Grantham years ago. He wants to keep up to date' replied The Assistant.

'It's not enough for them to have us on the floor. They won't rest until they've trodden us under' said The Branch Secretary.

'You surely don't see the hand of Coca Cola in this?' said The Assistant.

The Branch Secretary went across to the map.

'The bastards are everywhere. Nothing that happens anywhere is too insignificant to be part of their global strategy' said The Branch Secretary.

'Not the Station Shitehouse surely' said The Assistant.

'I know you think I'm paranoid' began The Branch Secretary. He waited for The Assistant to contradict him. When he realised he wasn't going to he continued.

'But this is not theory, it's fact. The evidence is here' he concluded with a wave of his arm which covered the entire world.

'There'll be Coca Cola signs up in space next' said The Assistant ironically.

'Yes there will' said The Branch Secretary.

The Assistant felt that The Secretary was rather losing his sense of proportion.

'We can't put everything down to the Conspiracy' he said.

'The Conspiracy sets the climate of the times. Everything is either the direct or the indirect result of what those bastards do' said The Secretary.

'So what's our policy regarding sandbagging the Station Shitehouse?' asked The Assistant.

'Sandbagging the Shitehouse is a vital health and safety measure. We back it' said The Secretary.

'Why don't we get them to play Vera Lynn over the loudspeaker' suggested The Assistant.

'We face a moral dilemma here' said The Branch Secretary.

'What might that be?' asked The Assistant.

'We've got a duty to protect our members' said The Secretary.

'No argument there' said The Assistant.

'But we need to know who is threatening to blow up the Shitehouse and what his motive is. What is his aim?' said The Secretary.

'We know his aim. He wants to send arses into orbit' said The Assistant.

'Yes, but why?' said The Secretary.

'We won't know that until we know who it is' said The Assistant. The Branch Secretary went across to the map of the world. He peered at it. Then he pointed at London and New York.

'That's where the bastards are' he said.

The Assistant looked puzzled.

'The White House and Ten Downing Street. That's where all the crap comes from' said The Secretary.

'So all we have to do is get The President and The Prime Minister on television and ask why they're keen to blow up the Platform Six Shitehouse' said The Assistant.

'And we won't get a straight answer' The Secretary told him.

The Assistant ventured a mild protest.

'Don't you think you're reading too much into all this?' he asked.

The Branch Secretary shook his head vigorously.

'For a start the reason there's no money to buy the sandbags to stick round the Shitehouse is that these bastards have imposed their half baked momentary policies on the entire shaggin' world', he said.

The door was flung open and The Truculent Man strode in.

'Are they sandbagging the Shitehouse or not?' he asked.

'It's been agreed in principle' said The Branch Secretary.

'So when are they going to do it? It's no good sandbagging the shagger when it's been shaggin' blown up' said The Truculent Man.

'It's a question of finding the money' said The Secretary.

'Finding the money!' exploded The Truculent Man.

The Branch Secretary nodded.

'We're talking about putting a few sandbags round The Shitehouse, not building a nuclear shelter' protested The Truculent Man.

'There's nothing in the budget' said The Assistant.

'They'll have to find something' said The Truculent Man.

'It's not that simple' said The Branch Secretary.

'Yes it shaggin' is' said The Truculent Man.

The Branch Secretary got up and went towards the map.

'I don't give a shag about The White House or Ten Downing Street. If those shaggers won't sandbag The Shitehouse what the shaggin' hell are we going to do about it?' asked The Truculent Man.

'What can we shaggin' do about it?' asked The Assistant.

'I'll tell you what we can shaggin' do about it retorted The Truculent Man.

The Branch Secretary and The Assistant hoped The Truculent Man had come up with a solution and waited eagerly to hear what he had to say:

'If they won't sandbag The Shitehouse we'll blow the bugger up ourselves' said The Truculent Man.

The Branch Secretary and The Assistant were somewhat taken aback.

'I thought our aim was to preserve The Shitehouse' said The Assistant.

'That's right' concurred The Secretary.

'We'll blow it to buggery then it'll be obvious they should have sandbagged it. It'll make it look as though they were prepared to risk lives to save the cost of a few sandbags. We'll have a public relations triumph. And it'll put the wind up the bastards' explained The Truculent Man.

The Branch Secretary was gazing at the map of the world deep in thought. The Truculent Man nodded towards him and tapped his forehead significantly. The Assistant shrugged.

The Branch Secretary turned from the map of the world and walked back to his desk rubbing his hands together. He beamed at The Truculent Man.

'I like it' he declared.

The Assistant opened his mouth to protest but The Truculent Man cut him short.

'We'll teach those shaggers at Birmingham they can't shag us about' he said.

'What do you know about explosives?' asked The Assistant.

'Shagall' said The Truculent Man.

'Never mind the logistics for the moment. Let's agree on the principle. Are we agreed that if they don't sandbag The Shitehouse we'll blow the bugger up?' said The Branch Secretary.

'All those in favour' said The Truculent Man and put up his hand. The Branch Secretary immediately followed and after a moment's hesitation so did The Assistant.

'Shouldn't we put this resolution to a full meeting?' asked The Assistant.

'Decision of a properly constituted sub committee, no problem' said The Truculent Man.

'So this is now officially a meeting of the Blowing Up The Platform Six Shitehouse Sub Committee?' said The Assistant.

'No minutes' said The Truculent Man.

'We should have done this years ago' said The Branch Secretary.

'What blown up The Shitehouse?' asked The Assistant.

'Turned to terror. Countered fire with fire' said The Branch Secretary.

'Talk's all very well, but if we don't know a thing about explosives, how are we going to get the job done?' asked The Assistant.

'No problem,' said The Truculent Man.

'We're having shagall to do with the IRA I hope' said The Assistant.

'We don't need those shaggers' said The Truculent Man.

'You think we can do the job In House?' asked The Branch Secretary.

The Truculent Man nodded.

'This office is full of old shaggers who beat Hitler on their own. It's full of young shaggers who recaptured The Falklands Islands, and it's full of wankers in The Territorial Army. If we can't get a squad out of that lot I'd be very surprised' said The Truculent Man.

'They're a bunch of bull shitters' protested The Assistant.

'We give 'em a chance to bring their fantasies to life' said The Truculent Man.

'We'd be better doing the job ourselves' said The Assistant, and immediately wished he had kept his mouth shut.

An unholy glint came into The Branch Secretary's eye. He went across to the map of the world and pointed to it.

'We'll send a message to the world. If we don't get some satisfaction from The White House we'll blow up The Shitehouse' he declared.

'There could be some very awkward questions about all this' said The Assistant.

The Truculent Man sat smiling happily.

'Suddenly life seems good' he said.

'You've hardly stopped smiling since you decked that Gaffer' said The Assistant.

'This could all end up in custodial sentences. We'll be famous. We'll be The Derby Three' said The Branch Secretary.

'If it comes to that there's one thing we can be sure of' said The Assistant gloomily.

'What's that?' asked The Truculent Man.

'We'll get absolutely no support from that stupid fat Shagger at The Trades Union Congress' said The Assistant.

CHAPTER
THIRTY ONE

Claiming Credit

'We've got another group claiming responsibility for blowing up up the Platform Six Shitehouse' said The Bomb Squad Sergeant.

'It's not been blown up yet has it?' asked his inspector.

'No' said The Sergeant.

'They're jumping the gun a bit aren't they?' said The Inspector.

'Not really. It's only a matter of time before the Platform Six Shitehouse joins the list of unsolved crimes' said The Sergeant.

'Think positive' The Inspector told him.

'There's nothing we can do about it. They can blow it up any time they feel inclined. We haven't got the resources to protect it', replied The Sergeant.

'I've got nothing in the kitty. I don't know how I'm supposed to operate with the budget they've given me' complained The Inspector.

'Where's all the money gone?' asked The Sergeant.

'What do you mean all the money? I had shagall to start with' said The Inspector.

'What happened to the North Sea Oil money?' demanded The Sergeant.

'You tell me' replied The Inspector.

'And what about all the sell offs?' Where did all that money go?' asked The Sergeant.

'What am I the bloody state auditor?' said The Inspector.

'She must have done something with all that money. It can't have just disappeared' persisted The Sergeant.

'She did. She buggered everything up' said The Inspector.

'Yes. Give credit where credit's due. She did bugger everything up' conceded The Sergeant.

'She's buggered me up. We've got no funds to feed the sniffer dog' complained The Inspector.

'We'll have to run another sweepstake' said The Sergeant.

'On what?' asked The Inspector.

'On who eventually comes to blow up the Platform Six Shitehouse' said The Sergeant.

'How many runners?' asked The Inspector.

'Everyone is guaranteed a horse The Sergeant told him.

The Inspector looked dubious.

'If this gets into the papers there could be some awkward questions' he said.

Before The Sergeant could put his mind at rest the phone rang. The Sergeant answered it. He handed it to The Inspector.

'It's for you' he said.

'Who is it?' asked The Inspector.

'Chief Constable's office' said The Sergeant.

The Inspector hastily took the phone.

There followed a somewhat one sided exchange in which The Inspector was restricted to making affirmatory noises. To his obvious relief the conversation was terminated.

'What does he want?' asked The Sergeant.

'He wants a full report on the Shitehouse Bombings' said The Inspector.

'There haven't been any Shitehouse bombings' protested The Sergeant.

'I know' said The Inspector.

'Why didn't you tell him that?' asked The Sergeant.

'I tried. He didn't want to know' said The Inspector.

'This is bloody stupid' complained The Sergeant.

'I know it's bloody stupid' said The Inspector testily.

'What's he ringing us for? As soon as they blow up The Shitehouse we'll let him know' said The Sergeant.

'That's no good. He wants a report on his desk first thing in the morning' said The Inspector.

The Sergeant's jaw sagged. A thought struck him.

'Had he been drinking?' he asked hopefully.

'I couldn't ask him that' protested The Inspector.

'Did he sound as though he'd been drinking?' asked The Sergeant.

'He always sounds as though he's been drinking' said The Inspector.

'What's he flapping about?' asked The Sergeant.

'He says he's under a lot of pressure' explained The Inspector.

'Who from?' The Sergeant wanted to know.

'Who do you think?' countered The Inspector.

'Rich shaggers' snorted The Sergeant.

'Rich shaggers' confirmed The Inspector.

'No-one else matters do they?' said The Sergeant.

'We administer the law impartially' said The Inspector primly.

'Like bloody hell we do,' snorted The Sergeant.

'Write out a report. Keep him off our backs' said The Inspector.

'This is a waste of police time' protested The Sergeant.

'It's a direct order' said The Inspector defensively.

The Sergeant was furious.

'I've got to sit down there as though I was Jeffrey Shaggin' Archer and write a load of crap just because some rich shagger at that shaggin' Golf Club has got onto The Chief Constable' he hissed.

'It's good public relations' said The Inspector.

'It's crawling. Those rich shaggers at that shaggin' golf club think we're their private shaggin' force' complained The Sergeant.

'Dots on the landscape' said The Inspector.

'You what?' asked The Sergeant.

'We're just dots on the landscape' said The Inspector.

The Sergeant didn't know what to make of that so he went across and sat in front of the typewriter. He put in a sheet of paper.

'Shall I put some sex in?' he asked.

The Inspector considered the idea and decided against it.

'Best not make it too interesting or they'll want regular progress reports' he said.

The Sergeant began to hammer the keys as though they were members of The Shaggin' Golf Club.

The Inspector stood staring gloomily at a map of the County.

'Nothing but unsolved crimes. It's a shaggin' catastrophe' he sighed.

The Sergeant was looking alarmingly cheerful. He typed like a man possessed.

'I could take to this shaggin' writing lark. It's got to be better than shaggin' about trying to defuse shaggin' bombs' he said.

'I've had an offer from a security firm' The Inspector told him.

'Take it. It's the growth industry. There's more private security men than police officers now' said The Sergeant.

'I'd be a consultant' said The Inspector.

'You'd earn more money. You'd have a business card. You'd get a mobile phone and you wouldn't have wankers of Chief Constables breathing down your neck' said The Sergeant.

'It's tempting' said The Inspector.

The Sergeant read what he had written with obvious satisfaction.

'This is bloody good' he said.

'Let's have a look' said The Inspector.

The Sergeant took the sheet out and handed it to The Inspector. The Inspector read it. He handed it back.

'What do you think?' asked The Sergeant.

'It's a bit far fetched' said The Inspector.

'What do you expect? It's a work of fiction' bridled The Sergeant.

'There's no need to get stroppy. I'm only giving my opinion', said The Inspector.

'What do you want for those fat shaggers at The Golf Club? Hard realism? Gritty analysis? The ring of truth?' asked The Sergeant.

'Avoid the truth like the plague and you won't go far wrong' said The Inspector.

The Sergeant thought for a moment then furiously resumed his typing.

'Tell The Chief Constable and his rich fat shaggin friends what they want to hear' advised The Inspector.

The Sergeant broke off for a moment.

'As soon as I've sold the film rights for this shagger The Chief Constable and his rich fat shaggin' friends can get bollocksed' he said.

Then just as he was about to resume work at the typewriter a thought struck him and he glanced at The Inspector with what could only be called a wicked gleam in his eyes.

'If I get much more crap from The Chief Constable I'll blow up the shaggin' Golf Club Shitehouse and claim responsibility on behalf of The IRA' he said.

The Chief Inspector looked alarmed.

'I hope you'll be sending a warning' he said.

'It'll depend on how I feel' The Sergeant told him and continued typing.

The Inspector decided not to pursue the matter. He was anxious not to create any more paperwork.

Unfortunately it was not the end of the matter since The Sergeant was obviously in a thoroughly bolshie mood.

'Another thing. That nutter writing on The Shitehouse Wall' he said.

'What about him?' asked The Inspector.

'He's bloody right' said The Sergeant.

The Inspector sat for a moment looking very thoughtful. Then he turned to The Sergeant.

'That Sweepstake to get food for the Sniffer Dog' he said.

'What about it?' asked The Sergeant.

'Best add Special Branch to the list of runners said The Inspector and left.

The Sergeant looked at his literary effort in the typewriter in near despair.

'How can you compete with that sort of thing?' he asked himself. He glanced through his report.

'This is not far fetched. Compared to the reality it's bloody pedestrian' he decided.

In the Union Office The Blowing Up The Platform Six Shitehouse Sub Committee was holding a somewhat turbulent meeting.

'Our security has been breached' complained The Branch Secretary. He glared round accusingly.

'It's shagall to do with me' said The Truculent Man.

'I've been the soul of discretion' claimed The Assistant.

The Branch Secretary looked exasperated.

'Either someone's been opening his big gob or we're being bugged he said.

'There's no budget for bugging' said The Assistant.

'Wrong. There's no budget for essentials. There's always money available to shaft us' said The Secretary.

'The office is full of bloody informers. We should never have tried to recruit those ex army men,' said The Truculent Man.

'I've been on to Union Headquarters' said The Branch Secretary.

'Much good that'll have been' said The Truculent Man.

'They don't want to know about us' said The Branch Secretary.

'They uphold the rule of law' said The Assistant.

'How did you know they'd said that?' asked The Branch Secretary.

'When do they ever say anything else?' asked The Truculent Man.

'They can't do anything to us' said The Assistant.

'Why not?' asked The Truculent Man.

'We haven't actually done anything yet' explained The Assistant.

'The best thing we can do is deny everything' said The Truculent Man.

'If those bastards had done the decent thing and sandbagged The Shitehouse in the first place we wouldn't be in this position now' said The Branch Secretary.

'If these bastards had any decency there'd be no need for us' said The Truculent Man.

The telephone rang. The members of The Blowing Up the Platform Six Shitehouse Sub Committee stared at it in horror.

'They'll probably write songs about us' said The Assistant.

The Branch Secretary picked up the phone. The other two members of The Blowing Up The Platform Six Shitehouse Sub Committee watched him closely. The Branch Secretary's face confirmed their worst fears.

'I'm a bit tied up now' he said without much conviction.

He listened in silence for a moment then asked:

'Are you giving me a direct order?'

The Truculent Man and The Assistant groaned. The Branch Secretary rang off.

'We're to report to The Head Postmaster's office immediately' he said. The Truculent Man shook his head gloomily.

'Ain't life a bitch' he said.

The Branch Secretary could see no hope. He took a look at the map of the world.

'Bastards!' he said and left the office.

'I'd feel more happy about our chances if he'd shut up about those bastards in Washington' said The Assistant.

'Is he trying to work his ticket?' enquired The Truculent Man.

They held a hasty conference outside The Head Postmaster's Office.

'Admit shagall' said The Truculent Man.

'You're right. It's not us who's guilty, it's those bastards in Ten Downing Street and The White House' said The Branch Secretary.

The Truculent Man became even more convinced The Branch Secretary was trying to work his ticket.

The Assistant knocked on the door.

'Come in!' bellowed The Head Postmaster.

They filed in and stood facing The Head Postmaster. To their astonishment he was all affability.

'Take a seat gentlemen. No need to stand on ceremony here. Will you have a drink?' he asked.

The Union Men were flabbergasted. This wasn't what they'd expected at all. They wondered if they were the victims of a cruel joke.

'I wouldn't say no to a whisky and soda' said The Truculent Man.

The Branch Secretary and The Assistant thought they might as well have a whisky and soda as well. When they all had their drinks The Head Postmaster sat at his desk and beamed at them.

'So gentleman what have you got to tell me?' he asked.

They'd decided to tell him as little as possible for fear of incriminating themselves so they were reluctant to speak. The Head Postmaster continued to beam at them. The Union Men remained silent, unwilling to speak for fear of dropping themselves further in it than they already were. The Head Postmaster continued to encourage them to get it off their chest.

'Anything you think I ought to know?' he asked.

'The Union Men remained silent. The Head Post Master leaned towards them and lowered his voice.

'Whatever you say here is in the strictest confidence' he said.

'What like the bloody confessional?' asked The Truculent Man.

'Exactly' said The Head Post Master.

The Sub Committee for Blowing Up the Platform Six Shitehouse sat sipping their whiskies. The Head Post Master decided that a broader hint was required.

'What I'd like is a progress report' he told them.

'What I'd like is a refill' said The Truculent Man.

'Certainly' said The Head Postmaster.

He gave The Truculent Man a generous measure, somewhat to the unease of the other two Union Men. The Truculent Man set about his refill as though it was the last drink he'd get for some time.

The Head Postmaster looked The Branch Secretary in the eye:

'When can I expect results?' he asked.

The Union Men were alarmed but managed not to show it.

'I'm not with you' said The Branch Secretary.

The Head Postmaster decided it was time to stop fencing.

'I am speaking to the properly appointed Sub Committee for The Blowing Up of The Platform Six Shitehouse aren't I?' he asked.

'Is there any shagger in this shaggin' building who doesn't know our shaggin' business?' asked The Truculent Man.

'Your security has been a bit lax' said The Head Post Master.

'Why don't we put an advert in the local paper?' asked The Truculent Man.

'So gentlemen I take it the arrangements are well in hand. Soon we can expect pieces of masonry flying through the air' said The Head Post Master.

The Branch Secretary was mystified.

'I find your attitude somewhat surprising' he told The Head Post Master.

'Surprising. It's bloody irresponsible' snorted The Truculent Man.

'The Platform Six Shitehouse has become a source of embarrassment to me' explained The Head Post Master.

'I wish I'd never heard of The Platform Six Shitehouse' said The Assistant Secretary.

'Those bastards at Birmingham won't allocate me any funds for sandbags. British Rail aren't prepared to meet the full cost from their budget, and they're threatening to sandbag two walls, and paint up a notice on the two remaining walls to the effect that I'm not prepared to meet my responsibilities for the safety of the travelling public. One way or another that Shitehouse has to go', said The Head Post Master.

The Truculent Man sat staring at his empty glass. The Head Post Master quietly refilled it for him. The Truculent Man took a drink. He looked first at The Branch Secretary and then at The Assistant.

'Let's see if I've got this right. We're sitting here in the Head Postmaster's Office and he's telling us he wants us to blow up the Platform Six Shitehouse' said The Truculent Man.

'That would appear to be the situation' said The Branch Secretary.

'Why do I get the feeling someone's pulling our strings?' asked The Truculent Man.

'It's got to be those cunning bastards in Washington and Downing Street' said The Branch Secretary.

'There's a cunning bastard a lot closer to us than Downing Street' said The Truculent Man, glaring at The Head Post Master.

'Are you actually instructing us to blow up The Platform Six Shitehouse?' asked The Assistant.

'That would be most improper' said The Head Post Master.

'Yes, but is that what you're doing?' persisted The Assistant.

'He's having us for a load of wankers, that's what he's doing' said The Truculent Man as he helped himself to another whisky.

'Blowing up Shitehouses is obviously against the law' said The Head Postmaster.

'Entirely illegal' agreed The Branch Secretary.

'So we mustn't get caught' said The Truculent Man.

'Suppose we did get caught? Could we rely on your support?' asked The Assistant.

'You must appreciate I'm in a delicate position' demurred The Head Postmaster.

'In other words you'll be as much use as that Fat Useless Shagger running the Trades Union Congress' said The Truculent Man.

The Branch Secretary stood up.

'It seems to me gentlemen that the future of the Sub Committee For The Blowing Up Of The Platform Six Shitehouse is in a very parlous condition. So far as I'm concerned Head Postmaster this meeting never took place.' he said and headed for the door with the Truculent Man and The Assistant at his heels.

'What about my shaggin' budget?' wailed The Head Postmaster.

CHAPTER
THIRTY TWO

Look Happy At Work

It was Team Talk Night at The Station. The Dim Manager sat staring at the sheet of paper he'd been issued with as the men filed in and sat down, half of them bolshie the other half much inclined to take the piss out of the proceedings.

The Dim Manager looked up.

'Where's George?' he asked.

Paddy glanced at his watch.

'Six thirty. Where do you think he is?' he asked.

The Dim Manager sighed.

'There's one item on the agenda tonight' he began when Paddy interrupted.

'Where's the Shaggin' Ghost Squad?' he asked.

'Aren't they here?' said The Dim Manager.

'You know bloody well they're not here' said Paddy.

'They're up to their old shaggin' tricks' said Joe.

'They're on undercover work' said Paddy.

'They'd be good at that' said Joe.

The Dim Manager felt on weak ground where the Ghost Squad were concerned and decided to get the meeting officially under way. He read laboriously from the paper.

'Everyone can make a contribution towards improving the image of the Royal Mail' he began before he was stopped by a barrage of laughs, jeers and insults.

'What shaggin' crap are they sending out now?' asked Paddy.

'It's not shaggin' crap. Image is important' said The Dim Manager.

'Bollocks!' said Joe.

The Dim Manager looked at his sheet of paper. There wasn't much there likely to be of assistance.

'Look happy at work. Happy postmen create a favourable impression' on the public' he read.

'Is this a shaggin' windup?' asked Paddy.

'It's not supposed to be. I think the wanker who wrote this believes it' said The Dim Manager.

'Where do they find these tossers?' asked Joe.

'Shagged if I know' said The Dim Manager.

'So we've all got to walk round grinning like a bunch of shaggin' eejets' said Paddy.

'That's about the size of it' said The Dim Manager.

'Spread a little happiness as you go by. Shaggin' 'ell' said Joe.

'So they're concentrating on the image?' said The Union Man.

'Seems like it' said The Dim Manager.

'I suppose they have to. The substance isn't too good' said The Union Man.

'The image isn't too hot either' said Paddy.

'Stick a cucumber up your arse and smile' boomed The Player King.

The Dim Manager winced.

'Then we'll all fly round the Station on our broomsticks with our trouser legs rolled up singing' said The Player King.

'Singing what?' asked Paddy.

To The Dim Manager's horror the Player King rose to his feet and began to sing:

'Heigh ho heigh ho

It's off to work we go

Heigh ho heigh heigh ho

This was bad enough but worse was to follow. Paddy rose to his feet.

Heigh ho heigh ho

To make the Ghost Squad go' he sang.

Just get a bit of glass

And stick it up their arse

Heigh ho heigh ho heigh ho'

Joe was delighted.

'Should have been done years ago' he declared.

'I take it you're still looking for feedback from these talks?' said The Union Man.

The Dim Manager remembered what he'd been told at one of the weekend courses.

'What the staff think is very important. Everyone has a contribution to make' he said.

The Player King rose to his feet again. He struck a pose. Everyone waited.

'You may tell our revered Masters that we were hewers of wood and drawers of water will follow them to the very ends of the earth' he declared.

'Write that shagger down' said Joe.

The Dim Manager dutifully wrote the shagger down.

The Player King hadn't finished.

'Illusions are what sustain us. They shield us from the grisly realities of life' he said.

'Sit down you daft old shagger' Joe told him.

'Such is the stuff of life. We begin rich with promise and become all too soon daft old shaggers' said The Player King mournfully.

'Right that about wraps it up' said The Dim Manager.

'Any word about the Platform Six Shitehouse?' asked Paddy.

'We're expecting it to be blown up any moment' said The Dim Manager.

'What are the Police doing?' asked The Union Man.

'They're busy breathlysing railwaymen and postmen. You can't expect them to do anything about Mad Bombers' snorted Joe.

'They're feeding all the available information into the computer' said The Dim Manager.

'They should bring back the Bobby with a bicycle' said Joe.

'Was he the one who used to keep giving you clips round the ear?' asked The Union Man.

'Never did me any harm' said Joe.

'Never did me any harm either' said The Dim Manager.

'The teachers used to clip you round the ear as well' said Joe.

'Never did you any harm' said The Dim Manager.

'And when your parents heard you'd had a clip round the ear they gave you one as well' said Joe.

'Was there anyone that didn't give you a clip round the ear?' asked Paddy.

'Not that I can remember' said Joe.

'It sounds shaggin' awful' said The Long Haired Git.

'They used to know how to treat people in those days' said Joe.

'They should bring in corporal punishment here' said The Long Haired Git as a joke.

To his horror this was taken up as a serious suggestion.

'They should flog The Ghost Squad for a start' said Joe with relish.

'We could have the stocks in the foyer' said The Long Haired Git.

'At least we'd know where the bastards were if we shoved them in that shagger' said Joe.

The Dim Manager looked as though he thought the idea might well prove to have some merit.

'What about the Do Gooders?' he asked.

'Shove them shaggers in as well' retorted Joe.

'But what will they say?' asked The Dim Manager.

'Shove 'em in the stocks a few times and if they've got any sense they'll say shagall' said Joe.

'They'll send that shagger down from The Sun again' said The Dim Manager.

'He'll be no problem. We'll build a cross and stick him up on it' said Paddy.

'That's it. Crucify the shagger' said Joe.

'Won't do him any harm' said The Long Haired Git.

'While he's hanging up there he can answer enquiries' said The Union Man.

'Like what happened to the Platform Six Shitehouse' said Paddy.

The door was flung open and George marched in. He found an empty chair and sat down.

'What's happened? Have you been barred?' asked Paddy.

George ignored him. He fixed his gaze on The Dim Manager.

'What's the latest on the Platform Six Shitehouse?' he asked.

The Dim Manager glanced at his sheet of paper.

'I've been given no information regarding the Platform Six Shitehouse' he said.

'You must be bloody deaf' said George.

'That'll be all those clips round the ear' said The Long Haired Git.

'There's shagall wrong with my hearing' said The Dim Manager.

'I heard nine groups have claimed responsibility for blowing it up' said George.

'It hasn't been blown up' said The Dim Manager.

'You wouldn't know if it had' George told him.

The Ghost Squad appeared in the doorway.

'Where have you two shaggers been?' asked The Dim Manager.

'Where they've been for the last twenty years' said Joe.

'Sorry we're late' said Len.

'We had to report for instructions' said Arthur.

'Who to?' asked The Dim Manager.

'We're not allowed to say' said Len.

'What do you know about the Platform Six Shitehouse?' George asked them.

'It's still there' said Len.

'For how much longer?' asked The Union Man.

'That's a tricky one' said Arthur.

'It's all these Do Gooders' said Joe.

There was an expectant silence and to his surprise and gratification Joe realised the meeting was waiting for him to enlarge on his theory.

'They stopped corporal punishment in schools and now all the kids are going round stealing cars and blowing up Shitehouses' he said.

This conclusion drew general assent. It was then noticed that The Ghost Squad had disappeared.

'Did anyone see them go?' asked The Dim Manager.

No-one had. There was an animated discussion as to whether The Ghost Squad were human or supernatural. Joe insisted they were a pair of Useless Shaggers and wouldn't shift from that position.

George asked for clarification regarding the future of the Platform Six Shitehouse. The Dim Manager decided his best course was to lie. Barefaced lies would get him out of an embarrassing situation and would demonstrate moreover that he was genuine Executive Material.

'I must remind you all that you've signed The Official Secrets Act' he said and did his best to look as though he considered the subject closed. He was soon disabused.

'So shaggin what?' said Joe.

'Shag the Official Shaggin' Secrets Act' said Paddy.

'I'm buggered if I can see how the shaggin' Shitehouse can come under the terms of The Official Secrets Act' said The Union Man.

'The Official Secrets Act covers everything' said The Dim Manager. That was the one thing he had grasped about The Official Secrets Act. It seemed to him to be beautifully simple, and expressly designed to help Dim Managers.

'So the Platform Six Shitehouse is a secret?' said The Union Man.

The Manager nodded.

'Why is The Shitehouse a secret?' asked The Long Haired Git.

'I'm not allowed to say' said The Dim Manager.

'Will it still be a secret if it's blown to buggery?' asked Paddy.

'It's best not to ask. The less we know the better for us' said The Dim Manager.

'The Police are giving up on it' said George.

'Too busy handing out clips round the ear' said The Longhaired Git.

'It's the same as the pedestrian precinct. They tell you not to walk in that shagger because you'll get run shaggin' over' said Joe.

'What a shaggin' town. You can't walk in the shaggin' pedestrian precinct without being run over by some shagger speeding, you can't go to the shaggin' Platform Six Shitehouse without being blown to buggery, the shaggin' Police can do shagall and if you ask questions you get some shagger pratting on about the Official shaggin' Secrets Act' said George.

'Do you feel better now?' asked The Dim Manager.

'No' said George.

'There was a knock on the door and Ivan walked in.

'Is your vending machine working?' he asked.

'We can't tell you' said Joe.

'Why not?' asked Ivan.

'Official shaggin Secrets Act' said Joe.

'I had to sign that shagger' said Ivan.

'We all have to sign it' said The Dim Manager.

'What for? We know shagall' said Ivan.

'In case we find out something' said George.

'So no-one can tell me if the shaggin' vending machine is working or not' said Ivan.

'More than my jobs worth' said Joe with a kind of grim relish.

'Can I find out for myself?' asked Ivan.

'Ever heard of commercial confidentiality?' asked The Union Man.

'What can you tell us about the Platform Six Shitehouse?' asked George.

'What do you want to know?' countered Ivan.

'That's an irresponsible attitude. Supposing everyone went round blabbing' said Joe.

'The Platform Six Shitehouse is safe in our hands' said Ivan.

The door was flung open and an agitated Leprauchan rushed into the room.

'Two men have just come rushing out of the Shitehouse' he yelled.

'So what?' said Ivan.

'They're blowing the shagger up' said The Leprauchan.

'I hope they've signed The Official Secrets Act' said Joe.

'I tell you they're blowing up The Shitehouse' yelled The Leprauchan.

'We know shagall' said George.

'We want to know shagall' said Joe.

'If you know shagall you can't tell anyone' said George.

'We want to keep our noses clean' said Joe.

'What are you shaggin' talking about?' shrieked The Leprauchan.

'Commercial confidentiality' said George.

'I have signed The Official Secrets Act' said Joe.

'Our lips are sealed' said The Union Man.

There was an almighty bang that rattled the windows. The men sat and stared at each other in silence. Then a second bang followed.

'Hit the shaggin' deck' howled Paddy and immediately followed his own advice.

The rest of the men flung themselves flat, apart from Ivan who headed for the door.

'Where are you going Ivan?' asked The Dim Manager.

'I have to make a public service announcement. Put the customers in the picture' said Ivan.

'They're in the shaggin' picture. Get on the shaggin' floor' said George.

There was a series of bigger bangs. Ivan got on his hands and knees.

'I'll appeal for calm later on' he said and flattened himself as there was a whole series of explosions.

The explosions went on for some time. After a while George started to get impatient.

'How long does it take to blow up a Shitehouse?' he asked.

'Why? Are you in a hurry?' asked The Dim Manager.

'I bloody am. There's aint waiting for me over at the Institute' said George.

'Why don't you make a dash for it?' asked Joe.

'I think I will' said George and headed for the door.

'Come back here you prat' called The Dim Manager.

George ignored him, turned up his collar and ran out.

Joe glared at The Dim Manager.

'Go after him' he demanded.

'Shagoff' said The Dim Manager.

'You're supposed to look after the welfare of your men' said Paddy.

'I've got a wife and kids' countered The Dim Manager.

'So's George' said The Union Man.

'If you're so concerned you go after him' said The Dim Manager.

The explosions continued unabated. Then there was one much louder than all the others. They all stared at the door but George did not return.

'That's another shaggin' postman who won't live to draw his pension' said Joe.

'Alas Poor George, I knew him well' intoned The Player King.

'Do you suppose they'll ever find his arse?' said The Longhaired Git.

'He wasn't such a bad shagger' said Joe.

The telephone rang in The Dim Manager's office. He pretended not to hear it.

'Have you gone shaggin' deaf?' asked Paddy.

'What?' said The Dim Manager.

'We'd best see who it is' said The Union Man.

He left the room and went to the Manager's office. Soon he returned looking very serious.

'I'm afraid it's bad news. It's George' he said.

'Is he dead?' asked The Dim Manager.

'No. Worse than that. Someone's drunk his pint' said The Union Man.

'Truly there is no limit to human perfidy' said The Player King.

'There's some rotten bastards about' said Paddy.

'It's gone quiet' said Joe.

'I reckon it's all over' said Ivan.

'The venerable Shitehouse that hath met man's needs for decades is now no more' said The Player King.

'We might as well go and piss on the embers' said Paddy.

They made their way gingerly out onto the platform. They lined up outside the door and stared over to Platform Six. Their mouths sagged open. The Player King broke the silence:

'Truly it is a prince among Shitehouses. It has withstood the battering' he said.

Everyone stared.

'He's right. The shagger's still there' said Joe.

'What about all the explosions?' asked The Dim Manager.

'We all heard 'em' said The Long Haired Git.

As they all stood staring at the plainly intact Shitehouse there was another explosion. Something shot from The Shitehouse window rose up and exploded in a blaze of glorious colour.

'It's a shaggin' firework' said Joe.

A second firework followed the first and then suddenly the sky was full of exploding starshells which they all watched descending slowly to earth.

'What day is it?' asked Joe.

'It's not November the Fifth' said The Union Man.

Joe gazed entranced as rockets and starshells flew out of The Platform Six Shitehouse.

'I wonder who sponsored this?' he said.

His curiosity was shared by a well dressed Would Be Traveller.

'To whom are we indebted for this splendid display?' he asked.

'Shagged if I know' said Joe.

'It's really first class' said The Would Be Traveller. He looked at his watch.

'If the bloody train finally arrives I'll have had a perfect evening' he said and left.

'He'll get no shaggin' trains here' said Joe.

'Some shaggers are never satisfied' said Paddy.

George came walking quickly down the platform. He glanced across to The Platform Six Shitehouse which was still ablaze with exploding rockets and starshells.

'Someone's claimed responsibility' he told the group.

'Go on. Surprise us' said The Dim Manager.

'It's the Sons of Erin' said George.

Everyone looked at Paddy.

'Never heard of the shaggers' said Paddy.

'We'd best tell that bloke' said Joe. He spotted The Would Be Traveller.

'Hey Guvnor' he called.

'The Would Be Traveller looked up. Joe pointed at the Platform Six Shitehouse.

'It's the Sons of Erin' he called.

'More power to their elbow. Any news of the train?' replied The Would Be Traveller.

'I don't know anything about trains' Joe told him.

'Neither does The Station Manager' said The Would Be Traveller, looking resigned.

The Long Haired Git turned to The Union Man.

'I think I know the Sons of Erin' he said.

'I didn't know you followed Irish politics' said The Union Man.

The Long Haired Git shook his head emphatically.

'I don't. They were on at Nottingham last week. I saw them' he said.

'Doing what?' said Joe.

'They're a Pop Group' said The Long Haired Git.

'It's another shaggin' windup' said Paddy.

Joe looked over to The Shitehouse.

'If they got in there and started blasting with their amplification they'd soon blow The Shitehouse to buggery' he said.

CHAPTER
THIRTY THREE

A Way Out

The Bomb Squad Sergeant sat reading through his latest report. He was pleased with it. He had no doubt The Chief Constable's posh friends would be most impressed. More importantly it confirmed his view that he had literary abilities. He could see a way out of the Police Force.

A Uniformed Officer came in. The Sergeant put his report out of sight.

'They've arrested The Sons of Erin' said The Uniformed Officer.

'Who are they?' asked The Sergeant.

'They're a Pop Group' said The Uniformed Officer.

'Are they any good?' asked The Sergeant.

'No they're crap' said The Uniformed Officer.

'You can't charge them with being crap' objected The Sergeant.

'They've claimed responsibility for blowing up The Platform Six Shitehouse' said The Uniformed Officer.

'It hasn't been blown up' said The Sergeant.

'So they're crap at blowing up Shitehouses as well' said The Uniformed Officer.

'There must be something they can do' said The Sergeant.

'There is. They can sign a shaggin' confession' said The Uniformed Officer.

'What's their motive?' asked The Sergeant.

'They can't get in The Charts' said The Uniformed Officer.

'You mean all the crap Pop Groups who can't get in the Charts are going to start blowing up Shitehouses?' asked The Sergeant.

'There's going to be a lot more of this sort of thing' said The Uniformed Officer.

'How many Crap Pop Groups are there?' asked The Sergeant.

'Enough to blow up every Shitehouse in the country' said The Uniformed Officer.

The Sergeant glanced longingly at his report. The life of a Literary Gentleman seemed ever more desirable.

He had no wish to spend the rest of his working life defusing bombs in Public Shitehouses. The Superintendent came in.

'I want a report on my desk first thing in the morning' he said.

'What about?' asked The Sergeant.

'Everything you know about The Sons of Erin' The Superintendent told him.

'I know shagall about The Sons of Erin' protested The Sergeant.

'That's not good enough for the members of The Chief Constable's Golf Club' chided The Superintendent.

'What am I supposed to do?' asked The Sergeant.

'Use your imagination' said The Superintendent.

The Sergeant smiled and put a piece of paper into the typewriter.

'Special Branch are sending us everything they've got on them' said The Superintendent.

The Sergeant looked up. He peered closely at The Superintendent.

'You're having me on' he said.

The Superintendent shook his head.

'Special Branch attach great importance to the surveillance of Dissident Groups' he said.

'What like Crap Pop Groups?' asked The Sergeant.

'Anyone with a grievance' said The Superintendent.

'They'd better open a file on me then' muttered The Sergeant. He wondered how the work of fiction he was engaged on could possibly compete with the the sheer preposterousness of the truth.

'I always thought The Beatles were crap. Is there a file on them?' he asked.

'Of course there is' said The Superintendent.

'Are they blowing up Shitehouses?' asked The Uniformed Officer. The phone rang. The Uniformed Officer answered it.

'Can I ring you back?' he asked and then rang off. He looked at The Superintendent.

'That was the IRA sir. They deny responsibility' he said.

'That means nothing. Even if they were responsible they'd deny any connection with a shambles' said The Sergeant.

The phone rang again. The Uniformed Officer answered it. He spoke to The Superintendent.

'That was the Manager of Derby Station sir. He wants a bomb squad officer at the scene of the crime immediately' he said.

'He wants an Officer there immediately. Who does he think he is? One of The Chief Constable's Posh Friends?' asked The Sergeant.

'I think perhaps it would be best if we were seen to be taking an interest?' said The Superintendent.

'Just in case one of The Chief Constable's Posh Friends starts poking his nose in' said The Sergeant.

'It's always best to cover your back Sergeant' said The Superintendent, blind to the irony.

'I'll take the dog. Give him a chance to cock his leg' said The Sergeant.

'Take some photos' instructed The Superintendent.

'What's he think I am? A shaggin' Tourist?' muttered The Sergeant.

Meanwhile there was great excitement at the scene of the crime. The Leprauchan was the first to enter The Shitehouse. He came out looking shaken.

'That Shitehouse is in a terrible state. I'd best put up the sign - 'Closed For Cleaning' he said and wandered off. Rod Williams refused to leave his office. He was writing a report to Region. The Dim Manager decided on a business as usual approach.

'Right come on lads. Back to work. Get stuck in.' he urged.

'What were we doing before we were so rudely interrupted?' asked The Player King.

'We were having a shaggin' team meeting' said Joe.

'The Sons of Erin want shaggin'. If they'd done a halfway decent job the Shitehouse would be flying over the town centre and we could knock off for the night' complained Paddy.

'Talking of knocking off for the night, anyone seen the Ghost Squad?' asked Joe.

No-one bothered to answer the question and before Joe had a chance to repeat it George came down the platform.

'The Sons of Erin' deny responsibility' he said.

'They've denied the shagger?' said Joe.

'Yes' said George.

'What are they shaggin' about at? Just now they claimed the shagger' said Joe.

'They say they didn't. They say some other shagger must have made the call' said George.

'You don't know who to shaggin' believe do you' said Joe.

Before a discussion could ensure as to who exactly was and was not responsible for the attack on the Shitehouse, if attack it was, Joe's jaw dropped in amazement and he stared incredulously up the platform.

'I can't believe I'm seeing that. Not those shaggers' he gasped.

The sight that caused Joe's amazement was truly remarkable. The Ghost Squad were sprinting up the platform. The reason for the unprecedented turn of speed was soon obvious. A dog was in hot pursuit. This spectacle caused Joe great delight. He urged the dog on.

'Come on boy, kill!' he shouted.

'Wanker!' howled Len.

Arthur suddenly swerved to the right and to his obvious relief the dog continued in a straight line and got a grip on the seat of Len's trousers. Despite Len's bellowed protests it showed no sign of letting go.

'What a lovely dog' said Joe.

'Wanker!' howled Len.

'What me or the dog?' asked Joe.

'Both' bellowed Len.

'Heel boy, heel!'

The cry came from a man who had come up the platform with no sign of urgency. The dog immediately let go of Len and went and sat by the man.

'Look at that. That's what I call a well trained dog' said Joe.

'Well trained dog! It's a bloody menace', cried Len.

'Sergeant Baxter, Bomb Squad. My ID' said The Man.

'You're a bit late' said Joe.

'The trouble is there's more of them than there is of us' said Sergeant Baxter.

'I suppose you've got troubles with the Budget' said The Union Man.

'It's all we ever hear about. That and The Chief Constable's Posh Friends' said Sergeant Baxter.

'Not the shaggin' Golf Club' said The Union Man.

'When dissidents start blowing up golf clubhouses I'll know the true revolution has finally come' said Sergeant Baxter.

'Are you really a copper?' asked Joe.

'I am. There's my ID' said Sergeant Baxter.

'You sure you're not one of those Agent shaggin' wotsits?' asked Joe.

'No. I'm just pissed off' said Sergeant Baxter.

'Join the Club' said The Union Man.

'We're being shat on from a great height' said Len.

Sergeant Baxter took a keen look at Len.

'The question is, why did my dog chase you?' he asked.

'Am I supposed to answer that?' asked Len.

'He's a trained sniffer' said Sergeant Baxter.

'He's a Big Shagger' said Joe looking approvingly at The Dog.

'He's shagged up my trousers' complained Len.

'Now why would my Dog notice you?' repeated Sergeant Baxter.

Len opened his mouth to speak but was drowned by The Player King.

'Oh thou whose lot is not a happy one,
I recommend you to consider the case of
Macbeth' he said.

'Was he being shat on from a great height?' asked Len.

'Macbeth and the weird women' said The Player King.

'Weird women. I've come across plenty of them in my time' said Joe.

'Join the Club' said everyone present, apart from Len who was feeling got at.

'Those who are on the earth but not of it' explained The Player King.

'He means they're unnatural' said Paddy.

'They infest the orb but belong not to it' boomed The Player King.

'Shaggin' vampires' said Joe.

'I can't charge them with that' said Sergeant Baxter.

'No but you can trace the sods back to their tombs and drive stakes through their hearts' said Joe.

'Shagoff' protested Len.

'Are you Vampires?' asked Sergeant Baxter.

'No we're shaggin' not' said Len.

'It's my duty to warn you that your particulars will be going into the Police Computer' said Sergeant Baxter.

'What particulars?' asked Len.

'Size of fangs. That kind of stuff' said Joe.

The Leprauchan came down the platform more or less driving Rod Williams before him.

'You have to assert yourself' The Leprauchan insisted.

'I was told to expect a Sergeant Baxter and a Constable Rawlings' said Rod.

'I'm Sergeant Baxter. Who are you?' said The Sergeant.

'I am The Station Manager' said Rod.

'Ask him where Constable Rawlings is?' hissed The Leprauchan.

'Where is Constable Rawlings?' asked Rod.

'He just bit Len's arse and he's about to piss on your leg' said Joe.

Rod leapt back hastily. Sergeant Baxter indicated The Ghost Squad.

'In your view are these men supernatural?' he asked.

'The Sun' have already investigated this Station for signs of The Occult and given us a clean bill of health' claimed Rod.

'What about the cucumbers up the arse?' said Joe.

'That was never proven' countered Rod.

'Then there was the Freemasons' Lodge' said The Longhaired Git.

'Best leave the Freemasons out. I think all The Chief Constable's Posh Friends are Masons' said Sergeant Baxter.

'Does The Chief Constable go round with a cucumber shoved up his arse?' asked The Union Man.

'He does walk a bit funny now you come to mention it, but I don't really want to pursue this line of enquiry until I've ensured my future elsewhere in a more congenial line of work' said Sergeant Baxter.

'So he does go round with a cucumber rammed up his arse. They're all the same' said Joe.

'And we're all supposed to be Male Witches' said The Longhaired Git.

'These are all very serious matters but fortunately nothing to do with me.' said Sergeant Baxter.

'What brings you here then?' asked Joe.

'I'm visiting the scene of the crime' Sergeant Baxter told him.

'What crime?' asked Paddy.

'The blowing up of the Platform Six Shitehouse' said Sergeant Baxter.

'The Shagger hasn't been blown up. See for yourself. The shagger's still there' said Joe.

The Sergeant looked.

'You're shaggin' right. The shaggers still there' he agreed.

'The Sons of Erin must be shaggin' useless. Couldn't organise a shaggin' pissup in a shaggin' brewery' said Joe.

'Their music's crap too' said The Longhaired Git.

'I'd better carry out an inspection' said Sergeant Baxter.

'That lad's never a real Copper' said Joe.

'You've seen his ID' said Paddy.

'It's a shaggin' forgery' said Joe.

Sergeant Baxter turned towards The Shitehouse and faced it resolutely.

'I want you all to stand well back' he told the men.

'How far guarantees safety?' asked The Union Man.

'A couple of miles should do it' said Sergeant Baxter.

Accompanied by the dog he went into The Shitehouse. The men remained where they were.

'Shouldn't we go back a bit?' asked The Longhaired Git.

'What for? It's a shaggin' windup' said Joe.

'We don't know that for sure' said The Longhaired Git.

'You please yourself. I'm stopping here' said Joe.

A few minutes passed and then Sergeant Baxter and the Dog emerged.

'I'm happy to report The Shitehouse remains an ongoing concern' he announced.

'What does that mean exactly?' asked The Union Man.

'Apart from some cracked porcelain the facilities are still functional' replied Sergeant Baxter.

'You mean there's nothing wrong with it?' asked Joe.

'You can bring in a Consulting Engineer if you want to but he'll only confirm my diagnosis. The Shitehouse remains structurally sound' said Sergeant Baxter.

'Consulting Engineer. What do we want one of those shaggers for? What we need is a shaggin' plumber' said Joe.

'There is scope for a plumber. I can assure you there are no bombs waiting to go off. The Shitehouse does not have to be designated a no go area' said Sergeant Baxter. He walked off followed closely by The Dog.

'Where are you going?' asked Joe.

'I have to write a report on this outrage' said Sergeant Baxter.

'He's never a proper Copper. It's another shaggin' windup' said Joe.

The Player King nodded his head.

'It occurs to me that the entire last twenty years have been a windup' he said.

'It'll get worse for the next shaggin' twenty' said Joe.

'It can't get any worse' said The Longhaired Git.

'That's what we keep shaggin' saying and we're always shaggin' wrong' retorted Joe.

Meanwhile The Sons of Erin were ruffling a few feathers at the Police Station.

The Desk Sergeant resented the fact that they looked so scruffy they created a bad impression on anyone entering the Station.

'Take this shower to the Interview Room' he ordered.

'Are they being charged?' asked a Constable.

'They're cluttering the place up' said The Sergeant testily.

'Yes but are they being charged?' persisted The Constable.

'They're assisting with enquiries' said The Desk Sergeant.

'You'll get no help from us' said The Lead Singer.

'It's not your assistance I'm after. It's your absence' said The Desk Sergeant.

'We never asked to come here' said another member of the Group.

'You confessed to a felony' The Desk Sergeant told him.

'No we never' said The Lead Singer.

'Yes you did' said The Desk Sergeant.

'What are we supposed to have done?' asked The Lead Singer.

'Blown up a Shitehouse' said The Desk Sergeant.

'Why would we do that?' asked The Lead Singer.

'You tell me' replied The Sergeant.

'This is a load of bollocks' said another member of the Group.

'It might be a load of bollocks but you lot are right in the shit' said The Desk Sergeant.

'You wait till our fans find out about this' said The Lead Singer.

'Why did you blow up The Shitehouse?' asked The Constable.

'We didn't blow up the shaggin' Shitehouse' protested The Lead Singer.

The Dog came in closely followed by Sergeant Baxter. Baxter tried to avoid The Desk Sergeant. He was unsuccessful. The Desk Sergeant spotted him with obvious delight.

'This is the shower that blew up The Shitehouse' he said.

'No it's not' said Sergeant Baxter.

'The wankers have confessed' said The Desk Sergeant.

'The Shitehouse is intact' said Sergeant Baxter.

'What's all this bollocks about a confession?' asked a Group Member.

'You are The Sons of Erin?' asked The Desk Sergeant.

'What about it?' asked The Lead Singer.

'The Sons of Erin confessed to blowing up the Shitehouse at 9.10 pm' said The Desk Sergeant glancing quickly at a report.

'We blew The Shitehouse up at 9.10 pm?' asked another Group Member.

'No you confessed to blowing up The Shitehouse at 9.10 pm corrected The Sergeant.

'But he says it hasn't been blown up' said The Lead Singer indicating Sergeant Baxter.

'That's not my fault' said The Sergeant.

The Lead Singer looked flabbergasted. Then a smile spread slowly across his face.

'It's a windup isn't up? You're all bloody kissagrams aren't you' he said.

'You'll all have to make statements' said The Desk Sergeant.

'About what?' asked The Lead Singer.

'If you didn't make the confession who did?' demanded The Desk Sergeant.

'What's the point of asking me that?' asked The Lead Singer.

The Desk Sergeant turned again to Sergeant Baxter.

'Sergeant Baxter. Take this shower to the Interview Room and establish whether or not we can eliminate them from our enquiries' he said.

Sergeant Baxter shook his head.

'I'm afraid that won't be possible' he said.

'Why not?' demanded The Desk Sergeant.

'I have to write a report for The Chief Constable's Posh Friends immediately' replied Sergeant Baxter.

The Desk Sergeant glared venomously at The Sons of Erin.

'If I let you lot off with a caution will you shag off and promise not to come here again?' he asked.

'We never asked to come here in the first shaggin' place' said The Lead Singer moving towards the door. The Constable spoke to him out of the corner of his mouth.

'Can you let me have a couple of tickets for your next Gig?' he asked.

The Lead Singer produced a couple of tickets.

'Here you are with my compliments. You can have them on one condition. Promise me you'll start looking for a proper shaggin' job', he said.

The Constable took the tickets and shook his head.

'Don't talk like a prat. If there were any proper jobs I'd never have come here in the first place' he replied.

CHAPTER
THIRTY FOUR

Dancing In the Dark

'A Branch Dance!', exploded The Truculent Man.

The Branch Secretary was somewhat taken aback by this plainly hostile reaction but remained calm in the face of fire.

'Yes a Branch Dance' he repeated.

'Have you gone stark raving dolally?' asked The Truculent Man.

'Not so far as I know' replied The Branch Secretary.

'We've never had a Branch Dance before' said The Assistant.

'Then it's high time we did' replied The Secretary.

'What the bloody hell for?' howled The Truculent Man.

'To show the bastards we're not defeated' said The Secretary.

This took a while to sink in. The Truculent Man glanced at The Assistant. The Assistant shrugged. The Truculent Man was baffled but determined to try and explain his point of view.

But we are defeated. Management are running amok. The discipline code comes straight from Saudi Arabia. They're doing what they like. We're powerless' he protested.

The Assistant nodded his assent.

'Quite right' agreed The Branch Secretary.

This wasn't what The Truculent Man expected and he was nonplussed. He stood with his mouth hanging slightly open. The Branch Secretary turned to The Educated Shaggin' Idiot.

'Enlighten them' he asked.

'We need to make a gesture of defiance' said The Educated Shaggin' Idiot.

The Truculent Man and The Assistant Secretary waited for him to continue. He took out his Guardian and read. The Truculent Man coughed. The Educated Shaggin' Idiot sighed and looked up.

'I don't get it' confessed The Truculent Man.

'We know we're beaten but we mustn't let them know' explained The Educated Shaggin' Idiot.

'They know already don't they?' asked The Truculent Man.

'They know they're winning. They don't know just how down we are' said The Educated Shaggin' Idiot.

'If they don't know, we don't want the bastards to know' said The Truculent Man.

'Exactly' said The Educated Shaggin' Idiot.

The Truculent Man sat with knitted brow. He was thinking hard. His brow cleared. He had come to a decision.

'I'll buy it' he declared.

'We'll need to set up a Sub Committee' said The Assistant.

'Sod that!' We've already got a Sub Committee' said The Truculent Man.

The rest looked puzzled.

'The Sub Committee For Blowing up The Platform Six Shitehouse' explained The Truculent Man.

'We can't do everything' protested The Assistant.

'The Shitehouse can go on the backburner' said The Branch Secretary.

'Right. Let's get down to the nitty bloody gritty' said The Truculent Man.

The Educated Shaggin' Idiot put down his Guardian and took out his pen.

'Are we going in for a modest function or something on a grand scale?' he asked.

'No point in effin' about. Let's do it properly' said The Truculent Man.

'I agree' said The Assistant.

'The bigger the better' said The Branch Secretary.

'Music to my ears' said The Educated Shaggin' Idiot.

'Where shall we hold it?' asked The Branch Secretary.

'Labour Club?' ventured The Assistant.

'Labor Club be buggered. Let's have The Assembly Rooms' said The Truculent Man.

'I thought we might ask Jack Tanner to come along as Guest of Honour' said The Branch Secretary.

'We'll never get Jack Tanner' protested The Assistant.

'We don't want Jack Tanner' said The Truculent Man.

'Why not?' asked The Branch Secretary.

'He's too political' replied The Truculent Man.

'How can he be too political? He's fighting for the workers' said The Branch Secretary.

The Truculent Man shook his head in exasperation. He turned to The Educated Shaggin' Idiot.

'If we get Jack Tanner he'll get up and tell we all we're a load of wankers and we need to get up off our knees' he said.

The Educated Shaggin' Idiot nodded his agreement.

'What's wrong with that?' asked The Branch Secretary.

'I thought the whole point was not to let management know we're on our bleedin' knees' said The Truculent Man.

The Assistant nodded sagely.

'He's right. And if Jack Tanner gets up there and says we're on our knees it'll be in the paper' he observed.

They all looked towards The Educated Shaggin' Idiot. He smiled benign at them.

'You're all right' he said.

This was too much for The Truculent Man.

'You talk like a twat. How can we all be right?' he demanded.

The Assistant was quick to agree with The Truculent Man.

'He's right. You talk like a twat. How can we all be right?' he wanted to know.

The Educated Idiot was used to being told he talked like a twat and remained perfectly calm.

'Jack Tanner has a list of speaking engagements for the next three years' he started before he was interrupted by The Truculent Man.

'So shaggin' what?' he asked.

'We've got no chance of getting Jack Tanner to come to our Dance' said The Educated Shaggin Idiot.

'So what are we arguing about?' demanded The Truculent Man.

Before The Educated Shaggin' Idiot could reply The Truculent Man burst out again:

'No wonder we're on our shaggin' knees, we spend all our time arguing about sodall' he complained.

'We're not arguing about sodall' said The Educated Shaggin' Idiot.

'Yes we are. We're arguing the toss about whether or not to invite Jack Tanner and he can't come anyway cos he's booked up for the next few years' said The Truculent Man.

'The fact that he can't come is beside the point' said The Educated Shaggin' Idiot. He waited for The Truculent Man to interrupt but since he contented himself with snorting and glaring The Educated Shaggin' Idiot continued.

'What matters is we invite him and issue a press statement to say we've invited him' he said. He then sat back and waited to see what response he got.

'So we invite a bloke we know can't come and we tell the press. What's the point?' asked The Truculent Man.

'We're sending out a signal' The Educated Shaggin' Idiot told him.

'What signal? SOS?' asked The Truculent Man.

The Branch Secretary decided it was time he took a hand.

'Who's the most militant Labour MP?' he asked.

'Jack Tanner' replied The Truculent Man.

'So we let the world know we've invited Jack Tanner' said The Branch Secretary.

'To declare our militancy' said The Educated Shaggin' Idiot.

'But we're not militant' pointed out The Assistant.

'We're a dispirited shaggin' rabble' said The Truculent Man.

'But Management don't know that' said The Branch Secretary.

'They must have a bloody good idea' retorted The Truculent Man.

'Put it to the vote' said The Branch Secretary.

'All those in favour' said The Assistant.

The Branch Secretary and The Educated Shaggin' Idiot raised their hands. The Truculent Man glanced at The Assistant Secretary. The Assistant shrugged. The Truculent Man looked at The Educated Shaggin' Idiot.

'You're sure he won't come?' he asked.

'Not a chance' said The Educated Shaggin' Idiot.

'Let's invite him then' said The Truculent Man and raised his hand. After a moment's hesitation The Assistant also raised his hand.

'Right that's carried? What's next?' said The Branch Secretary.

'I thought you were telling us' objected The Truculent Man.

Before The Branch Secretary could reply The Educated Shaggin' Idiot broke in.

'Cabaret' he said.

The Truculent Man's jaw sagged.

'You what?' he said.

'Cabaret' repeated The Educated Shaggin' Idiot.

'What's in the Kitty?' asked The Assistant Secretary.

'Not a lot' said The Branch Secretary.

'That's what I thought' said The Assistant.

'We could have a few strippers' suggested The Truculent Man.

The Assistant Secretary shook his head. 'We don't want trouble with the wives' he said.

The Truculent Man was having none of that. 'If there's trouble with the wives it's up to the bloody blokes to sort them out' he said.

'The funds won't run to professional cabaret' said The Educated Shaggin' Idiot.

'Right then. Next business' said The Truculent Man.

'We'll do our own cabaret' said The Educated Shaggin' Idiot.

'That definitely rules out the strippers then' said The Assistant.

'Just what do you have in mind?' asked The Assistant.

'Satire' said The Educated Shaggin' Idiot.

The beginnings of a smile played at the corners of The Truculent Man's mouth.

'Do you mean piss taking?' he asked.

The Educated Shaggin' Idiot nodded. The Truculent Man raised his hand. 'I'll vote for that shagger' he said enthusiastically.

'Who's going to perform this satire?' asked The Assistant.

'The Platform One Repertory Company' said The Educated Shaggin' Idiot.

The Assistant Secretary looked horrified. 'You're never going to let that mad old shagger loose' he gasped.

The Truculent Man on the other hand was delighted. He smashed his fist on the table. 'Bloody great! Let that old sod loose and they'll never know what's hit 'em' he enthused.

'Just so long as Jack Tanner doesn't turn up as well' muttered The Assistant.

'Which room are we having at The Assembly Rooms?' asked The Truculent Man.

'We're taking the Main Hall' said The Educated Shaggin' Idiot.

'But that holds thousands' said The Truculent Man.

'We'll have to sell thousands of tickets then' The Educated Shaggin' Idiot told him.

The Assistant and The Truculent Man were about to launch a concerted protest when The Branch Secretary cut them off.

'We've got nine hundred and eighty seven members' he said as though that settled the matter.

'And they've all got families and friends who'll buy tickets. It could well turn out to be the social event of the year' said The Educated Shaggin' Idiot.

'The social event of the year. Our Branch Dance. You talk like a twat' said The Truculent Man.

'A lot of our blokes are so knackered they'll never make it to The Assembly Rooms. We'll have to have 'em stretchered in' said The Assistant.

'So much the better. Let the people see what's going on?' said The Secretary.

'They know what's going on. They don't give a sod' said The Truculent Man.

'We'll need posters and leaflets' said The Educated Shaggin' Idiot. The others nodded assent.

'I thought something like this might fit the bill' said The Educated Shaggin' Idiot passing round some specimens.

'Coruscating wit. That's piss taking is it?' asked The Truculent Man.

The Educated Shaggin' Idiot nodded.

'What'll we say when Jack Tanner doesn't turn up?' asked The Assistant.

'By that time everyone will be so pissed they won't care if he turns up or not' said The Branch Secretary.

The Truculent Man gleefully picked up a poster. 'I'll stick this phucker up on the notice board right away' he said and left looking uncharacteristically at peace with the world.

'Have we got a spare copy?' asked The Branch Secretary.

'You can have this one' said The Educated Shaggin' Idiot.

The Branch Secretary took the draft poster.

'I'll just take this round to show The Head Postmaster' he said.

...   .

The Chief Inspector knocked on the door of The Head Postmaster's office and walked in. The Head Postmaster was pacing up and down looking as though he needed heavy sedation. The Chief looked at him expectantly. The Head Postmaster continued to pace up and down. The Chief felt he could spend his time more profitably than watching these perambulations.

'You sent for me' he said.

'The Union's having a Branch Dance' said The Head Postmaster.

'Branch Dance! Branch bloody wake more like' scoffed The Chief.

'Do you know who's coming?' asked The Head Postmaster:

The Chief Inspector shook his head.

'Jack Bloody Tanner' said The Head Postmaster.

The Chief Inspector was visibly shaken. 'Jack Bloody Tanner' he echoed, as he half sat, half collapsed, into a chair.

'And you know what that means' said The Head Post Master.

'Jack Bloody Tanner can only ever mean one thing and that's trouble' said The Chief Inspector.

'Too bloody right' said The Head Postmaster.

'What did they want to invite that bastard for?' asked The Chief Inspector.

'Who knows how the devious sods minds work' said The Head Postmaster.

'I bet The Educated Shaggin' Idiot is at the bottom of this' said The Chief Inspector.

'Well what are we going to do about it?' asked The Head Postmaster.

'I don't know what you're going to do but I'm going on leave' said The Chief Inspector.

'You can't do that' said The Head Postmaster.

'You watch me' said The Chief Inspector.

'Jack Bloody Tanner's an absolute maniac' said The Head Postmaster.

'That's why I'm going on leave. If you've got any sense you'll do the same' said The Chief Inspector.

'The bugger's dangerous' said The Head Postmaster.

'He's lethal' agreed The Chief Inspector.

'If he ever got into power he'd start evening the score. He'd have that lot at Region behind bars for a start' said The Head Postmaster.

'And I wouldn't complain about that if he did' said The Chief Inspector.

'Best bloody place for 'em' concurred The Head Postmaster.

'He's way over the top but not all his ideas are loony' said The Chief Inspector.

'I've always had a sneaking admiration for him myself' said The Head Postmaster.

'At least you know where he stands' said The Chief Inspector.

'On our necks if he gets half a chance' said The Head Postmaster.

'Jeezuzwept! Look at this!' cried The Chief Inspector as he waved the poster aloft.

'What's up?' asked The Head Postmaster.

'There's going to be a bloody cabaret. Performed by The Platform One Repertory Company. You know what that is don't you?' demanded The Chief Inspector.

'Not that mad old sod that used to be an actor?' gasped The Head Postmaster.

'Used to be! The old bastard does more acting now than he ever did when he was a pro' said The Chief Inspector.

'Let me have a look at that' demanded The Head Postmaster: The Chief Inspector handed over the poster.

'Do you see what he's going to do?' asked The Head Postmaster.

'No. What is he going to do?' asked The Chief Inspector.

'Satire!' yelled The Head Postmaster.

'That's taking the piss isn't it?' The Chief Inspector asked.

'Yes and you know who they'll be taking the piss out of don't you?' said The Head Postmaster:

'You and me' said The Chief Inspector.

'And where is it going to be?' demanded The Head Postmaster. The Chief Inspector gazed at the poster in horror.

'The bloody Assembly Rooms' he gasped.

'Every bugger'll be there. We'll be a laughing stock' said The Head Postmaster.

'What are we going to do?' asked The Chief Inspector.

'What can we do?' countered The Head Postmaster.

'We could have a dance. Take the piss out of them' suggested The Chief Inspector.

For a moment a glimmer of hope flitted across The Head Postmaster's face, then he slumped.

'We can't do that. We don't have a mad old sod'.

'We've got plenty of mad old sods' retorted The Chief Inspector.

The Head Postmaster shook his head sadly. 'You'll never learn to tell the difference between a mad old sod and a mental defective' he said.

CHAPTER
THIRTY FIVE

Command Performance

After having heard of Jack Bloody Tanner's impending visit The Chief left The Head Postmaster's Office still clutching the poster. He accosted the first Dim Manager he saw.

'What's coruscating?' he demanded.

The Dim Manager was nonplussed. He wondered if it might be something you did on ice but thought the best thing he could do was admit his ignorance.

'I don't know Chief' he said.

'Well friggin' well find out' instructed The Chief.

The Dim Manager decided to ask around. He asked a postman who happened to be in the vicinity. 'What's coruscating?' he said. The postman's response was immediate and dismissive. 'Fucked if I know he told him. The Dim Manager snorted.

'You know effall' he said scornfully.

'You're so bloody clever. Why are you asking me?' demanded the postman. 'I know what it is, I wanted to know if you knew' said The Dim Manager.

'Pull the other bugger' said the postman.

As soon as The Chief Inspector reached his office he slammed the door, kicked the desk and phoned The Dim Manager at the station.

'Chief Inspector here. Tell that man old sod I'll sue him' he ordered and rang off.

The Dim Manager stared aghast at the phone. 'What the bloody hell has happened now?' he wondered. He decided to see if The Union Man had any idea as to what was happening. He found him over on Platform Six where Rod Williams was keeping an eye on the toilets while pretending to read a paper.

'I've just had a call from The Chief' he began.

Rod Williams caught this opening and pricked up his ears while still keeping a sharp eye on the toilets and pretending to read the paper.

'Oh yes' said The Union Man noncommittally. He knew there was no need to press for information since it was perfectly obvious The Dim Manager was anxious to talk.

'I've got to tell! The Mad Old Sod he'll sue him' said The Dim Manager.

'Who's The Mad Old Sod?' asked The Union Man.

The Dim Manager looked at the men. 'You tell me' he said.

'The way things are now anyone over fifty could well be a Mad Old Sod' said The Union Man.

The Dim Manager nodded. 'Not to mention at least half the under fifties' he sighed.

'Then there's Rod Williams' said The Union Man.

'I can't understand why he's still loose' complained The Dim Manager.

'Care in the Community' The Union Man told him.

'Things never used to be as bad as this' said The Dim Manager.

'And what happened to all the North Sea Oil Money?' asked The Union Man.

'Christ knows!' said The Dim Manager.

'I reckon the Old Bitch has buried it in her garden' said The Union Man.

'She's just the sort who would try and take it with her' said The Dim Manager.

Rod Williams marched up and accosted The Dim Manager.

'When are the Goddamed Post Office going to stamp up their share of the sandbag money?' he demanded.

'Ask those prats at Region' The Dim Manager told him.

'Are you going to spend the rest of your working life standing guard over the Shitehouse?' asked The Union Man.

'Someone has to' Rod told him.

'We've had a message from The Chief Inspector' and The Dim Manager.

'Is it to do with the sandbags?' asked Rod.

'No' said The Dim Manager.

'Then I'm not interested' said Rod.

'Aren't you a bit limited?' said The Dim Manager.

'I keep my eye on the ball' said Rod.

'I don't see how I can pass this message on' complained The Dim Manager.

'Why not?' asked The Union Man.

'If I go up to one of them and say I've a message for The Mad Old Sod he'll most likely sue me' said The Dim Manager.

'Has The Chief started drinking again?' asked The Union Man.

'I didn't know he'd stopped' said The Dim Manager.

'Best put it in the pending tray' advised The Union Man.

'I think you're right' said The Dim Manager.

George marched up the platform. He accosted Rod Williams.

'Do you know what they call a bloke who's obsessed with Shitehouses? He demanded.

'I don't know and furthermore I don't want to know' said Rod

'Ignorant and proud of it' said George.

'What do they call him?' asked The Dim Manager, glad of something to take his mind off the message.

'Scatological' said George.

Paddy sought this and immediately took exception to it.

'It's a fine state of affairs when I'm under the jurisdiction of a man who's plainly scatalogical' he complained.

'I am not scatalogical' bellowed Rod, who was rapidly losing his temper.

'Why don't you get on the public address and save yourself the trouble of bawling?' asked George.

'That's not a bad idea' said Rod preparing to leave.

'Sit down. That's what he wants you to do' hissed The Leprauchan.

'Don't you tell me what to do' said Rod and sat down.

George produced a leaflet from his pocket. 'These are all over the Railway Institute' he said.

'So are you' said The Dim Gaffer.

George ignored the jibe. 'We're going to have a Branch Dance' he said.

'Oh yes' said The Dim Manager, not particularly interested.

'And Jack Tanner is going to be there' said George.

'Jack Bloody Tanner!' shrieked The Dim Manager.

A Passing Business Man turned somewhat pale.

'Did you say Jack Bloody Tanner?' he asked.

'He's coming here' said The Dim Manager.

'Don't panic' said The Passing Business Man and rushed off.

'Why would Jack Tanner bother to come here?' asked The Long Haired Git.

'He's probably coming to tell us to stop being bloody wankers and get up off our knees', said George.

'It's all right for him to talk' said Joe. He was feeling gloomy as The Ghost Squad were still allegedly working with him and he hadn't set eyes on them for three days.

'If Jack Bloody Tanner is coming here it means trouble' said The Dim Manager.

'For you. Not for us' said George.

'Jack Tanner is a Communist' said Rod Williams.

'No skin of your nose. Just so long as he doesn't blow up the Shitehouse' scoffed George.

'Just let him try' said Rod.

'If all he does is blow up the Shitehouse we'll have got off lightly' said The Dim Manager.

Joe was peering at the leaflet. 'What's this about a cabaret?' he asked.

'We're going to have satire' said George.

'That's piss taking' said The Long Haired Git.

'I wonder who they'll be taking the piss out of' said George.

'It had better not be me' said The Dim Manager.

'What's coruscating?' asked Joe.

'I don't know but I can't wait to see it' answered George.

'And it's going to be at The Assembly Rooms' chortled Joe.

'There'll be thousands there. I'm glad it won't be me they'll be taking the piss out of' said The Long Haired Git.

'I'll be there with The Missus' said Joe.

The Long Haired Git turned to The Player King.

'Will you be going?' he asked. The Player King smiled.

'I have been summoned to appear' he said.

Hearing this Rod Williams put away his newspaper and turned to The Player King.

'You've been summoned?' he asked.

'Summoned to appear' confirmed The Player King.

'It's high time some of you were summoned' said Rod.

'I am to appear before The Incomparable Jack Bloody Tanner' declared The Player King.

'You're going to do a turn?' asked Joe.

'I have been given a script and entrusted with the task of preparing the players to appear before The Man of The People.' said The Player King.

'Do you mean that bloody shit stirrer?' asked The Dim Manager.

'I mean sir, The Peoples' Tribune' said The Player King.

'What's he want to come here for? We can manage without him?' said The The Dim Manager.

'He is no doubt coming to clean out The Augean Stables' The Player King told him.

The Dim Manager shook his head baffled. He turned to The Union Man. 'What do you reckon to this then?' he asked. The Union Man was about to reply but The Player King spoke first.

'Led by The Incomparable Jack we will doubtless be shaking the bars of our cages and rattling our chains while our oppressors cower in their festering boltholes', he declaimed.

The Dim Manager felt he had to put his foot down, Jack Bloody Tanner or no Jack Bloody Tanner. He went up to The Player King.

'Now just you look here' he started.

'Go thou and putrefy' roared The Player King, and turned on his heel and left.

'Don't forget the bloody train' Joe called after him.

'Seems to me you're losing your grip' said Rod Williams.

'At least I'm not scatalogical' retorted The Dim Manager.

Meanwhile The Chief Inspector had got together as many of his Dim Managers as he could find. He glared at them all while they shifted uneasily wondering what was afoot.

'Right what's going on?' demanded The Chief Inspector.

There was an awkward silence. The Chief Inspector's glare became even more alarming. In desperation a Dim Manager spoke up.

'We're moving the Post Office into the twenty first century Chief?' he said.

'Bringing in customer orientated management techniques' piped up another Dim Manager.

'Is that what's happening?' demanded The Chief Inspector.

There was a general murmur to the effect that that was indeed what was happening.

'Then can someone tell me where exactly Jack Bloody Tanner fits into the leap into the twenty first century?' asked The Chief Inspector.

'I told The Head Postmaster we'd crushed all opposition. I told him the Union was on its knees, the staff were grateful to be in a job, they'd take any shit we cared to chuck at 'em and now what?' he demanded.

He waited. No-one dared speak.

'Now we've got Jack Bloody Tanner, The Che Guevara of Britain, coming down here. The Union's having a Branch Dance. At the bleedin' Assembly Rooms and there's going to be a cabaret. Not strippers. Satire, coruscating wit'.

The Dim Managers looked thoroughly bemused. They couldn't take in so much news at one time. They shuffled about and stared at their feet.

'What have you got to say for yourselves?' howled The Chief Inspector.

'What's coruscating Chief?' asked someone.

'I'll ask the bloody questions' The Chief Inspector told him.

'Does this mean the soddin' Sun will be back' asked The Potbellied Gaffer With Acne.

'It means we'll be coming under the spotlight' and The Chief.

'I thought they'd lost interest in cucumbers up the arse' muttered someone.

The Chief Inspector glared round. 'I hope none of you sods have any skeletons in the cupboard' he said. No-one spoke.

'I should be so lucky' said a voice from the back.

'What can Jack Bloody Tanner do?' asked a Dim Manager.

'The bugger's only human' said another.

'He can do what he always does. He can cause trouble' said The Chief Inspector.

'Why did that prat of a Branch Secretary invite him here?' asked The Dim Gaffer with Acne and a Pot Belly.

'Cos he thinks the bloody Union run the office. But it doesn't. We do,' said The Chief Inspector.

There were murmurs of assent followed by another awkward silence. The Dim Managers shuffled about uneasily. The Chief glared at them.

'Do you know what I want you all to do?' he asked.

Hoping he didn't require them to do something gross they all shook their heads.

'I want you all to buy tickets for the Union Dance and take your families' The Chief Inspector told them.

'Why do you want us to do that Chief?' asked a Dim Manager.

'Because I'm going to sue that Mad Old Sod' The Chief told him.

The Dim Manager waited for The Chief to enlarge on this statement.

'And I want you and your wives and families to appear in court as witnesses' said The Chief. The Dim Managers were not a lot wiser and continued to wait.

'That will be all gentlemen' said The Chief Inspector and they all filed out.

'What was all that about?' asked a Dim Manager.

'Something about one Mad Old Sod suing another Mad Old Sod' said The Potbellied Dim Manager With Acne.

'I don't want to go to the Union Dance, do you?' asked a Dim Manager.

'No I bloody don't' replied The Potbellied Dim Manager with Acne.

'So what are you going to do?' asked The Dim Manager.

'I'm going to do what I'm bloody told' answered The Potbellied Dim Manager with Acne. The Dim Managers wandered off looking for hapless postpersons to persecute with impunity.

In the Union Office The Sub Committee for the Blowing Up of the Platform Six Shitehouse, which was now The Sub Committee for organising The Branch Dance, were making final arrangements. The Educated Shaggin' Idiot was very pleased with the progress. News of Jack Bloody Tanner's attendance had first spread through the office like a forest fire and in no time at all over the town. There was a big demand for tickets.

'I suppose we'd better invite The Head Postmaster as a courtesy measure' said The Assistant Secretary.

This suggestion infuriated The Truculent Man.

'Courtesy measure my shaggin' arse' he said angrily.

'It's protocol' said The Assistant.

'We're having no bloody management' said The Truculent Man.

'How are you going to keep them out?' asked The Assistant Secretary.

'Ban the Bastards!' roared The Truculent Man.

'If they do come they'll only get thumped' said The Branch Secretary.

'Who's going to thump them?' asked The Assistant Secretary.

'Me for one' said The Truculent Man.

The Branch Secretary looked to The Educated Shaggin' Idiot.

'Are they in or out?' he asked. The Sub Committee waited for The Educated Shaggin' Idiot to give his judgement. He thought for a moment.

'There's no need for a learned address. Yes or no?' said The Truculent Man.

The Educated Shaggin' Idiot put down his pen. The Truculent Man sat poised on the edge of his chair ready to launch a protest if the decision was not the one he wanted.

'The point of all this is to make a gesture of defiance. We're throwing down a gauntlet' said The Educated Shaggin' Idiot.

The Truculent Man remained perched on the very edge of his chair:

'So are the rotten bastards in or out?' he asked.

'The rotten bastards are out' said The Educated Shaggin' Idiot.

'They're too uncouth. They'll lower the tone' said The Truculent Man. The Educated Shaggin' Idiot smiled and wrote something down.

'Managers will be refused admission' said The Assistant Secretary.

The Branch Secretary smiled happily. It was all going well.

The phone rang. The Truculent Man picked it up. 'Union Office … … who wants him?' He handed the phone to The Branch Secretary.

'It's The Head Postmaster. He sounds pissed off', he said.

'So he should' said The Branch Secretary as he took the phone.

'Branch Secretary here' he said and then held the phone away from his ear to avoid being deafened. The Head Postmaster was bawling to the extent that every word could be heard clearly by all in the room.

'This is The Head Postmaster speaking. I shall be suing you all individually, particularly The Mad Old Sod, and I shall also be suing you collectively, that is to say I shall be suing The Union of Communication Workers. If the invitation to Jack Bloody Tanner is not withdrawn immediately I will suspend all Branch Officials. You will kindly reserve me two tickets for the Branch Dance. Is that all clearly understood?' he said.

The Truculent Man was not to be intimidated. 'You can suck my bollocks. Is that clearly understood?' he retorted.

'Who said that?' asked The Head Postmaster.

'I did' replied The Truculent Man.

The Branch Secretary had had the presence of mind to make a note of the various points The Head Postmaster had raised. He glanced at them.

'Don't you think you might be going a little over the top here … ' he began, when The Head Postmaster's shriek again filled the room.

'Don't you take that tone with me' he howled.

The Branch Secretary remained calm. 'If you want to sue us all including The Mad Old Sod, whoever he may be, that's entirely up to you, but I think your solicitor might advise against it. The two tickets are quite out of the question,' he stated.

'What are you talking about?' demanded The Head Postmaster.

'Management are barred from attending this function' said The Branch Secretary.

'They lower the tone' said The Truculent Man.

'You can't bar management. That's discriminatory' protested The Head Postmaster.

'I think you'll find we can' said The Branch Secretary.

'I think you'll find management are classified as a minority and we're protected by anti discriminatory laws' said The Head Postmaster.

'That sounds like a load of crap to me' said The Branch Secretary.

'I'll bury the Union in writs' threatened The Head Postmaster.

The Branch Secretary began to look slightly uneasy.

'Why do you want to come to the dance anyway?' he asked.

'Coruscating wit' hissed The Head Postmaster.

'I'm not with you' confessed The Branch Secretary.

'If this so called coruscating wit is aimed at me and my management of this office I want to see for myself and I've told all my Managers to attend, with their families, so I've got witnesses' said The Head Postmaster.

'I'm afraid that's contrary to Branch policy' said The Branch Secretary.

'This is a matter of principle and I am prepared to take it to the highest court in the land' said The Head Postmaster. Before The Branch Secretary could reply he rang off. The Branch Secretary stared at the phone.

'I missed that last bit' said The Truculent Man.

The Branch Secretary shook his head. 'I can't decide if he really is off with the fairies or if he's trying to work his ticket' he said.

'Most likely both' said The Assistant Secretary.

'He says he's prepared to take the matter to the Highest Court in The Land' said The Branch Secretary.

'This gets better and better' said The Educated Shaggin' Idiot.

'Why's that?' asked The Truculent Man.

'It begins to look as though we may have Jack Tanner and The Attorney General' said The Educated Shaggin' Idiot.

'Bloody great! They can do the first waltz together' said The Truculent Man.

CHAPTER
THIRTY SIX

The King is Dead

"He's shaggin' what?" bellowed The Truculent Man.

The Branch Secretary repeated the news.

The Truculent Man was reluctant to accept the situation.

"He can't do that shagger" he howled.

"We know he shaggin' can't but he has" said The Assistant.

"What a complete gutless shaggin' wanker" shouted The Truculent Man.

"He was always that" said The Assistant.

"I always knew he was a wanker but I thought at least he had some bollocks" said The Truculent Man.

"If he had any bollocks Region would have got rid of him years ago" said The Branch Secretary.

"I blame the Mad Witch of Grantham" said The Truculent Man.

"What for?" asked The Assistant.

"Every shaggin' thing" said The Truculent Man.

"It's not her fault nobody's got any bollocks" said The Branch Secretary.

"Yes it is. She put a spell on them and they all shrivelled up and dropped off" said The Truculent Man.

"What?" asked The Assistant.

"Bollocks" said The Truculent Man.

"Can we get down to business" said The Branch Secretary.

"Yes. Let's decide something" said The Assistant.

"What's this about?" asked The Truculent Man.

"His going away present" said The Branch Secretary.

"His what!" shrieked The Truculent Man.

"His going away present" said The Assistant.

"What's he supposed to be? A bloody bride?" howled The Truculent Man.

"We always send the useless shaggers on their way with something to remember us by" said The Branch Secretary.

"What for?" The Truculent Man wanted to know.

The Branch Secretary was nonplussed. He looked to The Assistant for help. The Assistant looked blank. He shrugged his shoulders.

"We've always done it" he said.

"I know that shagger but why?" demanded The Truculent Man.

"To show our appreciation" said The Assistant.

The Truculent Man snorted.

"Appreciation for what?" he shrieked.

The Branch Secretary said nothing. The Assistant shook his head.

"Phucked if I know" he conceded.

"We usually give the shaggers a garden seat" said The Branch Secretary.

"If he wants a shaggin' garden seat he can go to the shaggin' garden centre and buy a shagger same as everyone else" said The Truculent Man, and left slamming the door behind him.

"We've got trouble with him" said The Assistant.

The Branch Secretary nodded glumly.

"He'll go round stirring up the blokes" said The Assistant.

Meanwhile the subject of the controversy was sitting at his desk talking to The Chief Inspector.

"I don't mind admitting I did a lot of heartsearching before I came to a decision Chief" said The Head Postmaster.

The Chief nodded encouragingly. He was hoping to hear what terms had been offered.

"I've been between the shafts for so long it took a lot of strength of will for me to break free" said The Head Postmaster.

The Chief Inspector wondered how he could come out with such crap but he still hoped to hear what the terms were, precisely how much cash was involved? Was there any chance it might run to a swimming pool? The Head Postmaster looked thoroughly pleased with himself, in fact he was infuriatingly smug. Self satisfaction positively oozed out of him. He was reluctant to divulge the financial details of his pending exit, preferring to burble on about what a wrench it was going to be and what a good thing it was he had so many interests. Since he'd always struck The Chief as being someone with a complete lack of interest in anything this seemed an entirely unwarranted claim, but The Chief didn't care what the old sod proposed to do with his years of unlimited leisure. He wanted to know about the money.

'How much are the bastards paying you?' he asked, having decided against the oblique approach.

'Not nearly enough for thirty five years dedicated service but we'll manage' was the wholly unsatisfactory reply.

The Chief was not too nonplussed. He'd expected an evasive answer. He knew he was dealing with a very devious character. Any revelations would have to be prised out of him.

'So long as your Bank Manager is happy' he tried.

'He's taking early retirement' said The Head Postmaster.

This rather took The Chief aback. He tried another tack.

'Your wife will have to go easy on the shopping' he said.

The Head Postmaster looked even more smug.

'Her inheritance left her comfortably off' he said.

The Chief decided to try a little none too subtle flattery.

'You'll be a hard act to follow' he said

The Chief decided there was no chance of getting any information from The Head Postmaster. He had no doubt his unofficial sources at Region would provide accurate figures that would enable him to plan his own future. He was sure his time at the Post Office was nearly over. He awaited the end eagerly.

Meanwhile The Truculent Man was stirring it up over the garden seat to the point where a lot of people were regarding the proposed presentation as an affront that bordered on a crime against humanity. The air of the canteen was rent by howls of indignation.

'Shaggin' garden seat!'

'I don't pay my union subs to buy garden seats for arseholes'

'What's he ever done for us?'

'What's Shaggin' Jack Tanner going to say about it?'

'What's it got to do with Jack Shaggin' Tanner?'

'Shag Jack Shaggin' Tanner'

'I'd sooner give Jack Shaggin' Tanner a garden seat than that useless effer'

'Too bloody true'

'Jack Shaggin' Tanner speaks up for the shaggin' workers'

'He's the only shagger that does'

In no time at all a consensus was formed to the effect that the garden seat should go to Jack Shaggin' Tanner and The Head Postmaster would be presented with a can of petrol and a box of matches and given a choice of either setting light to himself or shagging himself. Opinion was equally divided as to which option was preferable. After incoherent and furious exchange it was generally agreed that both were too good for him. While the controversy raged signatures were gathered demanding an emergency meeting of The Branch

The Truculent Man was delighted. He held the list of signatures aloft.

'We'll make the shagger official' he bellowed.

There was a most gratifying roar of acclamation. The Truculent Man felt that for once the public sympathy was moving in the right direction. If Jack Shaggin' Tanner turned up anything could happen. He put the paper in his pocket and headed for the Union Office. He looked forward to a thoroughly enjoyable row.

The Chief was in a state of sheer euphoria. His informant at Region was proving a mine of information. The figures being mentioned made it obvious that the last vestiges of financial sanity were being blown to the four winds. Whatever demented forces were now running The Post

Office were prepared to fork out fabulous sums to get rid of the people who actually knew about the business. He got out a pocket calculator in a state of feverish excitement and rapidly punched in figures.

A Dim Manager timidly knocked.

'Come in' bellowed The Chief. The Dim Manager stood in the doorway. The Chief glared at him.

'They're going to set light to The Head Post Master' said The Dim Manager.

'That's his problem' said The Chief as he continued to punch buttons. The Dim Manager opened his mouth to speak, but decided that if The Chief wasn't concerned about the impending incineration of The Head Post Master then he too could face the demise of his Commander with indifference.

'It's his fookin' problem' he concurred and left.

The Chief, engrossed in entrancing calculations, didn't notice him go. He'd worked out how much he was liable to get and his one concern now was to get the money as soon as possible. He was looking forward eagerly to what promised to be a blissful future.

The mood in the Union Office was considerably less rosy. Once the practice of sending Head Post Masters on their way with a tribute had been challenged it proved very difficult to defend. Indeed after an hour's heated debate they had been unable to come up with a single convincing argument. They agreed that they could not confront critics by citing precedent, and that nothing else came to mind. All they had been able to do was convince themselves that The Truculent Man was right. If anything they felt he had perhaps understated his case.

'The bastard should be giving us a garden seat' concluded The Assistant Secretary. Just as The Branch Secretary was peering at the map of the world, wondering just how Coca Cola fitted into the picture, The Truculent Man kicked open the door. He thrust the list of signatures under The Branch Secretary's nose.

'That useless shagger is getting no shaggin' garden seat' he bellowed. The Secretary and The Assistant were taken aback by the purple faced ferocity of the attack. The Secretary reluctantly abandoned his examination of the world map and faced The Truculent Man. He was about to launch into a tirade about the iniquities of Coca Cola when he was cut short.

'Fuck Coca Cola' said The Truculent Man.

The Branch Secretary felt that this was in essence a statement of his own position and nodded.

'And fuck MacDonalds too' said The Assistant.

'While you're at it shove Disney Land up your arse' added The Truculent Man.

No dissenting voice was raised and The Branch Secretary reached for the petition. The Truculent Man handed it over with much pride. The Branch Secretary read the motion.

'He can incinerate himself or fuck himself. I see nothing there to object to' he said.

The Assistant glanced down the list of signatures.

'Some right wankers here' he observed.

'Wankers are entitled to representation same as everyone else' countered The Truculent Man.

The members will expect us to make a recommendation' said The Assistant.

The Truculent Man raised his eyes. 'It's there. Incinerate himself or fuck himself' he said.

The Branch Secretary cast a critical eye over the paper.

'This needs setting out properly' he said.

'How?' demanded The Truculent Man.

'Option A and Option B' explained The Branch Secretary.

'So which is which?' asked The Truculent Man.

'Option A is fuck himself, Option B is set light to himself' said The Branch Secretary.

'And which are we recommending?' asked The Assistant.

'Option A followed by Option B' said The Truculent Man.

'Plus an acknowledgment of his crimes against the workers and an apology' said The Branch Secretary.

'And the shaggin' garden seat goes to Jack Shaggin' Tanner' added The Truculent Man.

The Assistant was writing furiously.

'So it's Option A, Option B and Option C. First he tells us what a twat he is, then he fucks himself, and then he sets light to himself' he said.

The Branch Secretary and The Truculent Man nodded their approval.

'We should have done this years ago' said The Assistant.

The Branch Secretary went to his map of the world. He prodded furiously at London and Washington.

'The bastards think they're unassailable but we will bring them down. This could be the start of the new world order' he declared.

The Truculent Man glanced at The Assistant and tapped his forehead.

An hour later a white faced Head Post Master rushed into The Chief's office.

'We have to stand together' he gasped as he slumped into a chair.

The Chief was thoroughly immersed in figures and had a pile of brochures advertising swimming pools on his desk. He was obsessed with the prospect of a large pay off and immediately sprang to the alarming conclusion that the Post Office was attempting to reduce the amounts being handed over.

'If they won't pay up sit tight' he said.

'We've got a mutiny on our hands' said The Head Post Master.

'Bollocks' said The Chief.

'It's not bollocks it's official' The Head Post Master told him.

The Chief shook his head. 'A mutiny can't be official' he said and punched in some more figures.

'It's on the Union noticeboard' said The Head Post Master.

'The Union doesn't run this office, we do' said The Chief.

'Not if there's an uprising' said The Head Post Master.

'There'll be no uprising here. All they care about is their overtime. There is no revolutionary fire on these premises' said The Chief.

At the mention of fire the Head Post Master became even more agitated.

'There will be if I have to set light to myself' he said testily.

'If it comes to that our firefighting techniques will rise to the occasion' said The Chief as he gazed with shining eyes on the columns of figures he had compiled.

'You do not appreciate the gravity of the situation' The Head Post Master told him.

Outside the rain poured down relentlessly. Half drowned postmen hobbled back from their deliveries. The Chief peered down at them.

'You're not telling me those poor downtrodden sods are going to raise the flag of revolution' he said.

The Head Post Master looked down. He had to admit the Chief had a point. A more disconsolate cowed and defeated bunch than the postmen would be hard to find. He was momentarily reassured but then gnawing doubt struck. Obviously they were a mere rabble, crushed and full of despair, but they were also seething with resentment. All they needed was a leader, some mad monk to stir them up. He feared the effect Jack Shaggin' Tanner might have. The time could come when the downtrodden masses would decide they would stand for no more. The likelihood was someone was going to get it in the neck, and the best he could hope for was that it would be somebody else. Clutching at straws he said:

'We could issue a joint statement'.

The Chief was brutally frank.

'I'm not in the shit' he said.

'You could be' said The Head Post Master.

'Only if I'm associated with you' The Chief told him.

'I always thought I was popular' said The Head Post Master.

The Chief gave a snort of derision.

'What gave you that idea?' he asked.

'This always used to be a happy office' said The Head Post Master.

'Bollocks." said The Chief.

'Well at least the blokes were not mutinous' said The Head Post Master.

'They're not mutinous now. They're just a bit pissed off' said The Chief.

'They want me to confess, fuck myself and then set light to myself' protested The Post Master.

'Like I said they're a bit pissed off' said The Chief.

'I am looking to you for advice' wailed The Head Post Master.

'Don't admit anything' said The Chief.

'So it's allright to fuck myself and set light to myself' spluttered The Head Post Master.

The Chief sighed heavily. He wondered how he had put up with this prat for so long.

'Clauses B and C of this resolution can only be applied following a full confession' he said.

'I've got nothing to hide. I've done nothing wrong' said the Head Post Master, looking so insufferably pious The Chief was tempted to withdraw his previous advice and urge The Head Poster Post Master to get it all off his chest so that clauses B and C could be applied as soon as possible.

'What we've done to these blokes is a crime against humanity' said The Chief.

'You can't say that' gasped The Head Post Master.

'I'm not going to' said The Chief.

The Head Post Master's relief was only temporary as The Chief added grimly:

'That's what Jack Shaggin' Tanner is going to say'

'We don't want that bastard here' said The Head Post Master.

'We bloody don't, but we've got the bastard just the same' said The Chief.

'We'll refuse him admission' said The Head Post Master.

'What to The Assembly Rooms?' said The Chief.

'Why not?' asked The Head Post Master.

'We're only the bloody Post Office, how are we supposed to keep Jack Shaggin' Tanner out of the Assembly Rooms. The shaggin' Union won't let us in' said The Chief.

'We'll force our way in' said The Head Post Master.

'You can if you like' The Chief told him.

The Head Post Master glared at The Chief.

'I don't like your attitude' he told him.

'I am not your problem' said The Chief.

'I have done nothing wrong' said The Head Post Master.

'If you say so' said The Chief.

'I'll put my case before the people' said The Head Post Master.

'What shaggin' case? What can you possibly say?' asked The Chief.

'I'll tell them the truth' said The Head PostMaster.

The Chief turned pale. 'If you do that we're all shagged' he said.

'No honest man need fear the truth' said The Head Post Master as he stalked out of the room.

'Oh Kerrist!' He's really flippped' said The Chief.

The glorious sunshine, the villa set in its own spacious grounds and the swimming pool suddenly had as much solidity as a mirage. It was beginning to look as though his chances of enjoying an early retirement under the blue Mediterranean sky were nil. All he could realistically hope for was a few forlorn fortnights. Something had to be done, or rather prevented. He decided to summon The Dim Managers. Gradually they all sidled in. The Chief glared at them. To a man they quailed. The Chief thumped the desk. They all jumped.

'These are your instructions' The Chief told them. He paused for effect. They leaned forward.

'You do fuckall, you say fuckall' said The Chief.

The Dim Managers looked even more blank than usual. The Chief sighed. The Dim Managers winced.

'Can you manage that?' asked The Chief.

The Dim Managers nodded. The Chief wasn't convinced.

'What are your instructions?' he asked.

'Do fuckall, say fuckall' chorused The Dim Managers.

'Any questions?' asked The Chief

A Dim Manager timidly raised his hand.

'Yes?' said The Chief impatiently.

'What are we to say fuckall about?' asked The Dim Manager.

'Whatever anyone asks you on whatever subject you know fuckall' said The Chief.

Since they genuinely knew fuckall The Dim Managers were at a loss to understand why they had been summoned. They gazed at The Chief hoping for some enlightenment. The Chief gazed back at them alarmed that his future should depend on such a bunch of cretins. He knew he must not overburden their meagre brains, but there was one fact they had to grasp.

'The Head Post Master has gone bonkers' he told them.

He wasn't sure if the complete lack of response to what was surely alarming news was because they were all brain dead or if they were dumbstruck by horror. He was amazed when A Dim Manager spoke.

'Is that why he's going to fuck himself?' he asked.

The Chief sighed. They weren't capable of grasping a glaringly obvious point.

'He can fuck himself any time he likes' he told them.

'It's The Permissive Society' said a Dedicated Brown Noser hoping to ingratiate himself by showing how tolerant he was.

'He's going to confess' said The Chief.

'What to?' asked A Dim Manager.

'Crimes against humanity' said The Chief.

'Is that why he's going to fuck himself?' someone asked.

'And set light to himself' added another Dim Manager.

The Chief was beginning to wish he had a box of matches and a can of petrol so he could set light to them all Spain seemed ever more enticing.

'If he confesses he'll be in the shit' he told them. They all looked blank. 'And we'll be in the shit with him' said The Chief. After a few moments of incomprehension The Dim Managers started to look frightened.

'Any ideas?' asked The Chief.

An Acting Dim Manager renowned for being a particularly slimy specimen spoke up.

'Denounce him' he said.

CHAPTER
THIRTY SEVEN

Sued and Suspended

"Our masters not unreasonably assume that the law is solely an instrument for their convenience. Another stick with which to beat us, but it is a double edged weapon and I shall certainly be bringing a counter suit" said The Player King, his stentorian voice echoing all round the station.

"What will you accuse him of?" asked Paddy.

"Crimes against humanity" declared The Player King.

"You'll have a job making that bugger stick" said Joe.

"Are we not human?' asked The Player King.

"I suppose so" said Joe without a great deal of conviction.

"And are not crimes committed against us on a daily basis? Do we not suffer constant provocation, regular humiliations? Are we not under the lash?" asked The Player King, his voice continuing to rise.

"I'm not saying it isn't true. I just think you'll have a job proving the bugger" said Joe.

"I am prepared to bring my case before the highest court in the land" said The Player King.

His voice carried effortlessly from Platform Six to The Dim Manager's office on platform one.

"'Kin'ell! said The Dim Manager. He came out of his office, looked across to platform six and was horrified to see The Player King standing on a barrow, arms raised aloft, surrounded by a crowd of railwaymen, trainspotters, postmen and a number of Would Be Travellers.

"Let the world take note" declaimed The Player King.

He paused and looked at his audience.

"I will no longer remain mute beneath the slings and arrows of outrageous fortune. From now on those who choose to heap indignities upon me do so at their peril" he continued.

The Dim Manager scurried back into his office. He needed a few moments to himself to decide what course of action he should take. He opened a drawer and had a look through the notes of the various courses in contemporary management techniques he had been sent on.

They contained nothing that was even remotely connected to the situation he faced.

There was a knock on the door and Rod Williams walked in.

'There's a lunatic at large on platform six' he said and sat down.

'Has he got a ticket?' asked The Dim Manager.

'It's one of your guys' said Rod remorselessly.

'Which one?' asked The Dim Manager.

'Which one do you think?' said Rod. The Dim Manager was at a loss to know what to do. He played desperately for time.

'It could be any one of them. It's the strain of modern life' he said.

Rod snirked in a way that made The Dim Manager wonder if he could cite the strain of modern life as a mitigating circumstance if he removed Rod's teeth with a good right hander.

The voice of The Player King resumed. 'Let them take note. The spirit of my forefathers rises within me. Ancestral voices call to me and urge me to bear no longer the insolence of office. They bid me rise up and cringe no longer'. Shouts of acclaim rent the air and both Rod and The Dim Manager turned somewhat pale.

'It's a Goddam mutiny' breathed Rod as he made for the door intending to seek sanctuary in the Executive Shitehouse.

'And Jack Bloody Tanner isn't even here yet' said The Dim Manager.

From outside the station a chorus of voices rose: 'I am Spartacus' they cried in unison.

'Oh God! We're back to Spartacus' said Rod. He scurried out.

'Come back here. You're supposed to be in charge' shouted The Dim Manager. Rod decided not to hear and carried on as fast as he could without actually breaking into a run. A Would Be Traveller in search of information attempted to stop him. Rod brushed him aside. The Would Be Traveller approached a railwayman. 'What time is the London train due?' he asked. The railwayman shook his head.

'Can't tell you that. More than my job's worth' he said.

'That's bloody stupid' protested The Would Be Traveller.

So's The Official Secrets Act but they made me sign the bugger' said The Railwayman.

The Would Be Traveller thought for a moment. Then he decided on a different approach. 'I do realise that the penalties for passing on information gathered in the course of your work can lead to very serious consequences, but this is after all a free country and you can express an opinion without fear of prosecution' he said.

The Railwayman considered this and after a while nodded his head emphatically.

'This is a free country and I am entitled to express an opinion' he said.

'Then in your opinion when is the London train likely to arrive?' asked The Would Be Traveller.

'Your guess is as good as mine' said The Railwayman and left The Would Be Traveller wondering what state of affairs Great Britain Limited had reached.

Rod Williams entered The Executive Shitehouse and turned off the light. Despite covering his ears with both hands he could hear demented cries of 'I'm Spartacus' coming from outside The Station, while over on platform six the crowd, including several Would Be Travellers, were shouting: 'We want Jack Tanner. Bring us Jack Tanner: Long live Jack Tanner and Jack Tanner speaks for the people.'

Realising he could expect no help from Rod Williams The Dim Manager decided to put a bold face on things and leaving his office walked briskly over to platform six where The Player King was still standing on the barrow surrounded by a sizeable crowd that showed no sign of dispersing. He had exhausted the subject of his own persecution and was now holding forth about the plight of humanity in general. The Dim Manager found himself standing by Paddy. Paddy was gazing at The Player King with something akin to awe.

'When the mood takes him that old fellow is inspiring' said Paddy. That wasn't the word The Dim Manager would have chosen but he thought it best not to argue so he made a vague noncommittal sort of sound and looked round to see if he recognised anyone in the throng. He was astonished to see The Ghost Squad standing in the front row directly opposite him.

The human dilemma The Player King was lamenting seemed to them to amount to being shat on from a great height so they were applauding enthusiastically. The Dim Manager saw them so seldom he decided to seek confirmation from Paddy that it was indeed the elusive pair.

'Isn't that The Ghost Squad over there?' he asked.

'Over where?' asked Paddy. The Dim Manager looked again. They had gone. 'I thought I saw them' he said lamely. 'Joe thinks they've taken early retirement' said Paddy. 'Perhaps they have and they really are ghosts' said The Dim Manager.

The Player King was drawing to a close. 'Don't forget the Branch Dance. Come and hear The Incomparable Jack Tanner, the man who speaks to and for the downtrodden masses' he said. The Union Man strolled round handing out leaflets. A number of Would Be Travellers bought tickets there and then. The crowd dispersed somewhat reluctantly. The Dim Manager approached The Union Man.

'I'll have a couple of those tickets' he said.

'Oh no you won't' The Union Man told him.

'Why not?' asked The Dim Manager.

'Management are barred' said The Union Man.

'That's bloody discrimination' protested The Dim Manager.

'I know. Great isn't it!' said The Union Man and walked off.

The Dim Manager approached George. 'Any chance of a couple of tickets?' he asked. George shook his head. 'It's all over town Jack Tanner's coming. There's a black market in tickets. It's worse than Winbledon' George told him.

'What for a bloody Union Branch Dance?', gasped The Dim Manager.

'Don't forget the cabaret with coruscating wit' George told him.

'What's coruscating?' asked The Dim Manager.

'I don't know, but there's obviously a big demand for it' said George. 'The sooner I'm retired the better' The Dim Manager sighed and made his way back to the office.

First thing next morning The Head Postmaster sent for The Chief Inspector.

'I hear The Mad Old Sod started a riot on the station last night' he began. The Chief shook his head. 'Hardly a riot, nothing was broken' he said. The Head Postmaster was not satisfied.

'I want him disciplined' he said. The Chief Inspector waited. The Head Postmaster grew impatient.

'You heard what I said. Discipline him' he instructed.

'What do you want me to do with him?' asked The Chief Inspector.

'Suspend him' said The Head Postmaster.

'On what grounds?' asked The Chief Inspector.

'Bringing The Post Office into disrepute' said The Head Postmaster.

'We'll have a job to make that stick' said The Chief Inspector.

'I don't see why' said The Head Postmaster. Seeing The Chief Inspector still looked dubious he added: 'After all who decides if he's guilty?'

'We do' said The Chief.

'Exactly. We can do what we like' said The Head Postmaster.

'Are you sure of your facts?' asked The Chief Inspector.

'Of course I am' said The Head Postmaster.

The Chief waited. The Head Postmaster evidently thought the matter was settled.

'So I charge him with bringing the Post Office into disrepute' he said.

'Correct' said The Head Postmaster.

'Suppose he asks what he's done' asked The Chief Inspector.

'Then tell him' replied The Head Postmaster.

'Exactly what has he done?' asked The Chief Inspector.

'He's threatened to sue me' said The Head Postmaster.

This puzzled The Chief Inspector somewhat. 'But you've threatened to sue him' he said. Seeing The Head Postmaster obviously didn't think this was relevant he added. 'I think we could be on dodgy ground if we're not careful' he warned.

'I don't see why' said The Head Postmaster.

'It could look like persecution' said The Chief Inspector.

'Am I the bloody Head Postmaster or not?' asked The Head Postmaster.

The Chief felt on sure ground here. 'Certainly you are' he conceded.

'Well then' said The Head Postmaster.

'Perhaps you should consult someone' suggested The Chief Inspector.

'Such as?' enquired The Head Postmaster.

'Someone at Region' said The Chief Inspector.

'What for?' asked The Head Postmaster.

'In case you end up with egg all over your face' said The Chief Inspector.

'We've got to show this lot who's in charge' said The Head Postmaster.

Since this was what The Chief Inspector was always saying himself he felt he could not argue with this bald assertion.

'Allright. I'll suspend The Mad Old Sod' he said.

'We'll make an example of him' said The Head Postmaster. The Chief Inspector left The Head Postmaster looking very pleased with himself and went back to his own office. He sat at his desk and wondered just exactly what was going on and where he fitted into the picture. He did not think suspending The Mad Old Sod was at all a good idea. Long experience had taught him that Mad Old Sods were best left alone. He wasn't at all sure the way events were going to turn out, but he was sure the less he was involved the better it would be for him. However he had been given a direct order and would have to carry it out. He frowned, then a happy thought struck him.

'I won't suspend The Mad Old Sod, I'll get The Dim Sod to do it' he told himself, and picked up the telephone.

The Dim Sod was sitting in his office at The Station when the phone rang. 'Station' he said. Then he turned pale.

'Chief Inspector here. Suspend The Mad Old Sod' he heard to his horror. Before he could say anything The Chief had rung off. The Dim Sod sat wondering what he should do. He knew he was being invited to stick his head in a noose. 'You can't just suspend a bloke' he muttered. The door opened and Joe walked in.

'The blokes want to know if there's a shaggin' team talk or not' he said.

The Dim Sod made an effort to pull himself together. 'Certainly there is' he said and started looking for his briefing sheet. 'Is this what you're looking for?' asked Joe.

The Dim Sod took the piece of paper from Joe, but not before Joe had had a chance to see what was on it. Joe snorted contemptuously.

'Not worth getting the blokes together for that load of bollocks' he said.

'I just follow orders' said The Dim Sod.

'Do you ever feel like telling 'em so to shagoff?' asked Joe.

'All the time' said The Dim Sod fervently.

'So do I' said Joe. The Dim Sod entered the room followed by Joe. A derisive cheer greeted him. The Mad Old Sod beamed at him.

'Unfortunate indeed is he who is lumbered with a bad script' he declared.

'This is all a complete waste of time' said Paddy.

'How can you say that before you've heard it?' asked The Dim Sod.

'I don't have to hear it. I know it's a complete waste of time' said Paddy.

'Yes but how can you say that before you've heard it?' persisted The Dim Sod.

'We have to sit here every week and listen to you reading out a load of shite' said The Long Haired Git.

'You don't believe it. How can you expect us to?' asked The Union Man.

'You might at least keep an open mind' said The Dim Sod.

George glanced impatiently at the clock. 'For Christ's sake get on with the crap' he said.

'They want suggestions' said The Dim Sod.

'No they don't' said Joe.

The Dim Sod had another look at the briefing sheet.

'Yes they do' he said.

'It might say that on the bumpfh, but every time we make suggestions you threaten to discipline us' said Joe.

'They're looking for constructive suggestions' said The Dim Sod.

'Ideas that'll benefit the service' said The Union Man.

'That's right' said The Dim Sod.

'We've been giving you ideas that will benefit the service' said Paddy.

'When?' asked The Dim Sod, genuinely puzzled.

'Every shaggin' week' said Paddy.

'Such as?' asked The Dim Sod.

'Don't you keep a note?' said George.

'I don't have to keep a note. You say the same bloody thing every week' said The Dim Sod.

'Truth can never be spoken too often' intoned The Player King.

'Exactly, and the truth is ninety nine per cent of management in the Post Office is superfluous' said The Union Man.

Before The Dim Sod could protest The Long Haired Git cut in.

'But instead of getting rid of the parasites we keep getting more' he complained.

'Every week another useless prat shows up in a suit' said Joe.

'Instead of us getting rid of them, it's them that's getting rid of us' protested Paddy.

'If the public knew what was going on they'd be horrified' said Joe.

'But we can't tell them' said The Union Man.

'Because we're all gagged by the Official Secrets Act' said The Long Haired Git.

'Has anyone got any sensible suggestions?' asked The Dim Sod.

'You wait till they privatise. Your feet won't touch the ground.' said George.

'And you won't get a job anywhere else' said Paddy.

There was a chorus of assent. The Dim Sod began to feel he was being got at.

'I could get another job, no doubt about that' he claimed.

This statement provoked a chorus of jeers.

'When the Post Office slings you out you'll be unemployable' said Paddy.

'No Post Office Gaffer has ever got another job' said Joe.

'Yes they have' contradicted The Dim Sod.

'All they ever get is jobs as doorkeepers' said Paddy.

The Dim Sod knew this is to be the truth and didn't wish to continue the argument. He decided to tell The Mad Old Sod he was suspended and get it over with.

'You're suspended' he said bluntly.

'The Player King alias The Mad Old Sod gazed steadily at him.

'Did I hear you right dear boy?' he asked mildly.

'You're suspended' said The Dim Sod again.

The Player King took it very calmly. He sat back in his chair, placed the fingertips of both hands together so as to form a pyramid and asked:

'Is that instead of being sued or in addition to?'

'As well as' said The Dim Sod.

'So I'm being sued and suspended?' asked The Player King.

'I said so didn't I?' said The Dim Sod.

'I am most flattered, but might I ask why such distinction is being conferred upon me. Why in fact am I thus being singled out?'. asked The Player King.

The Dim Sod knew enough to avoid admitting The Player King was being singled out.

'You're not being singled out. You're being treated the same as everyone else' he said.

'Do you mean we're all shaggin' suspended then?' asked Joe.

'No' said The Dim Sod.

'You wait till Bloody Jack Tanner hears about this shagger' said Joe.

Suddenly Paddy lost his temper. He leapt to his feet. The Dim Sod was understandably alarmed and convinced that Paddy was about to thump him.

Joe also rose and backed away holding up a deprecatory hand.

'It's a shaggin' scandal' said Paddy.

'Bloody disgusting' said Joe.

Paddy pointed to The Mad Old Bastard. The Mad Old Bastard looked back at him calmly.

'This man is being crucified' said Paddy.

'I trust not' said The Player King, alias The Mad Old Bastard.

'Try and make sure you're on double time when they nail you up' said George.

Paddy rounded on George. 'This is no laughing matter' he told him.

'They can only crucify him if they're paying him, if he's on duty, and all I'm saying is if he is going to go up on the cross he might as well make the most of it and be on double time' George explained.

Paddy had to admit there was some sense in this reasoning.

'You're right. Once they find out it's shaggin' up the budget having him hanging up there they'll have him down in no time' said Joe.

'He's not going to be crucified' protested The Dim Sod.

'Get it in writing' George urged.

'I know you're a man of your word old chap, but not all your colleagues are as scrupulous. I would like the guarantee in writing' said The Player King.

'What guarantee?' asked The Dim Sod. He felt he was being somehow manipulated.

'He wants a paper to say he's not going to be crucified' said Paddy.

'I never said anything about crucifixion' said The Dim Sod.

'You never said anything about slave labour either but it's here' said Joe.

'Where?' asked The Dim Sod.

'In the Friggin' Delivery Room' said The Longhaired Git.

'If there's any prospect of my being transferred to The Delivery Room I think I'd rather be crucified' said The Player King.

'Don't talk like a prat!' said The Dim Sod.

'To the terminally deluded the words of truth will always sound like the ravings of a prat. Metaphorically speaking those poor bastards have been hung on crosses for years' declared The Player King.

'Write that shagger down' Joe instructed The Dim Sod.

'You write the shagger down' retorted The Dim Sod. He knew Joe couldn't begin to spell metaphorically either.

Paddy glared at The Union Man.

'What are you going to do? Shagall?' he asked.

The Union Man shook his head. 'This is completely beyond me' he confessed.

'You're resigning?' asked Paddy.

The Union Man shook his head again.

'I'm bringing in Union Headquarters. We'll see what they've got to say about this' he said.

'That's right. Bring in the shaggin' Headquarters' said Joe.

Paddy could see no point in bringing in Union Headquarters.

'Union Headquarters! Union Headquarters! Ask those wankers what they think! You might as well ask my bollocks!' he concluded.

George was about to comment but a glance at the clock showed The Stew was open and he got up and left. The Player King looked round at the gathered company. 'I trust one is not becoming paranoid, but one does form the impression one is being shat open from a great height' he said.

CHAPTER
THIRTY EIGHT

Rocking The Boat

'Jeezuswept! You've done what?'. The Branch Secretary held the telephone away from his ear while the agonised screech from Union Headquarters continued. The Full Time official was beside himself with fury.

'You've invited Jack Bloody Tanner!' he howled.

The Branch Secretary attempted to get a word in but the Full Time Official was just getting into his stride. The outraged howls reached such a pitch that The Assistant Secretary sitting opposite could hear every word. He thought he was listening to the ravings of a wanker and indicated this to The Branch Secretary in a graphic nine. The Secretary agreed wholeheartedly and joined him in the mime. While they were demonstrating their unanimity in this manner the door opened and The Truculent Man walked in. He looked enquiringly at The Assistant Secretary.

'Headquarters' said The Assistant indicating the phone.

'Wankers!' snorted The Truculent Man and joined in the mime.

'We're trying to improve the image of The Union, show we're moderate and you go and invite a maniac like Jack Bloody Tanner. He's a bloody Militant' yelled The Full Time Official.

'The Truculent Man took the phone from The Branch Secretary.

'And you're a bloody wanker! he shouted and rang off.

'He always was a bloody wanker' concurred The Assistant.

'It didn't take him long to cross over' said The Branch Secretary.

'It's always the same. We send a good man up to London. That shower of shite get to work on him, send him round to C and A, get him a poncy haircut and the next thing you know he's a Pillar of the Establishment, one of the Undead' said The Truculent Man gloomily.

'Perhaps we should go up to Headquarters with pointed stakes' said The Assistant.

'If only we could' said The Branch Secretary.

'What's stopping us?' demanded The Truculent Man.

'The Mad Witch of Grantham' explained The Branch Secretary.

'It's nothing to do with her. If we want to put The Undead to rest it's between us and Hammer Films' asserted The Truculent Man.

'Quite right' said The Assistant.

'I think you're both forgetting the latest anti Trades Union Laws' said The Branch Secretary.

'There's sodall there about vampires' said The Truculent Man.

'If freeing Vampires from their bondage is in the interests of our members she'll have passed a law forbidding it' said The Branch Secretary.

'She's given the Unions back to the members' said The Assistant.

'Like The Russians gave the people back Hungary in 1956' snorted The Truculent Man.

'We have to keep fighting' said The Branch Secretary. He got up and went across to the map of the world.

'It's happening everywhere. The whole world is groaning' he said.

'MacDonalds, Coca-Cola and Disney' said The Assistant.

'But we'll keep fighting' said The Branch Secretary.

The phone rang. The Branch Secretary ignored it. He was trying to locate the spot where the latest atrocity against the people had been perpetrated. The Truculent Man took up the phone.

'Peoples' Liberation Army. Down with the Multi Nationals' he said.

The Representative of the Undead from Union Headquarters was not amused.

'What's going on up there?' he yelled.

'You might well ask' The Truculent Man told him. He held the phone away from his ear so that The Branch Secretary and The Assistant could hear what was being said. The Representative of the Undead was ranting about image. The Truculent Man cut short the tirade for a moment.

'Fuck the image' he said and rang off.

'What did you ring off for? There's some things I wanted to tell him' protested The Branch Secretary while he peered at the map wondering if there was anywhere that the Americans weren't crushing Human Rights.

He found China and pointed it out.

'They'll be there next' he predicted.

'Who The Undead?' asked The Truculent Man.

'No the bloody Americans' said The Branch Secretary.

'Pay your money take your choice' said The Assistant.

The phone rang again. This time The Branch Secretary was the first to respond. He held the phone out and the same outraged voice could be heard. If anything it was even more hysterical. The Branch Secretary waited until there was a pause.

'You lot up there are doomed to wander through the shades of eternal night. But help is on the way. The wooden stakes will put you out of your misery' he said in sepulchural tones. There was a pause. Then the voice was heard again, somewhat quieter now.

'He wants to know if we're threatening him' said The Branch Secretary.

The Truculent Man grabbed the receiver. 'If the cap fits wear it' he said somewhat enigmatically. He waited for a response. When it came it was obviously not to his liking and he flung down the receiver.

'What's he say?' asked The Assistant.

'He says not to rock the boat wait until we get a Labour Government' said The Truculent Man.

The Branch Secretary picked up the receiver.

'The bloody gaffers are strutting round here in jackboots. It's The Third Bloody Reich reincarnated. And you want us to tell our blokes to stay on their hands and knees until we get a bloody Labour Government. You want to get out into the sticks and see what's going on. And another thing. What about Guatamala?' He slammed down the phone.

"That's knackered him. He'll think Guatamala's somewhere up north" said The Truculent Man. The Branch Secretary went across to the map.

"Now then about the raffle prizes" he began. The Assistant Secretary had a suggestion.

"First prize twenty bottles of Coca Cola" he proposed.

"What about the second prize?" asked The Truculent Man.

"Forty bottles of Coca Cola" said The Assistant Secretary.

Before they could begin to discuss the question of raffle prizes in a serious way they heard a ringing voice outside.

"Sanctuary! Sanctuary! I claim sanctuary!"

"It's the mad old effer" said The Truculent Man.

"Let him in for Chrissake" said The Branch Secretary.

The door was flung open and The Player King swept in.

"Our mad masters are going to sue me first and then crucify me" he said.

"They can't do that" protested The Truculent Man.

"I could be wrong. The plan may be to crucify me first and sue me afterwards. In any event it is obviously their intention to piss on me from a great height" said The Player King.

"What are they playing at?" Why are they going to do this?" asked The Branch Secretary.

"My dear boy need you ask? It is the nature of the beast" said The Player King.

"He's right. If you're an arsehole it stands to reason you act like an arsehole" said The Truculent Man.

"And they're all arse'oles" said The Assistant Secretary.

"I'm not worried about a law suit, but can I assume they can't crucify me without going through certain procedures?" asked The Player King.

"I promise you one thing" said The Branch Secretary.

"And what might that be?" asked The Player King.

"If they crucify you it'll be on national television" was the reply.

'That will be most gratifying' said The Player King. He then added as an afterthought. 'I trust it will be shown at peak viewing times and you will of course negotiate an appropriate fee and ensure I get paid for repeats'.

The Truculent Man thought a wrong approach was being adopted and said so in no uncertain terms.

'Look you old prat' he began.

'That is no way to address one who is shortly to make the ultimate sacrifice for the good of the cause' The Player King admonished.

The Truculent Man was having none of it.

'They are not nailing you up' he declared adamantly.

'I'm sure they're entitled to. It seems there's nothing they can't do. Perhaps if you were to appeal to The Archbishop of Canterbury' suggested The Player King mildly.

'That's no good. He'll probably prosecute you for some form of blasphemy' said The Assistant.

'When troubles come, they come not in single spies but in battalions. First I am to be sued by my Honoured Masters here at The General Post Office, next I am to be nailed to the cross, I trust in the centre of the Station Foyer, and provided I survive that novel experience, I will then be hauled before a learned Judge accused of presumption' he said.

'Has anyone actually said they're going to crucify the old sod?' The Assistant asked The Secretary.

'Not in so many words' The Secretary replied.

'Best get it in writing. You can't rely on their word' said The Assistant.

The Truculent Man was convinced that the atrocity was imminent.

'We've got to stop this. If they get away with it once we'll have our members on crosses all over the town' he roared.

'And blokes saying 'excuse me postie where's my gito?' said The Assistant.

There ensued a somewhat heated exchange as to whether or not crucifying a postman would come within the terms of the latest piece of anti Trades Union legislation, or whether it would be considered to be in fact illegal. The Player King stated that if it came to a choice between crucification and having to work in The Delivery Room he would opt for crucification every time. The Truculent Man said he thought any sensible person would make the same choice. The arguments were still being hurled to and fro when the telephone rang again. The Branch Secretary managed to grab it first.

'Branch Secretary speaking' he said. There was a shriek that caused him to once again hold the receiver well away from his ear. The Branch Secretary waited until the speaker had seemingly run out of breath before he attempted to reply. Then his reply was short and to the point.

'Send up a team of investigators by all means, but remember we'll be ready with our garlic, sharpened stakes and silver bullets' he warned and rang off.

'Team of investigators! They don't even know where this place is' snorted The Truculent Man.

The telephone rang again. The Branch Secretary picked up.

'Anti Dracula Society. I'm afraid Peter Cushing is no longer with us. Van Helsing here. Can I help you?' he said.

A puzzled sounding voice at the other end said 'sorry wrong number' and rang off. The Branch Secretary replaced the receiver.

'That was The Head Postmaster' he said.

'Tell him to bollocks' said The Truculent Man.

The telephone rang again. The Assistant Secretary picked up the receiver.

'Union Office' he said. He turned to The Branch Secretary.

'It's The Head Postmaster. He wants to see you immediately in his office.'

'Tell him to bollocks' said The Truculent Man.

The Branch Secretary took the phone.

'We're not available at the moment. We're about to be attacked by The Undead' he said and rang off.

The Head Postmaster sat staring at the telephone. He felt as though his world was entirely without foundation. Nothing was as it had been. Strange mysterious forces were all about him, closing in. A disturbing thought struck him. Was his mind going? He decided not to seek medical advice for fear the diagnosis would confirm his worst suspicions. He thought it best to consult with The Chief Inspector.

There had never been any possibility of The Chief becoming The Brain of Britain but at least he had his feet firmly on the ground.

The Head Postmaster replaced the receiver. He left his office and made his way to The Chief's Office. When he entered The Chief was berating a Dim Manager.

'I've told you before. Keep your hands off the women' he said. The Dim Manager, a particularly unsavoury looking specimen, shuffled about uncomfortably.

'She led me on' he bleated.

'If there's an official complaint don't expect any support from me. You're on your own' The Chief told him. He waved his hand dismissively and The Dim Manager scurried out. The Chief was about to put The Head Postmaster in the picture concerning the little matter of yet another Dim Manager accused of sexual harassment when he noticed that he was staring at him in a way The Chief found somewhat alarming. He was also very pale.

'Put the do not disturb notice on the door Chief' instructed The Head Postmaster. The Chief did so and returned to his chair, keeping a watchful eye on The Head Postmaster. He stood behind his chair, gripping the back ready to use it for protection if he had to.

'Sit down Chief, sit down' said The Head Postmaster. The Chief waited until The Head Postmaster had collapsed into a chair and then sat himself. The Head Postmaster leaned forward.

'This is to go no further' he cautioned.

The Chief nodded. The Head Postmaster stared at him intensely.

'What do you know about The Undead?' he asked.

The Chief was thoroughly nonplussed.

'What have they recorded?' he asked.

The Head Postmaster shook his head in exasperation.

'They're not pop stars Chief. They're vampires' explained The Head Postmaster.

The Chief remained in his chair but wished he was standing behind it again. He tensed ready to leap away. What The Head Postmaster said next far exceeded his worst fears.

'They're vampires and they're attacking the Union Office' he said.

This revelation set The Chief's heart thumping. He took a few deep breaths the way his doctor had told him to and eyed The Head Postmaster steadily. It was important not to show fear and not to appear threatening. While he was composing himself he thought the matter through and decided there was no immediate threat to the all prevailing dominance of market forces. He decided to seek verification of the facts. It was always best to be sure.

'Vampires are attacking The Union Office?' he said.

The Head Postmaster nodded. 'That's what The Branch Secretary just told me' he said.

The Chief sat back and grinned from ear to ear.

'More power to their elbow' he declared.

The Head Postmaster was horrified. 'But Chief, you don't seem to understand. They'll turn the Union Men into zombies' he said.

The Chief continued to look very cheerful. 'So what? That's what we've been trying to do for years' he said.

This all struck The Head Postmaster as being somewhat callous.

'But what about their souls?' he asked.

One thing The Chief had never lacked was a clear idea of the limits of his role.

'Nothing to do with me. That's up to The Vicar' he said firmly.

'But they'll be doomed to wander round in the shades of eternal night' said The Head Postmaster.

'No-one asked 'em to go on the bloody Union' said The Chief.

CHAPTER
THIRTY NINE

Beware the Fangs

'I take it you're all Church of England' said The Chief Inspector.

The rows of Dim Managers standing before him wondered what was afoot. The Chief handed over a cardboard box to a Dim Manager in the front row.

'Pass these round' he told him. The Dim Manager glanced inside the box. It was full of crucifixes. He took one look at The Chief's face and decided not to argue. He handed round the crucifixes.

'Has everybody got one?' asked The Chief. There was a murmur of assent.

'Well don't stand there like a collection of pillocks. Put them on' instructed The Chief. Obediently The Dim Managers did what they were told. The Chief gazed at them bleakly.

'Why have you put those on?' he asked. There was an uncomfortable silence. Then a Dim Manager whose name The Chief could never remember put up his hand. The Chief nodded at him.

'Because you told us to' said The Dim Manager.

'And why do you think I did that?' asked The Chief.

There was another uncomfortable silence. Then another Dim Manager raised his hand tentatively. The Chief turned to him.

'Yes?' he asked.

'To see if any of us has an attitude problem Chief' replied The Dim Manager.

The Chief shook his head. 'If any of you had an attitude problem you'd have been out of here long ago' he told them.

They all knew this to be true and so kept quiet lest they should unwittingly demonstrate the sort of outlook that would be the cause of official displeasure. The Chief realised none of his Dim Managers was capable of giving him a sensible answer so he decided to put them out of their misery.

'Those are for your protection' he told them. The relief in the atmosphere was plain. One Dim Manager felt sufficiently emboldened to ask.

'Against what Chief?'

'The Undead' The Chief told him. There was another awkward silence. Then a Dim Manager began what was clearly a forced laugh. Seeing The Chief did not show any annoyance a few more Dim Managers produced false laughs. Eventually they all joined in the doleful din until The Chief bellowed at them.

'Shut up!' The sad attempt at mirth died on the instant The Dim Managers were convinced The Chief was barking mad, but he was still The Chief Inspector. Barking mad or not what he said went.

'Pay attention' The Chief demanded. They all did so, straining to look more attentive than the next man. The Chief produced a pair of fangs he'd bought in a Joke Shop. The Dim Managers stared at them aghast. What was coming next?

'I want you to keep a sharp look out for anyone with a set of these. Got it?' said The Chief. The Dim Managers nodded eagerly. They were trying to force what passed for their minds to come to terms with what was happening. Surely there had to be an explanation. For a moment it began to look as though The Chief was about to provide it. He seemed to go off on a tangent. Placing the fangs on the desk he saids.

'We are entering into a new stage in industrial relations'. A Dim Manager particularly keen for advancement ostentatiously made a note. The Chief nodded his approval, a couple more Dim Manager scribbled on the back of fag. He looked round until he spotted the particularly repellant looking Dim Manager with a penchant for sexual harassment and addressed his next remark directly to him.

'If any woman no matter how desperate she may be shows the slightest sign of finding you attractive' she's a bloody vampire. She'll turn you into one of The Undead and I will personally track down your lair and ram a wooden stake up your arse' said The Chief.

The Dim Manager quailed. 'That won't be necessary Chief' he said.

'It better not be' warned The Chief.

The Chief looked at the gathering of Dim Managers and thought that regardless of whether The Undead launched an attack the game was already up. He decided it was time to start planning his retreat. He waved his hand dismissively and The Dim Managers were only too keen to get out. As soon as they had gone The Chief picked up the phone and ring an Estate Agent. He asked them to send him details of villas in Spain and said he'd like one with a swimming pool. Then he rang the Union Office. The Branch Secretary answered.

'The Head Postmaster has now gone completely round the bend and you drove him there' said The Chief.

'The Head Postmaster has been round the bend for years and it's nothing to do with me' countered The Branch Secretary.

'Lately there has been a sharp decline in his condition. He used to worry about Union Militants taking over the office, now he's worried about vampires' said The Chief.

'You know as well as I do he's trying for a medical discharge' The Branch Secretary replied.

'That's what I used to think but now I'm convinced he's completely bananas. What are you going to do about it?' asked The Chief.

'It's a management problem' said The Branch Secretary.

The Chief decided it was time to make an appeal to The Branch Secretary's sense of compassion.

'Surely this is a matter of our common humanity' he said.

'Bollocks!' said The Branch Secretary and rang off.

The Chief nodded his head. 'That's what I thought he'd say' he told himself, put his feet on the desk, closed his eyes and wondered what life would be like when he was sitting beside his own swimming pool.

'Just so long as the nutcase doesn't move in next door' he murmured.

The Branch Secretary had an uneasy feeling that forces had been unloosed that he had no chance of controlling. There was a knock on the door and The Dim Manager with a penchant for sexual harassment sidled in.

'What would you do if The Chief Inspector threatened to trace one of your members down to his lair and ram a wooden stake up his arse?' he asked.

'I'd tell him there's no provision in the Postmasters' Manual for ramming stakes up workers' arses' said The Branch Secretary.

This reply seemed to take a great weight off The Dim Manager's mind. He thought that the crucifix and the regulations combined should be enough to literally save his arse.

The encounter with The Dim Manager made The Branch Secretary even more convinced that uncontrollable forces were being let loose upon his world. He was pleased to see the door open and The Assistant Secretary appear. The Assistant sat down and jerked his thumb over his shoulder:

'What's that wanker want?' he asked.

'He's got the wind up. The Chief has threatened to track him to his lair and ram a wooden stake up his arse' answered The Branch Secretary.

'Would it appear on his record?' asked The Assistant.

'His medical record?' asked The Branch Secretary.

'No. His disciplinary record' said The Assistant.

'Can he do that?' asked The Branch Secretary.

'What, put it on his record?' said The Assistant.

'No. Ram a wooden stake up his arse' replied The Branch Secretary.

'Perhaps we'll soon find out' said The Assistant looking suddenly cheerful.

'Supposing he rams a wooden stake up his arse and then finds out he can't do it?' asked The Branch Secretary.

'He'll get a severe reprimand and then get promoted' answered The Assistant.

'It's a bit excessive' mused The Branch Secretary.

'What the reprimand?' asked The Assistant.

'And the stake' said The Branch Secretary.

'Seems to me things are looking up' said The Assistant.

'The Head Postmaster has gone round the twist' The Branch Secretary told him.

'Is it official?' asked The Assistant Secretary.

'Not yet' said The Branch Secretary.

'Until we see it in writing best assume he's no more barmy than he's always been' said The Assistant Secretary.

'And we'll keep it to ourselves' said The Branch Secretary.

The door was flung open and The Truculent Man marched in grinning from ear to ear.

'The Head Postmaster tried to ram a wooden stake up The Chief Inspector's arse and they've taken him off in a strait jacket. It's all over the office' he chortled.

The Assistant Secretary shook his head in disbelief.

'I thought he was trying to work his ticket but I never thought he'd go this far' he said.

'The Chief Inspector is in shock' said The Truculent Man looking if anything even more delighted.

The Branch Secretary got up and stalked over to the map of the world. The Truculent Man pointed to him and turned his head.

'He'll be the next' he said. The Branch Secretary turned round and reached back indicating the map.

'The tide is turning. All over the world the bastions of perverted power are starting to 'crumble' he said.

'The sooner the better' said The Truculent Man.

'So what's our position?' asked The Assistant Secretary.

Before The Branch Secretary could reply The Truculent Man thumped his fist on the desk.

'We charge the old sod with desertion' he roared.

'Can we do that?' asked The Assistant.

'It's never been done before' said The Secretary.

'Then it's about time it was' said The Truculent Man.

'Suppose he's sick?' asked The Assistant.

'Suppose he is? He's a shaggin' deserter. Blokes were sick in The First World War but they still shot 'em. If it's good enough for them up to their nuts in mud and bullets it's good enough for him sitting on his fat arse in a nice warm office' said The Truculent Man.

In the face of The Truculent Man's conviction neither The Branch Secretary or his Assistant could come up with any objection.

'So we convene a meeting and recommend The Head Postmaster is charged with desertion' said The Assistant.

'And when the meeting has found him guilty, what then?' asked The Branch Secretary.

'Shoot the bastard' said The Truculent Man.

The Assistant was about to demur when The Branch Secretary cut him off.

'The same as World War One' he said.

The Truculent Man nodded emphatically.

'But we're not at war' objected The Assistant Secretary.

'Oh yes we are' said The Truculent Man.

The Branch Secretary strode over to the map of the world.

'He's right. It all comes back to Coca Cola. We're at war and there's no getting away from it.' he said.

'I don't know about Coca Cola. But management are always telling us we're in a war with all these shaggers trying to steal our traffic and destroy our jobs' said The Truculent Man.

'Who are these sods?' asked The Assistant.

'They never tell us that' said The Truculent Man.

'It'll never stand up in Court' said The Assistant.

'It will if it improves dividends' said The Assistant.

'What a bloody state of affairs' complained The Truculent Man.

'And we keep being told everything's improving' said The Assistant.

CHAPTER
FORTY

The Light Fades

The Head Postmaster sat glaring at The Chief Inspector.

"I've just had a hell of a bollocking" he fumed.

"Who from?" said The Chief, not looking particularly interested.

"Region" said The Head Postmaster.

"They're the least of our worries" said The Chief with a shrug.

That anyone should dismiss Region as being of minimal importance struck The Head Postmaster as shameless heresy. Region was the Deity before which they all bowed.

"Are you telling me Region's fuckall?" he asked.

"Region is no more than a government in exile" said The Chief.

"You've been listening to the Educated Effin' Idiot" accused The Head Postmaster.

"He talks a load of crap" said The Chief. The Head Postmaster nodded enthusiastically.

"But sometimes he makes sense" added The Chief.

"You've been reading The Shitehouse Poets said The Head Postmaster.

"Know your enemy" said The Chief.

The Head Postmaster didn't like the way the exchange was going. He decided to change the subject.

"I know they're a dozy bunch of sods, but Region say ramming wooden stakes up their arses isn't the way to liven them up" he said.

The Chief snorted. "No-one's had a stake rammed up his arse" he said.

"It's on the Shitehouse wall" said The Head Postmaster.

"So's your obituary" retorted The Chief.

"The bastard who wrote that should have a stake rammed up his arse" said The Head Postmaster.

"Only after a written warning" said The Chief.

"I blame that twat from The Sun" said The Headpostmaster.

This sudden change of direction left The Chief somewhat bemused.

"What makes you say that?" he asked.

"Everything was fine until he stripped off and did a streak" said The Head Postmaster.

"He didn't strip off, the bleedin' Union stripped him" said The Chief.

"They were provoked" said The Head Postmaster.

"Are you defending the bastard union?" demanded The Chief, as he glared furiously at his nominal boss.

The Head Postmaster quailed. "Of course not" he said.

The Chief continued to glare. The Head Postmaster looked haunted. "We don't want Region nosing round here" he said.

"Who cares about those twats? We've got Jack Bloody Tanner coming. The Sun will be back. There's The Shitehouse Poets, The Bastard Union, that bunch of nutters on the station, not to mention Count Dracula. We're right in the shit" said The Chief.

"The Forces of Darkness" The Head Postmaster gasped.

"And what have we got on our side?" asked The Chief.

The Head Postmaster looked at him hopefully. His hopes were quickly dashed.

"We've got a bunch of thick managers, The Mad Witch of Grantham, some garlic and The Industrial Relations Act" The Chief told him.

"What use is The Industrial Relations Act?" asked The Head Postmaster.

"It shags The Union but it won't be much use against Count Dracula" said The Chief.

"Don't suppose it will bother The Sun and Jack Bloody Tanner much either" said The Head Postmaster as gloom enveloped him.

"Perhaps if we all stick together … The Head Postmaster began, then lapsed into silence as he saw the derisive expression on The Chief's face.

"We could try The Vicar" said The Chief.

Since he was running out of friends The Headpostmaster felt that as a last resort he must seek help from his enemies.

"I'll talk to The Union" he decided, get up, straightened his back and headed for The Branch Secretary's office. He was about to knock on the door when the voice of The Truculent Man rang in in his ears. What he heard caused him to hastily retrace his steps.

"So far as I'm concerned the stake up the arse should just be the first step" The Truculent Man roared.

The news that The Chief Inspector had discovered a nest of female vampires and had eagerly taken on the role of Van Helsing had reached Union Headquarters like everything else by way of the train staff. As was customary reports from the train added a great deal of colour and variety to the report as a result of which a number of high ranking union officials were blundering round with their eyes heavily watering as they wondered how to respond to the appalling atrocities The Chief was alleged to have committed.

One official was particularly horrified as he read the report for the third time. "Some of this has to be physically impossible" he decided.

The General Secretary rose to the occasion. "This is a branch matter" he told The Executive Committee and moved rapidly on to next business.

Back in Derby The Branch Secretary was convinced Coca Cola were behind this latest outrage, but he realised he would have to deal with the matter on a parochial level so he called a Meeting of The Shitehouse Sub Committee.

It did not go as well as he would have liked. For a start no-one was prepared to accept the restrictions of the agenda.

"We need to respond to the latest atrocity" The Branch Secretary began.

"What bloody atrocity?" bellowed The Truculent Man.

"Wooden stakes up the arse" said The Assistant Secretary.

"That's not an atrocity" claimed The Truculent Man.

"Then what is it?" demanded The Assistant.

"Justice" said The Truculent Man.

The meeting then descended into pandemonium. Amid a tumult of angry voices phrases such as 'Some of these offers should have had stakes rammed up the arse years ago' were heard. When The Truculent Man thought The Educated Effin' said he'd had stakes rammed up the arse and it did him no harm it all threatened to turn nasty.

"Are you taking the piss?" roared The Truculent Man looking furious.

The Branch Secretary sought to calm the situation down.

"If we fight among ourselves we play right into the hands of Coca Cola" he told them.

"What's it got to do with those shaggers?" howled The Truculent Man.

The Branch Secretary opened his mouth and was about to tell him when he was cut short.

"We haven't come here to listen to you talking like a twat" bellowed The Truculent Man.

The ensuing uproar made it apparent that they certainly hadn't come to listen to The Branch Secretary talking like a twat so he sat down.

As tempers calmed the din subsided and a somewhat awkward silence ensued.

The Educated Effin' Idiot raised his hand.

'Oh kerrist 'ere we go!' groaned The Truculent Man.

Undeterred The Educated Effin' Idiot launched into an exposition of the situation as he saw it.

'When The Chief Inspector decided the best way to improve the efficiency of the office was to ram a wooden stake up a manager's arse he wasn't acting on behalf of Coca Cola' he begun.

The Branch Secretary got up and was, greeted by cares of 'Sit down you prat.' Realising that the feeling of the meeting was against him he resumed his seat, looking somewhat downcast.

What The Educated Effin' Idiot said next raised The Branch Secretary's spirits.

'However it is quite possible the corporate ethos may have influenced him' he said. Seeing the entire meeting looked puzzled he enlarged on his theme.

'What effect did having a stake rammed up his arse have on The Manager?' he asked.

'It made his effin' eyes water' said The Truculent Man.

'Apart from that?' said The Educated Effin' Idiot.

'It's given him an attitude problem' said The Assistant Secretary.

'And what else?' asked The Educated Effin' Idiot.

To avoid provoking cries of 'sit down you prat' The Branch Secretary resisted the urge to rise to his feet and spoke from a sitting position.

'Surely it's obvious … ' he began.

'Stand up you prat' said The Truculent Man. The Branch Secretary did so.

'The poor sod's terrified. He's had a wooden stake rammed up his arse for a first offence' he said before he was interrupted by The Assistant.

'What exactly did he do?' he wanted to know.

'He didn't do anything. That was the trouble' said The Branch Secretary.

'The stake up the arse was an inducement' said The Educated Effin' Idiot.

'Bloody 'ell' said The Truculent Man.

'It's a kind of perverted bonus' said The Educated Effin' Idiot.

'It's what?' asked The Truculent Man.

The Educated Effin' Idiot sought to clarify his theory.

'It's motivational' he said.

They all looked blank.

'Cost cutting' said The Educated Effin' Idiot.

This was something everyone was familiar with. Angry cries rent the air.

'Same bloody old story', bellowed The Truculent Man.

'It's clearly part of yet another economy drive' said The Educated Effin' Idiot. Seeing he had the attention of the meeting he continued.

'The twisted bastard who came up with this one is like as not an unconscious satanist.

'Has he got a cucumber up his arse?' asked The Assistant.

'Probably. Essentially we're looking at a negative bonus scheme. This is the new era. Before when you did well you got something. Now if you do well you don't.'

'You mean we all work our nuts off so we don't get the wooden stake up the arse' said The Truculent Man.

'The wooden stake is a bit extreme, I don't think The Chief has wholly grasped the concept' said The Educated Effin' Idiot.

'He was always thick' said The Assistant.

'But he is following the principle' said The Branch Secretary.

'This is bloody awful but what's it got do with Coca Shaggin' Cola?' said The Truculent Man.

'It's the new corporate strategy. Rule by fear' The Educated Effin' Idiot told him.

'So what it comes either drink that piss' or we get the stake up the arse' said The Assistant.

'It's Hobson's Choice' said The Truculent Man. "I'll go and get a crate" he said and went looking uncharacteristically subdued.

CHAPTER
FORTY ONE

The Big Picture

The Head Postmaster had decided that his best course was to try to rise above it all. It seemed to him that if he could somehow achieve a sense of detachment his troubles would seem less overwhelming.

'Historic perspective that's what one need' he told The Chief.

'And just what might that be? asked The Chief, obviously unimpressed.

'The Head Postmaster squirmed. He knew he was clutching at straws.

"What we have to think about Chief is our legacy" he said. Seeing The Chief looked mystified he added.

"What will we be leaving those who come after?"

"A right fuckup" said The Chief brutally. It was not yet mid day but he could see The Boss was well and truly pissed.

The Head Postmaster hastily swallowed a couple of pills and washed them down with a swig from a bottle marked sparkling water. The Chief could see no bubbles, nor any sign of sparkle and suspected his leader was knocking back gin.

The Head Postmaster took another swallow and grinned inanely. The Chief felt like thumping him. During his long career he had served under a succession of useless prats, but at least they hadn't been alcoholics.

'If he gets to Spain he'll drink himself to death within a year' The Chief told himself. He felt momentarily better. His improved mood was short lived.

'It could be a lot worse' The Head Postmaster claimed.

'I don't see how' said The Chief.

'Count your blessings' said The Head Postmaster sagely.

The sheer inanity of this took The Chief aback. Incredulity rendered him speechless. The Head Postmaster was obviously sublimely oblivious to the ghastly reality. He sat gazing into space with a faraway look in his eyes. He reached for the sparkling water. The Chief snatched the bottle from his grasp.

'You've had enough' he said.

The Head Postmaster did not argue. He sat there with a gormless grin.

'It could be premature senility' thought The Chief. He knew The Head Postmaster was a devious old sod, and that he would seek to advance his own interests to the exclusion of all other considerations, but he really had no idea what the crooked bastard's game was.

'Whatever it is money will come into it' The Chief mused.

The Head Postmaster's next remark did nothing to improve The Chief's humour.

"Vampires are all the rage at the moment" he said.

It was a matter of great regret to The Chief that us yet, despite what it said on the Shitehouse wall, he hadn't actually rammed a wooden stake up a manager's arse, and he found himself wondering what Region's attitude would be to a Chief Inspector who rammed a wooden stake up a Head Postmaster's arse.

He decided the pimply young squirts currently ruling the roost at Region would not look favourably on such an initiative, and it would be best to wait until he was working his notice.

The Head Postmaster took another swig at the sparkling water.

"They're all over the media" he said.

"Who?" asked The Chief.

"Vampires" said The Head Postmaster.

The Chief had no idea if The Head Postmaster was playing some sort of game or if he had, like most of the nation, taken refuge in barminess. One thing he was sure of was that he wasn't prepared to listen to any more crap about vampires, not even if they featured on the Shitehouse walls.

"Never mind what's on television. Deal with what we've got here" he demanded.

"There are problems, but we're gradually getting on top of things" said The Head Postmaster.

On hearing this fatuous claim The Chief jumped to the conclusion that The Head Postmaster was acting daft as part of a scheme to get a generous payoff on grounds of mental incapacity, but since the country had been run for years by people who were barking mad, and since they were regularly re-elected, it seemed derangement among those in charge didn't concern the people, so The Chief doubted if pretending to be daft would help The Head Postmaster.

Surely it was now taken for granted that anyone in charge would be mentally unbalanced.

"We're not getting on top of things. We're up to our necks in shit" declared The Chief.

"There are challenges, but we're overcoming them" said The Head Postmaster.

"Like hell we are" said The Chief.

"You have to look at the big picture" The Head Postmaster said.

"I don't have to look at it. I'm in the middle of the bastard. What about the bloody station?" said The Chief.

"The station is a mere outpost" said The Head Postmaster.

"Outposts are where the trouble starts" countered The Chief.

The Head Postmaster sat up proudly.

"We've saved the Shitehouse" he declared.

"That Shitehouse will be your monument" retorted The Chief.

"It's not just a Shitehouse, it is also a symbol" said The Head Postmaster.

"That's not you talking. The Educated Effin' Idiot has got to you. You've been brainwashed. You'll be joining The Labour Party next" scoffed The Chief.

The Head Postmaster was outraged.

"Just you remember who you're talking to" he said.

"Don't you come the high and bloody mighty with me" retorted The Chief. "It'll be on your headstone. He fucked up The Post Office, but he saved the Shitehouse" he added.

Hitherto The Head Postmaster had been solely concerned, to the point of obsession, with the size of his severance packet and the size of his retirement villa. He cared about the now, not the hereafter, but The Chief's claim that he'd be rembered as a complete pillock shook him somewhat, and he felt he had to justify himself.

The Chief, however, was in remorseless mood.

"The staff hate your guts" he said.

The Head Postmaster flinched, then attempted a rally.

"I might not be popular, but I am respected" he said.

The Chief snorted contemptuously.

"Read The Shitehouse Wall. The Voice of the People. The ones you haven't killed off you've pissed off" he said.

Before The Head Postmaster could rally the door was flung open and The Truculent Man stormed in.

"See how you like drinking this rat's piss" he bellowed, slammed the bottles of Coca Cola on the desk, and left leaving the door wide open.

"Close the bloody door" yelled The Chief.

"Bollocks" replied The Truculent Man.

The Head Postmaster edged away from the bottles.

"What's going on?" he asked.

"How would I know? I'm not a Shitehouse Poet. I'm just The Chief Inspector" said The Chief. He took up one of the bottles and took a sip.

"Bloody hell!" he spluttered. "This really is rat's piss" he added. He held the bottle up to the light. "We should get this analysed" he said. He took a small sip, swirled it round in his mouth and spat it out. The Head Postmaster winced.

"I don't gob on your carpet" he said.

"You would if you drank that rat's piss" The Chief retorted. He gazed at the pool of gob, then at the bottle, then sat gazing at the ceiling. Then he spoke.

"The Branch Secretary talks like a twat" he said.

"We know that fucker. He talks like a twat because he is a twat" said The Head Postmaster.

"Watch your language" said The Chief.

"Fuck off" said The Head Postmaster.

Any doubts The Chief had about the sparkling water being gin disappeared. The Head Postmaster was ratarsed.

"He'll be at Alcohol Anonymous before long" The Chief decided. He then returned to his assessment of The Branch Secretary.

"He talks like a twat all the time. That's why he's Branch Secretary, but he has got one thing right."

He paused and picked up the bottle of Coca Cola The Head Postmaster thought he might be going to use it to blow up the Platform Six Shitehouse, but The Chief was using it to illustrate a paint.

"Twat or not he's right about one thing. They'll have to achieve world domination. It's the only way they can get people to drink this muck" he said.

Realisation slowly damned on The Head Postmaster's face. He looked at The Chief horrorstruck.

"You mean all the crap he's been coming out with is true?" he asked. The Chief nodded.

"What can we do about it?" asked The Head Postmaster. The Chief looked unexpectedly confident.

"The pen is mightier than the sword" he said.

"You mean it's up to The Shitehouse Poets to save us?" said The Head Postmaster as he downed the last drop of gin.

The Chief nodded.

"I wouldn't say no to a glass of that sparkling water" he said.

The Head Postmaster took out another bottle.

CHAPTER
FORTY TWO

Pariahs

The Derby Office was now officially classified as an embarrassment. No-one wanted to know anyone even remotely connected with the bizarre events reported to have taken place there.

Despite many 'phone calls to Region The Head Postmaster could not find anyone in the upper echelons prepared to talk to him. He found himself having to listen to a series of junior executives who made it quite obvious he was now no more than an irrelevance, a relic, someone who could be treated with total disregard, even by newly recruited graduates with third class degrees. How had it come to this he asked himself.

Just when he came to feel he hadn't a friend in the world support came from an unexpected quarter. His door was flung open and The Chief walked in accompanied by The Branch Secretary, both holding bottles of what was neither sparkling water or Coca Cola. They sat down uninvited, put their bottles on the desk and waited. The Head

Postmaster eyed them apprehensively, wondering what catastrophe had brought them to see him. The Chief broke the silence.

"Are we going to drink from the bottle?" he asked.

The Head Postmaster get out some glasses and The Chief filled them. He raised his glass.

"Here's to Shaggin' George. May he never piss in the bottle" he said.

Although he was somewhat taken aback to find himself being called upon to toast Shaggin' George The Head Postmaster was so demoralised he didn't care who he drank to so long as he drank, so he swallowed the welcome booze with enthusiasm.

Nowadays he regarded The Chief with wariness, but as the alcohol entered his system he felt emboldened enough to ask why he had suddenly become an admirer of Shaggin' George.

"Shaggin' George is a pisshead, a compulsive gambler, he's permanently in the shit, nobody can change him, and thank God for that. George could be an endangered species. He's human" said The Chief.

By now The Head Postmaster had realised The Chief was awash with alcohol, and at least to an extent what he was hearing was the booze talking. Nevertheless he was keen to hear more as to why The Chief had come to regard Shaggin' George as a treasure.

The Branch Secretary was also eager to hear how Shaggin' George had managed to progress from being regarded as a right pain in the arse to a valued individual who had to be preserved as a possible last remnant of the human race. He doubted whether George would relish his new unsought role.

The Chief held up his empty glass and stared at The Head Postmaster who took the hint and poured out the remains of a bottle. The Chief raised his glass, then paused.

"Am I drinking on my bleedin' own?" he asked.

It was clear to The Head Postmaster and The Branch Secretary that they had some catching up to do, so they hastily filled their glasses and drank. The Chief nodded his approval, then leaned forward and gazed intently at them.

"Where do the arseholes come from? That is the question" he said.

This sounded like a quotation to The Branch Secretary, something Hamlet might have said if he was even more pissed off than usual, but he didn't think The Chief spent much time reading Shakespeare.

"Where do they come from?" repeated The Chief.

The Head Postmaster decided to seek clarification.

"Where do who from?" he said.

"The pimply little shits at Region" replied The Chief.

"From third rate universities" suggested The Branch Secretary.

The Chief gloomily shook his head.

"From a galaxy light years away" he said.

"Star Wars" said The Head Postmaster.

Normally The Branch Secretary would have scoffed at this as mere fantasy, but these were not normal times. He'd recently been approached by a driver who wanted to know whether The Union would support him if his van was enveloped by a large bubble and whisked away into the stratosphere while he was emptying a box.

At first he'd suspected it was a windup, but after considering the matter, he realised it was a serious question and he gave his assurance that any driver whose van was commandeered by aliens would receive the full support of The Union. He'd thought it best not to inform Union Headquarters of his decision. He doubted if they'd understand.

The Chief continued to air his suspicions.

"Body Snatchers! That's what the obnoxious little sods are" he muttered.

The Head Postmaster caught his drift.

"Giant pods! We need to find the giant pods!" he said.

"And incinerate the fuckers" said The Chief.

The Branch Secretary was beginning to find all this somewhat alarming. It was all very well having the occasional relatively convivial drink with top management, but it looked as though these two buggers were in need of professional help.

It seemed as though The Chief had given the matter serious thought.

"Somehow it's all starting to make sense" he said.

So far as The Branch Secretary was concerned it was all very confusing. He was convinced Coca Cola's tentacles were spread all over our planet and its ubiquity made it a formidable opponent. Frequent examinations of his map of the world reminded him of the vastness of the area under threat, but hitherto he had thought the battle had to be fought solely on earth. Now, according to The Chief, the conflict involved the entire universe. If this was the case he doubted whether The Shitehouse Sub Committee would prove equal to the task. It was pretty certain he did not have the necessary resources at his disposal to deal with the situation he faced.

Furthermore he could expect no help from Headquarters. A spate of unofficial walkouts by postmen driven to mutiny by the constant provocation inflicted on them by what it now appeared could be malevolent aliens had left The General Secretary feeling decidedly inadequate. If he was capable of grasping the magnitude of the challenge his Union now faced he would certainly throw in his hand.

The Head Postmaster's next contribution made The Branch Secretary suspect he had already been taken even by a giant pod.

"Time travel. That's the coming thing" he said.

"That'll sort out those stroppy bloody train drivers" said The Chief.

This was too much for The Branch Secretary.

"We're facing inter planetary conflict and all you can do is attack the unions" he said.

For the first time in his life The Head Postmaster was not interested in union bashing. He had other matters on his mind.

"What we need to know is are they from the past or the future?" he said.

The Head Postmaster's next remark did nothing to improve the Chief's humour.

"Vampires are all the rage at the moment" he said.

It was a matter of great regret to The Chief that as yet, despite what it said on the Shitehouse wall, he hadn't actually rammed a wooden stake up a manager's arse, and he found himself wondering what Region's attitude would be to a Chief Inspector who rammed a wooden stake up a Head Postmaster's arse.

He decided the pimply young squirts currently ruling the roost at Region would not look favourably on such an initiative, and it would be best to wait until he was working his notice.

The Head Postmaster took another swig at the sparkling water.

"They're all over the media" he said.

"Who?" asked The Chief.

"Vampires" said The Head Postmaster.

The Chief had no idea if The Head Postmaster was playing some sort of game or if he had, like most of the nation, taken refuge in barminess. One thing he was sure of was that he wasn't prepared to listen to any more crap about vampires, not even if they featured on the Shitehouse wall.

"Never mind what's on television. Deal with what we've got here" he demanded.

The Chief glared accusingly at The Head Postmaster.

"This bugger's empty" he said as he held a bottle of sparkling water upside down.

"All good things come to an end" said The Head Postmaster.

"Including our bastard jobs if we don't sort this mess out" said The Chief.

The Head Postmaster sat gazing vacantly into space.

"It all seems better when you've had a drink" he said.

"Drinking yourself legless might make you feel better, but it doesn't solve any of our problems" said The Chief.

The Head Postmaster continued to grin inanely. The Chief still couldn't decide if he really was cracking, or was putting on an act in the hope of working his ticket. He went to the drinks cabinet. It was full of empty bottles. He glared at The Head Postmaster.

"Since when have you been a pisshead?" he demanded.

Before The Head Postmaster could make a denial there was a diffident knock on the door.

"Come in" roared The Chief.

The Dim Station Manager came in looking terrified.

"Fuck off" bellowed The Chief.

The Dim Manager scurried out.

"Come back here" The Chief roared.

With obvious reluctance The Dim Manager did so.

"Where do you think you're going?" said The Chief.

"You told me to fuck off" said The Dim Manager.

"You've done that. Now do something useful "The Chief told him.

The Dim Manager waited for further instructions. The Chief sighed.

"Fuck off" he said.

The Dim Manager hastily started to leave.

"Come back" said The Chief.

The Dim Manager looked confused. He looked even more confused when The Chief continued.

"Fuck off. Find an off licence and come back here with a bottle of gin" he said.

"What brand?" asked The Dim Manager.

"Who am I?" "James Shaggin' Bond?" said The Chief as he handed over a note.

The Dim Manager left.

"That's the sort of useless wanker you promoted" said The Chief.

"I never promoted that tosser" protested The Head Postmaster.

"He's always been useless. He was a crap postman, crap driver, totally useless, so you made him a Manager" said The Chief.

"That's what we did then. If they were good for shagall else we made them managers. It was allright until The Bolshies started agitating" The Head Postmaster replied.

"We promoted arseholes. If they weren't arseholes to begin with he turned them into arseholes" said The Chief.

"Arseholes make good managers" said The Head Postmaster.

The Chief gave a mirthless laugh.

"That lot out there are arseholes, no doubt about that, but don't try and tell me they're good managers" he said.

"You have to be an arsehole to be a good manager" claimed The Head Postmaster.

"Let's advertise. Are you an arsehole? You are? Make it pay. Become a Royal Mail Manager" said The Chief.

Before The Head Postmaster could decide if this was a good idea there was a knock at the door. The Head Postmaster and The Chief simultaneously yelled 'Come in' and The Dim Station Manager sidled in holding a bottle.

"Keep the change" said The Chief.

"There wasn't any change" said The Dim Manager.

"Where did you go - effin' Harrods?" Asked The Chief.

"When did you last buy a round?" The Dim Manager countered.

This impertinence made The Chief decide that if having stakes rammed up the arse became officially accepted practice this particular Dim Manager would be the first recipient. However he had more pressing concerns and resolved to get The Dim Manager out of the way.

"Fill two glasses, then bugger off" he told him.

With trembling hands The Dim Manager filled three and took a gulp from one. The Chief was outraged. His face turned from red to purple.

"You cheeky sod! How dare you help yourself to my bloody gin? He said.

"I've chipped in for that bottle" said The Dim Manager, shakily defiant.

The Chief was too furious to speak. All he could manage was an indignant splutter. The Head Postmaster hastily swallowed his drink and went to pick up the bottle. The Dim Manager beat him to it. He finished his drink and poured himself another.

"It's a bloody mutiny" said The Chief. "He's another bastard looking for a medical discharge," he muttered to himself as another possibility occurred to him.

The Dim Manager appeared to have taken charge.

'Finish your drinks' he told them.

The Chief was outraged.

'Don't you tell me what to do' he bellowed.

The Dim Manager blanched but stood his ground.

'There's big trouble at the station' he said.

'Someone's finally blown up the bloody Shitehouse' scoffed The Chief.

The Dim Manager shook his head.

'Worse than that' he said.

'Well don't stand there like a twat. Tell us what's happened' ordered The Chief.

The Dim Manager hastily finished his drink.

'We're being sued' he said.

'If you're being sued that's your bloody problem' said The Chief.

'Not me, us. The Post Office' said The Dim Manager.

The Post Master was in an alcoholic stupor but this news made him sit up.

'Who is suing us?' he asked.

"British Rail" said The Dim Manager.

The Chief was astonished.

"British Rail! That bunch of wankers are suing us!" he said, shaking his head in disbelief.

"Why are they suing us?" asked The Head Postmaster.

The Dim Manager fished a piece of paper out of his pocket and read laboriously.

"For the wanton destruction of a valuable human resource" he said.

"What the bloody hell is that supposed to mean?" asked The Chief.

"The Educated Effin' Idiot says it's legalese" said The Dim Manager.

"That's his contribution is it?" said The Chief.

The Manager nodded.

"He's a twat" said The Chief.

They all agreed The Educated Effin' Idiot was a twat and felt momentarily better, but soon the gloom returned. The Dim Manager coughed.

"Have you got something to tell us?" asked The Chief.

"It's about Shaggin' George" said The Dim Manager.

"British Rail are suing The Post Office because of Shaggin' George?" said The Chief. The Dim Manager glanced at his piece of paper and nodded. The Chief was not impressed.

"Someone's taking the piss" he asserted.

The possibility of a court appearance did not appeal to The Head Postmaster. He hastily refilled his glass. The Dim Manager was bright enough to know that when trouble loomed the first response of those in charge was to look for a scapegoat and he was the most likely candidate to fill the role. He made an attempt to deflect the criticism that was bound to come.

"I offered George counselling" he said.

"What was his response?" asked The Head Postmaster.

"He said why don't you get your effin' fags out, stop talking like a twat, and how are you fixed, can you lend me a fiver?" said The Dim Manager.

"Does he realise the gravity of the situation?" asked The Head Postmaster.

Before The Dim Manager could reply The Chief butted in.

"Exactly what is the drunken prat accused of?" he wanted to know. The Dim Manager consulted a scrap of paper.

"He's accused of turning The Manager of British Rail's Derby Station into a mindless vegetable" he read out.

"The bugger was like that when he arrived" said The Chief.

"Then they can't blame Shaggin' George" said The Head Postmaster looking much relieved.

"If British Rail put nutters in charge it's their responsibility" said The Chief.

The Dim Manager peered at his piece of paper. The Chief glared at him.

"If you've got something to say for Chrissake say it" he said. The Dim Manager read from his paper.

"British Rail's top man is obviously scatalogical and should seek professional help" he said. The Chief didn't find that particularly illuminating.

"What the fuck is scatalogical?" he asked.

The Dim Manager consulted his paper.

"It means he's obsessed with the Shitehouse. He can't think about anything else" he said.

"Is that correct?" asked The Head Postmaster.

"Yes" said The Dim Manager. The Head Postmaster looked delighted.

"So their man in charge of a major railway station can't think about anything except the Shitehouse and he needs professional help, and they're saying it's all because of Shaggin' George" he said.

The Dim Manager nodded. The Head Postmaster turned to The Chief.

"This is all nonsense. They haven't got a leg to stand on" he said. The Chief was a little more sceptical.

"There has to be more to it. The Station Master may be a basket case, but he's not suing us. It has to come from Region. Have you told us everything or are you holding something back?" he asked The Dim Manager.

The Dim Manager looked as though he wished he was somewhere else, anywhere else. He squirmed in his seat and hoped he wasn't in line for a wooden stake up the arse. Summoning up the remains of his courage he blurted out:

"They've got medical evidence".

At the mention of medical evidence The Head Postmaster turned pale, but The Chief was not to be intimidated.

"What bloody medical evidence?" he demanded.

"The Doctor has signed him off because he's suffering from Shaggin' George" said The Dim Manager.

'What a load of bollocks!' roared The Chief. He turned to The Head Postmaster.

'He can't put George on a medical certificate. We all know he's a pain the arse, but he's not a disease' he said.

The Head Postmaster didn't have a clue as to what was going on, but felt he had to assert himself.

'What's George's work like?' he asked The Dim Manager.

So far as The Dim Manager was aware George didn't actually do any work, but he thought it best to be non commital until he could be sure which way the wind was blowing.

'He doesn't pull up many trees' he said.

'It's a good thing he doesn't. We've already got British Rail suing us, we don't want the bloody Forestry Commission suing us as well' said The Chief.

'What does Shaggin' George have to say about all this?' asked The Head Postmaster.

'He says they're not effin' up his social life and he's not pissing in the bottle' said The Dim Manager.

The Dim Manager could see that The Head Postmaster was affronted by George's attitude, and consequently he was even deeper in the shit than usual.

It was beginning to look as though the stake up the arse was the most likely outcome for him. He wondered if there was any point in seeing The Welfare Officer, but since everyone said he was a useless wanker he wasn't likely to get any help from him.

His prospects looked bleak, but relief came from an unexpected quarter.

"You'll never change George" said The Chief.

It seemed as though The Chief had given up on George. This didn't surprise The Dim Manager. After all he'd given up on George long ago, along with everyone else, apart from Rod Williams, on whose behalf British Rail were now seeking recompense through the acclaimed British legal system.

All could yet be well. Rod Williams was clearly deranged, George was being held responsible, and looked like being cast as the sacrificial goat. He felt emboldened enough to help himself to another gin.

His sense of euphoria was short lived.

"Where are they?" barked The Chief.

"Who?" said The Dim Manager.

"The bloody Ghost Squad" said The Chief.

"Do they still work here?" asked The Dim Manager.

"They're still being paid" said The Chief.

"I've been told not to discuss The Ghost Squad" said The Dim Manager.

"Who by?" asked The Chief.

"I don't know. It's to do with The Official Secrets Act" said The Dim Manager. He hoped his superiors were as terrified of The Official Secrets Act as he was. The Chief disappointed him.

"What a load of bollocks" he said.

The Head Postmaster was more cautious.

"The least said about The Ghost Squad the better" he said nervously.

"Best not get involved with the supernatural" said The Chief.

The Head Postmaster crossed himself.

"You mean they're not of this world?" he asked.

"They must have come from somewhere else and they keep going back there" said The Chief.

The Dim Manager liked the sound of this. If the bastards were aliens he couldn't be expected to keep track of their whereabouts.

"They could be space travellers" he suggested.

"With any luck they'll get in their ship and effoff" said The Chief.

"And take Shaggin' George with 'em" said The Dim Manager.

"Best not to antagonise them" said The Head Postmaster.

"What's Region's position on aliens? asked The Chief.

At the mere mention of Region The Head Postmaster looked panic stricken. The Chief, as so often, came to his rescue.

"We'll blame the Bastard Union" he said.

"And Shaggin' George" said The Dim Manager.

The Chief poured a small measure from the Coca Cola bottle, took a sip and spat it out onto the carpet. The Head Postmaster winced but kept silent.

The Chief held the bottle up to the light.

"Did you say George won't piss in the bottle?" he asked The Dim Manager.

"Every time he's asked to provide a sample he says it's postman prejudice" said The Dim Manager.

"It's probably not George then, but some sod has pissed in this" said The Chief, eyeing the coke bottle with distaste.

He handed the bottle to The Dim Manager.

"Have a swig" he ordered.

The Dim Manager blanched.

"Do I have to?" he asked.

"I'm giving you a direct order" The Chief told him.

Keen to avoid the wooden stake up the arse The Dim Manager followed instructions.

As soon as he swallowed his face convulsed, he shuddered, and spat the noxious brew onto the carpet. The Head Postmaster was the demoralised to protest. He looked resigned.

"Phuck me! Where's the bleedin' gin?" spluttered The Dim Manager.

The Chief poured him a shot of gin.

"Get that bugger down you" he said.

The Dim Manager sat slumped, wondering whether the wooden stake might have been preferable to the coke, and wasn't consoled by the thought that he might still experience both. He thought an attack on The Bastard Union might improve his prospects.

"The Branch Secretary talks like a twat" he said.

Encouraged by The Chief's approving nod he ploughed on.

"He talks like a twat because he is a twat" he said.

The Head Postmaster beamed. This was music to his ears.

"Only a twat would want to be Branch Secretary" said The Dim Manager as he poured himself some more gin. He wasn't used to basking in official approval, certainly not since he had been supposedly in charge at the station, so he sought to make the most of the sudden wholly unexpected change in his status.

He felt sufficiently confident to help himself to some more gin. He emptied his glass and tried to marshal his thoughts.

"The Branch Secretary is a complete twat" he began.

The Chief interrupted him testily.

"We know that" he said.

Several shots of gin on an empty stomach had an effect on what passed for The Dim Manager's intellect and he was seeing the world through an alcoholic haze. He started to giggle, then made a huge effort to regain control of his faculties.

He sat with a daft grin on his reddened face, then with a supreme effort he stood up.

"Even a complete twat once in his life talks sense" he said, and then fell flat on his face.

The Chief gazed at his prone form with utter contempt.

"That's the sort of prat you promoted" he said.

It was hard to justify advancing the inert lump on the floor, but the Head Postmaster felt he had to make some attempt.

"He was the best of a bad bunch" he said.

"He was so far up your arse we had to send in cavers to find him" said The Chief.

"I wouldn't put it quite like that" said The Head Postmaster.

"Look at him. He can't even drink. A few swigs of mother's ruin and he's paralytic" said The Chief.

The Chief punched some numbers into the phone, then barked.

"Two of you come to The Head Postmaster's office right away" He slammed down the receiver.

He pointed at the inert Dim Manager.

"The selection tests are useless. That idiot should never have been taken on. If you can't lift heavy bags and drink you're no good to The Post Office" he said.

"Our men can certainly drink" said The Head Postmaster.

"If the Post Office closed so would half the pubs in Derby" said The Chief.

There was a knock on the door.

"Get in here" ordered The Chief.

Two of the most junior Dim Managers sidled in The Chief wasted no time on pleasantries.

"Get that heap of shit out of here" he said.

The Dim Managers looked at their collapsed colleague with a total lack of sympathy.

"Shouldn't be on The Post Office if he can't hold his ale" said one.

"What shall we do with the wanker? asked the other.

"Shove the pissed up prat in a parcel bag and send him to Scotland" said The Head Postmaster.

The Dim Managers looked at The Chief for confirmation.

"Just get him out of here" said The Chief. This proved to be a task way beyond the Dim Managers' capabilities.

They hadn't lifted anything heavier than a pint pot for years and their pissed up colleague was grossly overweight so their efforts rapidly progressed from the ineffectual to the comic.

The Head Postmaster found the spectacle hilarious. The Chief was not amused. He turned to The Head Postmaster.

"Look at the useless sods! Call them Managers! Get out of the bloody way. Open the door" he told one useless specimen as he grabbed the drunkard's feet. The Useless Manager opened the door and The Branch Secretary came in followed by The Truculent Man.

The fiery temper of The Truculent Man was further inflamed by the sight that met him. His response was immediate and volcanic.

"Look at 'em! Bloody typical! Our blokes are out walking the streets, working their bollocks off, and this lot are here getting pissed" he bellowed.

"Don't you come in here making false accusations" said The Chief.

"False accusations!" howled The Truculent Man. He peered at the prostate figure.

"I think this effer may be dead" he said.

The Chief was shaken.

"He's not dead, he's resting" he said.

"He looks dead to me" said The Branch Secretary.

"He's never been very lively" said The Chief.

"He's either dead or comatose" The Branch Secretary told him.

"Is the bastard dead?" asked The Head Postmaster.

"Show some respect" said The Truculent Man.

"Should we start a collection?" asked one of The Dim Managers.

"You'll get effall from me" said The Truculent Man.

At this point the corpse sat up and rose unsteadily to its feet. The Head Postmaster gazed at him in fascination.

"The bastard's risen from the dead" he said.

The Chief was having none of it.

"He's not resurrected. He's pissed" he said. They were all staring at The Risen Manager, wondering whether he was proof of life after death, when Shaggin' George wandered in holding a sheet of paper. He bore down on the possibly newly arisen, ignoring everyone else.

"What's this shagger?" demanded Shaggin' George, waving the paper in front of his eyes. The Dim Manager was in no state to focus on moving objects so The Chief stepped in.

"Give it here" he ordered.

George handed it over. The Chief quickly read it.

"It's from some arsehole of a solicitor" he said, and handed it over to The Head Postmaster who laid it on his desk without looking at it.

"Is he in the shit?" he asked hopefully.

"If I'm in the shit, they're all in the shit with me" said George.

The Chief decided that the less the two Dim Managers knew the better.

"You two can bugger off" he said.

They left hurriedly. The Chief was determined to have no nonsense from George.

"Now look here George. There's only one bloke in the shit, and that's you" he said.

Memories of countless indignaties he'd endured because of George made The Dim Manager vindictive.

"You're going to be buried in shit" he told George.

George gave no sign of being bothered.

"If I'm in the shit so is everyone else" he said.

"That's a bloody solicitor's letter" said The Dim Manager.

"We've all got one. Even the bloody Ghost Squad" George told him.

The Chief couldn't believe his ears.

"What are you on about? British Rail are suing The Post Office, and it's down to you" he said.

"That's a corporate dispute" said George.

This was not what The Chief expected to hear and he was momentarily nonplussed. He rallied quickly and realised George must have taken advice.

"Have you seen your solicitor?" he asked.

"I haven't got a solicitor" said George.

"He's been talking to The Educated Effin' Idiot" said The Head Postmaster.

"We've had a chat" said George.

"That prat sees more people than The Citizens' Advice Bureau" said The Chief.

"Perhaps we could transfer him to Human Resources" said The Head Postmaster.

The Chief ignored this. He glared at The Dim Manager.

"Tell your blokes to say fuckall."

"Official Secrets Act" he said.

'You won't be able to hush this bugger up' said The Truculent Man.

The Chief was inclined to agree with him, but not prepared to admit it. He turned to George.

'What did The Ghost Squad say when they got their letter?' he asked.

'They said they were being shut on from a great height' said George.

'That's what they keep telling me' said The Branch Secretary.

'That's all they ever say. They're boring buggers' said George.

'We're all rather missing the point here' said The Branch Secretary, holding a bottle of coke.

'Look we all know that's piss' said The Chief.

'That's about all we're agreed on' said The Truculent Man.

'It can't be that bad' said The Head Postmaster.

'Try it' challenged The Truculent Man.

The Head Postmaster swallowed some coke and promptly gobbed it onto the carpet.

'Bloody hell!' he said.

'Fancy another?' asked The Truculent Man.

The Head Postmaster shook his head.

The Truculent Man nodded towards The Branch Secretary.

"I used to think he was talking like a twat, but I've changed my mind. Coca Cola must have world domination. Why else would people drink this piss?" he demanded.

All those who had tasted the noxious brew nodded their heads. A thought struck The Head Postmaster.

"This may be donkey piss, but he's still a twat" he said, pointing at The Branch Secretary.

Before The Branch Secretary could respond The Chief added fuel to the flames.

"He talks like a twat, and if you talk like a twat the chances are you are a twat" he said.

The Dim Manager spotted an opportunity to avoid the wooden stake.

"If it looks like a twat, talks like a twat, and acts like a twat, it's got to be a twat" he said.

The Truculent Man was going through the drinks cabinet. Each empty bottle he found caused his anger to rise. He tossed the bottles over his shoulder.

"Top management! Effin' pissheads!" he bellowed.

Having confirmed that the cabinet contained nothing but empties he turned accusingly towards The Head Postmaster.

"What about the guests?" he asked. Before The Head Postmaster could reply The Truculent Man turned on The Dim Manager.

"And who are you calling a twat?" he bellowed.

Normally The Dim Manager went out of his way to avoid confrontation, but he was full of alcohol fuelled courage and he found The Truculent Man considerably less frightening than the prospect of a wooden stake up his arse so he stood his ground.

"If the cap fits" he said.

The Truculent Man stepped towards The Dim Manager who hastily stepped back, trod on an empty bottle which rolled, throwing him off balance. He landed flat on his back.

"Look at that. Pissed on duty" yelled The Truculent Man.

"Bloody hell! Not again." said The Chief.

He then noticed The Truculent Man's clenched fists.

"Did you thump him?" he asked.

"Is he breathing?" countered The Truculent Man.

"Course he's breathing" said The Chief.

"If he's breathing I never hit him" he said.

"He'd be dead if I hit him" he added.

At this point The Head Postmaster decided to sum up the situation as he now saw it.

"We're all fighting for survival. We're being made to drink this piss, and all he can do is keep falling over" he said indicating The Dim Manager.

"And he's got the cheek to call me a twat" said The Truculent Man.

There was a chorus of condemnation directed towards The Dim Manager who was it was agreed responsible for all the ills affecting The Post Office. The one voice raised in his defence was George's.

"At least he gets his effin' fags out" he said, then looked round hopefully to see if anyone took the hint. No-one did. George had no idea what was going on. He decided to seek clarification.

"Am I in the shit?" he asked.

The answer he got was not reassuring.

"We're all in the shit. Why should you be any different?" said The Head Postmaster.

George was tempted to ask him how he was fixed, but thought it best not to push his luck, so he decided he'd go for a refreshing pint.

CHAPTER
FORTY THREE

Freedom of the Press

The Dim Station Manager sat at his desk deep in thought. He was contemplating his future with a great deal of alarm. His horoscope confirmed his misgivings. 'Troubled times lie ahead' it said. That was how it seemed to him.

Life was grim now but the future seemed to promise nothing but more horror.

Nothing was as it should be. The Chief's rapid descent into lunacy should have opened up career opportunities to his underlings, including The Dim Manager, but it was obvious being right off your chump was no handicap when you were in Post Office Management.

In any case The Dim Manager was pretty sure he was most likely to get a wooden stake rammed up his arse. His chances of promotion had always been remote, and recent events ensured they were now non existent.

The door opened and George stuck his head in.

"How you fixed?" he asked.

"Phuckoff" said The Dim Manager.

"I thought you said your door was always open" said George.

"It is. Phuckoff" The Dim Manager told him.

"If you change your mind I'll be over the road" said George and went.

The Dim Manager didn't have the slightest idea as to what was going on and he was beginning to think no-one else had.

He laboriously re read the bumph Region had issued for the team hulk. It was lamentable.

"Who writes this shite?" he wondered.

The door was flung open and Joe marched in.

"Are we having a shaggin' team talk or not?" he demanded.

The Dim Manager decided to assert himself.

"Knock on my door. Wait. When instructed to do so come in" he said.

"Bollocks" said Joe.

The Dim Manager saw no point in pursuing the matter.

"Tell the men I am on my way" he said. Joe left slamming the door. The Dim Manager sat gazing at the brief he had been given.

"Whoever writes this muck must have had a marrow up his arse" he muttered as he reluctantly left his office and went to meet his turbulent crew.

Before he could open his mouth Paddy bellowed at him.

"Never mind that crap. Are you going to sign the shaggin' petition?" he demanded, waving a thick sheaf of papers under his nose. The Dim Manager was taken aback.

"What shaggin' petition?" he asked, completely nonplussed.

"This effer!" howled Paddy.

The Dim Manager saw that Paddy was indicating a vast pile of paper. He peered at it and saw sheets covered in scrawled signatures. He knew nothing about this and quickly decided the less he knew the better. He feigned interest.

"What's it about?" he asked.

This confession of ignorance infuriated Paddy even more.

"Call yourself a shaggin' manager" he bellowed.

"Don't you read The Shitehouse Poets?" asked George.

"I read The Sun" said The Dim Manager.

"You mean you look at the pictures" said The Longhaired Git.

The Dim Manager did not want to have to attempt a defence against this charge and sought refuge in diversion.

"You've all signed The Official Secrets Act" he began before Joe interrupted him.

"So shaggin' what?" he said.

"Even a minute study of the inspiring work of The Shitehouse Poets does not amount to a contravention of the disreputable act" said The Player King.

The Dim Manager was not prepared to cross swords with The Player King and was relieved when the next attack came from The Longhaired Git.

"You can write your name can't you?" he asked.

The Dim Manager was floundering.

"Certainly I can" he said.

"Well put the shagger there" said Paddy, waving a sheet of paper under The Dim Manager's nose.

"What's it about?" he asked.

"Everyone's signed it" said Paddy.

"Yes, but what's it about?" repeated The Dim Manager.

"'Tis about parity" The Player King told him.

Incomprehension was written all over The Dim Manager's face. To his relief The Longhaired Git came to his rescue.

"It's supporting The Shitehouse Poets" he said.

This information did nothing to clarify matters in The Dim Manager's mind. It seemed The Shitehouse Poets now had managerial support. It had become very difficult to know who to suck up to. Were The Shitehouse Poets now his superiors? It was all very puzzling.

He noticed that The Head Postmaster and The Chief had signed. Despite not having a clue as to what was happening he added his name.

"When we get enough signatures those useless shaggers in Parliament will have to discuss it" said Joe.

The Dim Manager was even more puzzled.

"Those useless shaggers in Parliament are going to discuss The Shitehouse Poets. Why?" he asked.

"The Minister of Culture is going to make a statement" said Joe.

The Dim Manager decided he should clarify his position.

"We all support parity" he said, while wondering what it was.

"The Shitehouse Gazette should be on the BBC and Sky News with the rest of the papers" said Paddy.

The Dim Manager could scarcely believe his ears.

"You want The Shitehouse Poets on tv" he gasped.

"Should have been on years ago" said Joe.

"The voice of the people must be heard" thundered The Player King.

"Tests have shown they're mentally unstable" protested The Dim Manager.

"Exactly. The voice of the people" said The Player King.

The Dim Manager doubted if The Player King was qualified to judge the state of anyone's mental stability, but on balance it did begin to look as though the entire nation was demented so he did not argue.

"They might be round the bend but they've got millions of readers" said The Long Haired Git.

"You talk like a twat" said The Dim Manager.

"He might talk like a twat" but he's right" said Joe.

"How can millions read the Shitehouse wall?" said The Dim Manager.

"Technology" Paddy told him.

It was immediately obvious that The Dim Manager was none the wiser so The Long Haired Git attempted to give him some idea as to what was happening in the outside world.

"It's all changing out there" he began.

"I know that fucker" interrupted The Dim Manager.

The Long Haired Git ignored him and continued. "There's been a real breakthrough in communication. It's called social media" he said.

"What the fuck's that?" asked The Dim Manager.

"It's a bloody miracle" said Paddy.

"Oh Gawd! Get out the holy water" said The Dim Manager.

"He's right. It's a miracle of modern science" said The Long Haired Git.

Before The Dim Manager could speak he continued.

"One moment The Shitehouse Poets are writing on the wall that you're a fat wanker. Next thing someone in New Zealand is agreeing with him" he said.

"I'm not a fat wanker" protested The Dim Manager.

"It's either that or portly pillock" said Joe.

"I'll sue the sods" spluttered The Dim Manager.

"You'll get nowhere. It's freedom of the press" said Joe.

"Freedom of the press. To print shite" shrieked The Dim Manager.

"You must have freedom of the press" said The Long Haired Git.

"Even though they print shite and lies" said Paddy.

"It was ever thus" said The Player King.

CHAPTER
FORTY FOUR

Extreme Measures

The Inspector was immersed in The Bomb Sergeant's latest report. The Sergeant was delighted to see him eagerly turning the pages.

"What do you think?" he asked.

The Inspector shook his head. "It's a bit far fetched" he said.

"It's true to life" claimed. The Sergeant.

"I haven't met any lesbian vampires" said The Inspector.

"It's a work of fiction" The Sergeant told him.

"Strictly speaking its an official report" said The Inspector.

"Official report my arse!" snorted The Sergeant.

"Are you developing an attitude problem?" asked The Inspector.

"If that means am I pissed off with sucking up to The Chief Constable and his rich thick friends at the poxy golf club the answer is yes" said The Sergeant.

"They may be thick but they are born to rule" said The Inspector.

"Born to rule! That bunch of wankers?" said The Sergeant.

"They can make a lot of trouble" The Inspector warned him.

"Not for me they can't" asserted The Sergeant.

"For all of us" said The Inspector.

The Sergeant didn't see much point in prolonging what was obviously a futile conversation and turned his attention to his report, which he was beginning to think was far too good for a bunch of rich, fat useless thick shaggers.

"It might need toning down a little" The Inspector said diffidently.

To his surprise The Sergeant nodded his assent.

"It probably is a bit too imaginative for The Gin and Tonic Brigade" he conceded.

"I'll leave you with it" said The Inspector trying to quell the sense of disquiet that niggled away at him. The Sergeant was surely becoming weird. One weird sergeant was manageable, but it was obvious he was merely one of many, indeed it was beginning to look as though the problem amounted to contagion, the entire population seemed to be eagerly embracing lunacy.

"Can't say I'm surprised" muttered The Inspector. He wondered if he should raise his concerns at the next meeting of his Lodge. After a while he decided to keep his worries to himself.

"There's some real weird buggers in The Lodge" he muttered.

"Come to think of it there's weird buggers everywhere. It's modern life. It's driving people mad" he concluded as he decided to go for a drink.

The Sergeant watched him go, then turned with relish to his manuscript.

"Tone it down be buggered. It wants spicing up" he said as he took up his pen.

It wasn't only The Inspector who saw signs of a world gone mad. Like The Bomb Sergeant Doctor Llewellyn was yearning for the life of a literary gentleman. Every time he wrote out yet another prescription for some hapless victim of The Mad Witch's Carnival of Misery he found himself longing to be beaming at an admirer as he signed copies of his as yet unwritten book.

Following countless consultations with Rod Williams he had compiled a copious dossier on the saga of the platform six Shitehouse, and, as he listened to the patient's demented ravings, he had frequently felt that if he had to endure much more of this idiocy he'd blow the bloody thing up himself. He was also tempted to sign Rod off on the grounds that he was suffering from a probably incurable attack of 'Shaggin' George'."

He was also kept abreast of the crazed behaviour of various staff members at The Post Office, which in a possibly more enlightened past would have led to them being sent to Bedlam.

There was no shortage of informants as to the deplorable state of The Post Office. According to the postmen it was an "effin' mad house." Doctor Llewellyn had long since come to the conclusion that the entire country had been turned into an 'effin' madhouse," but it seemed clear that even by current British standards The Post Office was collectively spectacularly off its rocker.

He'd signed some more death certificates so he knew being a postman was a high risk occupation and he'd seriously considered contacting The Union to suggest they campaign for danger money, but since it was perfectly obvious no-one in power would admit how bad things were he decided there was no point.

One of his best informants now sat opposite him.

"Still alive Mr. Jenkins, despite all the odds" he greeted him.

The Doctor had decided long ago that only will power was keeping Mr. Jenkins alive, so he didn't examine his medical notes, but turned instead to the record of macabre events at The Post Office that he intended to be the basis of his book. He gazed at one entry in sheer disbelief.

"I'm told The Chief Inspector has ordered all his managers to wear crucifixes, and sprinkle themselves with garlic, and he's threatened to track one down to his lair and ram a wooden stake up his arse" he said.

"It took four of them to hold him down" chortled Mr. Jenkins.

'He screamed like a stuck pig' he added.

The Doctor was profoundly shocked.

'That's terrible' he said.

'Isn't it' echoed Mr. Jenkins, grinning from ear to ear.

'What hospital is he in?' asked The Doctor.

'He's at work' Mr. Jenkins told him.

The Doctor was astounded. 'How can he be at work?' he asked.

'When you've had cucumbers up your arse a wooden stake is just an escalation' said Mr. Jenkins.

'He must be in agony' said The Doctor.

'He's walking a bit funny' conceded Mr. Jenkins.

'I should think he is' said The Doctor.

'The Managers are all dead worried' said Mr. Jenkins, looking delighted.

'They're afraid he might end up in intensive care' said The Doctor.

'No. They're shit scared they'll be next' said Mr. Jenkins.

The Doctor was horrified. 'What do The Police say?' he asked.

'They say they're monitoring the platform six Shitehouse' Mr. Jenkins told him.

'Surely they'll make an arrest' protested The Doctor.

'There's been no complaint,' said Mr. Jenkins.

'What!' shrieked The Doctor.

'There's been no complaint' repeated Mr. Jenkins.

'A bloke's had a wooden stake rammed up his arse and there's been no complaint' yelled The Doctor.

'He wants to keep his job' said Mr. Jenkins.

'He's had a wooden stake rammed up his arse and he's scared of losing his job' said The Doctor aghast.

'If he brings The Police in he'll be accused of bringing The Post Office into disrepute' Mr. Jenkins explained, sounding as though this was all perfectly rational.

'But he's the victim' said The Doctor.

'It was for his own good' said Mr. Jenkins.

'He's had a wooden stake rammed up his arse for his own good. Is that what you're saying?' asked The Doctor.

'The Post Office is a caring employer. They take wooden stakes being rammed up the arse very seriously. They value their staff' said Mr. Jenkins.

'You don't believe this crap' implored The Doctor.

'They have the welfare of managers included in their mission statement and they have all been issued with crucifixes and garlic' Mr. Jenkins said.

'What for?' asked The Doctor.

'To protect them from the postwomen' replied Mr. Jenkins.

The Doctor was baffled.

'What about the postwomen?' he asked.

'They're vampires' replied Mr. Jenkins.

Seeing that The Doctor hadn't yet fully grasped the catastrophe that had befallen Post Office Management he continued.

'The Chief is afraid the office is going to be run by The Undead' he said.

'Surely that will be an improvement' ventured The Doctor.

'It won't make much difference to us we've been The Undead for years' said Mr. Jenkins gloomily.

Suddenly The Doctor cheered up. A smile slowly spread across his face.

'It's a wind up' he said.

'If only it was' said Mr. Jenkins.

'This can't be true' The Doctor protested.

'According to The Shitehouse Poets it is' said Mr. Jenkins.

The Doctor gazed in dismay at his copious notes.

'You mean this all comes from The Shitehouse Poets?' he asked.

'The Shitehouse Wall is where you go for the truth' said Mr. Jenkins.

Seeing the Doctor looked sceptical he added: 'It's much more reliable than The Sun or the BBC'.

The Doctor thought that was a justifiable claim. He heartily despised both organisations. In future he vowed that his search for the truth would include a close study of The Shitehouse Walks.

CHAPTER
FORTY FIVE

Nothing But The Truth

"According to The Mad Witch of Grantham and her disciples little shits like those sods at Birmingham are admired all over the world" said The Head Postmaster.

"Will sanity ever return?" asked The Chief.

"Not in our lifetime" The Head Postmaster said gloomily.

"We can live with lunacy" said The Chief.

"We'll bloody have to" said The Head Postmaster.

"Live with it! You've bloody well imposed it" said The Branch Secretary.

"We had to put up with it the same as everyone else. It was the tide of history" said The Head Postmaster.

The door was flung open and The Assistant Secretary rushed in followed by The Truculent Man and The Educated Effin' Idiot.

"Do you want the bad news first or the worse news?" asked The Assistant.

"Let's have the bad news" said The Chief.

"George has applied to go on the acting list" said The Assistant.

"He wants to be a shaggin' manager" said The Truculent Man.

The Head Postmaster was flabbergasted. He hastily refilled his glass, and emptied it in one swallow.

"I can't believe what I'm hearing" he gasped.

The Chief didn't look surprised. He took a sip of his drink.

"I don't call that bad news" he said.

The Head Postmaster was astounded.

"It's bloody outrageous" he said.

The Chief nodded his agreement. Seeing everyone looking baffled he sought to explain. "George is a credible candidate" he told them. This claim added to the general consternation. The failure to grasp what was to him blindingly obvious annoyed The Chief.

"He's got the main qualification" he said.

Everyone looked even more baffled.

Irritability threatened to overcome The Chief's alcohol induced good mood. He looked at The Educated Effin' Idiot.

"What do you have to be to be made a manager?" he asked.

"Effin' useless" said The Truculent Man.

"Thank Christ someone's got some intelligence" said The Chief.

The Truculent Man looked gratified.

"It's standard procedure. If you're good for nothing else you ascend the ladder" said The Educated Effin' Idiot.

"And if you're an absolute prat you rise to the top" said The Chief.

Apart from The Head Postmaster everyone murmured assent.

The Chief glanced at The Assistant.

"What was the worse news?" he asked.

"If George is made a manager the Committee at The Railway Institute are going to sue us" said The Assistant.

"On what grounds?" asked The Head Postmaster.

"Loss of earnings" said The Truculent Man.

"Loss of earnings!" echoed The Head Postmaster.

"If they lose George's custom it will tip the balance against them and they'll have to close" said The Educated Effin' Idiot.

The Chief poured another drink.

"Is there any bugger who isn't suing us?" he asked.

"I don't know what they're bothered about. We couldn't fuckup George's social life when he was a postmans, if we make him a manager he'll have more to spend on booze," said The Chief.

The Head Postmaster suddenly began to look a lot more cheerful. He tried not to smile. The Educated Effin' Idiot fixed him with a baleful stare.

"I know exactly what you're thinking" he said.

The Head Postmaster shifted uneasily in his seat. The Educated Effin' Idiot continued to stare steadily at him. Neither spoke.

The Chief broke the silence.

"What about telling the rest of us" he said.

"He thinks he's seen the solution to one of his problems. George becomes a manager, gets more money for booze and either drinks himself to death, or ends up in a clinic" he said.

"You bastard" said The Truculent Man.

The Chief was having none of it.

"If you're wanting George to drink himself to death you'll wait a long time" he said.

The Head Postmaster was genuinely indignant.

"I don't want George dead" he said. Then he added:

"But the prospect of him becoming a manager is enough to make anyone laugh. Why does he suddenly want promotion?

The Branch Secretary shook his head in disbelief.

"You really haven't got a bloody clue" he said.

The Head Postmaster's face confirmed this statement. The Truculent Man tried to shed some light.

"No bugger wants to work here" he said.

"Not even the bleedin' Martians" said The Chief.

"Everyone wants redundancy" said The Assistant Secretary.

"So why is George trying to be a manager?" asked The Head Postmaster.

The Educated Effin' Idiot tried to explain.

"The Mad Witch of Grantham has put half wits in charge. They got rid of useful people who were doing the work for a pittance and brought in hordes of useless wankers who were ridiculously overpaid

— RICHARD WALL —

and had no function. Having paid them huge sums for doing shagall you're now paying them huge sums to bugger off" he said.

"George wants a manager's payoff" said The Truculent Man.

"Cheeky sod!" said The Chief with a chortle. He refilled his glass. "Never mind Shaggin' George. One way or another he'll be allright. The rest of us are in deep shit. Apart from him" he said pointing at The Head Postmaster.

The Head Postmaster looked alarmed and was about to speak but The Chief had only just started. To the obvious delight of The Truculent Man he proceeded to dismantle his boss.

"We're fighting on all sides. They're coming at us from all sides. We're up against The Mad of Witch of Grantham, aliens, The Undead not to mention all those pimply little shits in Birmingham. We're completely outgunned, we're being overpowered, we've no chance, but we're not giving up, we've nailed our flag to the mast, then we'll cling to the wreckage. What's he doing? He's buggering off to Spain. They've bought him off. He's sold out. We're going down with the ship and he's in the lifeboat.

The Truculent Man was absolutely delighted.

"If you start out as an arsehole you end up as an arsehole" he said. He poured himself another drink. A wicked gleam came into his eye. He raised his glass to The Head Postmaster.

"When George gets his severance I hope he moves in next to you and pisses in your pool" he said. He then got up and headed for the door.

"Where are you going?" Asked The Chief.

"I'm going to report him to The Shitehouse Poets" said The Truculent Man.

The Head Postmaster turned deathly pale.

"What's up with you?" said The Chief.

The Head Postmaster looked stricken.

"I'm going to be exposed" he said.

"So what? You're going to Spain" said The Chief.

"I'll be a bloody pariah, an expatriate leper" said The Head Postmaster.

"Too bloody true" said The Truculent Man.

"Who cares about the Shitehouse walls?" said The Chief.

"We signed the petition. I'll be condemned in Parliament" said The Head Postmaster.

"You can't hide the truth forever" said The Branch Secretary.

"If you believe that you'll believe any effin' thing" said The Truculent Man.

The Chief nodded his agreement.

"It'll be a ten day wonder. Then everything will carry on as usual" he said.

The Truculent Man turned to The Educated Effin' Idiot.

"He's right isn't he?" he said.

The Educated Effin' Idiot shook his head.

"He's wrong. In the end the truth comes out" he said.

The Chief grinned.

"Thank God no-one will believe it" he said.

Printed in Great Britain
by Amazon

16376350R00246